JUSTIN DAVIS

Founded in 2020, and headquartered in Gainesville, Florida, USA, HDG Global Publications is a non-profit, independent publisher committed to publishing classic spiritual literature, in print and audio formats, that inspire the reader's spiritual evolution.

Based on the ancient Sanskrit literature of South Asia, and adapted for contemporary audiences both lay and academic, our publications make advanced concepts comprehensible and enjoyable.

JUSTIN DAVIS

THE SECRET OF THE FIRST AVATĀRA

HOWARD RESNICK

MANDALA

SAN RAFAEL LOS ANGELES LONDON

CHAPTER 1

Dressed in black, Justin Davis sat alone in a far corner of the bitter-cold high school yard. Another bad day. Wet fog stuck to the hills like a shivering disease. After his father was murdered and Justin rejected the world, old friends used to come out and urge him to come in. But he wasn't ready. They stopped coming. Better for everyone. Plato was right. This world is a dark cave full of shadows. Why cry over shadows? Plato's only mistake was to imagine a sunny world outside the cave. Obviously, Plato never saw Tucker County, West Virginia. Justin chewed a sandwich without tasting it. Then he broke his own rule and glanced at the noisy cafeteria where everybody else ate.

Justin cursed his life, and cursed it again as a pickle slice fell out of his sandwich. Then Sherri Bunton herself—former girlfriend Sherri—walked up and asked to speak to him. What did she want? He knew she despised him.

Sherri sighed, gathering her courage. For what? With a shake of those golden curls, she cast him a plaintive glance that only angered him, as most things did. She must really need something. He looked at the mask of her face. *Okay, girl, tell me that Billy is about to demolish your darling Ben.*

"I hate to bother you, Justin," she began, "but I'm so scared. That new guy, Billy Skinner, is going to kill Ben, and no one but you is tough enough to stand up to Billy."

Justin nodded, looked away, and tapped his foot to the beat of his shamefully outdated iPhone.

"Are you listening to me?" she demanded, as if she still had any rights with him.

He pushed his long, blond hair out of his eyes and shot her an angry glance. Sherri huffed, then took a deep breath and counted to five, as mandated by her therapist. So, she still did that.

Back in control, she forced a smile and tried again. "Justin, I know you hate me, though I don't know why. I always wanted to be friends."

The day they broke up, she had said, "Justin, you're really cute and all that, but you're just a dead end. You're a loser. You know I was there for you when...the tragedy occurred. But you won't let go of the past. I have to move on. I want to be somebody. Ben is going places and so am I. But you don't even want a career. You are going nowhere."

She actually said that then. And now...

"Justin, listen to me. I need your help. We're all afraid of Billy. His father's the county judge and always protects him..."

"Yes, I know that." He refused to look at her.

"...and Billy's bigger and tougher than the other guys, and he's bullying Ben and putting his hands on me. Did you hear that? He says he'll do worse if we tell anyone. No one can beat you in a fight."

"Call 911," Justin said, nodding to his music.

"Justin, listen to me! They say he raped a girl in Hardy County, and shot a boy in Parsons, and his dad got him off."

"Well, he hasn't shot Ben yet and he hasn't raped you, so there's nothing I can do. Is that all?"

Outraged, Sherri gasped. "Justin, don't be a monster!"

He stood up to leave. Her face turned from red rage to white fear. She grabbed his arm. He yanked it away. She burst into tears.

"Look," she cried, "I'm sorry for what happened. I'm sorry I hurt you. I really am. But you pushed me away, like you pushed everyone away. You know you did. You're the only one that can stop Billy. Please!"

She was getting to him. He had to end it.

"All right," he said. "Tell Billy I said to leave you and Ben and everyone else on earth alone."

"I already told him you said that."

"What?"

"I had to. But Billy just spit and called you names I won't repeat. I told him how tough you are and he swore at me and almost hit me. He's going to hurt us, Justin. Only you can stop him."

Justin shook his head. "So, I fight him and his father throws me in jail. Sure, I'll ruin my life for you. Any day. You can go now."

Tears streamed down Sherri's face.

"I don't fight anymore," Justin said.

"But you always fought for justice," she sobbed.

"There is no justice in this world. Didn't you notice? Look, I'll give it to you straight: I don't care what Billy does to Ben. And I don't care what he does to you."

Justin Davis turned up his music, hurled his unfinished lunch into a trash can, and walked away. After a minute, he turned around. Sherri was gone. Good.

Then Justin saw him, big Billy Skinner, shuffling toward the cafeteria with two friends. Billy always went in late and walked to the front of the line. Now, he spoke to his friends and they laughed. Billy seemed to have a plan. He and his buddies sauntered into the cafeteria.

A minute later, one of Billy's fast-talking friends led cafeteria monitor Ms. Bloony out into the yard. Smiling and busily chatting, he pointed out something she had to see. Now there was no teacher inside to see what Billy would do. Justin sighed, shook his head, cursed himself for being so sentimental, and trudged into the cafeteria. People got out of his way. He leaned against a pillar, nodded to the beat of his music, and watched.

CHAPTER 2

Billy and his friend Jaws, who had a large, square jaw, pushed their way through the food line till they stood behind tall, thin Ben Stecker, Sherri's current gentleman, who fearfully loaded up his tray. Still nodding to his music, Justin pushed his hair out of his eyes.

Billy smiled at Jaws, said, "Hey, don't push me," and lunged into Ben, who almost lost his tray.

Sweating and shaking, looking desperately for the strangely absent Ms. Bloony, Ben bowed his lanky frame and apologized, trying to placate his tormentor.

Sherri ran to Justin, grabbed his arm, and pleaded, "Can't you do something?"

He pulled his arm away. "Call a teacher."

"If I do that, Billy will kill me. Can't you do something? I'll do anything for you."

Justin yawned, opened and closed his fists, stretched his fingers. "If Billy attacks, I'll deal with it."

Jaws noticed Justin glaring at him and his square jaw dropped. He whispered to Billy, pointed at Justin, and shook his head.

Billy scowled at him and said, for everyone in the hushed hall to hear, "You mean little Justin Davis? That little girl with the long hair?"

Jaws did not reply to this apparently rhetorical question. Justin was short for his age, and his hair did go below his shoulders. By now, Ben was exiting the food line with a full tray, hoping to escape to a far table. That was not to be. Billy pretended to trip and smashed into Ben.

Ben's tray went crashing down, with Ben close behind. His thin, chalky, cologned face splashed into his bean soup. He moaned, turned his head, and plunged his styled hair into the spaghetti. Feigning a stumble over Ben's prostrate body, Billy kicked him viciously in the gut with a steel-toe boot.

Ben writhed on the floor. Girls screamed. Boys kept a distance. Some ran to find Ms. Bloony. Sherri rushed to Ben and wiped food off his dazed, terrified face. Billy glared at her and she flinched.

Justin wrapped up his old iPhone and placed it in his coat pocket. He had seen enough. He ambled over to Billy.

Billy clenched his fists. "Don't mess with me. I'll destroy you."

The cafeteria fell dead silent. Breathless students watched at a safe distance. Justin stared at Billy and said, "I want you to apologize to Ben, and then I want you to pick up this food. Now."

Looking down at Justin, two years his junior and half his size, Billy cursed him and shoved him hard in the chest, knocking him back several feet. Excellent. Billy struck first.

Justin strolled back up to Billy and said, "I told you—apologize to Ben and pick up the food, you ignorant sociopath."

Billy swung his big fist. Justin let the punch graze his cheek. Perfect. Facial contact. Now it was all self-defense.

As Billy finished his swing, Justin said, "It's over, caveman."

With extraordinary speed, he grabbed Billy's shirt with both hands and with a sweep of his leg, took the bully high off his feet and smashed him onto the floor, making sure his head didn't hit the ground. Justin didn't want a mess. Billy gasped for air. Justin flew onto his chest and with both fists beat the bully senseless.

By then teachers and staff swarmed over Justin, pulling him off Billy and wrenching him to his feet. He felt a painful grip on both arms and heard teachers rebuking him. His captors forced him along, lifting him off his feet. Justin recalled that today was his fifteenth birthday. This must be his party.

As they dragged him to the principal's office, students shouted all around.

"Stop Davis before he kills someone!"

"It's not Justin's fault. Billy started it!"

The voices stopped. He was pushed into a chair in front of Mrs. Patent, the principal's secretary.

"Justin Davis? Again?" She rolled her heavily mascaraed eyes and tapped her long green nails. "I thought you didn't fight anymore. Anyway, you'll have to wait. Principal Olsen is with someone."

Justin heard their voices through the door. Dr. Olsen was talking to a man with a loud voice. Still racing with adrenalin, Justin caught his breath and waited. And waited. He had never waited this long. Was this meant to humble him? It would not work.

He looked around the familiar office. Wow, an elegant new touch—plastic flowers in a Double Bubble gum carton. And the old elegance of plastic cartoon rabbits, ducks, and chickens plastered on the walls and main door. And a flyer with vital news—the winner of the Elkins, West Virginia beauty pageant gets a free local train pass for the summer. Why was he trapped in this world?

His stomach churned. He heard a sound from the hall and turned to a half-open door. Sherri was frantically trying to get his attention.

"I'm going to the bathroom," Justin said, and left the office before Mrs. Patent could look up. Outside, Sherri was holding Ben and cooing away his pain.

"We have to talk, Justin," she said. "Thanks so much for saving Ben and me. I really mean it. That idiot Billy is going to think twice before he bothers anyone in this school."

"Whatever," Justin replied.

Sherri looked down, looked up, looked sideways, everywhere but in his eyes. "Just one more little favor." She held up her thumb and index finger to show how tiny the favor was. "Please don't tell Dr. Olsen or anyone that I asked you to fight Billy. You know I'm trying to get into a good college and I can't have it on my record. You don't care about a career, so it won't matter to you."

Justin glared at her. "That's right. I'm going nowhere, so it makes no difference for me, right?"

"That's not what I meant."

"Of course not," he said with weary sarcasm. The Bunton family, Sherri strongly included, had always been social climbers, though there was precious little social terrain to climb in Tucker County. But they were ambitious, and had always envied the Davis family, whom they now considered beneath them. Bitterly brooding over this, Justin realized after a moment that Sherri was waving a manicured hand in his face to get his attention. Etching empathy onto her eyes and lips, she said, "I'm so, so sorry, Justin, but you won't tell anyone, will you?"

"No. Bye-bye. I'm busy."

Seeing that Dr. Olsen was still sequestered with his heavy-talking guest, Justin took a few steps down the hall and poked his head into the nurse's office.

Nurse Ruby scowled at him and barked, "What do you want?"

He scowled back and said, "How is that fine young man doing?"

"You mean the boy you almost killed?"

"Way to go, drama queen," Justin muttered.

"What did you say, boy?"

"I said life is a drama keen. I am paraphrasing Shakespeare; you know, that other Bill."

"Very cute," Nurse Ruby said. "So much wasted intelligence."

"At least I've got it to waste," he muttered.

"What did you say?"

"I said Skinner is okay, right?"

"He'll be all right, but no thanks to you."

"Of course it's thanks to me. Fighting is an art, nurse. You do medical arts and I do martial arts."

Nurse Ruby snorted with contempt. She was a total cave-dweller. What did she know about fighting? Or anything else? She was here less than a year. She didn't even know that he used to be normal, till his father was murdered. Did she think he liked being angry and depressed all the time? Fool.

"Do you even care about justice?" he said in a parting shot.

Another Ruby snort.

He muttered, "Cave-dweller."

"What did you say?"

"I said brave feller, that Billy Skinner. Later, nurse. And have a great day."

Returning to the principal's office, he found Mrs. Patent lost in her computer screen and Dr. Olsen still talking to that man, whoever he was.

Justin fidgeted in his chair. His mind raced back to the night of the murder. Damn! When would that image stop haunting him? It forced its way into his mind. He saw his father in his favorite chair, reading a book, when the killer burst into the room and pointed his gun at Justin's father. Justin gasped and shook.

"Are you all right?" Mrs. Patent said.

He looked up, hiding his trembling hands. "Of course I'm all right," he said. "I just got attacked in the cafeteria, that's all."

Mrs. Patent gave him a motherly glance. "I thought you vegans were peaceful. Are there many fighting vegans? Don't be offended; I'm just asking."

He looked away till she returned to her work. Then he wiped the sweat from his forehead and reminded himself that this world was unreal, a shadow in a cave. But philosophy did not remove the searing pain in his heart.

The other man walked out of the principal's office. He was tall and slim with thin wire glasses perched on a narrow nose. He gave Justin an unsmiling nod and left. What was that all about?

Finally summoned, Justin sat before Principal Olsen, who always said basically the same thing. The game was to guess exactly what Olsen would say.

"Justin, every test we give you shows you are a genius. You are the brightest student in this school. And the most violent. We all know about your skill in fighting."

Hundred percent so far. Nothing new.

"We know what you and your family have been through, but life must go on. That's what your father would have wanted. Make something of yourself! You could be a leader. All the kids would follow you, like before. Now they just fear you. You could do so much in this world. But you gave up on life."

No surprises there. But it hurt nonetheless. *I know what I've become,* Justin thought, *but I can't change. Okay, Dr. Olsen, now do the embarrassing mother line.*

"All I can say," Dr. Olsen continued, "is that you are so lucky to have such a great mom. She's a very fine lady. I know the life she was used to and what she's going through now. I know how hard it is for all of you. But it will all work out someday. Anyway, you've heard it all before."

"Correct, sir."

"And about this fight today—you'll say it was just self-defense. That's your usual plea."

"Yes, sir." Justin's stomach churned. "I have a right to defend myself. Billy struck first. In fact, he struck me twice. As we both know, according to Education Code 18A-5-1c, I have a right to attend a school free from bullying. And I have a further state right to use reasonable and proportionate force to protect myself. So I suppose you'll refer me to the psychologist."

Dr. Olsen looked down, twiddled his thumbs, and said, "That's exactly what I was going to do, though it seems that you and the school psychologist have read all the same books. I was going to do that, but we have a little problem this time."

"What problem?" Justin asked. This was not in the script.

Dr. Olsen shook his head. "The school superintendent, Dr. Green, is visiting today. I was just speaking to him."

"Oh. Well, so what?"

"The 'so what' is this—he happened to be near the cafeteria when you pounded Billy to a pulp and he saw what you did, or the result of it. Then, as I was speaking to him, Dr. Green got a call from Judge Skinner..."

"You mean Billy's father."

"Exactly. Superintendent Green feels that since you were a martial-arts champion, you were not in any real danger from Billy and thus did not act in self-defense, and thus did not use reasonable and proportionate force. So he suspended you from this school."

"What? He can't just do that."

"Oh yes, he can. And he did. You are to empty your locker and be off school property within half an hour, or the superintendent will have the police escort you off. Dr. Green knows what you've been through. He showed sympathy but did not change his decision because..."

"Because he's afraid of the judge."

"Justin, he is seriously considering expelling you as a threat to this school. God only knows what will become of you. I wish I could do more, but I can't."

"This is crazy..." Justin clenched his fists. "He can't do this to me."

"Justin, you're not going to fight your way out of this one. Write a humble apology to Dr. Green and ask for another chance. I know him and I think he'll let you back in. But you must humble yourself and apologize."

"Yeah, sure." Justin gritted his teeth. "As far as I care, Green can go and—"

"Don't say it, Justin. C'mon, let me help you."

"Thanks, but no thanks."

"What do you mean?"

"I mean I don't want to be here. Not in this school, not in this county, not on this planet. I don't want any of it. It was nice of you to try. Thanks for everything. Say hello to Mrs. Olsen."

Justin stomped out of the office. As he passed Mrs. Patent, she said, "Will we ever see the real Justin Davis again?"

She struck too close to home.

"What are you talking about?" he shouted. "This is who I am now."

"No. Not really."

"Mrs. Patent, no offense, but you're a secretary, not a psychiatrist, okay?"

Justin didn't wait for an answer. He stomped out, emptied his hall locker, and slammed it so hard that teachers ran out of their classrooms. He then stormed down the hall, kicking walls and cursing the world, as frightened students flew out of his path.

He marched up the mountain highway toward his humiliating home in Davis town. If only a car would hit him and end his misery.

CHAPTER 3

He tramped along, kicking stones, hardly seeing the monotonous forest's trees on both sides. It was six miles to Thomas, two and a half more to Davis. A billboard boasted of coming county events—the Spring Bird Walk; the Woodcock Round-up. He shook his head and rolled his eyes. They could have filmed *Groundhog Day* here. No actors, just film the town every day.

He hadn't always scorned Tucker County. As a child, he reveled in his life as a small-town celebrity in a town founded by and named after his family. A botanical garden, and even a college forty miles down in Elkins bore the family name. The Davis family lived in a great ancestral home, the finest in the county. Justin went with his dad to the golf-and-racquet club in Canaan Valley. Beyond Tucker County, at the university in Morgantown, Tark Davis was an academic celebrity, and Justin basked in family pride.

With all these blessings, Justin might easily have become an insufferably arrogant child. He did not, however, and for that the credit went to his parents. His mother, Star Davis, had grown up as a destitute orphan. Rather than make her a bitter or greedy adult, her past inspired in her a deep empathy for the less fortunate, and she taught this to her son.

Justin's father, Tark Davis, though wealthy and erudite, believed that his good fortune obliged him to serve others, and he too taught these lessons to his sons. Thus, when Justin decided at an early age to study martial arts, Tark made him promise to use his skill only to protect the innocent, never out of pride. Justin Davis greatly admired his parents, and he embraced their values.

Indeed, from childhood, Justin idolized his father. He walked and talked like Tark Davis. Everywhere they went together, people smiled and said that Justin was a perfect copy of his dad. And they told his father that Justin was a handsome, brilliant child. Father and son enjoyed the same sports, admired the same natural beauty, and laughed at the same jokes.

11

All of Tucker County called Justin the prince, a title he relished from early childhood. His little brother, Joey, almost from infancy, adored Justin. Crawling, toddling, or walking, Joey followed Justin, as much as Justin followed his father. Thus, from Tark, to Justin, to Joey, the Davis men were a very tight team.

Tark often took his older son on trips, which always had some beneficent purpose. Star Davis had not been a healthy child, and did not like to travel much. She was happy to stay at home on the family estate to engage her passion of writing, and look after Joey. When Star's career prospered, Tark built her a media room on their estate where she did frequent online interviews. Justin liked to sit and listen. He was fascinated by his mother's ability to tell delightful and meaningful stories.

At times, Tark would take his boys up in his plane and fly over the town, the high school, or Canaan Valley. If safety permitted, Tark let Justin steer the plane for a few minutes. If they had time, they sailed off through the blue to Morgantown. There they walked along the wide Monongahela River, walked on the lovely campus, visited Tark's office, and always made their final stop at Justin's favorite ice cream parlor. On their approach back to Davis, Tark would fly over Blackwater Falls, before landing on the private runway at his large country estate. The family had their routine. The men flew and Star wrote articles and books.

Weather permitting, the family held picnics on a favorite shaded meadow on the Davis land. Star would read from her latest writing, and the family listened eagerly. His mother was Justin's favorite writer. "And it's not because you're my mother," he always said.

Justin passed his childhood perfectly content with his life. He excelled at school, dominated regional martial arts as well as the youth social scene, and admired his parents above everyone he knew, or saw or read or heard about.

Around the age of thirteen, Justin made his first independent intellectual foray. He developed an increasing interest in movies and books about superheroes and higher worlds. Such interest, by itself, was normal. Much of humanity enjoyed such stories, and so did Justin from early childhood. But he now insisted, in talks with his parents, that he was developing a special theory to explain why so many people relished such stories.

Knowing that Justin consistently achieved genius scores on standard intelligence tests, and seeing his firm interest in this topic, his parents tried to understand exactly what he meant. Out of love and real respect for their son, his parents listened as he tried to articulate his new theory.

With parental help, Justin's theory took shape as follows. People all over the world were powerfully drawn to stories of superheroes and higher worlds. Justin believed that the standard psychological explanations for these phenomena were not the whole truth. In his view, people were fascinated by higher powers and worlds because they actually existed within the universe. People intuitively, though unconsciously, understand this. Therefore, it was easy and natural for so many people to suspend their disbelief when watching such movies, or reading such books.

Obviously, Justin acknowledged, Hollywood's versions of superheroes and higher worlds were fiction, but only in the details, only on the surface. The basic premise was true. Superheroes and higher worlds really existed, and Justin wanted to find them.

Star Davis, an avid reader of Plato in her youth, contributed an idea to Justin's theory. In his *Meno*, Plato presents the notion of anamnesis, the idea that we know certain things because we remember them from a past life. "I don't know if reincarnation takes place," Star said, "but at least Justin is in good company here. I mean, with Plato."

"I think we understand my theory now," Justin said.

"Fascinating," Tark added.

"I want to explore this further," Justin said, "but I don't know how. Maybe I should meditate."

"You could try that," Star said. "And you might also read more books on the subject. It would seem that if you're right, other souls over the centuries must have come to similar conclusions. Some of them probably wrote about it. We can look online together." Star Davis smiled. "I used to dream of being a librarian."

Justin effortlessly transmitted his interest in these topics to Joey, who demanded that Justin inform him of any new discovery in this area. Justin was happy to see that his entire family encouraged him in his new interest.

Soon after this, two new developments stressed the tight unity of the Davis family. The first was that Tark Davis grew in fame and popularity. His innovative programs to improve education in West Virginia gained national attention. Soon, Tark was crisscrossing the country, though not in his small plane. Around the nation, he became a most sought-after speaker at all sorts of academic and government seminars, conventions, think tanks, and more. The national press soon discovered him. A brilliant scholar and educator who served the poor, looked like a movie star, and spoke with heaps of country charm, could not fail to become a star commentator on endless national news shows. Both major political parties talked to him about running for office on their ticket.

Everyone seemed highly pleased with Tark Davis, except his own family, who complained about his frequent absence. During his short visits home, Tark asked Justin about his research in metaphysics.

Justin angrily said, "You don't have time to hear about it. You're always gone. You want to help everyone, but you have no time for your family."

Startled by these words, his father promised Justin that he would spend more time at home. "I have unavoidable commitments for the next few months," Tark said, "but after that, I promise things will be different. It will be like it was before. I promise you."

It had been a little over a year before Justin's suspension from Tucker County High School that Tark Davis had made this sincere promise to his son. Soon after that, a second new development stressed Davis family solidarity. Romance struck Justin in the form of his first girlfriend, lovely Sherri Bunton. His mother warned him that the Bunton family was very ambitious, and that Sherri possessed a generous portion of that proclivity. Tark also expressed concern. But all such parental caution was in vain. Sherri was, by wide consensus, a top-tier beauty at Tucker County High School, and her family was growing prosperous by county standards, though not on the scale of the Davis family.

Family gatherings now took on a new configuration. Tark was usually absent, and Sherri was always present. Already feeling the absence of his father, Joey now complained to Justin. "You act so weird around Sherri. Why can't you be normal?"

"I don't know what you're talking about," Justin replied.

"I mean you don't talk to me; you only talk to her."

Justin said he would be more careful.

The time that Tark had requested of his family, time to honor previous commitments, now passed. But just when his family expected him to return home to what had been their happy life, he revealed to his wife and elder son another, more serious problem.

The Davis family had previously suffered financial reverses in the Great Recession. Justin was too young at the time to hear about it, and Joey was not yet born. Since that time, Tark and Star had been rebuilding the family fortune, slowly but surely. But very recently, indeed in the last month, an apparently coordinated series of financial attacks on the family's investments and holdings again put them in financial difficulties.

"This is serious," Tark explained to his worried wife and son. "I swear to you, I had every intention to stay at home and only fly into Morgantown a few times a week for classes. But I have no choice now but to keep traveling. Of course, some of the programs I can do online, but many of them, especially those that pay well, I can't. At this point, I have to accept every paid appearance I can get. You can't imagine how disappointed I am. You cannot have wanted me to stay home more than I wanted it. I have no desire to be a famous talking head on television, or to appear at endless banquets and conventions. But these engagements pay well, and for my family's sake, for your sake, I have to push myself hard. I should have spent more time with you. You mean more to me than anything. I hate what's happening. But I owe it to you."

"Tark," his wife said, "we don't need to be rich. It doesn't matter to me. Really."

"That's right, Dad," Justin added. "It will be embarrassing here in Davis, but we can move to Morgantown, where we don't have an image to keep up. I like Morgantown."

"I appreciate both of you so much," Tark said. "I just need a little time to get us back in a safe position, and then whatever it takes, I will stay with you, I promise. Morgantown may be a good idea. I've been gone too much. Justin, you and Joey are growing so quickly, and I want to be there for you. I don't want to just feed and clothe you and tell you how much I love you, and then fly off again. Perhaps Wordsworth was right when he said, 'The Child is father of the Man.' Maybe I have to learn from you. We'll really talk about these things. I haven't been here for you. But I'll make it up to you. I give you my word."

These words both disappointed and pleased Justin. He didn't like the delay, but his father would keep his promise. Justin now looked forward to an intimate metaphysical discussion with both parents, since Star also gladly participated. Indeed, her interest in these topics preceded that of her husband or son. She had often escaped to other worlds, through books, in her unhappy childhood.

Justin increasingly saw what he wanted in life—basically, to become a great man in the world, for the best of reasons. He would serve humanity in some way or other (to be determined), and exalt his family even beyond their present status.

In his childhood games, Justin had fought bravely to protect the innocent, rescue fair maidens, and bring justice to Earth. In early adolescence, his dreams began to take more serious shape. He would go to one of the best colleges, and one day become, at the very least, a US senator, if not something higher. Like his father, he would fight for justice, for the innocent and the needy.

All these noble dreams ended in his fourteenth year, on a cold, dark, moonless night.

On that cold, moonless night, Justin went with his mother and Joey to see a movie down in Elkins. Tark Davis stayed home to work on a legal case. At the movie, Joey didn't feel well, and so the family returned early. Star and Joey went upstairs, and Justin stayed in the great room with his father. His father smiled at him and returned to his legal papers. Justin took a book off the shelf and read. Occasionally, he looked out through the large picture window that faced the street. Soon after, Justin heard a burly engine that broke the still air. He looked out and saw a large SUV parking across the street, opposite the Davis estate. Justin had seen that car several times during the last week, always at night, always parked opposite the Davis mansion. He assumed the large vehicle belonged to a friend of the Wyndhams, who lived across the street.

After several minutes, Justin heard heavy footfalls coming up the steps, making the old wooden porch groan. Who could it be at this hour? Justin stood and looked out the window, but the visitor was already at the door.

A large masked man pushed his way past the unlocked door and without a word, shot Justin's father at point-blank range. The killer then turned his gun on Justin. But the boy, a martial arts champion gifted with lightning speed, had instinctively grabbed an iron poker from the fireplace. With a furious cry he smashed the killer's gloved gun hand. The killer screamed, grabbed his gun with the other hand, and ran. As Star came screaming down the stairs and rushed to her husband, Justin pursued the killer, racing down the steps and dealing two ferocious blows to his upper back. The killer shrieked like an animal, fell into the waiting car with its masked driver and running motor, and the black SUV fled into the night.

Justin ran back to the house where his mother wailed, "He's gone! Your father is gone!" Joey cried uncontrollably. Justin could not breathe or see anything in front of him. Neighbors began pouring into the Davis house. Soon, state police arrived from Parsons. Star Davis held her husband in her arms as if he were still alive.

As the ambulance took his father, as police investigated, as paramedics cared for his mother and brother, and as the whole town gathered outside his house, Justin sat alone, unmoving on a chair, watching the big front door swing blindly in the frigid wind. Over and over, his shocked mind vowed deadly vengeance against the killers.

The murder stunned Tucker County and most of the state. It shattered Justin's mother. Joey was traumatized and couldn't speak.

All of Tucker County seemed present at the funeral. A large contingent came from West Virginia University, including the president. The governor came with a contingent from the state capital in Charleston. Officials came from Washington, and around the country. Visitors filled the area hotels.

Most prominent of the mourners was Senator Hunter Clay of Virginia, a leading national politician who seemed headed for a run at the presidency. About Tark's age, tall and imposing, the senator came with his lovely wife, Barbara. At an appropriate moment, they offered consoling words to Star Davis, who hid her grief behind a black veil. Senator Clay explained that he met Tark in Washington and was very impressed by him. He came to offer comfort to the family and to honor the memory of the departed. The pastor asked the senator to speak, but he declined, saying that he wanted to hear from family and close friends.

National, regional, and local news teams were there, remaining at a respectful distance. County and state police were out in force. Star Davis was too grief-stricken to mind Joey, and that task fell to Justin. He held Joey's hand, but released it to shake hands with Senator and Barbara Clay when they approached him.

"If I can help in any way," the senator said, "don't hesitate to call me. Here's my personal card."

Justin took the card, thanked the senator, made a polite bow to his wife, and watched as the senator walked with his wife toward their reserved seats. Joey watched them go with a mixture of grief, confusion, and awe.

The funeral went on and on. Many people wanted to speak. Justin knew his father was widely admired, and he had always liked to hear his father praised. But he could not pay close attention now. His own feelings and thoughts overwhelmed him. He was asked if he wanted to speak. He did not. The funeral ended. Close friends accompanied the grieving family back to their home in Davis, where food was spread on tables. Justin tried to be polite. He thanked those who offered condolences, but he could say nothing beyond that.

After the funeral, Justin sank into dark despair. He stopped cutting his hair. He dressed in black. He went deep into the woods where no one could see his anguish. And anguish flared into rage. Revenge possessed his mind. Hour after hour, relentlessly, he practiced deadly arts with daggers and guns. He steeled and strengthened body and mind into a calm killing machine.

His mother urged Justin to be noble and work for the good of others like his father, to make something of himself. "You can't give in to anger and hopelessness," she said. "You could do so much for this world."

"I don't care about the world."

The town and county rose up in support of the Davis family, but the family's troubles were only beginning. Within weeks of his father's funeral, a new crisis struck the grieving Davises. Star confided to her elder son that the family finances were in grave danger. "I feel terrible to burden you with this news," she told him, "but I fear you would not forgive me if I did not tell you. You must remember that your father spoke of an apparently coordinated series of attacks on our family investments."

"Yes, I remember," Justin said.

"Justin, those attacks have resumed. We are being attacked legally on many fronts. Our lawyers assure us that everything your father did was perfectly legal. But, we are being attacked with title challenges, lawsuits that attach our property, all our assets."

"Who is attacking us?"

"That's the problem. The aggressors are corporations registered in Delaware, which protects the anonymity of corporate directors. One corporation owns another, and the first is owned by a third, and all the corporate officers are anonymous. These corporations have armies of sophisticated lawyers."

Star explained to her son that the loss of one asset, like a falling domino, precipitated the loss of another. In a matter of several weeks, a cascade of financial blows hopelessly tied up, or definitively wiped out, the Davis fortune, leaving the grieving family destitute.

"What about our lawyers?" Justin asked.

"They tried their best, but the enemy has unlimited resources. I can't pay our lawyers anymore. They are good people. They've donated time to us. But they too are exhausted. They have to earn money for their own families. Justin, we are bankrupt."

"What will we do?" Justin asked.

"We have to sell our house, and our land. We'll have to live in the trailer for now."

"I would rather die," Justin said.

"How can you say that, after all I've been through? Don't you know how I feel when you say that?"

"I'm sorry." He looked away.

His mother looked at him with deep pain in her eyes. And soon after, proud Justin Davis watched in horror as vulgar men barged into his ancestral home and carried away fine old furniture and costly appliances. The house itself went next. Poverty drove the noble family into their last remaining asset—a ramshackle trailer his parents once provided to indigent families.

The family's disgrace, coming as it did when Justin was still grieving for his father, was more than he could bear. His many friends rallied to his side. But as the family status plummeted, the slightest hint of pity or condescension in their looks or voices, real or imagined, hardened Justin's bitter resolve to reject the world. The Prince of Davis would fall on his own sword. He would never be dethroned. At an age when he craved peer respect, Justin burned with shame.

Now, he was suspended from school. How would this affect his mother's health? She did not deserve this. Justin now brooded over topics he could not mention to his mother. He knew that whoever had caused the bankruptcy of the Davis family must have also killed Tark Davis.

"I swear to God," Justin said, "that someday I will find you and I will destroy you. I swear to God I will, and no one will stop me."

His mother kept trying to encourage him. She offered to read to him Plato's cave myth.

"You always liked that," she said.

"Not anymore. I don't believe in those things."

"I beg you," she said, "try to find good in this world. Why don't we go to the bookstore in Elkins? You always liked to go there."

"I told you, I'm not interested."

"Justin, your life is not over. When I was your age, I didn't even have one parent, but I kept trying to find meaning in life and now I have two beautiful sons. And I thank God every day that I had the best husband for many years. I miss him as much as you, but he wants us to go on with life."

Suddenly a loud truck horn startled Justin, who had been lost in these thoughts as he walked up the highway toward Davis. The truck swerved to miss him on the narrow highway, and the driver shouted in anger.

Justin kept walking, numbed by his grief. He walked through the town of Thomas, along the Blackwater River. Two miles later he saw Davis ahead. And who was Justin Davis now? The prince of Davis was just a teenager with emotional problems, someone to avoid. Justin was the image of his father, and he felt that a big part of him also died in that room that night.

Reaching Davis town, he walked past Henry Street, and looked toward the Davis Cemetery a mile away, where his father was buried. He would always stop there on his way to and from the Blackwater Falls where he did his serious thinking. But today, he felt too ashamed to face his father. He had promised his father to use his martial power only to protect the innocent. But today, Justin knocked Billy the bully out cold. He didn't have to do it, but he wanted to. Had he failed his father? Was he more lost than ever?

He dreaded going home. His mother might be there, and how would he face her? He walked a few blocks to the little city park where volunteers festooned a bandstand for weekend festivities. Tucker County would honor its best student scholars and athletes. In the past, Justin always won many awards. This year, he would not attend.

He walked back down to the main street, and passed the Tucker County Convention and Visitors Bureau located in a tiny, one-story building. He stopped and read the new flyer on the door. "Pitiful," he said as he read the words:

Welcome to Davis, the top of the Mountain State! This unhurried high-mountain paradise, the highest incorporated town in the state, offers family adventures unequalled in the region!

Paradise? Unequalled adventures? He couldn't breathe here. Cheery talk of paradise infuriated him. He almost punched the Visitors Bureau bulletin board.

He looked back toward the high part of town, up to lofty Blackwater Avenue, and stared at the Victorian mansion that floated above the other houses. For generations, the Davis family lived there. His father grew up there.

Since childhood, Justin gazed through its windows at the city below, at the Blackwater River that ribboned round the town's southern edge, at the wooded hills beyond the water, rippling in waves to the horizon. That grand old mansion pained him as much as the blighted trailer they now so absurdly called home. Sherri Bunton's father bought the house. Sometimes he saw them through the windows, looking down at the city, looking down at him. He kept walking.

Life would always fail him and he would always fail life. He walked to the cold, grassy riverbank and watched the Blackwater run. Even the moody river held him in contempt and he returned the favor. He could not bear this world. And there was no better world.

He kept walking, eyes down, seeing no one, and letting no one see his face. He reached the family trailer and kicked away a beer can that a drunk dropped in their so-called yard, which in fact was a miserable weed patch.

Justin entered the trailer and threw himself on the trashy sofa. His eyes moistened. He looked at a little bookshelf in the corner. Star Davis lost almost everything the Davis family owned, but somehow, she kept her little library. Her children and her books were her only consolation. Her dream was to write more books. Justin dreaded her return. She might know he was suspended.

He looked at a good-looking young man and a pretty young lady who smiled from a picture in a silver frame that sat on a corner table. It was his mother and father on their wedding day. They seemed pleased with all the world. Justin knew their story well. He tried not to think of it. The charm of their story would only heighten the pain of his loss. He looked again at the picture. He felt as if the attractive young couple in the picture were forcing him to listen, as they themselves told the story of their meeting.

CHAPTER 4

J ustin's mother, Star Davis, endured a very unhappy childhood as an orphan, with no memory of her parents. She had always suspected that they abandoned her, and no one ever denied it when she asked. People said they couldn't say, but they *did* say it, by their nervous silence.

She grew up in a crowded, foul-air facility on the wrong side of Chicago, encircled by menacing streets. She hungered for books and good food and true friends and peace and safety, and got precious little of any of them. Ever in poor health, she was still made to scrub and fold and lift and cook and carry. She was a sort of a sickly, latter-day Cinderella. And *Cinderella* was her favorite childhood story. But neither the fairy godmother, nor the ball, nor the prince ever appeared.

Then one day in early adolescence, as she rummaged in the attic, the only peaceful place she knew, Star discovered a new favorite book— *Jane Eyre* by Charlotte Bronte—the tale of an oppressed orphan girl who intelligently and courageously fights her way to a life of love and plenty.

Star saw the light. She would no longer passively wait for a fairy godmother. She fiercely resolved to study, to learn, and above all to write. She would escape to a fine college, hone her skills, make contacts, and burst upon the world. And she would help others escape their sorrows, and never forget to give back. In short, she would build a great life!

Her dream began to come true. She earned a full scholarship to a most respectable Midwest school, Northwestern University, where she exulted in the kind, learned culture, the magnificent old buildings, and lovely lakefront. The only drawback was that she still resided in the Chicago area, with its metro population of nearly nine million. Still, she was far more peaceful and energetic on campus, though the physical and mental strain of her childhood still at times left her prone to bouts of exhaustion. She dreamed of living in a bucolic cottage by a clear stream, placed pastoral pictures on her walls, and pushed on.

Her studies excelled; her writing flourished. She kept her vow and did not forget those who still suffered. Active in social justice issues, she won a grant to attend a national conference on public service law, hosted by the prestigious law school of the University of Virginia.

As she eagerly attended sessions, furiously taking notes, she found one lecture particularly brilliant, given by the handsome student president of the law school, Tark Davis. She felt an inexplicable bond with Tark, but his lecture, and her discreet inquiries, showed her that sadly he was her opposite. He was heir to a family fortune. She had no family. He was bold and charismatic. She was painfully shy. Indeed, her courage extended only to the keyboard of the computer the university kindly gave her.

She dreamed of speaking with him, but he was always surrounded by friends and admirers, a significant portion of whom were brilliant young ladies as charming as himself. He would never notice her.

Yet in this bleak calculation, Star overlooked an important fact that she had not fully grasped. She herself had grown into a very intelligent and beautiful young lady. Her beauty was not the result of painstaking grooming and dressing. It was natural, unstudied, and unadorned, but it was beauty indeed; modest and intelligent beauty that emanated from a virtuous soul. Apart from that, her figure, though not of the hourglass variety, did her no disservice.

She had been invited to speak at a small subsection of the conference and went to the room in great anxiety. Eight people attended, more than she expected. Even more surprising, one of the eight was Tark Davis. Intrigued by the abstract of her talk, and by her appearance, he had been discreetly watching her as much as she watched him.

He invited her to lunch after her talk, which he praised without a trace of merely polite or, worse, scheming flattery. He really just liked it. And he really just liked her.

Lunch was like a reunion of old friends. They laughed together at the same absurdities, and dreamed the same dreams of a better world. They both passionately cared about social justice. They were both convinced that a better world required a reawakening of basic virtues. They both wanted to dedicate their lives to such causes. And they both could hardly believe they had not always known each other.

For the rest of the conference, they conversed at every spare moment. Star's departure after a few days hardly lessened their communication. Tark came from a wealthy family and was only too happy to pay for daily long-distance phone calls to Star's dormitory room. The rest can be imagined. He graduated law school; she received her bachelor's degree at Northwestern. And they happily married.

Tark Davis was an only child, born late in the lives of his parents, who owned a good deal of Tucker County, West Virginia. He had first studied at nearby West Virginia University, keeping an old family tradition, and then studied law at Virginia. Earning numerous honors, he then received generous offers from universities and law firms around the country.

But Tark Davis chose to return to West Virginia for three important reasons: first, he wanted to stay near his aging parents, whose health was rapidly declining; second, his beloved wife, anxious to finally live with real family, happily helped care for her aging in-laws; and third, Tark yearned to bring his skill and training in public service back to his home state, one of America's richest in natural beauty, but one of its neediest in education and income. And so, he accepted an offer from the West Virginia University law school to lead their public service law program, one of the best in the country.

As a suffering inner-city child, Star dreamed of green valleys with flowing rivers and waterfalls. She found it all in Tucker County. Finally, she could live in the tranquil countryside as her doctors had always urged her.

Justin's elderly grandparents both passed away when he was still a child, and Justin then felt even more his father's regular absence from home.

Having escaped a dark childhood, Star never forgot her dream to write books, stories, and essays—both fiction and non-fiction—with an inspiring message. She spent joyful hours at her desk. Her well-crafted words flowed into journals and magazines. She outlined her first novel. Then she entered her first pregnancy, endured complications that affected her still-recovering health, and writing was suspended, but never forgotten.

Begetting two sons, and carefully raising them, put a strain on Star. Because of her own difficult childhood, she always worried about her children, that they not suffer as she did. This worry took its toll and she did not recover full strength as she hoped. Her husband urged her to relax more. Her children needed her. She tried, but with limited success.

Her children were the joy of her life, but caring for them took all her energy, and writing became a cherished hope for the future.

However, as her children grew, her strength increased, and she was busily and happily outlining her first novel when she lost her husband, her financial independence, and her health. The misery of her childhood revisited her in a terrible new way with the murder of her husband, and the family's steep descent into poverty.

Before the tragedy, Justin's mother led charity drives and graciously presided over the county social scene. Now in desperation, she took whatever jobs she could find in a town of 655, in a county with less than seven thousand people. Sometimes this meant cleaning other people's houses. Wherever she went to clean, Justin avoided that part of town. He could not bear to see it. The day his mother cleaned Sherri's house was the day he and Sherri broke up.

Justin begged his mother to move the family to Pittsburgh, less than a hundred miles away. No one knew them there, and they would find better jobs. But they could not afford to move, and Star was too weak anyway.

They considered a move to smaller and closer Morgantown, but life there was far more expensive than Davis, and jobs were not plentiful. The university did help the devastated family, and campus friends gave private gifts. But all the money was swallowed up in debts and lawsuits. Star Davis could neither request nor expect more money from her friends in Morgantown. The family was trapped in Davis.

Justin then begged his mother to let him drop out of school and work to support the family, but she wouldn't hear of it, and anyway, it was legally impossible. The minimum dropout age in West Virginia was seventeen. He must finish school.

Still, he struggled to help. He took out garbage and shoveled snow for families that once felt honored to speak to him. Then word got out that Justin was angry and dangerous, and no one wanted him in their home or shop. He was a bad influence. His fall was complete.

For her children, Star Davis labored beyond her strength, desperately trying to shield them from unavoidable miseries. Terrible stress again left her mentally and physically exhausted. She was again plagued with nervous exhaustion, sometimes severe, and this ruled out a regular job with normal hours.

Watching his mother and brother suffer with no way to help them, Justin grew increasingly depressed. Seeing this, Star Davis tried to keep alive in her family the vision that originally brought Tark and her together—the vision of helping the world. For now, writing was out of the question. She had no time, no energy, and almost no hope.

There were no relatives to help, no way to escape to a place where they could suffer their shame anonymously. They were trapped in Davis and must suffer there.

Justin sank into dark despair. Yet his mother, having survived so many troubles in the past, kept telling him, "Our fortunes will change; they will improve. I know they will. We must be patient."

Hearing these words, his heart held on to a faint hope that one day he would save his family from their troubles, that a glorious destiny awaited him. This dim hope kept him in school, though his dispirited performance there boded ill.

But high school suspension was not part of the plan. He dreaded the effect on his mother and feared for her life. What if expulsion followed suspension? He would take it as destiny, flee to Pittsburgh, and send money to his family. He hung on to life for his mother and Joey.

CHAPTER 5

A school bus broke the silence and rumbled to a stop. Eight-year-old Joey Davis ran into the house and embraced Justin. Whatever crazy thing he might be or do out in the crazy world, Justin could never let Joey down. He was almost a father to his kid brother.

Joey was not strong. After the shock of his father's death, he suffered from childhood depression and could not eat or sleep enough to maintain his health. Star did her best but there were few professional options in Davis, and none she could afford outside Davis. And so Joey suffered what Star and Justin believed to be a treatable debilitation, a fact that haunted them both.

Joey now burst into the house with this news: "My friend Bobby said you saved his brother Ben and beat up that cave-dweller bully."

Justin shrugged. Despite Joey's urging, he wouldn't talk about it. He didn't want Joey to become violent like him.

"Then tell me the cave story!" Joey said.

"Again? Not now, Joey."

"Please!"

Justin sighed, took Plato's *Republic* from the little bookshelf, opened it to the cave myth, and abridged it as follows in the dramatic voice Joey loved:

"Behold! Human beings living in an underground cave. Here they have been from childhood, with their legs and necks chained so they can only see in front of them.

"Far behind them a fire blazes, and they see only their own shadows, or each other's shadows, which the fire throws on the cave wall in front of them. To these prisoners, life is nothing but the shadows of the images. With their necks chained, they can't even turn to see themselves or each other.

"And when any prisoner is freed, he leaves the cave and outside, his eye turns to a greater reality. But he must grow accustomed to the sun's light, to the sight of the upper world.

"And when his eyes see that greater world, he remembers his old home in the cave, pities his fellow prisoners, and says, 'Better to endure anything than to think and live as they do.'

"This is the upward journey of the soul."

Joey applauded. But the truth here was that having thrilled his brother for years with stories of other worlds, and life outside the cave, Justin no longer believed in such things. After the murder, terms like *cave-dweller* became mere rhetorical weapons used to ridicule and dismiss antagonists. There was no other world, nothing beyond the dark cave of this world.

Joey said, "You got kicked out of school."

"What are you talking about?"

"C'mon! Everybody knows."

"It's no big deal," Justin said. "I can go back if I write a stupid letter to the stupid superintendent. But I'm tired of Davis. I may just leave."

Joey turned white, grabbed Justin's arm as if to physically restrain him, and begged, "Don't leave."

"Okay. I'm not leaving. I was just saying that. Now get ready for soccer practice. Steve's mom is picking you up."

Despite his depression, Joey tried to follow his brother by playing sports. Coaches allowed him on the team, though he rarely played in games. Today, however, Joey had no interest in sports.

"I want to stay for your birthday," he told Justin. "Can we have a party? Please…"

"I don't want a party. You think I would invite anyone to this dump? Besides, I already had my party at school. Now get ready."

"We're not trailer trash, are we?"

"What did you say, Joey?"

"One of the kids said I was trailer trash. Teach me to fight so I can make him eat his words."

"Forget it. Just get ready."

"Have a party with just me and mom."

"Joey, enough. Please."

Joey soon left and minutes later, Justin heard his mother's old car limp and wheeze into the dirt driveway. She walked in with a cake box in one arm and a wrapped gift in the other.

"I got some things for your birthday," she said with a smile.

Justin knew the indignities and physical hardship she endured at work to buy these things, not to speak of the humiliation dealt to her by those who had always envied her education and wealth. It was these people who hired her to clean their houses or watch their children, for no other purpose than to demean a lady who had once stood so far above them. This above all disturbed him greatly. He could not tolerate that she did it for him, though he knew it was an act of love. And the very idea of celebrating at a time like this aggravated him beyond his endurance.

"I told you," he said. "No party."

"Right. No party. It's just us. When Joey comes back, the three of us will—"

"Will do nothing. Don't you ever listen to what I say?" he shouted. He hated himself as he spoke, but he couldn't stop.

"Look." His voice rose with agitation. "I don't want a cake and I don't want a gift. I know you mean well, but I don't want to be here on this planet. I'm messed up. I'm just a freak out of a psychology book."

"Justin, that's not at all true, and don't shout at me," his mother said.

"It is true," he shouted. "And take back the cake and the gift."

His mother placed both items on the table, went to her room, slammed the door, and began to cry. This was bad. She never cried.

A sound startled him. He turned. Oh God! Joey stood there staring in disbelief. Justin never shouted at his mother in front of Joey.

"What are you doing here?" Justin asked, sick with guilt.

Joey spoke in a suffering voice. "Coach is sick. There's no practice."

"What did you hear just now?"

"Everything." He ran to his room and slammed the door. Justin knocked, but Joey told him to go away.

Justin said, "All right. Don't talk to me. Maybe I will go away and you'll never see me again."

The lock turned and the door cracked open. "Don't go…"

Justin entered the room.

Joey cried out in fear, "Are you leaving?" Seeing Joey's little body tremble, and the tears gliding down his freckled cheeks, Justin rushed to him, picked him up in his arms, and held him tight, saying, "No, I'm not leaving. I'm going to the falls. Look, I love you, and I'm never going to leave you. But I need a little time to think. I'll be back late. Just do your homework or something. Don't wait up."

Justin placed him gently down, but seeing that Joey still breathed heavily, Justin said, "Joey, I said I'm coming back. Okay?"

Joey nodded. "Okay."

Justin had long ago made clear to his family that when he went to the falls, he needed to be alone. He walked past his mother's door, intending to leave, but her phone rang and he stopped to listen. She said, "Hello...Oh, hello, Dr. Olsen. How are you? What? Justin suspended? But why?"

Justin ran out the door. He ran for miles till he reached Blackwater Falls. His heart ached. He hurled stones into the seething waters, tried with the usual futility to think of a plan to save the Davis family, remembered his father and wept bitterly.

Justin went home by starlight. He wore daggers on his belt, daring the bears and wildcats lurking in the dense, dark woods. He reached the trailer and waited outside in the cold till the lights went off. He was in no mood to explain anything to anyone.

In the small, shabby space his mother called a living room, he found the untasted cake with fifteen unlit candles, set on his mother's best platter. A neatly wrapped gift with fine ribbon and bow lay neglected and expectant. No gift could help him, but he took it in his hands.

Obviously, a book. Probably a self-help book, full of the same canned wisdom found in greeting cards and newspaper astrology. Still, it came from the only people in the world who truly loved him.

He slid off the ribbon and removed the wrapping paper without tearing it. It was a book. A strange book. *The First Avatāra*.

I don't need this, he thought. *I already saw the* Avatar *movie. And this book doesn't even spell the word right. They put an a at the end:* Avatāra.

His mother had tried many times to take him to the bookstore in Elkins, or to let her read to him from the books he used to like. And now this. How could she think that books like this could still interest him? He looked down at it.

On the cover a handsome young prince with large eyes and rain-cloud-blue skin walked through a tall forest. This, Justin presumed, was the First Avatāra. Sages in saffron robes watched and admired him. Among them, a fair young female sage caught his eye with her soft but stern features.

The Avatāra's world was crafted of bright, clear colors, and peopled by beautiful men and women. Justin gave a soft, cynical laugh. It was like the heroic, elegant world he dreamed of as a child, the world he rejected as a cruel fiction the night of the tragedy. Once he had yearned to be a hero, a true prince in a magical world. Now that vision angered him by its cruel impossibility. He shut the book and replaced it on the table.

But it could not stay there. It was a gift from his family. He picked it up again and read the cover flaps. The handsome, striding prince on the cover was indeed the Avatāra. His name was Kṛṣṇa. Perhaps it was the late hour, or the dim light, but when Justin stared at Kṛṣṇa, Kṛṣṇa stared back. Justin wondered if he had gone mad in his depression. He looked again. So did Kṛṣṇa. He put down the book and breathed deeply.

He looked around the room, wretched but familiar with its bending walls and collapsing furniture. The spell broke. A mere storybook could not spook Justin Davis. And it was a birthday gift from his mother, for God's sake. He forced a whispered laugh.

To complete his conquest of irrational fear, he looked back at the book. Kṛṣṇa looked back at him, this time seeming to invite him to enter through the book's cover into an uncanny, luminous world.

As he often did, Justin summoned courage with irreverence. "Well, Mr. Avatāra, since I'm not going to your world, let me be the first to welcome you to Davis, West Virginia."

A voice spoke in reply, not the voice of Kṛṣṇa, but of Joey, who came in pajamas, rubbing his eyes.

"Who are you talking to?" he asked.

"Nobody. I was just…talking to myself."

"Sounded like you were talking to someone."

"Joey, go back to sleep."

"What's that? Is that what Mom got you?"

"Yes."

"I want to see it. She wouldn't let me see it till you did."

Justin shook his head. "Go back to bed; I'll tell you about it tomorrow."

Joey shook his head and took the book in his hands.

"I like the picture," he said, eyeing Kṛṣṇa. "It looks like he's really there. Were you talking to the picture?"

"Are you crazy, Joey?"

"But he's looking at us. Tell me about the book."

"I haven't read it."

"Read it to me."

"All right, for one minute, and then you're going to bed."

Justin read:

Long ago, in time beyond memory, dark Asura forces attacked Bhū-loka and threatened to enslave its inhabitants. At the darkest hour, Kṛṣṇa, the First Avatāra, descended to the planet of Bhū-loka and fought the Asuras.

Centuries passed, then millennia, till history decayed into legend, legend into myth. Now, sadly, that world has forgotten how the First Avatāra fought to save it. This book will remind the people of Bhū-loka how Kṛṣṇa fought to save them. By reading this book, the people of Bhū-loka will take courage and strive with the Avatāra's help to save their planet. For once again their world is gravely threatened.

"Did that really happen?" Joey asked. "Did Kṛṣṇa fight to save Bhū-loka? Is Bhū-loka a real planet?"

Justin rolled his eyes. "I don't want to pop your bubble, Joey, but this particular literary genre is called fable, mythology, an imaginary story. There is no Bhū-loka."

"But the book said it's not a myth. What if Kṛṣṇa really fought for that world and they all forgot? Anyway, why did Mom get you this book? We never talk about warriors anymore."

"I have no idea. We'll have to ask her."

"Read more." Joey squeezed his arm.

"Just a few more words and you are going to bed," Justin said.

He read, "Learn from this eternal classic how you can awaken your real power and know your real self as you assist the Avatāra. We are confident that you will be delighted with your choice."

"Let's do it!" Joey said. "Let's go to Bhū-loka. We'll bring Mom."

"Joey, no more fairy tales, please. Don't you see they want to sell us something? It sounds like a car commercial. I can't believe Mom got this for me. Watch, at the end of the book, they'll try to sell me an Avatāra computer game where I save the world. Pathetic! And such hyperbole: Eternal classic. Not cool."

"One more sentence," Joey begged.

Justin read, "To fully participate in this unique adventure, you must learn the contents of this book from an authorized Teacher."

"Don't you see?" Justin said. "They want our money, so they'll sell us a course with a so-called Teacher. This is all crazy. I'm going to bed."

"But what if those people need our help? You could fix things, Justin."

"The world can't be fixed, Joey."

"But who is that girl? She looks so smart."

"I don't know. That's it." Justin closed the book, picked up his brother, carried him to his room, and gently placed him in his bed. Then he grabbed his book, put it on the remnant of his nightstand, and lay brooding in bed. He could not get the cover out of his mind. The girl, too, was lifelike. *Good artwork*, he admitted.

Justin closed his eyes, but still saw Kṛṣṇa watching him. The girl sage turned and noticed him. Her beauty haunted him. It might be nice to live in a world like that. Anything to escape this miserable, boring earth.

With such thoughts in his mind, he grew drowsy and fell fast asleep. He slept until a hand touched his shoulder and woke him. He yawned and rubbed his eyes. Why did his mother wake him? Did she forget that he was suspended from school?

He opened his eyes. He was in the forest! Who had carried him out of the house? Who woke him? Where were Joey and his mother? Were they all right?

The forest was lush and tropical, with waving banana leaves and palm fronds, and big, bright flowers of every hue. He must have been drugged, kidnapped, and flown to Latin America! How else could he be here? His father's killers had done this. But how did they do it without waking him? He must find a weapon to defend himself, a stick, a rock, anything!

CHAPTER 6

J ustin jumped to his feet and hit his head on a low-hanging mango. He cried out and rubbed his head. *There are no mango trees in West Virginia!* Where was he?

He rubbed his eyes, trying to wake up. But assiduous eye-rubbing and head-shaking did not return him to Davis, West Virginia. Confused, he reached into a little pond to his side and ladled water into his eyes. That did not bring him back to Davis, but it did show him his own reflection in the water. He saw a handsome face, all that he could wish for in personal beauty. It just wasn't exactly the face of Justin Davis. The skin was slightly darker. The hair was darker. The eyes were large and bright. He looked down at his body and saw he was dressed in red silk with a gold crest. A sword and assorted knives hung from a jeweled belt.

He stood in an emerald-green meadow, canopied by a deep-blue sky. Balmy breezes made palm fronds wave and wildflowers caper.

"My poor dear prince," came a lady's amused voice. He turned to face a remarkably lovely young lady who smiled affectionately at him. "You were sleeping so long," she continued. "I had to wake you. I'm sorry that mean mango attacked you." She laughed gaily.

"Yes, it did," he said, frantically trying to understand where he was and how he got here. This was definitely not West Virginia. Clearly, this lovely girl thought she knew him well. He considered what to do with rapid and rational calculations. He must conceal his confusion till he knew more about this place, and how to get back home to West Virginia.

"Anyway," the girl said, smiling, "wherever you went in your dreams, welcome back to Bhū-loka!"

Bhū-loka? This was impossible. Bhū-loka was a name in a storybook. He must wake up and get back to his family. But the girl spoke as if that life in Davis was a dream.

"Welcome back?" he asked. "Where was I?"

The girl was amused by what she clearly considered to be his feigned confusion. "You were dreaming of another place, dear prince. My poor Prince Jaya!"

"Prince Jaya…"

"Yes, you, Prince Jaya. And I am your beloved princess Su Varṇa. Do you always joke? Or did the mango really scramble your head?"

"Excellent question," he replied, with a sudden, pleasing sensation that he knew this girl. Of course, Su Varṇa. He remembered her. He knew her. But how was that possible? It was all like a dream, yet Justin felt as if waking from a dream, as if he really were Prince Jaya. For now, he would play the part, lest he go mad.

"Well, well," he said, matching Su Varṇa's playful tone, "so this is Bhū-loka, the land of the Avatāra."

"Now that is a hotly debated topic," she said, "whether there really is an Avatāra or not; and if there is, whether he really is coming to our planet."

"That's right," Prince Jaya said, for he must act as Prince Jaya for now, as he continued to remember this world. "Some deny the Avatāra. Others accept him as real. What do you think, Su Varṇa?"

"I don't know. Do you?" she asked in a light but challenging tone.

"No, I don't know." He was hardly going to tell her that he read about the Avatāra in a book in West Virginia. He intuited that he could not mix the two worlds.

Justin, or Prince Jaya, feared that despite his high status in this world, and its genteel civility, one wrong word might arouse suspicion and possibly endanger himself. He must not convince these people he was mad, or an alien who possessed the real prince's body. The result could be deadly. For now, he must play his part here.

Hollywood had prepared him for this situation. He'd seen so many movies where a hero from another dimension suddenly awakes on earth, usually in Manhattan, and stupidly keeps telling everyone, "I'm not from here," though no one believes it, and they are about to lock up the hero in a psychiatric facility. No, he must play it smart. He must convince everyone around him that he *was* Prince Jaya. He could not imagine the consequences if he failed in his performance.

And despite the familiarity of this fabulous world, he was desperate to find a way home to West Virginia. His mother and brother must have already discovered his absence. What would the shock do to them? Both were still weak and sickly from the loss of a husband and father. If Justin did not find a way back to them, his mother and brother might not survive the shock. The very thought made his heart tremble. But how?

He must understand his relationship to this world, how he got here, and how to escape. Was he an alien here? If so, why did he increasingly remember this world, its people, and his place in it, as if he were awaking from a dream? Indeed, this world precisely matched the higher world he envisioned and longed for in his childhood. A terrifying question entered his mind—was Davis, West Virginia a dream? His family? The earth itself?

But this was too shocking an idea. He would not consider it. His mind clung to the reality of his mother and brother and the world he shared with them. His quick mind came to a determined resolution: For now, he had no choice but to survive in this world. But he must somehow find a way to return to his family. Every moment he was away was causing them cruel suffering.

In the meantime, the beauty of this world, of Su Varṇa, threatened to overwhelm him. A fear shook his heart. What if he could not resist this world? What if it erased his memory of his real home? If this was ultimately a dream, it promised to be a dangerously seductive, long-lasting dream. A part of Justin was thrilled with his life here as a prince, the beloved and betrothed of Su Varṇa. That part of him feared waking too soon, if it was a dream. But could it be a trap, and he might never wake again? If so, it was a deadly trap indeed. In Bhū-loka, he felt as if a screen were lifted from his senses and for the first time he truly saw, tasted, heard, smelled, and touched. For the first time, he saw flawless feminine beauty.

Su Varṇa enchanted him. He knew her. He loved her as she loved him. He had never felt such strong attachment to a girl. He prayed it was not a dream, and that he could bring her back to West Virginia, as bizarre as that juxtaposition of images now seemed.

Prince Jaya, as he increasingly thought of himself, now recollected that he would inherit a minor kingdom. But Princess Su Varṇa promised that her elderly, sonless father would add to that his larger, richer throne. In return, Prince Jaya must be strictly faithful to her. That was an absolute, perpetual condition. No problem there. Jaya was truly attached to her.

These thoughts unfurled in his mind like a riveting movie, till Su Varṇa broke his reverie. "What are you thinking of, Jaya?"

"Of you, of course. And forgive me," he said.

"Forgive you for what?"

"For my silly questions. Forgive me and my heart is yours."

"But your heart is already mine. You tell me that every day. Oh Prince, it's a lovely day and you must help me to enjoy it."

She smiled and ran away from him. He gladly ran after her as she led him through a green meadow ablaze with wildflowers. She stopped and fell laughing on the soft earth beneath the shade of an ancient tree. He fell at her side and moved close to her.

He reached for her hand. She pulled it away, laughed, and said, "Wait till we are married. It won't be long now."

"It would be even sooner if we didn't have to make this silly trip," he said, for he now knew everything about his situation in Bhū-loka.

"Oh yes," Su Varṇa agreed. "If only I could embrace you now. Oh, why do we have to wait for our marriage?"

"Yes, why?" Jaya echoed.

"Why?" said a young man walking up to them. "Because you are both respectable, civilized royalty, sworn to uphold Dharma, the sacred Law."

"Oh Lokeśa," Su Varṇa said, "who asked you? You are supposed to be our dear friend."

"I certainly am," Lokeśa said, laughing at his cousin's fiancée.

Jaya knew Lokeśa as his first cousin and best friend, his most intimate confidant. Lokeśa was not as handsome as Jaya, but he was an attractive young man.

"What would we do without Lokeśa?" Jaya asked.

"Don't tempt me with that question," said Su Varṇa, who really did love Jaya's cousin.

Despite their intimacy, Jaya and Lokeśa differed in many ways. Jaya was bold, Lokeśa cautious, even shy. Jaya eagerly sought to enjoy the world. Lokeśa was rather austere. Jaya adored Su Varṇa and counted the days till they could live together. Lokeśa preferred a single life of study and contemplation, unusual qualities for a prince. He even declared that he would never marry. Jaya laughed at this and Su Varṇa teased him. It was perhaps in their complementarity that an unbreakable bond was forged between the cousins. And for all of Jaya's grumbling, he knew he could not avoid this trip.

"I hate to interrupt true love," Lokeśa said, "but we must resume our journey."

"Why do I have to go up the mountain?" Jaya moaned. "I want to stay here with Su Varṇa, and you, of course."

"Exactly." Su Varṇa flashed her quick and bewitching smile. "You and I both know the nearly lethal boredom you will suffer up there with some old teacher's pious lessons, but you will gladly do it to win me, your fair princess."

Jaya smiled. She was right. He knew he must make this trip. In Bhū-loka, both his father and hers insisted he follow ancient custom and learn from a Teacher before he married Su Varṇa. Both fathers, in their youth, followed ancient custom and lived the austere life of an ascetic student in the mountains.

"It builds character and strength," Jaya's father told him. "I always wanted that for you, but you avoided it for years. You only think of pleasure, not discipline and duty. You will be a king someday and you must prepare."

Both fathers insisted that Jaya not accept any so-called Teacher, but that he follow their example and journey to the great mountains to learn from an exalted guide. Neither Su Varṇa nor Lokeśa could accompany Jaya up the mountain, but they both chose to accompany him to its foot.

Lokeśa urged his cousin to remember that a king's first duty is to serve his people, and for that he must study ancient Law, Dharma, and ensure justice, not merely enjoy his opulence and power.

Jaya acknowledged the wisdom of Lokeśa's words, but continued to complain.

"It's a sacred duty," Lokeśa said.

"But I have no interest. Of course I'll be a kind, just king. I don't need all this ritual. You know that this religious stuff bores me to death. Why do I have to leave Su Varṇa? Okay, I know, I know because the tradition is to go alone to the mountains. Don't tell me again."

Lokeśa warned, "Be cautious in the mountains. You know there is talk of an Asura invasion."

Jaya laughed. "Bhū-loka does not look like an invaded world. There is peace and beauty everywhere." He smiled at Su Varṇa.

"Yes," Lokeśa agreed, "but it may not last. Asuras thrive on deceit. They may be here and we don't know it. Be careful. We still don't know if the Avatāra has really come, and even if he has, whether he can defeat the Asuras."

That caught Su Varṇa's attention. "Jaya," she said, "let's be serious now. I'm worried about you going alone in the mountains. There are dangerous animals. And what if you meet a powerful yogī who demands that you renounce the world as he did? What if he won't let you come back to me?"

"Now that," Jaya said, "is absurd. I would never renounce you. Believe me, I will be back as soon as possible and not one second later."

"You promise on your royal honor?"

"Yes, with all my honor, and all my heart."

"But why have we come so far?" Su Varṇa insisted. "There are teachers in our kingdoms."

"Su Varṇa," Lokeśa said, "you ask that question every day. I don't think the answer will change."

"Perhaps it won't," she snapped, "but I still don't believe that Jaya must ascend the mountains to find a so-called Teacher. It's all a little pompous for me. And you, Lokeśa, must tolerate my asking that question just once every day."

Lokeśa smiled. "Dear Su Varṇa, I do not merely tolerate you. I admire you and love you as my sister. And I tell you daily that our local teachers cannot unleash all of Jaya's powers. Only special Teachers can do that. That is why Jaya's father sent him to the mountain to study with the illustrious Dhī-mān and his celebrated wife, Cāru-dhī. No Teachers in our region compare to them. It is an honor that they agreed to teach Jaya."

Su Varṇa shook her head and turned to Jaya. "My love, learn the rituals and dogma, and we can all go home. Do it quickly."

As they boarded their open royal carriage, they saw handsome men and women in fine robes walking about. Jewels shone on their bodies, virtue in their faces. The gleaming sun played on distant domes of silver and gold.

These fine people bowed their heads to Jaya as he passed.

"Look at how these good people bow their heads to me," Jaya marveled.

"Yes, Lokeśa said, "but keep your own good head bowed to the sages. May we now proceed?"

They resumed their journey. Whenever they stopped to let the horses rest, Jaya got down from the carriage and tried out his weapons. To his delight, he found that he possessed amazing abilities in Bhū-loka. Eager to impress Su Varṇa, he pointed out an apple tree fifty yards away and shot an arrow dead center into an apple swaying in the wind. He threw daggers in rapid succession, with both hands, with pinpoint accuracy. Su Varṇa was a warrior's daughter and Jaya's prowess captivated her. He was not merely a normal warrior in a super world.

"What a fortunate birth I have in this world," he said.

"There is no one like you," Su Varṇa said, "but please don't let it inflate your head. I will have to live with you."

"Oh, don't worry about me." Jaya laughed, bursting with pride. And he said to himself, *If only Tucker County could see me now!* But this thought quickly led back to his dread of never returning. What if Tucker County never did see him again? But the demands on his attention were too great now to think about that.

In a quieter, more pensive moment, when Su Varṇa was resting, and the two cousins sat around a campfire, Prince Jaya again thought with dread about his mother and brother. He missed them all the more for his fear of never seeing them again. How would they go on? No matter how natural and familiar his Bhū-loka life felt to him, his life as Justin Davis was always more real in a way that Justin, operating now as Prince Jaya, could not fully understand. But to the extent that he had a most real worldly identity, it was Justin Davis of Davis, West Virginia. If he could not find a way to return to that life, he and his family might all be lost. The thought was too frightening to dwell on. For now, he must somehow accept the strange circumstance that in Bhū-loka, he had a different father and mother, and different siblings, who were also somehow real.

How many lives did he have? Was his love for his family in Davis a mere illusion? This thought made him shudder. He rejected the thought because it violated his deepest intuition. When they were alone, he asked Lokeśa, "We have many lives, don't we?"

"Of course. Everyone in Bhū-loka knows that. We are not ignorant."

"Yet in each life, we love the family of that life."

"But that's natural," Lokeśa said, "since in each life, we owe a special debt to that family. They are the ones who care for us in that life. After all, we are all souls, and so the universe is but a single family. Therefore, it is easy and natural to love other souls that love and care for us, even if they see us as bodies, and do not see our true soul."

This reply comforted Jaya. He was more determined than ever not to forget his earthly mother, brother, and late father. He formed a resolution that at the right time and moment, he would risk asking Lokeśa if he knew about Earth, and how Jaya might go there. But what if he returned to a different time, a different century or millennium? If Earth time and Bhū-loka time were not calibrated, his family's might have already passed on Earth. These scenarios frightened him so much that Lokeśa asked him if he was feeling well.

"Of course," he said, desperately trying to play his role. "I never felt better." Yet despite these fears, the celestial beauty of Bhū-loka began to take over his mind. He found himself eagerly looking forward to the pleasures of Bhū-loka. He feared his power to resist total identification with this place was waning, and with it, he would lose his memory of Davis, West Virginia.

For now, he must be Prince Jaya, as the small group of friends continued their trek. And as he played the part, he became the part. After some time, they reached the path up the mountain.

"Lokeśa," Su Varṇa said in her last protest, "it's rather silly that you and I can't go too."

"Dear sister," he replied, "to journey alone to the Teacher is ancient family tradition."

"Yes," Jaya added. "I know, yet another old rule."

"Jaya, just do your duty," Lokeśa said. "And we can all go home. As we agreed, Su Varṇa and I will wait for you in this neighboring kingdom. We have friends and allies there."

The time had come. Inspecting his weapons and tightening his belt, the former Justin, and present Prince Jaya, bid an affectionate farewell to both Lokeśa, who embraced him, and to Su Varṇa, who embraced him with her eyes. And with many backward glances at Su Varṇa, he took to the ancient trail that rose through thickly forested hills to the great mountains.

CHAPTER 7

E ager to finish this duty and return to Su Varṇa, Jaya ran quickly up the mountain, confident that with his powerful body, he would soon reach the hermitage of the celebrated brāhmaṇa couple, Dhī-mān and Cāru-dhī. He spared little time to eat or rest. But the mountain path was longer and steeper than he expected. His meager provisions were soon exhausted, and even his powerful body grew weary as he trekked for many days and miles through lonely wilderness. This was aggravating indeed. Why didn't sages build their hermitages in more convenient locations?

He must soon reach his Teachers. He would rest and eat in their ashram. He pushed his endurance to the limit. At last, he saw clear signs—a smooth, narrow trail leading to a wide riverside clearing—that he drew near the ashram.

But when he entered the hallowed hermitage of Dhī-mān and Cāru-dhī, he found it eerily deserted. He assumed they went into the forest to gather firewood, or to fill their pitchers at the river, or gather nuts and berries. He waited. And waited. But they did not return.

He touched the firepit. It was stone cold. No one had been here for days. There were no provisions in their huts. It was cold! The abandoned ashram was adorned with fruit and flower trees, framed on three sides by a lovely bend in a clear mountain stream. Yet abandoned it was, deserted for some reason.

Now what? On the very ground where he was to hear sacred lessons, he sat alone hearing nothing but the haunting wind, the shrieks and cries of birds and beasts. He shivered in the high, cold air and brooded over his options.

He could not return without a Teacher's blessing. That was impossible. He would rest briefly, then resume his search. People said there were Teachers in these mountains. He must find one. He would take the first Teacher he saw, whether famous, infamous, or unknown. He just wanted to finish and go home with Su Varṇa and Lokeśa. Then he chided himself for coming under the spell of Bhū-loka and forgetting his dear family in Davis. It was to them he must return, despite the celestial charms of this realm.

After resting, he gleaned wild nuts and berries, drank cold creek water, and set out on his search. His life as Justin Davis drifted through his mind. He worried about his family. Were they still alive? If only he could speak to them across worlds. But his only hope to return was to somehow learn more about this world. Surely the portal through which he arrived here could also take him back, if only he could find it. In the meantime, he must live or die here as Prince Jaya.

He found no one that day, and spent a chilly night under a blanket of leaves. He set out again in the morning, walking miles through uncaring wilderness. Again, he found nothing. After many hours, as the sun sank in the west, his hope sank with it. But as long as he was alive, he must try. He climbed the highest crest in the area to survey his surroundings and plan the next day's trek.

Then he saw it in the distance—a small fire blazing magically in a sheltered clearing. He thought he saw a figure near the fire. A few lower hills separated him from what must be a sage's abode. Gathering his last strength, he eagerly descended one hill and ascended another, approaching the clearing. A closer view confirmed that two sages in white robes sat by the fire. They could be his Teachers!

He climbed the hill that bordered the clearing and descended toward the sages through thick woods that blocked his view. In the last few minutes before their meeting, he practiced his appeal to the sages, choosing fine words to show a respect and sincerity he did not feel, or had not yet learned to feel.

Emerging from the thick woods, he was startled to see how close he was to the sages. They stood about thirty feet away. A sudden, steep drop in the hillside, and a similar drop in the sages' clearing, formed a small ravine that bordered the ashram. A stony stream flowed through the chasm. That ravine separated Jaya from the sages.

In the day's last golden light, he saw that the two sages were not the couple chosen by his father. They were young girls about his age. Why were they alone in this remote place? They were too young to be Teachers, but surely they could direct him to a Teacher, or even inform him about Dhī-mān and Cāru-dhī.

To reach them, he must descend the steep hillside, cross the stream, and climb back up the slope of their ashram. This annoying topography dashed his hopes for an elegant, princely entrance. Oh well. He would enter the hermitage sweating and climbing in a most absurd way. But he must do it.

His entrance, however, was to be far worse than he imagined. As he descended the steep hill, he took a closer look at the girl sages. One was perhaps a bit younger, and seemed to be tidying the ashram. The slightly older girl sat in a graceful yoga posture, back straight, with half-open eyes staring intently into the fire. Her pure white cloth glistened in the twilight. She softly chanted hymns and ladled fragrant melted butter into dancing flames that pulsed with power. Her free hand rested in her lap. This would be easy. He would befriend her, charm her, as he charmed all girls, and even convince her to certify him immediately. Back home, no one would know her age. He wouldn't even have to take the course!

Buoyed by this brilliant plan, he made his way down the tricky slope. But he inadvertently kicked a stone that rolled down the slope and crashed into the stream just below the meditating girl.

Instantly she stood up and opened wide her large eyes, piercing him with her gaze. Her lips parted silently. Every feature of her face showed angry agitation.

She didn't understand. He took a step toward her. Her eyes fell with an almost audible thud upon his rich array of weapons.

"Leave! Now!" she yelled.

"You don't understand…" Jaya shouted. Now was the time to charm this young, disturbed lady. Since royalty must honor sages, in good humor he made a grand bow, and flashed his most charming smile. He had just begun to introduce himself when the older girl raised a menacing staff and cried, "I told you, leave at once! Stay at your peril!"

"What? Seriously? You don't understand." He stepped forward. He could teach her a lesson by knocking her staff away with an arrow. He decided against it. Sages must be respected. Princes never attacked them. And he was too tired to play with this overwrought adolescent. But she just wouldn't stop.

"This is your last civil warning," she said, raising her staff as if to attack him. "You must leave now."

Prince Jaya raised his open hands and laughed. "Would you please stop all this drama, young lady? I won't hurt you. I'm a humble prince, looking for a Teacher. I'm delighted to meet such lovely sages in this rather remote location. You are a bit young, like me, but if you would kindly certify me as your student, you could earn a sweet reward. So, what do you say?"

The girl stared at him, incredulous. He took her silence as permission and stepped toward her.

"I warned you." She again raised her staff. This time, its tip burst into flames and a fireball shot across the creek straight at his head. With the lightning reflexes of a trained warrior, he dodged, and the racing flames singed his ear. He cried out in pain. Was this girl an Asura? Had he stumbled into a demon camp?

"That was not amusing," he shouted, raising a shield. She moved her hand and the shield flew from his grasp.

"Very, very clever," he said with a trace of anger. "Nice tricks. Look, you have no reason to fear me. I will not use my own powers on you, so please calm down!"

Jaya was a brilliant fighter, but he could not attack a girl or a sage, and she was both. Though he was confident he was not in real danger from her magic, she did have some power, and she did seem crazy, and that was a bad combination. He realized he had startled her and so he again resorted to his powers of persuasion. "I am most sorry that I startled you. Forgive me. I truly mean no harm."

She shook her head. "Asuras always say that before they strike. Leave. Now."

Well, at least she was probably not an Asura. In fact, something about her seemed familiar, but he had no time to think about that. Hungry and tired as he was, he chose to retreat at once before she attacked again and forced him to subdue her, which would be extremely awkward.

"All right, I'm leaving," he shouted, taking a step back. "And I am not an Asura! What can I do to convince you of that?"

"You can leave quickly before I slay you. If you are truly innocent, your death here would be most unfortunate."

"But if you kill an innocent," he said angrily, "how are you better than an Asura?"

"Because I offer you a chance to leave," she said. "If you are innocent, you will go."

"I'm going," he replied. "And thanks for the saintly reception."

He could not turn his back to her. Locking his eyes on her, he stepped slowly backward, up the hill, hands guarding his face. But in his anxious state, walking backward in fading light, he stepped on a slippery, round rock. He fought for balance, twisting his body and swinging his arms. But with a cry, he tumbled backward head over heels down the hill, crashed into the creek, and struck his head with an awful crack on a granite rock. For a moment, he saw the stream turn red with his blood. Thinking, *I will die*, he sank into the rushing water and lost consciousness.

He knew not how much time passed before he opened his eyes to find himself lying on the creek bank. It was night and a lovely, moonlit face hovered above his. It was the face of his attacker. Flowing silken tresses framed her flawless features, and cascaded over delicate shoulders. Seeing her face so close, he shuddered. How could it be?

"Why do you stare at me?" she asked.

"I…I'm sorry."

She was the girl on his book cover in Davis, the girl sage who watched the Avatāra stride through the woods, the girl he meditated on as he fell asleep that night. But this was not the time to tell her about West Virginia.

She looked into his eyes and said, "You are healed."

Jaya reached up and touched his head. There was no wound, no pain. He slowly sat up and asked, "Did you do that?"

She nodded. Seeing him well, she moved to a respectful distance.

"I sincerely thank you," Jaya said. "You saved me. But why did you try to kill me?"

"I didn't," she said calmly. "Had I tried, I would have killed you. I just wanted you to leave."

"But why?"

"Because you may be an Asura who came here to kill us."

"That is crazy," Jaya argued. "Why would you think that?"

Her face flushed and tightened and she looked away as if his words aroused a most painful memory. Regaining composure, she turned to him, and said, "Asuras menace the world. Sometimes they dress as princes and murder unsuspecting sages. You entered a sage's dwelling with weapons, like an Asura."

"I'm sorry," he said, "truly sorry. I didn't know. I come from a distant country." If only she knew how distant. "Look," he continued, "I don't really know what Asuras are, or what they look like. Some say they invaded this world, but I took that as a story, a myth. And if you truly suspect I'm an Asura, why did you save me just now when I fell in the river?"

"You may be innocent. I could not let you drown."

"So, you didn't know. That means you risked your life to save mine." The thought struck him deeply.

"Yes," she said. "That was my duty. All souls are united in Kṛṣṇa. So if I unfairly harm you, I harm myself."

Jaya would have to think about that. He heard footsteps. The younger girl sage approached and shyly peered at him.

"It's all right," the older girl said. "You can come now." As the younger girl slowly approached, the older said, "This is my younger sister, Sarit. And I am Devī."

"I am Prince Jaya," he said, "and despite these unusual circumstances, I'm happy to meet both of you." He saluted them with folded hands and they returned his gesture. Sarit now smiled and came closer. More relaxed than her older sister, her eyes were playful.

Prince Jaya took advantage of this thaw in their relationship and explained politely that hunger assailed him. "I have not had a meal in several days, and I walked up here from the wide valley below."

"Of course." Devī nodded to Sarit, who brought forest fare, placing a bamboo tray of wild fruits, vegetables, and nuts before him. Because of Devī's initial attack, Jaya was still a bit wary. What if they poisoned the food? He had no choice. He must eat or die. Happily, he ate and did not die. The simple food, like Devī's healing power, worked its magic. His fatigue was gone.

By now, darkness spread everywhere. Only the sacred fire gave light. He now had to raise a delicate question—would the girls permit him to stay the night, and if so, where? The girls discussed privately and awarded him the far end of their clearing, with a thick blanket for the mountain cold.

"We know you are accustomed to luxury," Devī said, "but this is all we have to offer you."

He thanked them. He had avoided these austerities for his entire youth, but no longer. He looked at the positive side—he would grow tougher. The sky was clear and white with stars, so no rain would torment his rest.

Jaya prayed intensely to awake as Justin in Davis, West Virginia. But he awoke as Prince Jaya in a mountain clearing in Bhū-loka. Devī and Sarit were already awake. They sat facing their holy fire, chanting mantras and offering clarified butter into the dancing flames. He approached them, and stopped at a respectful distance. Devī was absorbed in her offering, and so he could discreetly study her face in the light of fire and dawn. There was no doubt. She was the girl on his book cover, even more beautiful in person, angelic and dangerous.

CHAPTER 8

J aya walked quietly to the fire and sat across from Devī and Sarit. He watched their faces through the flames, and they glanced at him when the fire offerings did not require their attention.

Still seeing suspicion in their eyes, he waited till their duties were done and then boldly said, "Please let me tell you my story, who I really am. We need to clear this up now, if you will be so kind as to hear me."

Devī looked up at his sudden request, spoken with a martial passion to which, he sensed, she was not accustomed. Sarit, looking eager to hear a good story, gently nudged her older sister, who remained stoic and silent.

"Please," Justin said. "It is necessary that I tell you."

Feeling Sarit gently tugging her hand, Devī said, "All right, Prince. We will hear you."

He must be open and honest with Devī. She first suspected him of evil intent, and he could not forever lose her trust with a clumsy lie or half-truth. So he told his story, minus West Virginia, recounting how his father and future father-in-law insisted he learn at the feet of a teacher. A humble, austere life in the cold mountains, under strict tutelage, would teach Jaya discipline and austerity, virtues he had not yet learned to love. If he was to claim Su Varṇa's hand, inherit a throne, and rule a realm, he must submit to this ancient, ascetic custom, at least for a short while.

At the same time, his most pressing goal was to return to his family in West Virginia. All the beauty and pleasure of Bhū-loka, no matter how familiar and real it seemed, could never compensate for the loss of his family in West Virginia. Were he to fail to return to them, all three lives would be devastated.

As a powerful king, Jaya might have access to knowledge and power that would carry him back to West Virginia. In the meantime, he must continue to play his role here, a role he could not honestly say he disliked. After all, he first saw Devī on the cover of a book that his dear mother gave to him. This thought gave him hope. It must all be somehow connected. And even Devī might have the power to send him home, once he gained her confidence.

"I will be honest," Jaya said to Devī and Sarit, "all I want is to return to Su Varṇa, marry her, and inherit my throne. I'm desperate to find a Teacher who will just certify me. I know I will be a just and merciful king. And I have the power to protect my people. I don't see what else I need to learn."

"But why did you come here?" Devī asked.

"Yes, exactly," Sarit echoed. "Why here?"

"Well, both my father and Su Varṇa's insisted that I not accept any so-called Teacher. Rather, I must follow their example and journey to the great mountains to learn from an exalted guide. They emphasized that our local teachers could not unleash all of my powers. I tried to convince them that I had all the power I need, but they insisted that I needed a special Teacher. I am not exactly convinced, but I had to obey. They said they knew of a brāhmaṇa couple who were excellent Teachers, and they sent me here to study with them. Both are renowned for their knowledge and character. No Teachers in my country compare to them, or so everyone said. But when I reached their hermitage, a few days ago, they were gone with no trace. I was deep in the mountains and tired from my trek, with little food left. I could not turn back. Even if I made it back down, it would be defeat and shame, worse than death for a prince. As you may know, once a prince ascends the mountain, he can only return with the blessings of a Teacher. I then searched for another worthy Teacher. I literally stumbled into your midst. And as true sages, you must know that I speak the truth, with no motive other than what I already described."

Devī followed his narration with rapt attention. When he finished, she said quietly, "What are the names of the illustrious sage couple that you could not find?"

"Their names are Dhī-mān and Cāru-dhī, his wife."

Devī's face suddenly turned pale. And Sarit seemed to be holding back tears. Jaya waited in silent suspense, till Devī looked up and said, "Dhī-mān and Cāru-dhī were our parents. They left this world a year ago."

Shocked at this news, Jaya expressed his genuine sorrow at the girls' loss. With kind, eloquent words, he repeated his condolences, emphasizing that he had only heard the highest praise of their parents.

"I assure you with all my heart," he promised, "I meant no disrespect to your most dear and venerable parents, when I expressed my eagerness to finish the course and return to Su Varṇa. I beg your forgiveness if I gave any offense, implicit or explicit. I deeply regret that I spoke as if I didn't value the instruction I might have received, had I enjoyed the great fortune of learning from your parents."

Devī assured him that she took no offense since he had spoken without personally knowing her parents, nor even that they were her parents.

Jaya thanked her. She smiled sadly, and her smile only increased her beauty. He began to see that her grave reserve concealed, and probably protected, strong noble affections. It was clear that she had deep feelings for her parents and sister. And she risked her life to save his.

But as much as he appreciated Devī, a new possibility opened to him. He had been sent to study with a saintly couple, but that couple had passed away. Jaya now had a perfectly good reason to go back down the mountain and find an easy Teacher. He need not stay here. But since he was already here, the simplest solution would be to study with Devī, if she accepted him. And life in the mountains did have its charm. It was peaceful.

No, actually it was boring and cold. And the food here was impossibly plain. He longed to return to his warm southern home, and even more so to Davis, West Virginia. He must not be seduced by this realm, however familiar, celestial, and gratifying it was.

But Devī and Sarit did intrigue him. And Devī was on his book cover in West Virginia! He had thought of her, fallen asleep, and then awoken in a strange, beautiful world. Devī might well hold the key to his return to West Virginia. So for now, he would stay and see what he could learn from Devī about returning to Davis, and about battling those demons the girls seemed to see everywhere. If Devī was too difficult, he would head down the mountain and seek help elsewhere.

Now was the time to ask her to teach him. He hoped for full cooperation. After all, Devī even smiled once. For now, he would only request that she teach him. Tomorrow, he would request, most delicately, an abbreviated course of study. If things went well, he would eventually broach the topic of West Virginia.

But if Jaya thought that Devī's brief, lovely smile signaled a budding friendship between them, a new spirit of easy cooperation, that hope ended as quickly as her smile. He asked her to teach him and Devī, who had now reassumed her impenetrable reserve, replied coolly, "Everything you told me about your purpose and actions matches what we heard from our parents. They once spoke to us of your father and future father-in-law as good people. I have no reason to doubt your identity. But there may be serious reasons to doubt your seriousness as a student. I will think about your request and we can discuss it tomorrow."

Without waiting for a reply, she gave him a curt bow of her head, and walked into the forest, presumably to have quiet time away from him. This delay disappointed Jaya, but he knew he could not press Devī, especially now when his mention of her parents aroused her grief. He must wait till the next day. Even as she began to trust him, Devī was still Devī. She kept an unvarying emotional distance from him, yet she seemed to look into his soul. She was unlike any girl he had ever met. If her answer tomorrow was unfavorable, he would request her help in returning to Davis. If that failed, he would return at once to his friends.

In the meantime, he would take advantage of Devī's temporary absence to speak with Sarit and hopefully learn more about the situation, since the younger girl seemed more open and relaxed than the elder. Still, it was with some shyness that Sarit agreed to speak with him.

"I am grateful that Devī is considering my request for instruction," he began, "but I don't understand why I was so strongly suspected of being an Asura and driven away with, let us say, controlled violence? Why such strong suspicion? I mean no disrespect to you or your sister. I simply want to understand."

"We do regret that we drove you back last night and precipitated your fall, but it was not out of malice. We had a reason. You see, when our parents departed for the World Beyond, they believed that Devī and I were ready to take care of ourselves, and we were prepared at that time. But soon after that, we heard from sages that Asuras had invaded Bhū-loka, placing us all in danger, even the sages. The invasion began secretly, some time ago. The first Asura wave took birth in royal families and now by Dharma, by Law, they are inheriting kingdoms and armies. Their power grows in a most frightening way."

"Are you sure of this invasion? Do Asuras look different than normal people?"

"No, they look like us. That's why they are so dangerous."

"But in my kingdom," Jaya said, "and in all the kingdoms we crossed, we saw no sign of an Asura invasion. In fact, in the two great kingdoms of Śūra-sena and Kuru-kṣetra, everyone seemed happy and at peace."

Sarit paused for a moment, as if to consider his words. Colorful singing birds darted about the ashram. On a facing hill, a family of deer stopped to watch them, and then made their way slowly toward the ever-rushing creek below.

Sarit had gathered her thoughts. "But you must have heard that evil King Kaṃsa rules Śūra-sena. He is an Asura invader," Sarit insisted.

"I heard that he is a severe king who suppressed family rivals to seize the throne. But those things are all too common among royalty. I confess I did not think that Kaṃsa is an invading Asura," Jaya said.

"Oh, but he is. Devī confirmed it and she knows these things."

Jaya now saw that the girls, for all their purity, were frightened young ladies, alone in the mountain forest. They believed they could live alone, but now they saw Asuras everywhere, and embraced an invasion theory, for which Jaya could see no evidence in the hundreds of miles and many kingdoms he recently traversed. Indeed, this talk of Asura invasion amused him, though he would never offend the girls by revealing his skepticism about it.

Sarit had more to say on this subject. "I've heard of terrible incidents," she continued anxiously, "in which Asura princes approached kindly Teachers, praised them, touched their feet, gave them gifts, gained their confidence, and then cruelly murdered them."

"Oh God!" Jaya cried. "That would be unspeakable evil. Are you sure that happened?"

"Of course. Devī told me. She heard it from traveling sages, though I don't remember their names. We grew up in the lovely ashram that you found abandoned. We lived with our parents, of course, and we were always very happy in our daily duties and our spiritual practices. But when my parents ascended to the World Beyond, and Asuras invaded Bhū-loka, Devī feared for my safety. Asuras might come. So she decided we should leave our home and go higher in the mountains where we are now. And she also learned mystic weapons to protect us."

Sarit's naive narration increasingly entertained Jaya, and it took some effort to remain serious when Sarit mentioned Devī's weapons. Devī and Sarit could hardly understand the powers and weapons of real warriors. Little fire tricks with a staff impressed them and made them feel safe. Still, Sarit's credulous tale was delightful in its own way, and a welcome relief from Devī's unmitigated gravity. Jaya wanted to hear more. "So," he said in a concerned tone, "what will happen to Bhū-loka, according to Devī?"

"Oh, you need not fear," Sarit assured him. "The sages say that the Avatāra is coming, and he will save Bhū-loka. Kṛṣṇa himself, the original Avatāra, will come very soon, any day now. But at least you can understand why we were so suspicious when you first came. We're sorry now, but Asuras often lie, and if you had been an Asura, you would feign innocence to gain our trust. And I'm sure you understand that Devī feels responsible for my safety. She is my only family now. So she had to be cautious. Please don't think badly of her for that."

"Of course I don't. She acted as a loving sister and I honor her for that." Much as this topic interested him, Jaya then said, "Could I ask you about another topic, which perhaps is related to the first?"

"Yes, please." Sarit pushed her long, smooth hair away from her face, and tied it with a string. She opened her eyes wide, inviting his question.

"I mean no offense," he began, "but even now, when we seem to trust each other a little more, Devī seems, well, so distant and aloof with me. I feel I can never speak to her as a friend, though we are near the same age. I beg you not to take this as a criticism of your sister."

"I understand your feelings," Sarit said. "I might feel as you do were I in your place. But please consider that Devī grew up in a tiny hermitage in the mountains and in her whole life, she never met a boy or young man near her age. You are the first. She has dedicated herself since childhood to advanced and, perhaps from your viewpoint, severe yoga practices."

"Yes, I understand," Jaya continued. "It is an honor to be the first boy to speak with such an extraordinary girl."

"I think it's an honor for anyone to speak with Devī. I feel so fortunate to be her sister." Sarit flashed her spontaneous, innocent smile that Jaya found charming. Were she not a sage, he would see her as a dear younger sister.

"I'm sure you are fortunate," Jaya said, finding this talk with a brāhmaṇī girl to be unlike any previous conversation. "It's easy to grasp that my presence here would be quite awkward for Devī, as it would be for me had I never met a girl. But to be fair, you and I are able to easily converse. But didn't you also grow up in the same high mountains?"

"For some time, I did. But I wanted to see the world, so when I was ten, my parents let me stay with my aunt and uncle in the foothills, where there are villages. I spent a year there and met many people."

"And Devī never desired to see the world?" Jaya asked.

"No, she didn't. I asked her to come, but she was always engaged and happy in the spiritual dimension that lies within each of us. Devī is a very advanced soul. She thinks more of the World Beyond than of this world."

"The World Beyond? Isn't that where your parents went?"

"Yes, that is the real home of all souls. But we must be pure to go there. Devī is so eager to return to the real home of every soul, that she vowed she would never descend to the world below. She is preparing to rejoin our parents."

"And you will follow your sister?"

"Of course. It will take me a little longer, but Devī is so kind, she said she would wait in this world until I am ready. That's why I try hard in my spiritual practice. I don't want to keep Devī waiting."

Jaya smiled, and nodded his appreciation of Sarit's devotion to her older sister. "Sarit, I deeply respect Devī's purity, her spiritual achievement, and yours. But was she never curious at all about this world?"

Sarit smiled. "As children, we learned that the world below is a place of illusion and selfish pursuit, and that even religion down there is often mere ritual and dogma with little deep concern for the pure soul."

"There is some truth in that. But tell me honestly. Do you and Devī see me as merely part of the corrupt material world?"

At this question, Sarit laughed so innocently that Jaya found himself laughing with her. With a smile, he waited for her answer.

"Oh, we know there are good people below," she said. "In fact, some wise saints live there to help and teach those who suffer. Perhaps you are one of the wise."

"You are very kind, Sarit, but I cannot call myself wise. Not yet."

She raised her eyebrows, as if to say, "Well, you know yourself best."

Sarit's kind, open nature emboldened Jaya to ask a final question. "Sarit, are you really happy with this life, living alone with your sister up in the mountains? Is this really all you want from life?"

"Yes, we are happy," she replied. Jaya had his doubts. He wanted to pursue this topic, but he heard Devī returning up the path, so he thanked Sarit for her time, and went into the woods to practice with his knives and arrows. As night fell, the air again turned cold and he returned to sit by the fire, watching Devī through the flames. She gazed at him, as if scanning his soul. He pondered his fate till he grew weary and retired for the night.

It was cold, too cold, in the high mountains. Jaya came from the warm south. And the food here was always the same, so plain, so austere, nothing but boiled vegetables, wild fruit, a few seeds and nuts. Jaya dreamed of fried cakes and vegetables, sweets, butter and yogurt, and...he stopped himself.

He must stay focused. If only he could be sure of returning to West Virginia, he would happily endure the austerity of this ashram. And he would not lament if Devī rejected him and sent him back down the mountain where Su Varṇa waited. If only he could be sure that his family was safe, he would not at all lament spending time with Su Varṇa. And yet, it would be something to learn from Devī. Thinking confused him, so he went down to the stream to practice his weapons.

The next morning, he met Devī at dawn, gave a polite bow, and said, "So, what is your decision?"

She began at once to speak of Asuras, invasion, and the Avatāra. This topic was good fun with Sarit, but far less amusing with Devī. She was too serious about it.

Jaya sighed impatiently. These girls were so easily spooked, so given to exaggeration. They'd seen so little of the world, despite Sarit's adventures in foothill villages. Jaya had seen many kingdoms, armies, heroic warriors. He was in a far better position to judge whether Asura fiends had invaded this planet. Devī's voice startled him. She was speaking to him. "So Prince Jaya," she concluded, "if you wish to serve the Avatāra and help him defeat the Asuras, I will teach you. Otherwise, find a Teacher who covets your gifts and agrees to a quick skim through ritual and dogma."

She knew just what he thought of religious teachers: ritual and dogma.

"Thank you," he said, well aware he had other options. "Thank you for that kind offer. Exactly what is involved in your course? How would you prepare me to help Kṛṣṇa fight Asuras?"

"It's quite simple. You must become a Rājarṣi, a Royal Sage."

"I've heard the term, but what does it mean?"

"What? Haven't you ever studied? It's part of our eternal culture. It's found throughout our sacred texts," she said.

"Of course. I meant, what does it mean to you? Devī, I came here to study, right? So just tell me. Please refresh my memory."

She shook her head with incredulity. "A Rājarṣi, a Royal Sage, is a king, with all the power, titles, and opulence of a monarch. But with all the wisdom of a sage. A Royal Sage sees himself as a soul, and thus as a selfless servant of all other souls. Only in that pure state can you receive the Avatāra's power and defeat the Asuras."

"I would like to be a Rājarṣi, but I don't exactly feel like everyone's servant. For my whole life, so many people have served me."

"I can imagine. But those relationships are based on the body, which merely covers the soul. In this life, you were born in a prince's body, and another soul lives in a servant's body. In the future, you will reverse roles. None of these bodies, high or low, rich or poor, learned or simple, are the eternal soul. Is that really so hard to grasp? It's pretty basic."

"I see that. I do grasp it. But I really enjoy my prince-life. I want to be honest with you. I know we're all souls. But I don't think at this stage of my spiritual evolution that I can give up the pride or pleasure of a prince. I just like it too much. Honestly."

Even as Prince Jaya spoke these words, another voice, the voice of Justin Davis, spoke within his heart that he, Justin, had known humiliation, poverty, and disgrace. It was Justin who now wanted to cry out to his incarnation as Prince Jaya, "You are mistaken in your pride. There are good people who are poor and forgotten. My mother is the best of ladies, yet she suffers in that condition. And Joey...do not be proud that in one life, you are a prince."

He preached these words to himself, for he was also Prince Jaya. Yet he felt powerless to restrain the pride of his Bhū-loka incarnation. He must merely witness what he, as Prince Jaya, would do. But now he must pay attention to Devī, who spoke to him.

"What will I do with you?" Devī said. "Why do I even try?"

"Okay, how about this?" said proud Prince Jaya. "I'm not a pure soul, but I will try if you will try to help me. Teach me, give me some little practice I can do, and I'll make an effort. I know I could go down the mountain and quickly purchase a teacher's blessing. But your message about the soul...well, it's interesting. Self-realization may not be all bad, after all. Hey, let's give it a try."

"That is quite generous of you," she said with blunt sarcasm. "But I am not your self-realization valet. I told you my conditions."

"All right. I agree to all that you said about serving. All of it." Jaya was eager to see what Devī would teach him, and he had a plan to satisfy her demand without giving away too much.

"You still strike me as extraordinarily whimsical," she said, "but I will give you a chance. You will aspire to realize your connection with Kṛṣṇa, of whom you are part."

"I am part of Kṛṣṇa? Then I can serve him by serving myself."

"True," Devī said, "but to serve yourself, you must know your real self, not just your external bodily identity."

Checkmate. "Good point," Jaya acknowledged.

"Do you promise to use all the powers I may give you—all of them—strictly in service to the Avatāra, to help him save Bhū-loka from the Asura invasion?"

"Oh yes," he said. "I vow that if evil Asuras have invaded Bhū-loka, and if the Avatāra's leadership alone can save this world, and if he comes for that purpose, I will use all powers that I receive from you strictly in his service."

"That was a fine legal answer." Devī crossed her arms over her chest. "Do you really mean it?"

"Of course I mean it." He crossed his own arms. "Do you think I would knowingly stand by and let evil flourish? Or that I would sit and watch innocents suffer at the hands of cruel oppressors? I hope you get to know me better. If all you say is true, I will devote myself to serving the Avatāra."

Devī listened carefully. "Thank you. You just swore a sacred oath."

"Sacred oath? Really?"

"Yes. And the Avatāra will never forget your vow. Ever."

This was way too serious. He feared this might happen. Sacred vows that last forever. That was precisely why he cleverly inserted three escape clauses in his vow. He would serve the Avatāra if Asuras had invaded Bhū-loka; and if Kṛṣṇa alone could save the day; and if Kṛṣṇa actually came to this world—all of which he seriously doubted. Further, he felt somehow that he would soon return to earth, and that would surely nullify his vow, though he would seriously regret leaving Su Varṇa, Lokeśa, and his kingdom.

In any case, Jaya felt he had outwitted Devī. There might even be more ways to undo a vow, but it seemed unwise at this point to consult Devī on the subject of vow-nullification.

Instead he asked, "How does Kṛṣṇa know what I vowed?"

"He is within you."

"What do you mean?" Jaya patted his arms and chest.

"Not physically," she said, almost laughing. How lovely she was when she smiled. "The Avatāra is spiritually present within your heart. You must reach pure consciousness to see him."

"Well," he said, "pure consciousness sounds…well, sublime, and I can always use spiritual power."

"Yes," she said, "I can imagine you like power."

"But I would like to speak personally to the Avatāra, to discuss my vow with him."

"Someday you can speak with him, but you must earn such a privilege by your devotion and service."

"Thank you," Jaya said. "If the Avatāra would simply speak with me, I'm sure we would agree on how to proceed."

"Undoubtedly," Devī said with palpable sarcasm. "But I must bring up another point. I am a young lady, perhaps a little younger than you. But as your Teacher, I must order you and you must follow. Are you sure that's not a problem?"

"Not at all. I'm delighted to accept a young, lovely Teacher. I'm glad you don't have a gray beard."

"You are hopeless." Devī sighed.

"Sorry," he said. "I meant no offense. I am faithful to my fiancée. It's just that I am, well…"

"Vain? Flirtatious? Frivolous?"

"Something like that, but I can improve."

"We will see about that."

"Of course. So, I don't want to rush you, but can we start now? I mean, right now?" Jaya folded his hands in supplication.

"If you like. But I must warn you—you will soon be tested and you must pass the test. If you fail, your lessons will end."

Enjoying what he saw as a kind of game with Devī, he implored her to tell him what the test would be, so that he might prepare. "I can only tell you," she said, "that your faith in your Teacher will be tested, and that the test will come soon. I promise not to waste your time or my own."

"Exactly," he said, "and in that spirit, let us begin." He almost said "fair maiden," but realized that one cannot talk that way to an austere sage, even if she is a beautiful young maiden.

"Wait here," she said. She went to her cottage and returned with folded white cloth. "Take this, Jaya," she said. "You cannot be a spiritual student in your silk and jewels. You will use a student's simple cloth."

"Seriously?"

"Yes, just like your father and his father. This is the tradition. To learn, you must humble the mind so that it opens to wisdom. Even you can see that."

She threw him the cloth and he caught it. He went into the woods to change, grumbling all the way.

CHAPTER 9

S he asked him to sit quietly on a kuśa grass mat. "Everything here is already quiet," he said. *And boring!* he said to himself.

"I meant you must quiet your mind. Now, sit firmly and comfortably on your seat with your head, neck, and back in a straight line. And do not smile at me like that. Please pay attention."

"I was paying attention," he grumbled. Was she always this serious?

She kneeled in front of him, held up her right index finger, and said, "Keep your eyes fixed on my fingertip. Please look at my finger, not my eyes."

He had never been this close to Devī. He snuck a glance into her eyes at close range. Her eyes were large and lovely, but they possessed a depth that unnerved him. He felt her power and feared falling under its control. He was trying to understand her, to fathom her. She took it the wrong way. He had no inappropriate intention with Devī. That was unimaginable. He fixed Su Varṇa's image in his mind, to ward off any possible attraction to this girl sage. And really, any thought of Devī as anything other than a temporary Teacher was absurd, considering her superior social rank of which she was so conscious, his aversion to her lifestyle, and indeed their utter disparity of interests and natures.

He saw in her eyes a determination as fierce as any warrior's. He knew it to be an unbreakable allegiance to a higher truth. For that, she earned his genuine respect. No man could control this girl. He feared she would mistake his intention, his fascination with her. Lost in thoughts, he suddenly realized that she had been speaking to him.

"Please pay attention," she ordered. "I repeat. Balance in-breath with out-breath and fix your mind on the self within."

"What does that mean?"

"Didn't anyone ever teach you these things? Every child in Bhū-loka can meditate. What is your excuse?"

"My excuse? I was never interested."

"Why am I doing this?" She sighed. "All right, mighty prince, try to listen." Her irony did not amuse him, but he let it pass. She went on,

"Focus your mind on Kṛṣṇa as the first sage, the great Teacher..."

"I see Kṛṣṇa as the greatest warrior, smashing evil Asuras," he said. *If they exist*, he said to himself.

"We will get to that, but Kṛṣṇa is not only a demon-smasher. He is also our highest, wisest Teacher."

"What does he look like?" Jaya asked.

"He has a celestial hue, like a rain cloud. He is luminous as the sun, with beautiful, perfect features."

Her description matched his book cover in Davis. So far, so good.

"Now, envision your self as a pure, luminous soul within the heart of your body. Do that until I return at sunset."

"What? That's hours of meditation."

She shook her head and went down to the creek.

He tried to withdraw his consciousness from his body and the external world it processed and focus it instead within, searching for the pure self in the heart. After an hour of meditation, he felt his mind separating from his body. He jumped to his feet. "I can't do this!" he shouted. "It's too strange."

Devī returned and said, "Where is your courage? You are so brave in the external world, yet you fear your own self within. What do you fear?"

"I don't know," he admitted. "It's disorienting."

"It is reorienting," she corrected him. "How can you fear your own true self? It's just you, the real you."

"I am already willing and able to fight the bad guys," Jaya argued. "Why are we doing all this?"

"Because a monarch is tempted by power and riches. If you see your self as a material body, you will fall under the spell of the body's desires. Attraction and aversion, greed and pride will control you. Thus, you will try to enjoy, that is, to exploit, other people, whom you will also see as mere bodies. Politically, socially, emotionally, physically, you will use others for your pleasure. You will be no better than Asuras, even if you fight them. When you see your true self, when you see that all other souls are equal to you and intimately related to you, you will act spiritually and not misuse your power. You will naturally serve the Avatāra, the source of all souls."

Jaya pondered her words. He thought he saw a flaw in them. "But the Asuras also have souls," he countered. "So why would I fight them?"

"To stop them from harming others, and thereby harming themselves."

It sounded true and worthy, but his attachments battled his reason. Still, at Devī's behest, he again tried to meditate. This time, he lasted a little over an hour, but he made little progress. He could not put his whole heart into submission to a greater being, nor could he let go of his bodily identity. Pride and attachment were too strong.

"I'm sorry," he told Devī, "I want to control my own life."

"You submit to a doctor to get free of disease. Follow Kṛṣṇa and he will lead you to real freedom, not to bondage. The more you try to control the world, the more you are controlled by Māyā."

"Māyā is illusion, right?"

She nodded. "Māyā is the power of illusion that pervades the universe. Māyā convinces us our body is our self, though the body merely covers the soul, like clothes cover a body. When we feel we are the center of reality, that is Māyā. When we try to exploit, rather than serve, that is Māyā. It is Māyā that makes us believe that this ephemeral world is our real home. In fact, our real home never perishes. It exists in the World Beyond. That is the real world. We can return there by selfless devotion."

Jaya said nothing, for he had nothing clever to say.

"I know you're thinking of your fiancée, your family, your kingdom," Devī said, troubling him with her insight. "I never asked you to reject your bride, nor your family and friends. I'm asking you to love them more. See them as eternal souls and help them awaken to their undying nature. That is true love."

He wanted to tell her that his fiancée and family were not in the mood to reject their present identities as aristocratic ladies and gentlemen in Bhū-loka, and awaken to a new life as embodied souls. They would all be furious and heartbroken if Jaya unilaterally and fundamentally changed his present relationship with them. And he was too attached to them to even attempt such a metamorphosis, especially since his real identity was still but an idea, vaguely glimpsed in meditation. He did not see it clearly, as he clearly saw this world.

But to avoid trouble with Devī, he said nothing. He didn't need to. She always seemed to read his thoughts, though she was too polite to tell him everything he was thinking.

For today at least, he was in no mood to debate metaphysics with Devī, nor indeed to fight for self-realization. Nonetheless, Devī fascinated him and he decided to stay an extra day with her. He made half-hearted efforts to meditate on the spiritual objects Devī assigned, but repeatedly found himself meditating on loveliest Su Varṇa, his future kingdom, the latest in weaponry, and the amazing heroic deeds he would perform as a king. If Devī read his mind, she said nothing.

That evening Jaya saw Devī sitting by the fire. He didn't want to bother her, but with a little nod, she invited him to join her. He sat at a respectful distance and watched the firelight dance on her high, handsome forehead. For a moment, he imagined she looked at him as he looked at her. As if reading his mind, she closed her eyes, ever the reserved yogī.

The night chill made him shiver.

"Aren't you cold?" he asked.

"No," she said. "All my life, I trained my body to ignore such things."

And you trained your heart to ignore people like me, he thought. *But somewhere inside, you must have a heart.* He hoped she did not read those thoughts. If she did, she gave no indication of it, continuing in her own meditation.

Her gravity affected him. He thought seriously about his family in West Virginia. Could Devī help him? It was best to ask her help after he passed her test. It was too early to seek her help, or indeed to bestow on her complete confidence. How could he explain West Virginia to her? How would she take it?

Another issue troubled him. His attraction to this world was growing. And perhaps worse, his identification with it grew as well. And yet, it was as if his identity as Justin Davis had little power to influence or change his feelings and behavior in his role as Prince Jaya of Bhū-loka. One world could not affect the other. One identity had very limited power over the other. He often felt like a witness of his own behavior and speech as Prince Jaya. He knew that the same soul (Devī would like that) ultimately was Justin and Jaya, but the two roles, the two incarnations were apparently not able to influence each other. If the two worlds, Bhū-loka and Earth, were really so separate, how could he ever get back to Earth? But if they were really so separate, how did he come from Earth to Bhū-loka? There must be a way!

He settled on a plan. Prince Jaya would pass Devī's test, and then beg her to help him return to West Virginia. Perhaps he would slay a few Asuras first, to make her happy (if there were any around), and in return she would use her power to send him back to his mother and brother in Davis.

Encouraged by this plan, he would ask Devī some preliminary questions, to better understand Bhū-loka.

"I have a question," he began.

"Yes, please ask."

"What is an Avatāra? What does that word mean?"

"Ava means downward, and tāra is to cross. So one who crosses down from the World Beyond to our world is called an Avatāra."

"I have heard Kṛṣṇa called the First Avatāra. Why?"

"Because he is the origin of all other avatāras."

"So it is quite an honor if Kṛṣṇa himself comes to this planet."

"Yes," Devī said, "that is the point."

"Another question, if I may…"

"Yes."

"Intellectually, I see your point. Your system of thought is coherent and consistent, given certain metaphysical assumptions about the soul and the Avatāra. But it seems so laborious, and even artificial, to bend my will, my feelings and emotions, to your teachings."

"If you had the courage to explore your inner self, you would not find my teachings so abstract and emotionless. You would find them tangible and inspiring. But that is your choice, isn't it?"

"Yes, it is. I admit that I have far more courage to fight out in the world than to seek a true self within. Perhaps I'm a material hero and a spiritual coward. I crave fame, female beauty, and power, and I fear losing them."

"Well, I respect your honesty. And your fear of losing lesser things," she said, "will prevent your achieving greater things."

They sat for some time in deep mountain silence pierced only by the crackling fire and the sporadic cry of a nocturnal bird or beast.

At last, Devī rose to retire for the evening. Sarit was already asleep. Devī stood for a moment before the fire, her face and figure golden in its glow, and said, "I tell you as a friend, that if you neglect your practice, you will not pass the test. And if you fail the test, you will not be able to serve the Avatāra in this life."

Her words jolted him for but an instant. He quickly recovered his pride and concluded that her statement was a bit dramatic, indeed hyperbolic.

Devī retired to her cottage and he to his makeshift camp at the opposite end of the clearing.

The next day Devī again assigned him his meditation and then went to do other things. He followed her instruction for half an hour, but could do no more. He needed a break. She returned without warning and found him practicing archery.

As she looked on incredulous, pride overcame him. He told her, "Watch this!" He shot an arrow into a target hung on a tree. He then split the first arrow with a second, and both of those with a third, so that all three arrows stuck together.

"Not bad!" he said. "And I did meditate for a while. Seriously."

"Jaya," she said with a tone so earnest, so imploring, it startled him. "If you refuse to be serious now, you will sink so deeply into illusion that for many lifetimes, you will forget the truth. Doesn't that worry you at all? Have you no fear of losing touch with reality for centuries?"

"It sounds simple, Devī. I accept in theory that I am a spiritual being in a temporary body. I know I'm attached to the body's identity. And those I love cling to their bodily identities that vanish when the body dies. But my attachment to these costumes is strong. I can't give them up. To say that Su Varṇa and my other loved ones are but fleeting external identities is fine philosophy. But my whole life, my emotional stability, my sanity, is built on these relationships. How can I give them up so quickly?"

"I understand," Devī said. "I never asked you to reject your loved ones, only that you try to see yourself and them as eternal beings in bodies."

"But Devī! Forgive me for giving this example, but you lost your own parents. And I again offer my sincere condolences. Surely, you saw them as souls, but did losing them mean nothing to you? You felt nothing?"

"Of course I felt their loss. But I know where they've gone. I know they are happy and enlightened."

"But what about parents who die unhappy or unenlightened?"

"Those parents are still learning. But all souls will reach perfection. Some just take a little longer."

"You are different, Devī. You are not like ordinary people."

"I know that's true," she replied. "As a child, I learned that the world below was a place of greed, lust, and illusion. So, attachment to that world was a betrayal of the soul."

"That sounds very…strict."

"It's all I've known. I was born in a strict ashram. We all had one goal–liberation from the world of birth and death. My home has always been the world within, the world of the soul. I choose not to descend to that world below."

"Yes, but down there is where all the people are suffering."

"Of course, and that is why I'm trying to teach you, so you can help them. And I can help them through you."

Jaya remained convinced that Devī could help most by going down into that world. But he did not speak. Anyway, the test was coming. He turned his face away and smiled. When it truly mattered, he would rise heroically to the occasion, fix his mind within, and pass her test. Perhaps he could not quickly sever material attachments, but to pass the test, he would focus intensely on the self. After all, how long could a test last?

Mere tedious practice did not motivate him. But he would come through in the clutch. Devī underestimated him. He could meditate when he had to. But Devī might delay the test. The delay itself might *be* the test. Jaya made up his mind. If the test did not come the next day, he would leave. What if the test comes in a year or more? When would he ever return to his mother and brother? He prayed they were alive. Who was looking after Joey when his mother was hard at work? And who really cared about Star Davis in that county?

And what about Su Varṇa? She would not wait forever. She loved him. He was sure of it. But Su Varṇa was high strung, and sought after by many princes far richer and more powerful than Prince Jaya. He knew that she would interpret a long stay with Devī as indifference toward their marriage. And if she discovered how beautiful Devī really was, God only knew what dark interpretation she might give to his long stay. Both on Bhū-loka and on Earth, a long stay here jeopardized his future.

Even if the Avatāra is real, Jaya thought, *I don't have time or patience for an endless course.* He was tiring of the game. He wanted the test. He turned back to Devī. Another question troubled him.

He said, "You reject attachment, but what about romantic attachment, falling in love? That's not so easy to give up."

"There is a higher love, a spiritual love between souls."

"Yes, but Devī, you are a renunciant from birth. How could you know what normal people feel when they fall in love?"

The moment Jaya launched these words into the ether and saw Devī's pained expression, he wished he had never spoken them. She stared at him with outraged disbelief that he dared presume to know her private feelings. Jaya tried to apologize. Devī insisted it didn't matter.

He fell silent. So did Devī. After a few terrible moments, which seemed like hours, she spoke with no trace of anger.

"Jaya, you may end your lessons at any time. I cannot force you. Nor would I ever wish to."

Jaya thanked her. They both knew he was thanking her for not rejecting him for the words he spoke. Still, it might be best to end his lessons here and leave. But that would mean he failed. He weighed the need to return to Su Varṇa, and to West Virginia, against his earnest desire to gain Devī's powers and use them for good. He decided. He would stay a little longer with Devī. If any other motive kept him there, he could not now admit it to himself.

He apologized again to Devī, returned to his seat, and tried to meditate. She left. He sat ramrod straight, breathed in rhythm, and tried to focus on the self. But the image of Su Varṇa and a splendid kingdom, not an eternal self, blossomed in his mind. Flattering future scenes came to his mind—King Jaya dispensing charity to the needy, slaying the wicked, graciously accepting the world's acclaim. His soul was eternal. He would find it later.

After an hour or two, Devī returned, took one look at him, and said, "This is not working. You will not pass the test. Remember that I warned you." She stood over him, shaking her head. Devī did not merely look at him, she x-rayed his soul, unmasking his heart. And whatever she saw in him usually annoyed her.

For Jaya, the experience was most unpleasant. He strongly preferred to do his own introspection in his own good time. Yet, he thought, despite her reproving words, her biting sarcasm and frosty reserve, might Devī believe that though in spiritual matters he was a clumsy caterpillar, he might someday soar as an enlightened butterfly? Or did she simply see him as a useless materialist? Jaya could not decide. After all, it was inscrutable Devī he was trying to decipher.

For now, Devī sighed, said, "I warned you," and walked away to her sacred fire. There she threw back her head, scattering long, silken tresses, and sat gracefully upright in perfect yoga posture. Jaya tried to meditate for a few more minutes, and then took a long walk in the forest, trying to decipher his own feelings and motives.

The next morning, at dawn's first glow, Jaya bathed in the cold creek, with much complaining, and came up to the clearing. Devī meditated by the fireside. She nodded to him but continued her meditation. He went back to the woods and practiced his weapons till he happily heard Sarit preparing breakfast.

When it was ready, he sat about ten yards from the girls. If he sat closer, hoping for conversation, Devī wouldn't stop frowning till he reached the ten-yard line.

When they met for the day's lesson, Devī said, "Jaya, you could be a leader for the Avatāra. If you would only devote yourself fully."

"Well," he said, "can't we be a little more positive? I did some decent meditation yesterday. I can't be perfect all the time."

"When you fight Asuras, the day you are imperfect is the day you die."

That startled him. But he recovered and said, "Devī, you don't know my martial skills. I'm not afraid of Asuras."

"Then you are naive and will not live a long life." She threw up her hands in aggravation. "If you face Asuras in your present state, they will devour you. Literally. You don't know their power. You must learn to be an instrument, to let Kṛṣṇa fight through you with his unfathomable power. Then you can defeat Asuras."

"But Asuras reject the Avatāra, and you claim they have powers."

"Yes, but they have been accumulating dark power for many lifetimes. You cannot match their power now. Anyway, that is precisely the problem—their power exceeds their purity. I will not add to the problem by giving you power beyond your purity. Earn your power by genuine devotion. If not, however else you obtain it, you will likely misuse it."

"Well, that's clear," Jaya grumbled. This was worse than church sermons in West Virginia. He tried but failed to suppress a yawn. She didn't know his power.

"Are you listening?" Devī asked.

"Raptly," he replied. "But you have the spiritual qualifications, and I mean that sincerely. So why don't you fight the Asuras?"

"I am a sage. I can only fight when attacked. That is Dharma, the Law."

"But I didn't attack you, yet you attacked me."

"I didn't attack you; I was just chasing you away. I serve the Avatāra by teaching warriors to access Kṛṣṇa's infinite power and thus fight with pure devotion, not with lust for power and glory."

Devī turned and walked away. It was hopeless. She would never believe in his strength and ability, nor in his sincerity. And she would never stop her sermons. He could never please her. He wasn't like her. How could he sit all day to meditate? Why couldn't she understand that and stop trying to make him like herself?

The test would come today, or he would leave. What would the test be? A full day of meditation without a break? A full day of Devī's sermons? Perhaps it would be a form of self-denial, like fasting all day or sleeping on bare ground? Maybe he would have to fix his mind on the self for an extended time. Whatever the test, he could handle it. He would surprise, he would amaze Devī, if she would only give him the test.

He chuckled thinking of what he would say to her when he passed the test. "I told you so" was an unimaginative cliché. He needed something far cleverer, but nothing mean-spirited. A clever phrase with a dash of sarcasm would do. And if she delayed the test, he was gone. His decision pleased him.

Devī and Sarit approached and explained that they would be gathering fruits and nuts in the forest and would return in several hours. This was most annoying. He wanted the test now.

He began a relaxed meditation, saving his energy for the test, if it came. But when he tried to meditate, West Virginia came to his mind. He felt his mother and brother near him, like when he first awoke in Bhū-loka.

He was impatient to leave the mountain. He valued the soul, but he had to go home, and he wasn't even sure to which world. He could not think of the soul now, so to relax, he stood up, stretched, and prepared to practice his weapons, which was what he really wanted to do.

He heard a sound from the deep forest and listened hard. Footsteps approached on the forest path. Devī and Sarit had returned early, probably to check on him. He sat down and acted as if he were intensely meditating. The steps came closer. It was not the girls' graceful glide. A heavier step broke the underbrush. Jaya pulled a dagger from his belt. Swiftly, silently, he moved behind a tree and waited.

CHAPTER 10

A man entered the clearing, shouting, "Prince Jaya! Are you here? It's me, Lokeśa." With a cry of joy, Jaya sheathed his knife and ran to embrace his dearest friend.

"Lokeśa," he cried, "I'm so glad to see you!"

"And I to see you!" said Lokeśa. "Su Varṇa misses you so much, and she looks lovelier than ever."

"Well, that is quite a worldly observation for you, Lokeśa."

The two friends laughed and embraced again. Lokeśa said, "Su Varṇa sends her love, of course."

"Thank you. But how did you find me? And what brings you here?"

"Your father sent an order for your immediate return. Hence I came."

"Is my family all right? Are they safe?" Jaya asked anxiously.

"Yes, everyone is very well. Don't worry about that. Your father wants you for another reason, which I will explain. Anyway, as to how I found you, I learned from a wandering sage who came down the mountain that the sage couple who were to teach you had passed away. The sage, who was a great yogī, had passed invisibly through these hills and happened to see that by chance you met the departed couple's daughters and were now studying with the elder girl. I believe her name is Devī."

"Perfectly correct! I guess we have no secrets from the great yogīs and sages."

"It would seem that way," said Lokeśa with a rather serious smile. "I quickly sent word to your father. I felt it my duty. And he ordered your immediate return. So, when your father's message arrived, I went up the mountain trail to look for you, following the sage's description. From a hilltop I saw a fire burning here and came to see if it was you."

"How amazing!" Jaya said. "That's how I found this place. And indeed, I have been studying with Devī, though I fear I have neither the patience nor the inclination for her particular course. I appreciate her very much, but I was thinking of leaving. And your arrival with my father's order must be a divine confirmation."

"Well," Lokeśa said with a smile, "I don't think I'm a divine messenger, but your father insists that you return at once. Su Varṇa awaits us down in the valley, and is most eager to see you, as you can imagine."

"Oh, lovely Su Varṇa!"

"Yes, indeed. But Jaya, I have something most serious to tell you. Can we speak here with absolute privacy?"

"That sounds dramatic. Yes, we can speak here. The girls won't be back for a few hours."

"Excellent. Jaya, when I learned with whom you were studying, I mentioned it to some brāhamaṇas who know about the girls. Those sages warned me that you must not stay here."

"Warned you? About what? What is this danger?"

Lokeśa said, "I heard below that since their parents departed and they were left alone in the wilderness, the two girls, Devī and Sarit, grew paranoid. They imagine Asuras everywhere, a full-scale invasion. Yet you and I personally saw on our trip that the world is going very well. Jaya, the sages insisted that Devī is not only paranoid, she is dangerous. You were to study under her parents, not her. Your father never authorized you to study with her. I spoke to sages who know Devī from her birth. They told me that she has always been mentally unstable, but that her parents' passing pushed her over the edge. Devī definitely has power, but in her hands, it is a threat to you and anyone that associates with her. I truly pity her. But she is extremely dangerous, Jaya, and we must leave at once."

This account of Devī confused and saddened Jaya, but he could not disprove any part of it. And he had always fully trusted Lokeśa. He told Lokeśa that Devī was soon to test him.

"Don't wait for a so-called test," Lokeśa pleaded. "You may not survive it. Or, Devī may keep you waiting for the test till she has full control over you. I fear it's a trap. We must leave now, before the girls return."

"I appreciate and share your concern," Jaya said. "It's just, well, Devī doesn't seem as bad as you say. And she once saved my life."

"How did she save your life?" Lokeśa asked, sounding suspicious. Jaya gave him the details.

"Don't you see?" Lokeśa argued. "She almost killed you so that she could save you and control you through your gratitude."

"I see. But Devī always gives me the freedom to leave when I like."

"Yes, only as long as she knows you will stay. Do not be reckless, Jaya. This is serious."

"So I cannot even say goodbye to the girls?"

"If you do, they will not let you leave. You must come now. Please trust me and come with me. I'll explain later. Devī is not who you think she is. Please! Trust me!"

"I would not advise trusting him," said Devī, who suddenly appeared in the clearing with her sister. Devī turned to Sarit and said, "Stand back, this may be a little unpleasant." Sarit obeyed. Jaya stared, wide-eyed.

Lokeśa whispered to Jaya, "Please be careful. Don't anger her. She has a crazy look in her eye."

"Jaya!" Devī said, "stay away from him. This man is an Asura."

"Devī!" Jaya shouted, "You don't understand. This is my cousin, Prince Lokeśa. He's more than a cousin, he's my brother and best friend. He is not an Asura."

"Would you like to reveal the truth, Lokeśa, or shall I?" Devī pronounced his name with sarcasm.

"There is nothing to explain," Lokeśa said. "I am Jaya's cousin, Prince Lokeśa, and he is needed urgently in his kingdom. His father sent word, and—"

"Please," Devī said, "don't pretend with me. Tell Jaya who you really are."

"Jaya," Lokeśa pleaded, "now you see for yourself. Please help me. I do not want to offend this sage, but you hear what she's saying."

"Fine performance," Devī said, "but forgive me if I don't applaud."

She raised her staff and shot a flame at Lokeśa, who shrieked in pain. Her unprovoked attack on Lokeśa confirmed Jaya's worst fears about Devī's mental condition. Special power in the hands of a crazy girl—a deadly combination.

"Devī, not again!" Jaya shouted. "You can't attack everyone that comes to your ashram. Please stop it. Now. Or I will have to stop you. I will not allow you to harm Lokeśa. This is a terrible misunderstanding."

"There is no misunderstanding." Devī shot another flame at Lokeśa, who again cried out in pain. Jaya was shocked. Devī was the real Asura. She tricked him all along. She fooled him completely. If necessary, he would attack her before she killed Lokeśa. But first, he tried to stop her with words.

"Devī, you need help. Seriously. Do not attack my brother."

"I am your Teacher," she said, "and I am protecting you."

"Have you gone mad? He is my brother. Devī, listen to me. I don't want your protection. If you want to protect me because I'm your student, then hear me. I reject you as my Teacher. I am no longer your student, and I do not want your protection."

"And that is your decision?" she asked gravely.

"Of course it is. What real Teacher would try to kill Lokeśa? You are the last person I would accept as my Teacher. So you have no reason to harm Lokeśa. We will leave at once and you will never see us again."

"Yes," Lokeśa said, "please just let us go. We pose no threat to you."

"Let us at least part as friends, Devī," Jaya pleaded.

"We are not all friends," Devī said. "Jaya, please step aside. I don't want to hurt you. Your so-called cousin cannot leave until he is honest with us."

Devī's refusal to make peace enraged Prince Jaya. He shouted at her, "If you had more compassion, Devī, you would not do this. Can't you see that all your austerities only hardened your heart? You talk about helping the world, but you don't care about the world. You stay up in the mountains and look down on all humanity. And in your isolation, you imagine that everyone is an Asura. You are so aloof, so out of touch, so cold to other souls who are not like you."

For a moment, Devī stood unmoving, staring at Jaya as if in disbelief. Her lips slightly parted but she did not speak. Her face turned pale, and she seemed not to realize that she was staring at Jaya. For just a moment, he saw that his words had shocked and wounded her. However, she quickly recovered. With frightening resolve, she turned back to Lokeśa. It would be a fight.

Jaya quickly signaled Lokeśa, who, though peaceful by nature, was an accomplished warrior. Lokeśa understood Jaya's signal and he assumed a defensive warrior pose. Lokeśa would handle this young lady. Jaya would help if needed.

Devī again attacked and Lokeśa deflected her flames. Jaya was proud of his cousin. Now Devī would learn what happens when a sage provokes a warrior who really fights back.

But to Jaya's surprise, Devī intensified her attack. She hurled shafts of invisible energy that knocked Lokeśa back, and threatened to knock him over. Devī's attack grew steadily heavier, and Lokeśa fell to one knee, struggling to hold on to his bow. Lokeśa was in danger. Jaya had to intervene. He knocked Devī's staff away with arrows. She wheeled around and said to him, "Are all princes as clueless as you?"

Jaya was about to issue a clever retort. But before he could, she raised her hand and Jaya's bow flew away, landing in the trees. He wanted to retrieve it but suddenly found he could not move. Devī had frozen him in place. He tried to grab his knives, but he could not move his hand or any other part of his body.

Not bothering to retrieve her staff, Devī held Jaya at bay with her left hand, and with her right, she pummeled his cousin with fire and wind that tossed him about the clearing. As she did so, she calmly spoke to Jaya.

"You clearly failed your test, and even rejected me as your Teacher. Had you practiced seriously, or had you simply believed me, you might have succeeded. I'm sorry. But in your present state, it would be dangerous for you to wield special powers. You mistake a good soul for an Asura and you take an Asura to be a good soul. You will soon understand."

Jaya struggled in vain to free himself from her control. She then said, "Enough of this. Jaya, I will show you the truth. The Asura is tiring and will soon not have strength to maintain his disguise."

Devī then hurled frightening flames at Lokeśa, whose scream suddenly turned into a terrifying roar that shook the forest. As Jaya's chin dropped and his eyes bulged, the so-called Lokeśa rose up in his true form as a huge, black-garbed Asura warrior.

"All right, Jaya," Devī said. "You boasted that you could defeat an Asura. Now is your chance. He's all yours. You are free to move now. Goodbye and good luck."

As Jaya regained control of his body, Devī took Sarit by the hand and walked away to the edge of the clearing. Still shocked, Jaya said to the Asura, "Who are you? Where is Lokeśa?"

"My name is Vyādha. Your cousin Lokeśa is below where you left him. He knows nothing of this. I took on your cousin's form for your good. I want you to work with me. The Asuras are meant to rule Bhū-loka, and you will rule with us. There are tens of thousands of us already on Bhū-loka, and together we will easily defeat all other kings, and even sages like her." He laughed at Devī. "You are alive, young lady," he said, "only because I was keeping my disguise. But now, I have no such concern. If your former student Jaya does not accept my generous offer, I will kill him and then I will kill you and your sister. Or, perhaps I will kill you first, young lady."

"But why would you kill a sage?" Jaya cried.

"For two good reasons," Vyādha said. "First, because she works with the Avatāra, our greatest enemy, and second, because she may someday work with you, and that combination is too dangerous. Jaya, you must decide. Come with me and I'll give you all your heart desires. I will even let these girls live. Work with me. Don't force me to slay all of you."

It was all true. All that his book in Davis said, all that Devī said. Asuras did menace Bhū-loka. For a moment, Prince Jaya noted that the Asura was handsome and strong. Had he devoted himself to virtue, he could have been a most impressive leader. But Vyādha had chosen a dark path. Rage filled Jaya's mind and body.

"I'm sorry," he shouted to the Asura Vyādha, "I cannot be like you and I will not go with you. Fight with me but spare those girls. Once I am dead, they are no threat to you."

"Oh, but they are." Vyādha took several menacing steps toward Prince Jaya. "They will empower another foolish prince against us. And the older girl seriously offended me. She will pay for that with her life, and her sister's life. Her death will please me greatly. In your case, I'm terribly disappointed. I want to treat you as a son, and give you power beyond what you can imagine. I don't want to kill you. But I certainly will. This is your last chance, my friend."

Jaya silently stared at the Asura and shook his head, rejecting Vyādha's offer. Devī stood and watched. She did nothing. Was she also afraid?

Without warning, Vyādha rushed upon Jaya so quickly that he could not react. Vyādha grabbed him by his white robe and threw him across the clearing. Dazed, Jaya shook off the blow, stood up, and took out two knives. "Stay away!" he shouted. "I warn you."

The Asura laughed and walked toward him. "This is your last warning," Jaya said. Vyādha kept coming. Jaya hurled a dagger at his arm. The Asura flicked it away and laughed. He grabbed Jaya and threw him back across the clearing. Devī and Sarit stood and watched. He wished they would run and not stay to witness his death. Why didn't they save themselves? He wanted to call out to them, but he was struggling just to breathe.

As Jaya struggled to stand up, Vyādha said, "It was rather imprudent of you to brag that you could defeat us. It really shows a critical lack of self-knowledge. Sadly, you have a fatal case of it. I will do you one favor—as you die, I will be the last thing you see and think of. That image will carry you to an Asura birth in your next life. That's the best I can do for now. I wish you all the best in your next life."

Vyādha unsheathed a razor-sharp sword and cried, "This is power!" With one blow, he cut a thick tree in half. The severed trunk and crown crashed to the ground. Jaya looked at the girls. Sarit was very anxious, but Devī, if she felt any emotion, did not show it. In the midst of this mayhem, she was Devī still, impenetrably grave, coolly observing the one-sided battle. Jaya understood her. She looked upon his death with the same calm she would undoubtedly look upon her own. Or perhaps, she welcomed his death after he rejected and insulted her.

But how could Devī be indifferent to Sarit's fate, unless Devī already knew the happy destination that awaited both sisters? Perhaps they would join their parents in the World Beyond and thus were happy to accept their fate. But Sarit did not look happy. Jaya would never understand Devī. All these thoughts raced through his mind in a moment. He must focus on his own death for now.

Vyādha raised up his sword, pointed it at Jaya's face, and came toward him. Jaya threw more knives at him. Some bounced off his chest. Others stuck in his body but did no apparent harm. The Asura laughed and kept coming. Jaya resigned himself to die and stood motionless. The Asura raised his sword and nodded to indicate that Jaya's death had come.

Jaya took a last look at Devī. She was indifferent. She would happily let him die! Was that her so-called spiritual consciousness?

But suddenly, she raised her arm and a blinding flash of light raced from her hand into the Asura's body. Vyādha screamed in pain and rushed at Devī. But Devī struck him again with her power of light and the Asura fell to his knees. "Sorceress!" he screamed. Devī struck him again. The Asura dropped his sword and fell facedown onto the ground, still breathing. He struggled to rise, but could not. As his life flowed from his body, he uttered a last defiant roar and shouted, "I vow by the dark and the shadow that I will take revenge on you, Devī, no matter how many lives it takes, no matter where in the universe you flee. And if Jaya will not submit to me, I will certainly slay him too. That is my vow."

The Asura gasped and slumped lifeless on the ground. Jaya's gaze flew from the Asura to Devī. He was too stunned to speak.

"I must burn his body at once," Devī said calmly, "or other Asuras will track him and come for revenge. That would be a mess. Stand back."

Jaya retreated. Devī stretched forth her hand and the Asura's body burst into unearthly flames. In a moment, only ashes remained. Devī murmured a mantra. Wind gusted into the glen, scattering the ashes far away in all directions. Still speechless, Jaya quietly picked up his knives from the black-scorched earth.

As he began to breathe, and to think, he remembered all the cruel words he spoke to Devī. Shame overpowered him. She turned away from him and, without a word, returned with Sarit to their cottage. Jaya felt so weak that he sat down on the ground.

After some time, he saw Devī enter the forest. He knew she did not want to see him, and probably hoped he would leave before she returned. Emotionally and physically drained, he sat there for some time, till Sarit came out. Kind Sarit approached him with pity in her eyes and asked if he was hungry. He could not eat. Sarit turned to leave, but Jaya called to her with such a suffering voice that she stopped and returned.

"I must speak to someone," he said. "Please, just for a moment, though I know you have every reason to despise me."

Sarit hesitated, then sat down at a distance. Jaya spoke at once before Devī returned and took Sarit away.

"Devī saved my life," he said, "and I will never forget it."

"Devī always does her duty," she replied.

"Yes, and I completely failed to do mine, something I will regret for the rest of my life. But how did Devī know Vyādha was an Asura, if she was not sure of my identity when I arrived?"

"Asuras are easier to detect when they present a false identity," she explained.

"I see," Jaya said. His mind was numb with shame, but he desperately hoped that Sarit would not leave. He needed to talk to an understanding soul. He knew that he had slandered and insulted Devī beyond what could be forgiven. He had formally rejected her as his Teacher and clearly, she had no wish to renew the relationship. It was over.

Jaya now apologized repeatedly, begging Sarit to convey his words to her sister.

Sarit nodded. "Devī spoke to me about this and she asked me to tell you that she releases you from all offenses, since otherwise nature itself would punish you terribly. But your relationship of student and Teacher has been severed and Devī has no wish to ever renew it. You may rest here to recover from the battle. But tomorrow noon at the latest, we must all leave. Asuras have inscrutable powers. Although we burned the body, they might find us here. Please do rest, but we must all leave by noon tomorrow. We will not leave you here alone until we see you are able to travel."

Sarit began to leave, but Jaya desperately called her back.

"Just one last question," he said. "The Asura's curse—what power does it have? Devī must know."

"Yes, we discussed it. The Asura will absolutely attempt to keep his vow. In some future life, he will attack Devī with greater power, and he will try to kill you if you do not submit to him."

"What can we do?"

"Someday, you must keep your vow."

Without waiting for his response, Sarit left him and went into the woods. Her last words struck his heart to the core. The girls were again risking their lives to save his. They could leave at once, but they would not abandon him in a weakened condition. All the remorse he felt over his treatment of Devī now returned with redoubled force.

Feeling weaker from shame than from physical injury, Jaya went down to the creek to wash his wounds. That night, as he lay under the censuring stars, he felt more alone than ever in his life. He thought of his home in Davis. The image of his lost father filled his mind. He envisioned his mother and brother. Were they all lost to him forever?

CHAPTER 11

J aya rose before dawn, still morose. He had failed in Bhū-loka and had no idea how to return to Earth.

He saw candlelight in the cottage. Today he would leave and never see the girls again.

Sarit came out and lit the sacred fire. Devī came out and sat by the fire, deep in meditation. He watched her from a distance. He dared not come closer. In the first light of dawn, Devī looked just as she had the first time he saw her in that fateful dusk when he approached the ashram. And she looked as she did on the book cover in Davis. How could he ever explain that? And how much had happened since he first gazed at that picture?

He brooded over the past till the growing light sent him down to the creek for a quick, punishing bath in frigid water. On the way back, he saw Sarit bringing his breakfast portion. She set it down in the usual place and greeted him with a most cursory nod. Gone was the smile and brief banter that enlivened their previous meetings.

Worst of all was the deep disappointment he saw in the eyes of an innocent girl who had once trusted him, befriended him. He could only imagine Devī's feelings, since he would likely never speak to her again.

It was still early morning, so he rested, preparing for his descent. They would all depart at noon. Devī and Sarit went into the forest. Perhaps they went to gather supplies for their trip, or perhaps to avoid any awkward contact with him. In either case, they were gone.

He now gathered his own few possession. He was about to change back into his royal garments and leave the white robes forever when he heard a faint rhythmic sound in the still forest. The sound grew louder. Two sets of footsteps came this way. How could the Asuras have come so quickly?

Jaya put down his princely clothes and grabbed his bow, prepared to die, if it came to that, battling the Asuras. He placed two arrows on the bow, one for each Asura. The footsteps came near. Two people walked into the clearing. It was Lokeśa and Su Varṇa! Or, it was two Asuras disguised as his dearest friends.

The newly arrived pair cried out in joy to see him. Fearing for his life, he did not put down his bow, nor approach them. He must confirm their real identity first.

"What is wrong, Jaya?" cried his fiancée. "It is me, Su Varṇa. What have they done to you? Did the sages force you to renounce the world? Will you not welcome us?"

When Jaya still hesitated, Lokeśa said, "Jaya, what is wrong? It is us!"

"I am glad...to see you," Jaya stammered, "but...why did you come?"

"I will explain everything," Lokeśa said, as if hoping to wake Jaya from his seeming fog. "We heard of the sad passing of Dhī-mān and Cāru-dhī, who were to be your Teachers. We knew you must find another Teacher. But when we received no message from you, Su Varṇa and I grew increasingly uneasy till Su Varṇa insisted that we look for you. She said she would go alone if I didn't come. We started up the trail, enquiring on the way. As we got closer, we heard sounds of a frightening battle up in the mountains. We feared for your safety. I urged Su Varṇa to wait below, but she insisted on coming and so we rushed on. We had to stop at night, but started again at the first light of dawn. And now, thank heaven, we have found you and you are safe."

In figure and speech, these two were indeed Lokeśa and Su Varṇa. But an Asura had fooled him before and almost destroyed him. He longed to tell his friends, if they *were* his friends, what happened yesterday, why he was wary. But if these friends were Asuras, they might fly into a rage at the revelation of their fellow Asura's death, and kill him at once.

What was Jaya to do? What could he say to them as they stared at him in disbelief? The tension was unbearable on both sides, and remained so for several moments, until Sarit suddenly walked into the clearing.

As royalty, Lokeśa and Su Varṇa bowed to her as a brāhmaṇī. Reminded of his own duty, Jaya did the same. Sarit seemed embarrassed by all this bowing, and humbly thanked them. Seeing Jaya too bewildered to speak, Lokeśa then followed the etiquette and introduced himself and Su Varṇa to Sarit as Jaya's cousin and fiancée.

Sarit listened so acutely to Lokeśa's words, and fixed him so sharply in her gaze, that Jaya felt certain she would now declare his friends to be Asuras, and cry out for Devī. Or, Jaya's friends, perceiving that Sarit had seen through their disguise, would throw off their disguise, manifest as Asuras, and attack Sarit.

Jaya braced himself for either traumatic event, determined to give his life in defense of Sarit.

But Sarit did not sound the alarm, and Lokeśa and Su Varṇa remained Lokeśa and Su Varṇa, at least for a few more moments. Jaya next feared that Sarit, having learned that these two were his intimate friends, would treat them with the same coolness she now bestowed on him. She might even expel them from her ashram, since they were his friends.

But none of that happened. To his amazement, Sarit turned to him and said, "I am very happy to meet your friends."

"So, they really *are* my friends," Jaya said.

"Yes, they are your real friends, just as they appear."

This brief exchange thoroughly confused Lokeśa and Su Varṇa. Jaya then explained all that happened the day before, and why he thus hesitated to greet them, for which he apologized. Hearing of the deadly attack of an Asura disguised as Lokeśa, the real Lokeśa was horrified. Su Varṇa rushed to Jaya and could not help embracing him. Lokeśa did not disapprove in these circumstances. So earnestly did Su Varṇa beg Sarit to convey her thanks to Devī for saving her prince that Sarit could not but be moved.

Lokeśa then explained to Sarit why he and Su Varṇa had come. Lokeśa always spoke well, and now, seeing Sarit's interest in the topic, he spoke at some length. He regularly apologized to Sarit for giving so many details, but she kept encouraging him to go on.

When Lokeśa spoke with reverence and regret of the passing of the sage couple Dhī-mān and Cāru-dhī, Sarit explained that she and Devī were their daughters. Lokeśa offered his heartfelt condolences, earnestly seconded by Su Varṇa.

Everyone listened to Lokeśa's words, but none so intensely as Sarit. Seeing her rapt attention, Lokeśa directly faced her as he spoke, and began to speak as if only he and Sarit were there. Su Varṇa and Jaya both noticed this. Lokeśa and Sarit did not notice the attention they were attracting.

Lokeśa finished his story. Sarit sighed, and then offered her guests refreshments, which they declined with many thanks. Sarit told them with kindness and gravity that this place was no longer safe, that more Asuras might soon come to avenge their fallen comrade. They all must leave by noon. Everyone readily agreed. Su Varṇa, no less than Jaya, was grateful for even an hour or two to rest before the strenuous descent.

Jaya led his friends to his side of the clearing. With his white robes and other cloth, he made a reasonably comfortable resting place for Su Varṇa. Lokeśa preferred to sit and lean back against the soft green moss that covered the trunk of a large, ancient tree. He rested in that position.

Jaya and Su Varṇa went to rest by the creek. Lokeśa had always claimed he would never marry, never settle down. So, what happened next astonished Jaya and Su Varṇa. Looking up at the clearing, they saw that Lokeśa had given up his rest. He and Sarit could not be separated. They sat by the fire, eagerly conversing like old friends. They smiled and laughed as Jaya had never seen either smile or laugh.

Jaya and Su Varṇa turned to each other and laughed quietly. But Jaya now had much to say in reply to her eager inquiries. They huddled together by the creek, talking about everything, yet hardly aware of what they said, simply happy to be together.

Jaya noticed that as the two couples eagerly conversed, only Devī was alone, somewhere in the deep woods. Jaya felt for her, but he was sure that he felt more for her than she felt for herself.

But he did recall that pained look in her eyes when he told her she could not understand what lovers feel. What did she feel now? It was useless to wonder. He could never pierce her emotional veil. Still he felt for her.

He could think no more of Devī. Su Varṇa demanded his attention. But she did say that she hoped to see Devī before they left. "I've heard that she is quite a lovely young sage. And you were with Devī all this time?"

"Yes, and with her sister."

Su Varṇa looked at Jaya suspiciously. He laughed. "You really don't know Devī. She barely tolerated my presence. She hardly spoke one kind word to me. She sees me as a degraded prince."

"Oh, so she's that kind of sage. Then it's best we don't meet."

"Exactly. Let's not talk about Devī. Let's talk about us."

After the two couples conversed separately for over an hour, Su Varṇa insisted on speaking with Sarit. Su Varṇa must have still harbored some jealousy or suspicion and wanted to investigate the girls further. Jaya agreed, to allay Su Varṇa's fears, and to have his own time with Lokeśa, who must have learned much from Sarit that Jaya was eager to know.

So, as Su Varṇa spoke with Sarit, Jaya met alone with Lokeśa, who was not as happy as Jaya expected to find him.

"Is everything all right?" Jaya asked.

"Yes, of course," Lokeśa replied. Jaya knew his cousin, and he saw at once that Lokeśa was unhappy and didn't want to disclose the reason. Not yet. Respecting his privacy and timing, Jaya asked his cousin what he had learned from Sarit. Jaya had quickly coached Lokeśa on what to ask her. The two cousins knew each other well and a word or two between them had sufficed.

Lokeśa explained that Sarit knew at once that his questions came from Jaya, but answered them anyway. Sarit did not tell Lokeśa about Jaya's offense. Jaya was grateful to her for that.

Jaya then asked, "How did that Asura Vyādha track me here, and why did he care about me?"

Lokeśa replied, "When we camped below the mountain in that village, he saw me with you and saw how close we are. He duplicated my body and followed you here. I knew nothing of it. He cared about you because he heard from sages that were you to join Devī, the two of you would be unstoppable in the service of the Avatāra."

Jaya struggled to conceal the remorse that filled his heart. He spoke in what he believed to be his normal tone. "Well, I shall return home, and Devī will travel north to the high mountains. So I will have to do my best without those special powers."

"You don't want to study further with Devī?"

"No. I'm not...ready yet to study with her. But let's not talk about that. What about you and Sarit? You seem to like each other very much."

"Yes, we do," Lokeśa said sadly, "but her older sister always warned her about princes, and after a recent bad experience, Sarit completely lost her trust in princes, even if they are not Asuras. She would not say what that recent experience was. Do you know?"

Jaya had to deviate from the truth here and profess ignorance of what that recent experience might be. He had never in his life seen Lokeśa so deeply unhappy and it was hard to bear. He blamed himself for Lokeśa's misery, but Lokeśa would suffer more if he knew that his closest friend had ruined his chance, perhaps his only chance, of finding a true loving companion in this life. Jaya could not bring himself to confess his role in the affair.

"Also, I could not separate her from her sister," Lokeśa added. "They are so close. I told Sarit that I will happily provide everything that both girls could ever need, at least materially. But years ago, Devī took sacred vows to never go down into the world. She cannot live in our world. And as we know, the righteous can never break their vows."

This cut deep, for Jaya betrayed his own vow by not taking his studies with Devī seriously and consequently failing his test. How could he ever explain all this to Lokeśa? Maybe in forty years at the earliest.

Lokeśa had more to say. He had to unburden his heart. "Jaya, Sarit and I just met, but I know that she cares for me as I do for her. When two souls are destined for each other, sometimes they see it in a second. Not in every case, perhaps, but in this case... Anyway, I'm sorry. I will never mention it again."

Jaya could hardly bear his shame. But what could he do? Su Varṇa now approached him. It was almost time to leave. Lokeśa went to say goodbye to Sarit.

Su Varṇa stared at them for a minute and then said, "I don't understand Lokeśa and Sarit. They have known each other for a total of one hour. But they clearly are in love. But they have no plan to meet again. Look at them sitting together in such silent misery. What is wrong with them, Jaya? It must be the caste question. He is a prince, and she is a brāhmaṇī. It shows that royalty should stick to royalty. Brāhmaṇas are too complicated for us, and too proud."

Jaya could only nod in silence. His heart ached for Lokeśa. They must all leave now, probably never to meet again. Jaya quickly changed to his royal garments and gathered his weapons.

Then Jaya, Su Varṇa, Lokeśa, and Sarit all assembled in the clearing. It was time to depart. Su Varṇa asked Sarit, "Where is your sister, Devī? We really wanted to meet her."

The question seemed to embarrass Sarit. "You don't have to tell us," Su Varṇa said.

"I will tell you," Sarit said, but she hesitated. Lokeśa and Jaya waited anxiously for the answer. Sarit looked quickly at all of them and said, "Devī went ahead, to our future home, to prepare."

"But what about you?" Lokeśa asked. "You can't go there alone. It's too dangerous."

"Thank you." Sarit blushed at Lokeśa's concern for her. "I am not going alone. Devī will come back for me now."

"Then she's not far from here?" Jaya asked.

"Yes, it's quite far. But we travel a different way. Wait just a moment. I think that she's coming now."

Devī suddenly appeared in the clearing. Her hair gently swirled as if she had descended from the sky. Sarit smiled and ran to her. Su Varṇa gasped, and Lokeśa held his breath. The manner of Devī's arrival amazed the royal friends, but no more than her beauty and grace. Jaya struggled to conceal the admiration and shame that filled his heart. Su Varṇa shot him a glance as if to say, "You didn't tell me how lovely she is."

Devī nodded kindly to Lokeśa and Su Varṇa, but did not approach them nor invite them to come near. She looked more distant and powerful than ever. For but an instant, Devī glanced at Jaya with an expression that he would long struggle to understand.

Devī then said, "The Avatāra has taken birth in Bhū-loka. Kṛṣṇa has come. Leave here at once and take care, for the Asuras will attack now while the Avatāra is still an infant. Beware in Śūra-sena. I wish you all well."

Sarit waved goodbye to Lokeśa. He waved to her. Devī and Sarit then clasped hands, and the two girls vanished as the three royal friends looked on in wonder. They stared at the exact spot where the young sages had stood a moment before.

But there was no time now for wonder. Su Varṇa demanded they leave at once, and so they did. As they descended the trail, Jaya tried to comfort Lokeśa as best he could, but knowing that he himself had caused Lokeśa's heartbreak weighed heavily on him and left him too depressed for much conversation.

Clearly, Jaya would never see Devī again, except on his book cover, if he ever returned to Davis. Here in Bhū-loka, their respective circumstances and plans, and their bitter separation, made any future meeting virtually impossible. Their paths could never cross.

Far away in West Virginia, Justin Davis had bitterly rejected the world after the tragic loss of his father. But now, as Prince Jaya of Bhū-loka, he wished he could have told Sarit, and even Devī, not to give up the world. "The world below is imperfect. But there is good there. You could help so much." That is what he wished he had told them, before he wounded them and lost their friendship.

But he could not dwell now on such miseries. Serious danger lurked all around. What if the Asuras recognized him as an accomplice in the killing of one of their own? As they made their way down the mountain trail, Jaya explained to Su Varṇa all that remained to tell of his time away from her. He concealed but a few things—his failure to seriously follow Devī, his offense against her, and her rejection of him. He said only that he began his course, and soon after, the Asura attacked.

As he spoke, he silently reflected on all that had happened since he met Devī. He was humbled and ashamed. Yet he could never be like Devī. Su Varṇa was imperfect, but open to the world like him. And she loved him, as he loved her. It was a good and proper match. Still, recent events troubled him.

Jaya had to throw off his low spirits. Su Varṇa watched him with a mix of fear, concern, and suspicion. To allay her anxiety, he would attribute his state of mind to the trauma of the Asura. Desperate to appear normal, he looked with feigned eagerness at the rich landscape all around them, praising its beauty. He began to chat affectionately with Su Varṇa. They planned their future happiness, the good they would do for their citizens. Jaya spoke with feeling of his love for Su Varṇa and soon stilled her disquiet.

Emerging from a dense forest onto a high ridge, they gazed down in awe at the Great River Valley, extending beyond the horizon, the mighty Kuru realm. After admiring the endless panorama, they descended further till the path widened and the slope flattened into a gentle descent to the valley.

They finally reached their royal carriage. Eager to ride after walking so far, they rode happily into the Kuru lands whose prosperity, natural beauty, and architectural wonders raised their spirits.

They entered the magnificent Kuru capital of Hastinā City. So lovely and peaceful was it that Jaya found himself almost doubting Devī's claim that Asuras threatened the world. Perhaps the Asuras, like cruel animals, committed only random acts of violence, as did Vyādha.

As they rested in Hastinā City, as guests of its monarch, Lokeśa went to consult with learned brāhmaṇas. He returned to his friends looking white with shock.

"We must talk. I have heavy news," he said.

His friends insisted that Lokeśa speak at once. He began. "The next kingdom south of the Kuru lands, is Śūra-sena. That country is extremely dangerous."

"Yes," Jaya confirmed. "Devī told us to beware in Śūra-sena."

"But we crossed Śūra-sena on our way here," said Su Varṇa, "and we had no difficulty."

"That is true," Lokeśa replied. "And at that time, we knew only that its ruler, King Kaṃsa, was powerful and cruel. But I have now learned more from the sages. King Kaṃsa is a mighty Asura, indeed one of the mightiest. For years, he has violently persecuted the princes and even the princesses of his own Yadu dynasty. He imprisoned his own father, Ugra-sena, the legitimate ruler of this land."

"We knew that Kaṃsa was cruel and powerful," Jaya countered. "But what has changed now? Why did Devī warn us?"

"Everything has changed!" Lokeśa said. "Celestial voices, heard but unseen, have declared that Kṛṣṇa will personally kill Kaṃsa and liberate his kingdom. You have already heard that Kaṃsa imprisoned his cousin-sister Devakī. Listen to this! Devakī gave birth to the Avatāra! He chose to appear inside Kaṃsa's prison. Thus, he shows that he is one with all those who are suffering the king's cruelty. The Asura king heard of Kṛṣṇa's birth and went to kill the baby, but the infant Kṛṣṇa escaped! And no one knows how. This threw Kaṃsa into a frenzy of murderous paranoia. He ordered his soldiers to kill every male child born in the realm within the last ten days. I'm stunned. The Asura soldiers are killing innocent babies."

Su Varṇa clutched her heart. "I can't bear to hear this. That such evil could exist in our world…"

"We must change our route at once," Jaya said. "We cannot go through Śūra-sena. None of us can bear to see such evil. And who knows what they might do to us in their madness. We will take a different route."

"It is too late," Lokeśa argued. "Asura spies are everywhere. They know we are coming. We are royalty, and if we change our route, they may fear a plot and attack us."

"But they may attack us in Śūra-sena."

"Not if we behave normally and don't arouse their suspicion. They no longer fear you. They know you did not receive Devī's power."

"I see." Jaya tried to conceal the tumult and pain in his heart.

Su Varṇa said, "We must not go mad worrying about this. Let us rest here in the Kuru capital, and speak of other things."

Jaya and Lokeśa agreed. They rested that day in Hastinā City as guests of the Kuru monarch, and visited the capital's famous markets, filled with opulent foods and clothing from around the known world. They strolled through endless parks and gardens, landscaped with exotic trees laden with fruits and flowers of all varieties of taste, fragrance, and color. Entering a residential quarter, they promenaded along a wide, shady avenue lined with marble palaces. Yet, when they had completed their grand tour, and Prince Jaya asked Su Varṇa how she liked it, she simply replied, "Jaya, what did you think of Devī? Be honest!"

"Oh, I respect her," he replied cautiously. "And I'm grateful to her for saving me from an Asura."

"Respect and gratitude!" said Su Varṇa. "Yes, that would be all that you would feel, if she were old or plain. But she is neither. Devī is young and beautiful. But knowing you, I'm sure you didn't notice that."

"My dear Su Varṇa," said Jaya, trying to keep the dialogue playful, "of course I noticed. But her beauty is not of this world. And I, in contrast, am most certainly of this world. So, we were quite incompatible. Let me also mention that Devī sees me as a lowly prince, hopelessly entangled in base, unworthy activities."

"Really?" Su Varṇa said. "You mean unworthy activities such as loving a beautiful princess?"

"Precisely," Jaya replied.

Su Varṇa gave Lokeśa a joking elbow in the side. "My dear cousin, am I low and unworthy? Be honest."

"My dear princess," Lokeśa said, "you are a true highness, not at all a lowness. You are most worthy, in your own inimitable way. Thus, you have captured the heart of our dear Jaya."

Su Varṇa enjoyed this repartee, but not exactly in her usual carefree way, for she too worried about the Asuras. Noticing this, Jaya tried to play his part to keep up everyone's spirits. But a new thought tortured him. Had he taken Devī more seriously, he might now save innocent souls, helpless infants, from Asura atrocities. And perhaps he might have saved his own friends from future danger.

CHAPTER 12

The next day, they resumed their journey, rolling south on the carriage road for two days till they reached the celestial Yamunā River, bordered on one side by velvet green pastures, on the other by fruit-and flower-bearing groves.

After resting on the riverbank, they traveled a full day along the lush river road, stopping to rest in a peaceful village. Halfway through the next day's journey, the road rose gently onto a plateau that gave an excellent view of the region that lay ahead. Lokeśa stopped the carriage, stepped down, looked around carefully, and said, "All the land you can see below is Śūra-sena. I remember this place."

Prince Jaya quickly got out of the carriage and stood with Lokeśa, gazing at the dangerous kingdom. From their vantage point, it was all beauty and peace as far as the eye could see. The land was a manicured quilt of rich farm fields, interspersed with wooded land and more extensive forests. A wide, glistening river meandered its way through the kingdom, stretching beyond the horizon.

"That is the famous Yamunā River," Lokeśa said. "Sages say it is as sacred as the Gaṅgā. And somewhere down there, Kṛṣṇa himself has taken birth."

Unwilling to sit alone in the carriage, Su Varṇa now joined the men. She stood next to her betrothed and looked out, her face tense with anxiety. "Oh, Jaya! Devī warned us to beware here. The wicked Asura Kaṃsa rules this land. I can't bear to see the Asuras killing babies. Do we really have to go through this land?"

"Apparently we do," Jaya replied. "I dread the atrocities as much as you. Hopefully, we will not see them. I pray we don't see them."

Su Varṇa moved her head slowly from side to side. "From here, it is all beauty and peace. How tragically deceptive."

The friends looked at each other. Jaya nodded, and they returned to their carriage and began the slow descent into Śūra-sena, all three passengers tense and wary. At the next village, Jaya consulted with local people, who confirmed all they had heard. The Avatāra had truly come and escaped Kaṃsa's power. The evil king sent his Asura legions to kill every newborn male infant.

Su Varṇa pleaded with the local people to suggest a route that would take them away from these atrocities. They replied that with extraordinary luck, they might avoid the evil, but it was not certain. The killing filled the kingdom.

One wise man suggested they drive to the west of the king's capital city, Mathurā. Once past Mathurā, their path would bring them near the border of the Virāṭ kingdom, ruled by a pious king. Indeed, it lay just an hour to the west. Crossing the border to Virāṭ, they would be safe. At that point, they would have passed through a good portion of Śūra-sena and their turn to the west, while still in Śūra-sena, would not offend wicked Kaṃsa, nor arouse suspicion that the travelers were avoiding his kingdom. And yet, they would minimize their time in his realm. With luck, they would avoid any unpleasant scene in Śūra-sena.

Everyone agreed to this plan and they resumed their journey. They left the river road and drove twelve miles west to a smaller southbound lane that ran parallel to the river road.

Despite the danger, the travelers appreciated the rich land with its neat rows of grains and vegetables, flowers and orchards. Fine houses bore trellises bursting with bougainvillea colored bright pink, purple, orange, yellow, and magenta. The manners of the people, and even their speech, were gentle and considerate. It was ten days since their departure from Devī's ashram. Traveling steadily south, they reached a point due west of the capital and stopped to rest by a lovely green hill with grazing cows. It stood alone among level pastures and clear ponds. They met a brāhmaṇa who said the hill was Govardhana. "Someday," he said, "Kṛṣṇa himself will come to this hill. The sages foretell it."

Hearing this, the three friends gazed carefully at the hill. "It does have a unique ambience," Lokeśa said. "It almost glows. I would like to see the Avatāra when he comes here."

"I could never return to this land, for all its beauty," Su Varṇa said. "I will never forget this terror."

Jaya tried to comfort her. He admired the hill's unique beauty but he did not want to seem indifferent to Su Varṇa's feelings, and so he said nothing in its praise. They were soon on their way.

Lokeśa was a skilled diplomat, and in each village and hamlet, he spoke with local people and gathered useful news. They passed Mathurā to their east, and were approaching the western turn toward the safe Virāṭa realm, when they stopped at a small town to water their horses.

As usual, Lokeśa spoke to the village elders. When he rejoined Jaya and Su Varṇa, who were sitting on the grassy bank of a clear stream trying to eat their lunch, the fear in his face was plain to see. He sat down close to them and said softly, "Listen carefully. The infanticide has begun. There are Asura soldiers just ahead on the road. Their spies are everywhere. It is likely that right now we are being watched."

Silently, Jaya bitterly reproached himself for having wasted his chance to gain power to battle the Asuras. For now, he must try to save Su Varṇa and Lokeśa. "Let's get going," he said, "and leave this land as soon as we can. The turn to the west cannot be far. We need to cross the border into Virāṭ."

"It is too late," Lokeśa said. "Asura troops have sealed the borders. We are trapped. We must somehow convince them to let us pass."

Su Varṇa began to softly weep. Jaya tried in vain to comfort her. Angry at the Asura's endless evil, Jaya said, "I would rather die defending these people."

"Noble words," Lokeśa replied, "but I cannot let you die. My duty is to keep you safe. And make no mistake—if any of us say one word against them, or resist in any way, they will kill us all. I trust we are all clear on that point."

Jaya and Su Varṇa nodded, their faces pale.

"Our best hope," Lokeśa continued, "will be to tell the truth, that we are on our way back to the Central Lands. You should add that your father is sick and you cannot delay an instant. After that, we can only pray. I'm afraid that everything Devī told us was true."

They moved forward. Su Varṇa did not look out the window, fearing what she would see. Jaya studied the landscape. They entered a prosperous village of fine homes and gardens. But for the first time in Bhūloka, Jaya saw no smiles, no happy citizens. The dark news was known to all. People conversed in tense little circles.

Reaching the next town, they found people even more disturbed and frightened, emotions he had rarely seen in this magical land. Jaya and his friends were riding toward the Asuras, not away from them.

When they stopped to briefly rest their horses, Lokeśa conversed with elders and returned with bad news: "Kaṃsa's troops are just ahead."

"How close are they?" Jaya touched his sword handle.

"No one knows. Let's move quickly. It could be a false rumor, and—"

Heart-stopping shrieks pierced the air. They came from the far side of the town. Lokeśa looked all around. Jaya placed an arrow on his bow. Su Varṇa froze and hardly breathed.

The cries grew louder. Desperate citizens ran toward them. Just weeks ago, on their journey toward the mountains, these same citizens strolled peacefully, joyfully about their Bhū-loka paradise. Serenity and joy were now swallowed in terror. Lokeśa grabbed Jaya's arm and tried to pull him away, but Jaya stood firm, desperate to help.

Then he saw them—huge, black-clad Asura soldiers, swords in hand, coming hard upon them. Jaya wanted to defend the people, but his mind flashed back to his humiliating defeat at the hands of the Asura Vyādha and his confidence collapsed. He could not fight them. Nor could he ever risk the lives of his friends. Ashamed, in agony over the people's fate, he grabbed Su Varṇa, motioned to Lokeśa, and they hurried back to their carriage.

The Asuras charged into a circle of trembling young mothers, ripped infants from their arms, ascertained their gender, and cruelly killed the males, throwing the females back to their mothers. Jaya stared in utter shock. Asura soldiers were searching for the newborn Avatāra.

If he had earned the powers Devī offered, he might have saved these poor infants. What had he done? It was better now to die with honor, fighting for these innocents. Jaya opened the carriage door. Lokeśa slammed it shut and shouted above the din, "You will get us all killed. Su Varṇa will die here with you. Is that what you want?"

A sage standing by the carriage said to Jaya, "Your friend is right. Only the Avatāra can stop this horror! Pray he has truly come, and that he lives."

"The Avatāra is born!" cried a young woman. "He is alive in this world and I live only to see his justice! I say it openly!"

"We must go," Lokeśa shouted above the din.

Jaya resisted. "It makes no difference whether we go or stay. They will kill us if they like. I must hear what these people say."

"Yes, listen!" the young lady said. "Kaṃsa is an evil Asura! Asuras have no mercy, no justice. They killed my infant son, beautiful as a Deva god, my only child. Now let the Asuras kill me. I already died to this world. I live only to see Kṛṣṇa destroy the Asuras. Otherwise I would enter fire this moment. Pray the king does not find the infant Kṛṣṇa! Pray, O pray, the Avatāra lives and grows quickly! Listen to that cry! Another mother has lost her child."

Then, an elderly sage tried to protect a mother, but Asura soldiers cut him down with swords. It was horrible beyond words. Everywhere, people screamed and ran. The three friends held each other as the world swirled around them. Jaya thought of his mother in Davis and dear Joey. Would he ever see them again? If he died in Bhū-loka, would Justin Davis also die at once? Prince Jaya would have gladly given his life to save these people, but such a sacrifice would help nothing, would save no one. Indeed, while it could do no good, his death might do great harm if he could never return to his family in Davis.

Lokeśa shouted at Jaya, "We must go now. You are a prince. If you listen to these people, or try to help them, the Asuras will come after you. Their spies are everywhere."

Jaya nodded and, with his heart in pieces, drove the carriage slowly forward through the terrified crowd. Then a deep voice ordered Jaya to halt. A platoon of black-clad Asura troops came up to the carriage. Jaya faced them and said, "I am Prince Jaya of the Central Lands, returning home from the great mountains to see my sick father. What do you wish?"

The Asura commander said, "Welcome, Prince. King Kaṃsa sends his greetings. He knows that you are traveling through his land. You will stay with us tonight as the king's guest. We want to talk to you."

"I would eagerly accept the king's kind invitation." Jaya hid his rage. "But my dear father is ill and I must hurry to his side. He begged for my immediate return. Please send my deep respects to King Kaṃsa and thank him again and again, on my behalf, for his generous invitation."

The Asura studied him carefully. Jaya nodded to him with apparent confidence. Merciless Asuras might slaughter them all at any moment. Jaya smelled the Asura's carnivorous breath and waited for him to speak. The Asura commander, who apparently knew nothing of Vyādha, smiled and said, "You may go to your sick father with the king's wishes for his recovery. Your father is our friend."

That could not be true. Jaya's father could not be Kaṃsa's friend. But for now, Jaya was glad he and his friends would escape with their lives.

Jaya nodded and the carriage began to move slowly. But suddenly the Asura leader shouted at him to stop. Jaya stopped the carriage. Its three passengers froze. The Asura marched back up to them.

"I forgot to ask," he said. "What is your route?"

Fearing a trap, Jaya thought it best to tell the truth. "We planned to take the western turn just ahead. We've heard much about the natural beauty of Virāta, but we've never seen it."

"Oh, nature lovers," the Asura said. "I see. Here, take this pass. You will need it to cross the border." He handed Jaya a light wooden pass engraved with Kaṃsa's royal insignia. "The border guard will collect this."

Jaya thanked him. The Asura signaled them to leave, and Jaya moved the carriage slowly forward. Su Varṇa dared not breathe. Lokeśa watched with unblinking eyes. This time, no one stopped them. They left the town and entered the grieving countryside.

"My father cannot be Kaṃsa's friend," Jaya said to Lokeśa.

Su Varṇa said, "What choice is there for your father or mine? Perhaps someday the Avatāra will change the balance of power, but for now none of us has any choice. We have no power to oppose the Asuras. If we do, all those whom we love will die."

The carriage rolled on. The cries and shouts faded. The cool air hushed into strange, sterile silence. Jaya looked back and saw only pastoral scenes. They were safe for now. But they could not rest till they left Kaṃsa's land.

Jaya's impotence before the Asura horror tormented him. This, and all the pain he caused dear Lokeśa—indeed, all his problems—sprang from his failure on the spiritual path.

"What are you thinking?" Su Varṇa asked him.

"Oh, nothing. I'm just anxious to get home."

As they entered the last village in Śūra-sena, Asura soldiers marched toward them holding black Asura banners. They were large and muscular, with ruggedly attractive features. Their disciplined movements betrayed a slight swagger. Desperate citizens saw Jaya's royal insignia and rushed to his carriage, begging him to help. Su Varṇa squeezed Jaya's hand, pulling it away from his sword.

"I know how you feel," she said, "but you know we can do nothing. We cannot help these people! Think of me and Lokeśa. Think of our families. Think how our citizens will be slaughtered in revenge if you fight now."

Jaya obeyed, but his heart was broken. Terrified citizens clung to his chariot, shouting and banging on the door, begging for help. He quickly offered a silent, desperate prayer to Devī. *Forgive me! Grant me now the power to save these people, and I will dedicate my life to your Avatāra!* The banging and shouting grew louder and louder.

He suddenly awoke in Davis, West Virginia. His mother and Joey were banging on his door and shouting, trying to get into his room.

CHAPTER 13

D azed, astonished, Justin opened the door and said, "I'm all right." His mother replied, "Your face is white. Justin, what happened?"

"I don't know. It must have been a dream, but it was more than that. I don't understand."

"Justin, I'm worried. I've never seen you like this. Did you read that book last night? Was it the book?"

"I can't explain now," he said, "but I'm all right. It must have been a dream, that's all. Don't worry."

Joey looked up fearfully at his brother.

"Don't worry, Joey." Justin ruffled his hair. "I'm okay. I'm back now."

"Where did you go?"

"Nowhere. We'll talk later. It was just a dream." Justin saw that any other explanation would provoke questions he could not answer. And that would just increase his family's anxiety. For now, it was best they believe he had had a very heavy dream.

Justin closed his door and looked at the clock. 11:45 p.m. It was impossible. He had been sleeping for thirty minutes, yet several weeks had passed in Bhū-loka.

A minute later, Joey snuck back in and asked, "Why were you scared? What did you see?"

"Look Joey," Justin put his arm around his brother's shoulder, "before I went to sleep, I read more of that book, and then I dreamed about it. It was just an unusually long, realistic dream, that's all. It was just a bad dream. I'm tired. Now go to bed."

"Did you go to another world?"

"Joey, go to bed. We'll talk later." Justin spoke in a tone that could not be refused. Joey begrudgingly returned to bed.

Justin was finally alone. Was it a dream? Dare he go back to sleep? Would he wake up again in Bhū-loka? He concluded that he dare not go back to sleep now. And anyway, he was frantic to learn the truth of his Bhū-loka experience. He sat at his computer and looked up key terms. He began with Bhū-loka. Amazingly, it was an ancient Sanskrit name for Earth. He had been on Earth! Of course! Kṛṣṇa appeared in South Asia, then called Bhārata. Thus, the great mountains where Justin met Devī must be the world's tallest range, the Himālayas. The Teachers were Vedic sages. All this matched.

But how long ago did the Avatāra come? Ancient tradition claimed that Kṛṣṇa appeared in the third or Bronze Age of a cycle of Gold, Silver, Bronze, and Iron Ages. This roughly matched the ancient Greek writer Hesiod and the Roman Ovid, both of whom spoke of similar Gold, Silver, Bronze, and Iron Ages.

Archeo-astronomical calculations of Kṛṣṇa's appearance gave a date of roughly five thousand years ago! Had Justin gone five thousand years back in time?

A chilling fact now faced him. If his dream was an ancient memory, he was now separated from Lokeśa, Su Varṇa, Devī, and Sarit by millennia. If they really had known each other, then countless lives had since passed. Were they even still in this universe? That was unlikely. Certainly Devī, and probably Sarit, would have gone long ago to the World Beyond.

If so, Devī and Sarit were far beyond the reach of the Asura Vyādha, but Justin was not. Also, Justin yearned to make up for his failure, on various levels, in his relationship with Devī. That was now impossible. Justin's vow to serve the Avatāra, if such a being actually existed, would still be in effect. But the thought of fulfilling that vow without Devī frightened him. Though he had rejected Devī, and was then rejected by her, he still felt he needed her to serve the Avatāra. But that could not be. How could he serve the Avatāra without her? It seemed unnatural, inconceivable. Worst of all, what if Vyādha sought his revenge not only against Justin, but against his family as well? Were his mother and Joey safe? He shook at the thought.

But he must not give in to these feelings yet. His dream might not be a memory. His Bhū-loka friends and Devī might not even exist. After all, the book spoke of Bhū-loka; Kaṃsa; his capital, Mathurā; the Asuras; and of course, Kṛṣṇa, the Avatāra. Justin's own mind might have created the rest, weaving fact and fantasy into a most amazing dream.

Yet the book did not mention the high mountains of Justin's dream. But mountains exist in many places, not only in South Asia. This alone could hardly prove his dream an ancient memory. He must look further. He eagerly pored over the book. Devī was on the cover, but not in the book. Su Varṇa, Lokeśa, and Sarit were not in the book. Did his troubled mind create them? He quickly checked their names and found that every name of every person he met in Bhū-loka was a real Sanskrit name. Justin had no previous knowledge of Sanskrit, nor had he ever read a book with Sanskrit names.

Anxiously investigating, he found that many more details of his dream were not in the book! Justin's geographical recollections, indeed, the exact location of mountains, rivers, valleys, plains, and ancient cities, were all accurate. The precise locations of ancient royal capitals like Hastinā City and Mathurā, well known to scholars today, fully matched Justin's dream experience. Satellite maps proved that his topographical memories were equally accurate. None of this information was in his book, nor had he learned it elsewhere. How could his mind know or invent such detailed information? Clearly, it was impossible.

Was Kṛṣṇa a real person? Did he really save the earth? Thrilling as this would be, it meant that Vyādha and his terrible oath were equally real. Justin heard Joey's labored breathing through the paper-thin walls. What if little Joey was in danger?

Justin now felt how exhausted he was. For all the excitement, he fell back on his bed, unable to keep his eyes open. If he woke up in Davis, he would ponder the matter further. Exhaustion overcame fear and he fell asleep.

Justin did find himself in Davis the next morning. As his initial shock at his dream, and return to Davis, subsided, he found that he still lamented his failures in Bhū-loka. He grieved for those he might have defended against the cruel Asuras. And he still feared for the future.

Lying in bed, Justin remembered his vow to serve the Avatāra, and Vyādha's curse. The Avatāra might demand that Justin keep his vow and take him away to another world. Justin's family would be left defenseless. But surely Kṛṣṇa was good, not cruel. Such thoughts crowded his mind and made it difficult to regain his energy. Assuming, as he now did, that he had experienced a world that existed five thousand years ago, a world he must have lived in, he despaired of returning there. But that world must live on in his mind. In a sense, he could not escape that world, since his vow to the Avatāra, and his danger from Vyādha, were still vividly present in his present life. And the lessons learned tragically through failure would never leave him. In that way too, he could not escape Bhū-loka.

On a more selfish note, he faced another problem. Having experienced life as a prince, he could not go back to his life as a miserable outcast in a tiny West Virginia town. In the face of larger issues, he was ashamed to still care about his status. But he was fifteen years old, and he did care, shameful or not. In various ways, Justin would never be the same after visiting Bhū-loka, meeting Devī, and experiencing life with Su Varṇa, with whom no girl he knew, or had even heard of, could be compared.

Only one girl could be compared with Su Varṇa, and that was Devī. He still yearned for a princess he could love and who would love him. Yet he now revered Devī's devotion, wisdom, and spiritual power, despite all his problems with her. He smiled to think that Su Varṇa and Devī had become key reference points in his life.

But such thoughts led to the same uncertainty and confusion now as they did in Bhū-loka. He must now focus on urgent, practical matters, which could be summarized in a single question: What was he to do with his life? He must not make the same mistakes in this life that he made in Bhū-loka. But what did that mean?

His mother knocked at the door and anxiously called his name.

"Come in," he said, and she entered.

"I'm afraid of that book." She nodded toward it on his desk. "We should get rid of it. I should never have bought it for you."

This was serious indeed. Justin sat up. "I have to keep it. But tell me, where did you find the book? I looked online and the internet has never heard of it."

"I know," Star Davis replied. "I discovered that myself after I bought it. I found it in that little bookstore outside of Parsons, on a shelf in the back. It caught my eye. The owner, Annie, said she'd never seen it before. She didn't recall how it got there. At the time, it struck me as mysterious but harmless. And I thought you'd like it. I'm sorry."

"Mom, don't be sorry. I do like it. But why did you buy that book?"

"It looked like ancient stories, the kind you used to enjoy. I hoped it would take your mind off our problems."

"Yes," Justin said, remembering Bhū-loka, "it definitely did that."

Seeing her son was well, she hugged him and rushed off to do the menial work that was killing her body and soul. Justin could not bear it. His mother deserved so much better in life.

How many times had he seen her sitting in despair at her little desk, struggling in vain to write? "I feel like Jane Austen in Bath!" she would exclaim. "Nothing comes. I can't write. I'm just so tired."

Yet he, her elder son, had been so self-absorbed, so obsessed with his own pain, he had neglected the greater suffering of his mother. When she went out every day to work, he had cared more about his own reputation than her grinding, devastating misery.

The shame he now felt equaled what he suffered on failing the innocent citizens of Bhū-loka. There, he failed deserving strangers. Here in Davis, he failed those most deserving of his compassion. His mother had asked so little of him, only that he try to be happy, yet he had blindly, obstinately refused to give her that simple satisfaction she so desperately needed to keep hope alive in her heart. He now saw as never before that his mother was literally working herself to death, physically and emotionally, because he was too angry and morose to keep a job. For his sake she didn't speak of her troubles, but the endless poverty and abject humiliation she faced daily ruined her health and robbed her life of joy. Behind the cheerful face she put on for her children was a broken heart and crushed hopes. She lost the man she loved. And the pride of her life, her first son, gave up on life and gave her only more pain and trouble.

In his selfish rage, Justin had even caused pain to brilliant little Joey, whose spirits and health had never recovered from the loss of his father, the first loss provoking the second. Previously blind to its harmful effects, Justin now condemned the proud self-pity that had driven him to create misery in his own life and the lives of those he loved.

Determined as he was not to fail again, as he most certainly failed in Bhū-loka, he vowed to himself that his first concern must be his family. He would not stop till he uplifted them. His mother would live in comfort and respectability, free to pursue her literary dreams. Joey would have the best medical treatment and anything else he needed or wanted. In short, Justin would restore his family.

But there was more. While his mother and brother had first claims upon his devotion and efforts, his father's legacy demanded that he also strive to make the world a better place. With burning regret, Justin now saw that on losing his father, he had given up his father's noble values and goals, when he should have honored and pursued them in his own life.

But what did that mean? What could he do for the world? No answer came to him. He knew he must honor his father by helping the world, but he had no idea how to do it. And Tark Davis himself had urged his son to pursue his own dreams, his own chosen career. Justin could only hope that in time, his path would become clear.

In the meantime, one fact was very clear. At present, Justin Davis was nothing but an impoverished teenage outcast, on the verge of expulsion from school.

He put his book and some food in a backpack and went to Blackwater Falls, where he could be alone and form a plan. Hiking down to the foot of the falls, he sat quietly, watching the waters dive and churn and flow into a calm, crystal river.

He recalled how weak and useless he had been when Asuras assailed the innocent, how he failed with Devī, and these visions made his mind churn like the waters. His troubled mind found peace only when it flowed into the calm of absolute resolve—in this life, he must not fail. He must not fail his family or the world. Or himself.

But he needed a practical plan. He came to the falls to devise one, and he now threw himself into that task.

To achieve specific career goals, whatever they might be, and whenever they manifested, Justin must excel in school. Before the tragedy, he had been deeply attached to following long family tradition and attending West Virginia University as an undergraduate and then doing his graduate studies at the University of Virginia. But now, the tragedy of his father made the notion of moving to Morgantown, where they had spent so much happy time together, unbearable. And the idea of going directly to the University of Virginia as an undergraduate was an impossible idea.

Surely, the path to help his family, and the path to honor his father, fully converged in a present duty. He must return to high school and achieve overwhelming success there. This would lead him to Virginia. And from those privileged heights, he would choose the best career to raise his family and honor his father.

To pursue his goals, he needed nothing short of an extreme makeover, a dramatic new plan for his life, with well-planned steps. If only Devī were here to guide him. But she was gone forever.

But what if other Teachers still lived on Earth? If he found one, he could acquire immense power. He could do so much good.

He opened his book, hoping for mystic confirmation, and read this:

Your world is spiraling out of control. The Avatāra will again save your planet, but only if good people like you are willing to follow him. But you must learn how to do this from a Teacher.

That was it! He had his confirmation. Only one problem remained.

Where would he find a Teacher?

On returning home, Joey attacked him with questions. Justin decided not to reveal his plan, lest he put Joey in danger. But Joey began to threaten to steal the book, read it anyway, and find out for himself. When Justin still refused, Joey turned pale and said, "You're going to go back to that world and never come here again. You're going to leave me and Mom. That's why you won't tell me the truth."

"That's absurd. I will never leave you and Mom."

"Then tell me. If you don't tell me, I'm going to jump into the falls."

"Joey, don't ever say that!" Justin cried. "How can you even think about such a thing? Don't ever say that again. And don't ever think about it."

"You can't stop me," Joey shouted, shaking uncontrollably. Justin had never seen him so disturbed and feared what he might do. Joey had never recovered from the trauma of his father's murder.

Justin went to hold him, but Joey pushed him away. He had never done that. Joey then ran into his room and slammed the door behind him.

Joey's unprecedented behavior deeply frightened Justin. And apart from what Joey might do to himself, his level of anxiety seriously threatened his health. Justin decided that not to include Joey in his plan was the greater immediate threat, and so resolved to reveal only as much as would satisfy and calm him. Justin knew that Joey was only happy when he saw his older brother inspired and confident, and when he was allowed to participate in whatever Justin was doing. Justin saw that he could not exclude Joey from his plans. He could hardly imagine the horror for himself and his mother if Joey were to harm himself, or if his health collapsed from stress.

Justin went to Joey's door and heard him crying in his room. Justin said, "Joey, I decided to tell you what I'm doing, and you can be part of it."

A moment later, Joey, eyes red and cheeks drenched in tears, opened the door. Justin picked him up, held him tight, and carried him to his room.

"Now, before I tell you," Justin said, "you must promise me never, ever to hurt yourself, and never even to say it. Promise me."

"I promise. Now tell me."

"Okay. I'm making a plan to help Mom, and our whole family. Then, we can help the world, like Dad did. As Plato said, we'll go back into the cave, to help everyone else."

"How will we do that?" Joey asked, eager to participate.

"Well, there are bad people—the book calls them Asuras—who don't like it when people do good things for other people, so we need power, in two ways. First, I'm going to return to school and do my best to be the top student there. That way, I can follow Dad to the University of Virginia, and I can have a real career and make real money for the family."

"But what about the bad people?" Joey asked.

"We'll try to avoid them, and hopefully they won't bother us. But in case they do, I experienced in my dream that a Teacher can bestow great power. And the book confirms it. So, I'll return to school and try my best, but in the meantime, we can look for a Teacher, who will explain what else we should do."

"But how can we find a Teacher in Tucker County?" Joey asked.

"Good question. I only know that the book told me to find a Teacher. That means a Teacher must already be here, or somewhere, waiting for us. But we might as well be practical and start looking here before we go elsewhere."

"I agree," Joey said. "That's a good plan." He gazed at the book cover and asked, "What were those people like?"

"Well, I never met Kṛṣṇa. But I did meet some sages who were devoted fully to understanding their own soul, and connecting with the Avatāra, the source of all. And the sages were powerful."

"Really?"

"Yes, and I admire their devotion, their courage in spiritual life."

"So, you did go to that world. I knew you did."

"Yes, in a dream. And the dream matched the book. So that's what we have to do."

"Tell me about the Avatāra," Joey asked.

"I never met him. But, if he exists, he's very powerful."

"But the sages, the Teachers said he exists, so he must exist, right?"

"Yes, basically, that's true. So, assuming the Avatāra is real, we will help him to save this world. But we need a Teacher first. And I don't know if there are any in this world. Not now. Tomorrow, when you come home from school, maybe we'll look for a Teacher."

Joey gave an excited *Yes!* He then begged Justin for a story.

"Consider this," Justin said. "What if, long ago, people had an entirely different kind of technology? It would have been…natural, not industrial. They used natural elements like water and fire, not steel machines, or even digital technology. They uttered mantras, powerful sound vibrations that tuned into the core vibration of matter and released great power. This is all in the book. And what if the myths and fables that come down to us today are faint memories, mythologized recollections of an ancient world that was more advanced than our own? What if we could invoke that world again, if we believe in it?"

"Just by believing it?" Joey seemed intrigued but doubtful.

"No, of course not just by believing. But if we believe, even a little bit, we will try to learn or relearn an ancient science more subtle than our own today. What if we could reconnect with souls far stronger and wiser than us and revive their ancient wisdom?"

"Yes, we should do that," Joey said. "But how?"

"How? It's obvious. We have to find a Teacher and learn from him, or her, and then teach the world. We'll make a plan tomorrow."

Justin lay in bed that night, trying to put his thoughts in order. Since childhood, he suspected there was something important about this world that he should know, but didn't. Then the book came. Now, he must act. The next morning, Joey came into his room and woke him.

"What are you doing, Joey? I was resting."

"Tell me what really happened that night," he said.

"I will, I promise." Justin jumped out of bed. "We have a world to save, and I have to get back in shape."

"You are always in shape," Joey argued.

"No, I mean super shape. I've got a mission."

Justin hit the ground and dashed through fifty pushups as Joey insisted, "We have to talk. Tell me what really happened that night."

"Just relax," Justin said, as he whipped through twenty-five pullups on a closet bar.

"This is not cool." Joey stomped his foot.

"Hey, relax, Joey. Today's a big day. We have to find a Teacher."

Joey acquiesced and asked for a practical plan.

"Well," Justin said, "Mom found this book in Parsons, and no one knows how it got there. So the Teacher might be in Parsons. Maybe it's Annie, the bookstore owner."

"I seriously doubt it's Annie," Joey said, "but I think you should start in Parsons. And by the way, why is Avatāra spelled that way?"

"I looked it up. That's the original Sanskrit spelling." Justin grabbed a towel and headed for the shower.

"That's what I thought," Joey replied.

Justin could not tell Joey that since his humiliating defeat at the hands of Vyādha, Justin had lost some of his old confidence in martial affairs. But a Teacher would solve this problem. He could then serve Kṛṣṇa and defeat Vyādha, or at least defend himself from the Asura. Joey went to school, and Justin set out for Parsons, seventeen miles down the mountain, with no idea how he would get there.

CHAPTER 14

A trucker from Maryland who knew nothing of Justin's local reputation gave him a ride down the mountain to Parsons, where he first tried the now-legendary bookstore where his mother bought the book. Annie wanted to help but had no clue as to the book's provenance. When Justin dropped hints about the book's contents, she seemed confused. The only spiritual Teacher she knew was that fiery preacher down in Elkins. Justin thanked her and went out to walk the town.

He searched for a Teacher in the faces he passed. Surely a real Teacher would recognize him, would see his soul, and signal him. Parsons is not a large town, with under fifteen hundred inhabitants. And Justin walked up and down virtually all of its streets. He crossed over the Cheat River to the tiny hamlet of Bretz and came back again. He entered stores and banks, schools and restaurants, and even spent extra time at the handsome Tucker County Courthouse, since a Teacher might be a judge. Result: No Teacher. Indeed, he saw not one mystic visage, and certainly no one like Devī. He began to feel very foolish and found his way back to Davis.

The next day was Saturday. Aided by Joey, Justin searched in Davis and neighboring Thomas, soon exhausting these resources. He next searched the nearby Canaan Valley area. No Teacher in Canaan Valley.

Justin even looked for a new Devī. But the Tucker County girls, though lovely enough, were not great sages. The search lasted five days and Justin was feeling desperate. He might well need a Teacher to protect his family, and his own life. How would he ever find a Teacher in little Tucker County, which had fewer than seven thousand inhabitants?

Then, Joey declared, "My teacher Mr. Blankenship might be a Teacher."

"Why?"

"He kind of looks like Gandalf the Wizard, but without the beard."

"Is that all?"

"No, it's not. I told Mr. Blankenship you were reading ancient stories to me, and he smiled, like he knew more than he was saying."

"Joey, we have to be thorough. Ask your teacher if he knows anything about the First Avatāra, Kṛṣṇa."

Mr. Blankenship turned out to be a total blank. Justin concluded there were no Teachers in Tucker County. What would he do now? What was the plan? To do nothing was not an option. Seeing Joey disappointed, and hiding his own frustration, Justin said, "We can't be sure that Teachers even come to this world anymore, if they ever did. We may be forced to act as our own Teachers. We'll have to seriously study the book."

"Do you really believe that will work?" Joey asked.

"Probably not, but it's the best I can do right now."

The next day, Justin took his book back to Blackwater Falls to inaugurate his new career as his own Teacher. If it worked, he would teach the world to self-teach, overlooking the intrinsic paradox in such a plan.

He sat by the falls in the yoga pose he learned from Devī and made a mild effort to meditate, as he had done in Bhū-loka. But his cell phone rang. It was Joey. Justin said they would talk later and resumed meditation. But then his mother texted him. He turned off his phone, but twenty seconds later, turned it back on and checked for messages.

Exasperated, he thought of Devī. He admired her now more than ever.

Devī had been young and attractive, yet she had taken the soul so seriously, as if she really knew her inner self. He saw no vanity in her, not even the vanity of thinking oneself free of vanity. He had not detected any of that hypocritical pride in one's humility that is observed so often in so-called enlightened beings.

But Devī was gone forever, and there were no other Teachers, at least not in Tucker County. So, Justin had no choice but to create his own path. He tried to recall what Devī taught him. He focused his mind on the true self within the heart. This effort garnered a dim, out-of-body experience, but nothing very empowering or impressive. He laughed sadly at himself. Just as Devī said, he had courage only for external things, not to explore the inner self.

He prayed, without knowing to whom, for determination and courage to discover the truth, whatever it might be, and then teach it for the world's good. But this too produced no result. His book declared that he must find a Teacher. And his attempt to be his own Teacher was going nowhere.

The sky darkened over the unrelenting falls. He felt lonely and useless. He had failed yet again.

Perhaps there were Teachers around him, but he could not see them, just as he could not see the true worth of Devī when he was with her. Perhaps after his offense to Devī, no Teacher would accept him. This idea, which struck him as highly probable, drove his spirits into deep despair. He could not drive it away, as he had once done, with irritation and pride. Irritation and pride now seemed absurd, given his situation.

He remembered Devī's warning, that if he failed her test, he would lose his knowledge for many lives. It must be true. He briefly thought of throwing himself into the waters, but the image of his mother and brother drove such thoughts far away. It would be the ultimate selfish act. Also, he was an excellent swimmer.

He had to do something to protect his family and himself. This was not a game. Everything was at stake. If the Avatāra was real, so was the Asura who would stop at nothing to get revenge. And after Justin's traumatic failure to help the innocent victims in Bhū-loka, he could not bear to stand by and again watch the world be savaged by evil men. The scene of his father's murder still haunted his memory. There were nightmares. In the worst of these, he saw the killer return to slay his mother and brother. He tried to save them, but his legs would not run; he could not lift his arms. All his family were gone forever. It was more than one night that he awoke covered with sweat, his heart beating wildly. He thought of Devī. If only he could acquire now the power she offered him then. He knew that other people loved their families as he loved his. He remembered the innocent victims of Bhū-loka, the terror in their eyes, their pleas for help, and his impotence in the face of it.

He recalled how proud his father was of him, how confident that Justin would make the world a better place. He imagined his father observing his failure in Bhū-loka, and he felt unbearable shame.

But how? How could he help his mother before she worked herself to death? How could he save Joey? And, if the Asuras did return to Earth, what could he do this time? Who would be his Devī?

One thing was clear. In this life, he would not let indolent self-pity cause him to fail all those he cared about. He got up and walked restlessly through the woods till a vague answer came. Even if he could not lead people to enlightenment, nor find it himself, he could at least materially uplift his family. Without a Teacher, he could never challenge the Asuras, nor change the world. He would focus exclusively on his own family. But he made this resolution only to abandon it the next moment as images of faces—heart-rending faces—of Bhū-loka's innocent victims filled his mind. He remembered specific faces, particular cries—last cries—of babies. He shook uncontrollably and wept for them. The thought of again impotently witnessing such human suffering shook him to his soul. If only he could find a Teacher. For now, he was powerless.

Devī taught that the true self, seated in a bodily machine, must learn to transcend this world and reach the World Beyond. But Devī also taught him, though he did not learn or believe it then, to submit to the Avatāra, and to use his power to defend the world.

Justin whispered to himself, "Is the Avatāra watching me now? Devī said he is everywhere. So, he must be here in the river, on the earth, in the sky?" He decided to address the Avatāra for the first time. With a deep breath, he looked into the churning waters and said, "Please send me a Teacher. Please give me power and I will serve you this time."

He glanced around, at the water, the trees, the sky. He looked with his heart. He heard no answer; at least he heard no voice. But in his heart, he felt that his appeal might have been heard. Time would tell.

For now, Justin would have to do what he could. If he excelled in school, he would earn a scholarship and give the money to his family. That was practical. That was all he could do for now. He would focus on earning a scholarship. This plan might not address the whole person, the soul, but he was very pleased with it. For now, he had no Teacher, no clear, spiritual path. Something was better than nothing. And to provide his mother and brother money was a huge something. It might save their lives.

Justin was delighted to have a vital, practical task. But to uplift his family, he must first excel in school, and then build a powerful, prosperous career. His mind moved quickly and confidently now, which he saw as a sort of blessing, or divine approbation. The immediate practical steps were obvious.

He must first write a fake, but apparently sincere, letter of apology and contrition to Superintendent Green. That was tough, but to save his family, and lead the world, he would gladly do it. His intense drive and ambition, repressed for years, were mightily reborn.

Once back in school, he must ace every class and win a scholarship to a top college. For that, he must also succeed in student activities. Election to high student office would certainly make a difference. For that, he must charm old friends, and win new ones. This last item pinched his pride, but a higher pride prevailed.

He still had limits. Before the tragedy, the kids would hang out at his family mansion. He would never allow anyone to visit his present home. But he could easily work around that.

After success in college, the sky was the limit. He would buy his family a beautiful house in a place far away from their shame. His mother had a little library in her room by the desk. Justin often saw her sit there, trying to find energy to write, always sighing at her failure to write, but trying again. She had sold almost all they owned, but somehow kept her library. This image of his suffering mother further galvanized his determination. Star Davis would have the life she dreamed of. She would write books. And she would know how much her son really loved her. Joey would have the best medical care in the world. And to make his father proud, he must achieve public recognition. A worthy goal would be election to the US Senate. But he could do more. And all the while, he would remain on the lookout for a Teacher. He had only to remember Devī, which he did often, to sustain his spiritual hopes.

He saw no flaw in the plan—moral or strategic. And if the opportunity arose, he would certainly fulfill Devī's loftier vision.

Returning from the falls, he revealed the external details of his plan to his family. Over and over again, he vowed to his mother that he would help her and Joey. His mother wept in joy to see her son revived and devoted to his family. Joey, too, rejoiced at the plan, but when their mother left the room, he confronted Justin with a concern.

He looked up into his big brother's eyes. "Are we going to be cave-dwellers? You said you would take me and Mom to a higher world. You promised. If we serve the Avatāra, won't he take us all there?"

"Joey, I didn't say I wouldn't serve the Avatāra. But there is no Avatāra in our world today. Or if there is, we don't know about it."

"Maybe he'll come if we want him."

"Life isn't that simple, Joey. The book said that to serve the Avatāra, we need a Teacher. So Kṛṣṇa has to send me a Teacher. And he didn't. So, we will not talk about that now. When a Teacher comes, we'll renegotiate."

Justin felt his father's presence as he wrote to the superintendent, with a copy to his ally, Dr. Olsen. And his eloquent, moving, insincere apology quickly reinstated him at school.

Friday, his first day back, he saw Sherri entering the campus. Trying to be the new Justin, he struggled to suppress the angry and wounded pride that the very sight of Sherri always aroused. Seeing that she saw him, he walked up to her, and said, "Good morning. It's nice to see you again."

Sherri stared, swallowed, and said, "Justin! I'm so glad you're back. I felt guilty." *Sure you did*, he thought. She was as insincere as he was. But then the new Justin smiled at her, which made her suspicious and fearful. She said something polite and hurried off.

He went to all his classes, unusual in itself, and greeted a few students in each class. This startled and frightened them as much as it had Sherri, as if he were marking them for future violence. Justin tried to conceal his discouragement. Now that he sought to reenter society, he saw how far out of it he'd gone, and how unwelcome he was.

In the cafeteria at lunch, he approached old friend Aaron, with whom he used to practice martial arts. When Justin suggested they train together again, Aaron hung his head and confessed that his parents forbade him to associate with Justin. "I'm really sorry..."

"No problem." Justin tried to hide his pain. He sat alone for a while in the cafeteria, then got up his courage and approached Denise Plimpton, who used to have a huge crush on him and who had grown into a fairly cute girl.

"Hey, Denise."

"Justin, how are you?"

Before he could answer, shouting and cheers erupted in the middle of the cafeteria. Denise excused herself and ran to see what was happening. Everyone crowded around Sherri's boyfriend, Ben Stecker, whom Justin had saved. They shook Ben's hand, slapped his back, and embraced him. The first embracer was Sherri.

Justin took a few steps toward the commotion and asked a boy what was going on.

"Ben got into the Hilltop Academy in Elkins."

"And...?"

The boy was about to say, "Are you serious?" but then he saw to whom he was speaking and quickly changed gears. "Oh hi, Justin. Sorry. I guess everyone thinks that Hilltop is a great school, I mean people who are into a career and all that." The boy quickly walked away.

That afternoon at home, Justin called old friends. He left messages, since no one answered his calls. A few called back and said they would love to spend time with him but right now were busy with school. One boy sounded particularly ashamed. He should be. Justin had risked his own life to save that boy's sister from drowning in Blackwater Falls. And that boy was too busy to spend time with him.

Fighting back tears, Justin hurled objects about his room and smashed his fist on larger objects, like walls and countertops. He even seized the Avatāra book, preparing to hurl it out the window.

But taking a deep breath, he recoiled from rage and lowered the book. After all, it was a gift from his mother. He tried to calm his anger. He sat down and tried to think.

Based on today's abject failure, he considered reinstating a total ban on social life, but rejected the idea. Not yet. He could not give up yet. What could he do? The answer came from an unexpected, but reliable source.

After soccer practice, Joey ran in and greeted Justin with this question: "Did you beat up any bullies today?"

"Why do you ask that? I'm different now."

"But you look the same."

A thought struck Justin. He looked the same. "See you later, Joey," he said. "I've got stuff to do."

Justin locked himself in his room and stared into a mirror. Voilà! He saw the problem. A menacing figure stared back at him, dressed top to bottom in vampire black; long, wild hair twisted about a face frozen in angry defiance, when he wasn't trying to smile. No wonder people feared and avoided him.

Now was the time for his extreme makeover. He took the little bit of money he had saved and hitched a ride back down to Parsons with yet another out-of-town trucker, straight to the nearest barber shop.

First came, or rather first went, his hair. He settled on a Caesar cut. He had studied Caesar's journals, and had always liked the Roman look. He left a hill of hair on the barber's floor.

At the thrift shop, Mrs. Starp didn't recognize him and was therefore friendly and helpful. He told her that he wanted to project success and she quickly fitted him up with preppy pants and shirts.

Right there in the store, he threw out his vampire attire and walked out as Earth's future leader. It was easy getting a ride back to Davis. He was respectable. No, he was more than that. He was impressive! Back home he liked what he saw in the mirror.

"Yes, ladies and gentlemen!" Justin said in his best orator's voice. "The all-new, unstoppable Justin Davis will appear tomorrow at Tucker County High School."

But queasy fear soon replaced giddy excitement. What if they all still rejected him, and even found him more ridiculous than before?

Joey walked into his room. This was to be the first test. It did not start well. Joey opened his eyes wide and his jaw almost bounced on the floor. He clearly considered Justin's makeover to be a disgraceful capitulation to the cave-dwellers.

"What happened to you?" Joey cried. "What are you doing?"

"Let's talk," Justin began, "just you and me."

"I knew you'd say that."

"I want to talk to you. Could you please relax?"

Justin then opened his heart to Joey, revealing his hopes and plans. With real concern, Joey asked, "Are you going to be a cave-dweller?"

"I knew you'd say that, Joey. You forgot your Plato. One who escapes the cave and sees the light outside then goes back to the cave to help those who are still suffering in darkness. Maybe it's time we go back to the cave and help people. And anyway, Mom is obviously not a cave-dweller and I'm trying to help her. Don't you see how hard she works and what it's doing to her? Do you even care about that?"

Joey hung his head. Tears fell from his eyes. "I'm sorry. What can we do to help Mom?"

"I have to crush my classes at TC, and then I win a big scholarship to some college, and I give the money to Mom, and she stops working. Do you get it?"

"Yes, but how will you live if you give her all your money?"

"Look, if I can live in this dump, a dormitory room will be heaven. And I just won't spend money. I don't need anything. Mom needs it."

Joey nodded. Justin remembered the innocent victims of Bhū-loka. "And what about all the people who suffer in this world? You may not remember, but Dad really cared about those people. He worked hard so that everyone could go to school and get a good job. Should we just forget everything that Dad worked for, or should we try to follow him and also care about the world? Well?"

"We should follow Dad," Joey said, afraid he had offended his late father. "But what should we do?"

"I'll tell you. And just one more thing. The book says that our planet is again in danger. The Asuras may come back; in fact, they are probably already in charge of some countries. You have no idea how people suffer under Asuras. I saw it in my dream, and I can't see it again. Even if we don't have a Teacher now, we have to be ready for one. Plato says that if good guys don't lead, bad guys will. Then everybody loses. That's the whole point of *The Republic*. That's what the Avatāra wants, that we be true leaders. And how can I lead if I scare everyone away?"

Joey ran to tell his mom that he needed new clothes like Justin's, and a Caesar haircut.

That night Justin again vowed to his mother that someday soon she would stop the hard labor that was ruining her health. She thanked him with tears in her eyes, said, "I know that all work is noble, but as a child in the orphanage, they forced me to do this same hard work. I was sure I'd left all that behind forever. I felt like Cinderella and your father was my prince. But now, it's all gone." Tears glided down her cheeks. "I feel like I'm back in the orphanage," she continued, "after all these years. I don't know how long my strength will hold out. But you will help us, Justin. I always knew you would. Your father lives in you."

His mother had never before opened her heart to him in that way. She had always tried to shield him from her suffering. Justin was too moved to speak. But now, with an iron will, he would redouble his efforts to help his family.

CHAPTER 15

Monday, Justin got on the school bus, excited and fearful. He quickly saw from the blank faces that no one recognized him. Even Sherri glanced at him in the bus's dim light and then asked a girlfriend in a voice meant to be overheard, "Who's that gorgeous new guy in the back?" Her friend didn't know. He smiled.

The terrible moment of truth came soon enough in his first class. The teacher, thinking him a new student, asked his name. Justin hesitated as students turned to look at him in the back corner. He said, "I'm Justin."

"Justin? Justin who?"

"Justin Davis."

Confusion. Disbelief. Murmuring. Buzzing. The teacher said, "Well. I guess…it is you, Justin. All right, class, let's get started."

Everywhere he went that day, both teachers and students gawked and marveled. Everyone talked about him, but few spoke to him, and no one fully welcomed him. It was too sudden, too strange. A few students wanted to speak to him, and almost did so.

By the end of his last class, he felt as alone as ever. Everyone doubted and even feared his motives. He sat alone on the bus home, like before. He thought of dropping out of high school.

"What is this?" his mother shouted that evening as she riffled through the day's mail. "Justin, what is this?"

She handed over an envelope addressed to him. The sender's name had clearly astounded her: The White Hall Academy. Justin took it with equal amazement. Why would the country's most prestigious prep school write to him? His mother hardly breathed as he took out the precious letter and read it to her.

The gist was this: The White Hall Academy, which monitored such things, had taken note of Justin's extraordinary performance on national standardized tests. The Academy then learned that Justin was a state martial-arts champion, and that he did not go to the national competition because of a family tragedy. Thus, the prestigious school had been tracking him as a most promising candidate.

Seeing his grades collapse, and his martial arts vanish along with other school activities, the great school investigated further and learned of his father's tragic death. After due consideration, and with a strong recommendation from Principal Olsen, White Hall had the pleasure to invite Justin to apply to study there. If accepted, he would receive a full scholarship and would begin at the start of the next academic year.

Star Davis fell, gasping, into a chair. "Oh my God, White Hall! White Hall! A scholarship! If only your father could see this letter. I pray he's reading it right now from heaven. Justin, do you know what this means?"

He did. US senators, corporate leaders, Nobel laureates, celebrated writers, and movie producers proudly traced their lineage to the White Hall Academy. To attend White Hall was to connect for life with one of the most powerful social networks in the country. Those who did well at White Hall went to the college of their choice. Nothing was impossible for a White Hall graduate.

Still incredulous, his mother read the letter several times and cautioned him. "Justin, White Hall did not accept you. They invited you to apply. It is so hard to get in there. I don't want to see you hurt and disappointed."

Too late. The letter inflamed his ambition. Now it was all-out war! He drew up tomorrow's battle plan.

Since White Hall sought students who excelled academically, Justin renewed his vow to be at the top of every class. White Hall sought leaders. As of now, he launched his campaign for class president. White Hall sought those who served society. Justin would do amazing service in the worthiest school clubs. This plan must remain secret in order to succeed. He must not be seen as manipulative or scheming. He knew he was, but it was for the best purpose.

The next day, walking to his first class, he saw Sherri and Ben. The word was out and this time she recognized him. Her wide-open eyes said it all. Justin hesitated, recalled his purpose, and warmly greeted them. This startled Sherri and frightened Ben, who dropped Sherri's hand as if fearing that Justin might be jealous. If Ben only knew that Justin had far better things to do than to covet small-town, small-time Sherri.

In a voice slightly above his normal pitch, Ben said, "Justin, hi, I didn't get a chance to thank you for saving me in the cafeteria. Thanks so much."

"No problem," Justin said, nodding so much in his old way that Ben flinched. Justin raised a hand to reassure him and Ben stepped back. Justin put his hands behind his back and said, "Hey, congratulations. I hear you're going to the Hilltop Academy."

"Thanks. I'll miss all you guys. I almost wish I was staying here at old Tucker."

"Yeah, almost." Justin smiled.

Sherri looked him head to toe and said, "Justin, what happened? Why this change?"

"I'm pursuing new options," he said with another smile. Sherri was not merely a girl who rejected him. More importantly, she was now a potential vote for student office.

"Options?" she asked.

"Yes, I've decided to...to make a serious effort to realize my potential."

"Amazing." Sherri sighed. "You look so good in...your new style."

"Thank you. Anyway, good luck, Ben. Actually, I may not be here for long either."

Sherri snapped to attention. "You really might leave? Where will you go?"

"As I said, I'm pursuing a few options." He was careful not to mention White Hall. "I'll be sure to let you know when I decide. Take care."

He walked off, mentally punching the air with jubilation. He didn't fall back. He didn't call her a cave-dweller, nor act like one himself. If he could be nice to Ben and Sherri, he could be nice to anyone. A real moral improvement. And Sherri began to see what she had lost. He could not avoid some silly satisfaction in that.

Later that day, he entered a lunch meeting of SEC, the Student Environmental Club. The faculty advisor, lanky, hairy-yet-balding Mr. Harris, stared uneasily at him and said rather stiffly, "Can I help you?"

Justin nodded. "Actually, I thought I could help you, as in volunteer." He raised his fingers in a V sign. Confused, Mr. Harris stroked his vanishing hairline.

Denise Plimpton spoke up. "Why can't Justin help? Our club is for everyone, isn't it?"

"Of course," Mr. Harris said, jolted back into the real world, where discrimination lawsuits happen.

Justin also joined the International Club, since he longed to act globally. Of equal importance, Sherri recently left the club.

His plan worked magnificently. After holding back and staying away for so long, he now unleashed so much pent-up energy, enthusiasm, and good ideas that before long, students begged him to lead these clubs. Other clubs recruited him and sought his advice. Justin felt the undertow of material success that long ago pulled him away from Devī and attached him to kind-but-worldly Su Varṇa. He felt the seductive power of White Hall. If he were admitted, he would meet extraordinary young ladies there. His career would rise. Would he succumb again; would he again forget his higher mission, as in Bhū-loka? Justin might succeed, but the world might not. And what of the safety of his family, and himself?

Another thought shook him. White Hall was a high-stakes institution, a place for children of powerful people. If Asuras did infiltrate this world, they would likely send a few of the cohort to White Hall. After all, five thousand years ago, a mighty Asura, Kaṃsa, seized the throne of Mathurā. Asuras coveting power in America would logically attend White Hall—at least a few of them.

Justin could not let down his guard. Two very different kinds of people must concern him for the rest of his life. Like it or not, he must search for a Teacher, and be constantly vigilant for the presence of Asuras. He laughed at the irony. He must appear to normal people as a normal person. And he must simultaneously be vigilant, ever on the lookout for two very abnormal kinds of people, without ever betraying his special knowledge. He had no choice. With his right fist, he punched his open left hand and ordered himself to stay focused.

Justin attacked his studies with ferocious energy and sailed to the top in every class. He again piled up medals in martial arts. He knew that White Hall embraced the Platonic ideal of the philosopher-athlete. Justin would exceed their standards. He had another reason to raise his fighting skill to the highest level—he had not forgotten his vow to hunt down his father's killer. Bad guys fight back. Justin would be ready. He could not shake a foreboding in his heart that the day of trial was approaching. Even as he worked tirelessly to elevate his mother and brother to health and comfort, he knew he would have to protect them one day. These considerations drove him on relentlessly. And in the midst of this, he never forgot the need for a Teacher. A Teacher would prepare him for what would likely be the greatest, most dangerous challenge of his life. Indeed, it might well be that only a Teacher could save his life, and that of his family.

For now, top grades, community service, and sports were good, but not enough for Justin Davis. Winning high student office would further enhance his White Hall candidacy. He must be elected class president.

Thus, at club meetings, in class, at local hangouts—everywhere—he was covertly on the campaign trail, but he would not declare his candidacy till urged to do so by the popular groundswell he was so assiduously orchestrating.

As he hoped, and planned, growing numbers of students urged him to run for class president. How could he ignore the people's voice? No, he must honor it.

"My friends, you spoke! And I heard you!"

He liked the ring of those words. He heard them in a movie, and used them in his campaign. He sought everyone's support. He took no chances. White Hall and his future were at stake. He was engaged in a type of self-gratifying altruism, and he would not worry about the paradox of the term. His family's future was at stake. He must not engineer a mere victory, but a landslide. Thus, when Billy Skinner, who had avoided him, now sought a formal peace treaty, Justin said, "Sure!" and gave him a friendly "you're okay" punch in the shoulder. Even Billy was a vote. And if elected, he would serve all students faithfully. It might not be selfless, but it was a lot better than his former estrangement and hostility. It was good enough.

"It's all in the Caesar cut," he joked to himself, running his fingers over his hair. The whole school was buzzing about Justin Davis! But a voice inside cautioned him not to forget the gravity of his mission. Success was part of the life-architecture he was constructing. But he must remember.

Just before the election, Dr. Green tried to derail his campaign, arguing that once suspended, a student could not run for student office. But many students and teachers rose to defend Justin, and Dr. Green was forced to back down. His attack had only strengthened Justin's candidacy. Justin told his supporters, from his heart, that he would never forget them, nor disappoint them.

All these events took place within a few months, during which Justin grew in spirit but also in body. He not only again ruled the social world, but also gazed at the physical world from a much higher vantage point. He was now taller, not shorter, than average. He was again prince of Tucker County. The prettiest girls, and even second-tier girls, pursued him. Many of them declared that even in Justin's troubled times, they always knew that he was tough but fair, and above all, misunderstood. He was actually crying out for help in his own way. Etc. Etc.

But romance could wait. Career was now everything. The landslide happened. President Justin was grateful for his victory and dreamed of White Hall.

About this time, Joey accidentally told a friend who accidentally told his brother that Justin would probably go to White Hall. The news went viral in Tucker County. Justin also heard from friends, for he had myriad, that Sherri dismissed his chances.

Justin understood her. She could not bear to think that she dumped a White Hallian in favor of a Hilltoppian. Thus, she secretly told friends, who told no one but their close friends, that Justin Davis would never make White Hall.

As the time neared for White Hall to send out acceptance and rejection letters, expectation mounted in Tucker County. A usually reliable source revealed that Sherri would die if Justin made White Hall, and thus with a natural desire to live, she prayed to God that he not get in. She also prayed that God forgive her for this wicked, but irrepressible, wish.

Sherri disclosed this to her best friend, who felt morally obliged to speak to Justin alone about such a delicate matter. Thus, he heard in detail of Sherri's dark night of the soul, as her best friend poetically described it.

The letter from White Hall arrived. Justin feverishly opened it. White Hall accepted him. Justin ran to tell his mother and Joey. The little family gathered in the living room. Justin read the letter to his mother, who listened with tears in her eyes. Then she embraced him, followed by Joey.

Star Davis tried to speak but was overcome with joy. Finally, she gasped through her tears, "Your father would be so proud of you. If only your father were here to enjoy this with us."

Justin could not hold back his own tears. In his heart he vowed and vowed again that he would raise his family, honor his father, somehow find a Teacher, and prepare for the Asuras. White Hall would present new challenges, perhaps new threats. In Bhū-loka, the Asura attacked when Justin was rising as a student of powerful Devī. He was rising again now. Five thousand years ago, personal power flowed from warrior might. In today's world, it flowed from connections, status, wealth. And White Hall meant that Justin would rise in all these key categories.

If Asuras were on Earth, they likely monitored him. If they did, they were already planning to deal with him at White Hall, even as he and his family and friends celebrated.

And there were other, more provincial concerns. Would the other students accept him? He must hide his poverty. He must conceal at all costs the fact that he lived in a broken-down trailer. To be thus humiliated at White Hall would be beyond his endurance.

Yet, despite his dread and worry, the news that he was headed to White Hall worked its magic, leaving Justin, his family, and all Tucker County awestruck. Justin would finish his semester as class president, and then ascend to White Hall. Everywhere he went, people told him how happy they were for him, how much his father would be pleased, and what this must mean to his mother. Even more than in his childhood, people cherished a word or a smile from him. The Davis mayor spoke of presenting him to the governor in Charleston.

Justin assured everyone that White Hall would not change him, though it already had. White Hall's offer confirmed his power to create his own future—if not in spiritual matters, at least in worldly concerns.

Of course, he was not all pride. He was grateful for his success, though he was not sure to whom he owed this gratitude. He did not rule out, or in, the Avatāra. And, despite his inexorably inflated head, his deepest joy was seeing his family's new hope. They were happy again! It meant the world to him.

He could not forget Bhū-loka. He dared not discuss it with anyone, not even Joey, who sometimes became too excited to keep secrets. If people knew of his fantastic dream, they would think him weird, or even crazy. That could overturn his career. White Hall might find out and withdraw their offer. Bhū-loka must remain his secret. But he did not forget his vow to the Avatāra, nor that his growing success could mean increased danger.

As the semester passed, and Justin prepared for White Hall, an important discovery absorbed his attention.

Justin discovered that one super prestigious student club, the Knights, reigned above all other men's clubs at White Hall. The Lorelles were the equally exclusive sister club of the Knights.

Justin forbade himself to even wish for Knighthood. To enter White Hall was extremely difficult. To be a Knight was virtually impossible. Knights only admitted their own siblings, offspring of former Knights, or children of important leaders in politics, finance, entertainment, or science. Justin lived in a trailer in Davis, West Virginia, and his mom cleaned the homes of people not much better off than she was.

Yet to become a Knight was to guarantee one's supreme success in life. He swore not to dream of Knighthood, only to break his rule. Dreams of Knighthood drove him like a drug. One particular White Hall student, Tom Walker, caught his attention. Tom would be the incoming Knight president and had also been elected student body president for the coming year. He was also captain of the football team. Justin gazed at his picture with much admiration.

Justin once casually mentioned the Knights to his mom. He thought he was being casual. But his mother heard the intensity in his voice.

"It's a wonderful goal," she said, "but don't set your heart on it, Justin. Please."

Perhaps more than anyone, one person had recently fixed White Hall in the public eye. White Hall alumnus and US Senator Hunter Clay lived on a vast estate near White Hall. Handsome, bright, still in his forties, he was heavily favored to be nominated by a major political party for next year's presidential elections and stood as the strongest overall candidate for the highest political position in the world. At present, he was one of the most influential senators, leading several key committees. He appeared all the time on major news networks. And that same Hunter Clay had come to the funeral of Tark Davis. Surely, he remembered Justin's father and would feel a natural sympathy toward Justin, and perhaps a desire to help him in his career.

Senator Clay's well-known Clay Campus, just over the mountain from White Hall, housed a large, devoted staff that managed the senator's huge and growing national political network. Clay Campus was also home to the senator's own think tank, staffed by prominent scholars who produced sophisticated position papers on national and international issues.

Equally famous was the senator's vaunted Youth Corps, composed of student volunteers from the nation's most elite political science programs. These students served a one-year internship at Clay Campus, then returned to their respective schools to serve local branches of the Clay Youth Corps.

A handful of the very best White Hall students also served the Corps at Clay Campus. Justin had his sights set on this position. The future rewards were incalculable.

The White Hall Academy was eager to cooperate with Senator Clay, for he was a loyal, dedicated White Hall alumnus, famous for large donations to the school. Thus, the magnificent new White Hall library bore the name Hunter and Barbara Clay Library. The intimate association of the White Hall Academy with Hunter Clay lent to both an aura of learned celebrity.

More than once Justin dreamed of meeting the senator, who sometimes visited the White Hall campus. A position for Justin in the Clay Youth Corps would lend a most powerful boost to Justin's career. Justin did not dare speak of this possibility with his family. His mother or Joey might mention it to someone in town, who might know someone in Virginia, who might have a third cousin near White Hall, who…in short, this ultimate option must be kept under tight wraps for now. Justin could not appear to be grasping or ambitious. And yet the great senator had come to the funeral of Tark Davis.

In the midst of these lofty calculations, little Joey suffered. Though extremely proud of his older brother, he dreaded losing him, a fear that haunted him since the loss of his father.

Justin swore they would be in touch daily, and that Justin was going to White Hall for Joey and their mom. Joey understood and accepted. He feared Justin's departure, but gloried in his good fortune.

As the time for departure drew near, Justin returned to the falls to think about it all. He knew that glorious as it was, White Hall was a bastion of materialism, a place of pride, snobbery, and unabashed worldly ambition. He expected to meet quite a few phony people there.

For a higher purpose, Justin must pursue his worldly goals. He still clung to Bhū-loka as a life-changing event and an ultimate reference point. Once he had belittled, practically mocked, Devī's teachings. Now, he longed to find a Teacher like her. When the Asura attacked him, Devī saved his life. The Asura would surely attack again. If he did not find a Teacher, and quickly, he would face the Asura alone. He, Justin, would die this time, and God only knew what would become of his family. His foreboding of danger at White Hall did not leave his heart. Yet he must go to White Hall. His pride and jubilation mixed strangely with dread and almost desperation to find a Teacher.

He still missed Lokeśa, and even Su Varṇa. Devī, of course, still commanded his highest regard. He wondered where in the universe, or beyond it, she might be, and whether she had ever forgiven him. Perhaps she did not remember him. That seemed more likely.

CHAPTER 16

For the first time in his young life, Justin was leaving his family behind, a mother and younger brother who struggled with health and spirits. But he must go. They insisted he go as much as they lamented his departure.

White Hall created a strong new possibility of failure. He could not fail in Tucker County, proud as that might sound. He was already a success here. But White Hall was different. White Hall created for Justin a new chance for humiliation. He would be the poorest of the poor. He came from one of the poorest, least educated states. Everyone would know that. If they found out how poor he was, it would be unbearable. Tucker County was safe. White Hall was exciting and dangerous.

During his last week in Davis, his mother said to him one day, "Justin, did you know that Senator Hunter Clay is a former White Hall student, who lives just over the mountain from White Hall? They say he visits the school regularly and is a major donor."

"Yes, I know," Justin said, hiding his own designs on the good senator.

"Who knows," Star Davis said, "you could even meet him one day."

"That would be nice," Justin said, his mind absorbed in calculations.

A less glamorous topic had to be considered. How would Justin travel to White Hall? Tucker County had no airport, no train, no intercity bus. His mother's health did not permit her to drive him. Many people with good cars offered to take him on the three-hour drive over the mountains to White Hall. But Justin could not risk going with anyone from Davis who might inadvertently reveal information about Justin's indigent state. White Hallians might notice the mountain accent that Justin carefully avoided. A driver from Davis might let slip that Justin lived in a trailer, or that his mother cleaned houses. No, much as he loved the local people, he could not risk any of them driving him to White Hall.

So he politely declined, and invented an excuse. Most students would arrive at the Charlottesville Airport. By flying in there, he would have a chance to make valuable contacts with other students.

First impressions were so important.

It was a poor excuse, but no one seemed to notice in the excitement of his journey to White Hall. The mayor offered with his personal funds to buy Justin a plane ticket from the nearest airport in Bridgeport. Thank God! He would arrive like other White Hallians. He could not thank the mayor enough.

Good friends drove him to the airport seventy miles away. His mom and Joey accompanied him. The only flight left Bridgeport at six a.m., so Justin and his family left Davis at three a.m. He carefully placed the book in his backpack.

Despite the early hour, a group of loyal friends got up or stayed up to say goodbye. Justin bid them farewell at the bridge over the Blackwater River. He would never let them come to his shameful house.

As he embraced his friends at the bridge, everyone prophesized great things for Justin. They urged him to write, promising to post whatever he wrote on the Tucker High site and in the county newspaper. Everyone wanted to visit him at White Hall. He told them that he would be too busy, at least the first year. He would come home for Thanksgiving.

As the boys saluted Justin with raised fists, and the girls blew kisses, and everyone waved, he bid them all goodbye with much feeling. He would never let them down.

Rolling by tiny, sleeping towns, winding through the endless hills of West Virginia, Justin gazed at his reflection in the car window. Who was Justin Davis?

The flight to Dulles Airport passed over Tucker County. Davis rejoiced in the symbolism as he flew high above his old life. And what could be more auspicious than to make a stop in Washington, DC, the world center of power?

But before that glorious stop could occur, Justin's flight hit a bad storm over the high mountains. The middle-aged lady next to him was busy at her computer till the small plane suddenly heaved and dropped a thousand feet. As passengers cried out, Justin gripped the armrests.

The lady gasped, closed her eyes, and began to chant: Hare Kṛṣṇa Hare Kṛṣṇa, Kṛṣṇa Kṛṣṇa Hare Hare; Hare Rāma Hare Rāma, Rāma Rāma Hare Hare.

She repeatedly chanted this mantra with increasing intensity. Justin stared at her as the plane bounced about. Suddenly, the turbulence ended as quickly as it began and the plane leveled off, flying through calm air.

The lady breathed out slowly, shook her head, and breathed deeply again.

"Well, young man, I'm glad that's over."

"Me too," was all Justin could manage.

"I'm a big Beatles fan," she said. "My favorite was always George Harrison."

"Really?"

"Yes. Can I read you what he said about a flight he once took?"

"Sure."

"I always bring this book with me on flights, so I can read it at times like this. Here's what George said:

Once I was on an airplane that was in an electric storm. It was hit by lightning three times, and a Boeing 707 went over the top of us, missing by inches. I thought the back end of the plane had blown off. I was on my way from Los Angeles to New York to organize the Bangladesh concert. As soon as the plane began bouncing around, I started chanting Hare Krishna, Hare Krishna, Krishna Krishna Hare Hare/Hare Rama, Hare Rama, Rama Rama, Hare Hare. The whole thing went on for about an hour and a half or two hours, the plane dropping hundreds of feet and bouncing all over in the storm, all the lights out and all these explosions, and everybody terrified. I ended up with my feet pressed against the seat in front, my seatbelt as tight as it could be, gripping on the thing, and yelling Hare Krishna, Hare Krishna, Krishna Krishna Hare Hare at the top of my voice. I know for me, the difference between making it and not making it was actually chanting the mantra. Peter Sellers also swore that chanting Hare Krishna saved him from a plane crash once.

She looked up at him. "Well, how do you like that?"

"So George Harrison believed in Kṛṣṇa," Justin said.

"Yes, and so did Peter Sellers."

"He was an actor, I believe."

"Oh yes, you know, *Dr. Strangelove*, *The Pink Panther*, and so many other movies."

"Very interesting. Thanks for sharing that."

The lady smiled and returned to her computer. Justin wondered if one of the Beatles, and a famous actor, knew the Avatāra.

He wondered about this until he entered Dulles airport, where the bustling scene captured his attention. Strolling down the long corridors, he smiled to think that here at the nation's capital, no one recognized him as a future world leader. They would all know him one day. He was going to White Hall. Other thoughts were less pleasant. Dulles reminded Justin of travels with his family in happier times. But even this sad memory toughened his resolve to restore his family to their rightful position.

Justin's long hour layover in Dulles assured him of ample time to savor the airport ambience, and ponder his future glory. The hour passed and an airline agent welcomed him to the departure lounge for his flight to Charlottesville. She asked if he was going home.

"No, I'm going to the White Hall Academy," he said, striving to sound casual.

"White Hall!" she said. "That is a real honor."

"I guess it is."

Justin knew that his life was about to change forever. He didn't know how. Would his next flight take him into an Asura attack? A brilliant new life? Both? Would he even succeed at White Hall? What if he failed? White Hall was not Tucker County.

CHAPTER 17

Justin ambled and rambled around the airport for a while, till he reached his departure lounge, where he settled in for some acute people-watching. After an hour or two—time melted away—he took out the book. He was struck by the contrast between its otherworldly message and the very this-worldly scene around him. He floated between these worlds till a stunning image pulled him decidedly into this world.

A fashionable young lady with a fine figure entered the lounge. Silky auburn hair framed her exquisite face. She struggled with two big, heavy carry-on bags. As she walked to the counter, one of her bags crashed to the floor. She rolled her eyes and gasped with annoyance.

The ticket agent crinkled her brow, shook her head and said, "Young lady, I hope you don't plan to carry both those bags on the plane. You must check one of them."

"Impossible!" the girl said. "I have important items here, and once your airline lost my checked bag."

The agent apologized for the loss, but again shook her head. The girl threw down her other bag with a bang, put her hands on her hips and said, "I'm sorry for the trouble, but my stepdad spoke to a supervisor in Florida and she said I could carry on both bags. Could you please call her? I have her personal number here. Thanks."

"Ma'am, either check a bag or skip the flight."

"Are you serious?" The girl, flushed with anger, pushed her hair from her face. "I am trying to be reasonable."

Justin jumped up and ran to the counter. "Excuse me," he said to the ticket agent, "I'm on this flight and I don't have a carry-on, so I'll just take one of this girl's bags. Then we're all happy, right? I mean, if you don't mind," he said to the girl.

The young lady looked at him and smiled. "I don't mind at all. Thank you so much!"

The speechless agent nodded. Justin grabbed the fallen bag, and the other bag as well. "I'd be happy to carry these," he told the girl.

"Well," she nodded, "you do look much stronger than me. That's very kind of you."

"No problem," he replied.

The girl found a seat to her liking, far from the counter. Justin put the bags down and hesitated. The girl said, "Please have a seat. We can talk if you like." Justin happily complied. The girl looked back at the ticket agent and said, "I could call my stepdad right now and get that lady fired. But she probably needs her job."

"Probably does," Justin agreed. "And if it wasn't for her, I wouldn't have had the chance to help you."

"What a sweet thing to say," she said. "By the way, I'm Scarlet."

"I'm Justin."

With mutual smiles, they shook hands. Scarlet had captivating blue-green eyes, a delicate nose, and full, expressive lips. Her sleeveless blouse and long, linen shorts revealed a smooth, tan complexion, and flawless figure. Tucker County girls were nice, but Scarlet had a refined poise and charm that fascinated him.

She soon told him what he longed to hear—she studied at White Hall. He blissfully told her that he would be there too. Instant elite camaraderie! They were happily the same age and happily agreed they would probably have classes together.

She lived in a Palm Beach mansion. Where was he from? Her query smothered his bliss. He tried to put on a confident face and said, "Davis, West Virginia."

"Oh," she said, "where is that?"

"Oh, two or three hours south of Pittsburgh."

She lived in one of the richest areas in America, he in one of the poorest. They both knew it. She said, "Oh, that's…nice! West Virginia is…a pretty state, isn't it?"

"People often say that."

"Then I will say that." She laughed. She picked up her iPhone and searched for pictures of Davis, handing the phone to Justin when she found a picture she liked. Blackwater Falls particularly caught her attention, along with the quaint downtown. She praised his town. Justin saw that she wanted to put him at ease, but she only increased his discomfort when she said, "Do you live in one of those beautiful old houses there?"

He tried hard not to sweat, squirm, or blush. "In fact," he said, "I grew up in a Victorian mansion, our ancestral home. My forefathers founded the town."

"That is impressive. Show me your house on Google Street."

Justin smiled and explained that, "Davis is a very small town and Google doesn't provide a street view of my"—he didn't say for-mer—"home."

Scarlet smiled and said, "And you still live there?"

Justin's creative mind went into overdrive and he quickly replied, "I grew up there, but a few years ago my dad passed away and my mom decided to live a bit outside town."

"I'm so sorry about your father," Scarlet said with real concern.

"Thank you."

She leaned over, unzipped her designer luggage, and pulled out a bottle of drinking water. "I only have one, so we can share." She drank from the bottle and then handed it to him, saying, "Don't worry, I'm healthy."

Justin drank, returned the bottle, and thanked Scarlet. She went right back to Davis. "How many people live in Davis?"

He couldn't lie here. She could fact-check him.

"A little over six hundred," he said.

"My, that is quaint. Well, quaint is good, right?"

"It can be. But only at times."

"I like you," she said. "You're clever."

"So how is your family doing?" he asked.

"Well, I live with my mother and stepfather. I won't talk about him. My bio-father lives in Chicago and he's fine. Always busy with his law firm, but fine."

"That's great. My father was a lawyer."

She looked in his eyes with enchanting empathy. He felt her growing power over him. "Hey Justin," she said, still probing, "trust me with your last name."

He was stuck. What if she researched and found out the truth? What if she found his mother's ad for domestic service? Disaster. No escape.

"Davis," he said. "Justin Davis."

"So the town really is named after your family."

"Yes, it is," he said, imagining her scorn when she discovered the family shame. "And what's your last name, Scarlet?"

"I thought you'd never ask. I'm Scarlet Walker. Oh, by the way, my older brother Tom also goes to White Hall."

A terrifying thrill swept over him. Tom Walker, Scarlet's brother, was president of the Knights. How many times had he admired his picture on the Knight-site? Innumerable. This casual, chance meeting with Scarlet was a high-stakes encounter. She must like him, or at least approve him. A single word from Scarlet to her brother might easily make or break his Knight candidacy. And for now, becoming a Knight was what he most desired in this world. It was a giant step toward fabulous success and family redemption. It meant fulfilling the destiny that called in his heart.

He now understood the gold locket with a jeweled letter "L" that hung around her neck. She was a Lorelle, a member of the Knight's sister club. Of course!

As these lofty ideas and visions wafted and whirled through his mind, Scarlet said, "What's that sticking out of your coat pocket? Is it a book?"

She playfully reached for it and before he could stop her, she drew it out and held it before her eyes.

"*The First Avatāra*! You read books like this?" Her tone did not approve or disapprove his choice.

"My mother gave it to me for my birthday, so I thought I should read it at least once." He would say no more till he knew how she really viewed such books.

"Very good!" Scarlet said. "I like that you honor your mother." Scarlet held the book up, studying the cover. Did Kṛṣṇa smile at her too? Apparently not. She opened the book and skimmed a few pages. "It's mythology, isn't it?"

"It's considered to be mythology, yes," he said.

Scarlet replied to his evasive answer with a knowing smile. Justin saw that White Hall students were very smart. He would not be Gulliver at this school.

Scarlet continued to probe. "Do you like mythology?" she asked.

"It often conveys wisdom—in its own way," he replied.

"True," she said, enjoying his craft. "It is an interesting genre. That must be a prince." She pointed to Kṛṣṇa. "Handsome guy, isn't he?"

"Ancient sources thought so."

"Yes, mythology can be quite interesting." Scarlet pointed at the cover. "That girl is striking. Do you find her beautiful?"

"In a way." He wondered if Scarlet could be jealous of a book cover. Just in case, he added, "But her beauty is a bit unusual…"

"As if she's from another world."

"I admire your perspicacity."

"And I admire your vocabulary." She laughed. "You'll fit right in at White Hall."

Tiring of the book, she replaced it in his pocket with playful politeness. She looked at her jeweled watch and said there was still time to visit the posh snack bar across the corridor. Scarlet was a vegan. So was he. They high-fived this discovery.

Sherri, who lusted after red, rare steak, bore no comparison to brilliant, vegan Scarlet. But when he looked at the wall menu, Justin's soaring heart sank. As a gentleman, he must treat Scarlet. As a poor student, still waiting to receive his scholarship money, he knew he could not afford it.

"What are you going to get?" Scarlet asked, tapping her fingers on the counter.

"Actually, I don't think I'll get anything right now. I ate a lot on the first flight."

Scarlet smiled and stopped tapping. "I'm not hungry either. Let's go back and sit down. Follow me." She playfully wheeled around and marched back to their seats. All of Scarlet's movements were somehow graceful.

Justin could not discern whether she realized his poverty, or if she did not want to appear hungrier than him, or if she truly was not hungry. In any case, he was grateful for her gesture. In lovely Scarlet's company, his own poverty mortified him more than ever. He dreaded endless repetitions of this scene at White Hall.

Still, he played his part well and eagerly conversed with Scarlet. They talked and laughed till their flight was called. "Justin," she said as they walked to the plane, "you are not a bad-looking guy. You must have a girlfriend in West Virginia, right?"

"I did, but we broke up. She's with another guy."

"Oh, I'm sorry to hear that," Scarlet said happily. "Aren't you going to ask me if I have a guy?"

"Actually, I would like to ask that," he said with a gallant nod. "Do you have a guy?"

"Not now, but I seem to be developing a special friendship with Mel Trayhem. I'll see where that goes, if it goes."

Mel was the Knight vice president. Arousing Mel's jealousy could be dangerous, neglecting Scarlet equally so. The situation required a level of diplomacy Justin had not exercised in Tucker County.

They boarded a small plane. With a word and a smile, Scarlet convinced the passenger next to her to trade seats with Justin, who joyfully sat by her side.

"So, what do you study?" he asked.

"My present focus is psychology as a life art, and visual art as a psychotherapy. What is your focus?" she asked with a bright smile.

"Very good question," he said with a smile no less bright. "First, let me say how fascinating I find your own intellectual focus."

He was stalling for time as he ransacked his brain for something that sounded like an intellectual focus. He came up with this: "Presently I am drawn to the liminal conceptual region that unites the physical with the metaphysical in daily life."

Well, well." Scarlet smiled. "I'm impressed. It's about time someone figured that out."

The two new friends chatted gaily during the short flight, both very well entertained by the other. Scarlet was more than just a pretty girl. She was smart, charming, and socially powerful. He would not use her in any crass sense, but rationally he must make sure that her power acted for him and not against him. A single false assumption on his part, just one displeasing word or action, could ruin his prospects for Knighthood. Then there was Knight vice president Mel Trayhem to worry about.

Remembering the story about George Harrison, Justin asked Scarlet if she liked the Beatles. "They're okay," she said. This lukewarm reply did not give him courage to retell what happened to a Beatle on a scary flight. He spoke of other things.

As they descended into Charlottesville, Justin felt a rush of anxiety when Scarlet mentioned that her brother Tom and Mel would be at the airport. What would Tom think of an unknown guy accompanying his sister? What would Mel think?

They deplaned and crossed the tarmac. Balmy late-summer breezes rustled his short hair, and lifted Scarlet's auburn locks, making her laugh. She laughed easily with true good nature. He had never been so happy in a girl's company since he was with Su Varṇa.

Justin sighed. He sighed for Scarlet and for what awaited. He was about to meet those who would decide his destiny.

CHAPTER 18

As Justin and Scarlet walked toward the baggage claim, Justin easily recognized Knight President Tom Walker. Tall and muscular with preppy good looks, he dressed well, and sported a black baseball cap with a gold-embroidered K. He moved with total self-assurance. As both Knight president and student body president, and captain of the football team, he was easily the most famous and influential student at White Hall.

With a kind smile, Tom embraced his sister and shook Justin's hand as Scarlet introduced him. Justin again felt he was dreaming. But he was sufficiently awake to scan the small terminal for Mel Trayhem, Knight vice president and special friend of Scarlet. Justin had seen his picture for months. He spotted Mel near the baggage claim, dressed in a White Hall sweatshirt and Knight hat. Just as in his pictures, Mel was reasonably good-looking, of medium height, with curly brown hair, and a serious, attentive gaze. Tom went to organize the arriving students. Justin slightly widened his distance from Scarlet as she led him toward Mel and the baggage claim. White Hall students greeted her with deference. Scarlet clearly reigned here. No other girl matched her in beauty and composure. And she chose to walk with Justin.

A very different sort of girl stood by a table outside the baggage claim area. She had jet-black, straight hair, chiseled features, and a shapely figure dressed in a tight gray skirt that rose above her knees, and a white blouse that was not adequately buttoned. On her table sat a cardboard box with a slit on top, and the word "Donations" in black letters on the front. Hanging from the table was a hand-lettered sign:

Donations Please
Stonewood School for Girls

The black-haired girl smiled, cocked her head, and beckoned young male students to her table. After a few failed attempts, she succeeded in motioning to her table three boys with matching blue blazers. They had been standing at the meeting point for the Blue Ridge Academy, a boys' preparatory school.

The boys each put a dollar in the box. Before they could leave, the girl whispered something to them and pointed to a paper tablet on the table. One by one, the boys leaned over and wrote something on the tablet. This aroused Justin's curiosity and he took a step toward the table.

He turned back and saw Scarlet urging Mel to stay away. Mel shook his head. "I'm sorry, but I can't see those boys victimized."

Mel then walked quickly up to the table and placed himself in front of the Blue Ridge Academy boys. He told them, "Listen, I'm from White Hall. Did you give that girl your contact information?"

Clearly impressed by this attention from a White Hall student, the boys nodded. Mel said, "I want you to take it back. That girl is from the Stonewood School. Stonies engage in drug trafficking and prostitution. They are violent and dangerous. Read it online. Do not leave her your contact information. It is against the rules of your school."

Awed and frightened, the boys demanded their papers back. The Stonewood girl cursed Mel and threw the papers on the floor. As the Blue Ridge boys stooped to retrieve them, a large young man with steel-tipped boots and an expensive black leather jacket walked up to the table and exchanged knowing looks with the girl. Glaring at Mel, he said to the girl, "Is this man bothering you?"

The girl nodded. "Yes, he is. Extremely."

The large man walked slowly up to Mel, and with a laugh, flicked off Mel's hat. It fell to the floor. A small crowd started to gather. By now, Scarlet stood next to Justin. Mel stood unmoving, looking up at the larger man. Justin rushed over, picked up the hat, dusted it off, and handed it back to Mel, who took it mechanically. At this, the large man came over and tried to knock off Justin's Pittsburgh Pirates cap. Justin quickly stepped aside and the big man looked foolish as he swatted the air. Justin began calculating how he would take him down if he moved toward Mel.

All this happened quickly. Tom rushed over, and an airport security officer pushed his way through the crowd and inserted himself in the middle of the confrontation.

"What is going on here?" he said in a stern voice.

Mel stated that the girl was soliciting private contact information from the students, against the rules of their school. The officer asked the girl if she had done that. She nodded. The officer forbade her to do it again. She cursed him under her breath and he told her to immediately leave the airport.

Under the officer's gaze, the girl angrily folded her table and left the terminal with her male friend, who glared at the White Hall men but said nothing. Mel then thanked Justin for his support, and said to Scarlet, "Please explain to…"

"Justin. Justin Davis."

"Thanks. Please explain to Justin."

Scarlet nodded, pulled Justin to a private corner of the hall, and said, "Let's go over this quickly. First, I'm truly sorry you saw that scene, but there's a tragic history to all this. Stonewood School girls, whom everyone, including themselves, calls Stonies, are very dangerous. In the past, Stonies made friends with innocent White Hall girls who wanted to help them. The Stonies stole their money and threatened to kill them if they told the authorities. And Stonies don't just harass White Hall girls. They push drugs and prostitution, and seek to entrap White Hall boys. In fact, that gentleman in the black coat is probably the girl's pimp. Sorry for the real-world language."

"Really bad," Justin said. "Are all Stonewood girls like that?"

"Who knows? We don't have the luxury of making such distinctions. It's too dangerous. In the past, every time a White Hallian tried to be nice and reach out to a Stonewood girl, tragedy ensued. But I didn't tell you the worst. You just spoke to Mel. There's a reason why he stepped forward to protect those three boys. He asked me to explain to you because it's too painful for him. Two years ago, a Stonie killed his older brother, Mike."

"Oh my God. What happened?"

Scarlet looked around to make sure Mel wasn't near. "It was awful. Mel's older brother, Mike Trayhem, was a Knight. That's how Mel made it. Anyway, this girl begged Mike for help, claimed she was different, just needed a break. She seduced him, got him intoxicated, and induced him to take a lethal overdose of drugs. She confessed to the police that she had always wanted to kill a White Hall boy. I can't tell you how much Mel loved his brother, and how much he suffered. It almost destroyed him. You can imagine how he feels."

"Yes, I can," Justin said. "I've got a brother."

Scarlet pressed her lips together, met his eyes, and said, "I know you can understand. Anyway, after that tragedy, the school and alumni association went berserk. The school forbade all contact between White Hallians and Stonies. For White Hallians, the penalty for breaking that rule is instant expulsion. Justin, I want you to succeed here, and you can be expelled for even speaking to a Stonewood girl. You will hear about it tomorrow at Orientation."

Justin earnestly told Scarlet how much he felt for Mel. He also meditated on Scarlet's words: *I want you to succeed here.*

By now, Mel had loaded up a luggage cart with Scarlet's designer things, which he apparently knew well, and approached her. As he pushed the cart, Scarlet playfully pulled it and led him to seats far from the other passengers. She whispered to Mel and he invited Justin to sit with them. Hopefully, Mel was not the jealous type.

As the three students sat and chatted, Justin noticed that one arriving student seemed to be watching him. Justin glanced at him and the boy looked away. He had short, light brown hair. His features and expression suggested sharp intelligence. He seemed to be Justin's age, of normal height, thus slightly shorter than Justin, and of medium build. He looked like a young scientist who might invent a time machine. But Scarlet was speaking to Justin and he needed to give her his attention.

When all flights had arrived and Tom was checking in the last White Hallians, Mel stood, told Scarlet he would drive her in his car, and said to Justin, "I'd be happy to take you, but I've got a two-seater."

Scarlet smiled and nodded her confirmation of that fact. Then she said to Justin, "Why didn't you drive here? Davis isn't far. I looked it up. The bus is mostly for students who fly in from other regions and freshman who aren't allowed to drive. But you're a junior like me."

Scarlet's question sent Justin brain racing into gear. "Actually, I chose not to get a car because I am determined to reduce my carbon footprint."

"I admire that," Scarlet said. "I really do."

Tom and Mel, with Scarlet and Justin, led the students out toward a luxury bus whose sides proudly displayed the White Hall Academy's name and coat of arms. As they all exited the terminal, Justin saw the Stonewood girl and her friend waiting on the sidewalk next to a large motorcycle. When Mel pulled up in his convertible BMW Z4 and jumped out to open Scarlet's door, the man with the black jacket, accompanied by the girl, moved toward him, clenching his fists. The girl came with him, as if ready to fight at his side.

Justin's disastrous combat in Bhū-loka with the Asura Vyādha made him wary of supernatural demons. But that setback could hardly affect him in an altercation with this gentleman and his lady, both of whose bodily movements clearly indicated that they knew little of advanced martial arts.

Justin boldly stepped forward in front of Mel, and faced them. The man cursed and puffed out his chest in a sort of primal invitation to battle. Scarlet looked on anxiously. But the airport security officer now came out and stepped between Justin and the man, ordering all concerned to calm down and exit the airport. Mel again thanked Justin for his help.

On their way toward the parking lot, the man shouted at Mel, "We'll get you, punk. You're finished. Don't think you're safe in your fancy school."

Justin took a step toward the man, but Tom put his arm around Justin and said, "Don't worry, it's over."

"It's not over!" the man shouted confidently. "It just started. And we'll finish it. When the cops aren't there."

Justin's muscles tensed for combat. But Tom again urged Justin to stay cool. Justin nodded, but he glared at the man, till Tom grabbed one arm, Mel grabbed the other, and they pulled him onto the bus and seated him there.

Then Mel leaned over and said confidentially to Justin, "I want you to know that I won't forget how you stood up for me." Justin said he was grateful for the opportunity to serve the Knights. Tom and Mel looked at each other and nodded with approval. They exited the bus as the sun dipped below the trees.

Astonished at all these events, and his sudden intimacy with the Knights, Justin sat quietly in the bus, scanning the parking lot to make sure the black jacket didn't return. He took Scarlet's warning about Stonies most seriously. He would never speak to a Stonie, though he wondered if there might be at least one or two decent, unfortunate girls at the school. After all, his own mother went to such a school, and she was the finest lady he knew.

CHAPTER 19

The White Hall bus glided over the glistening Rivanna River and headed west toward the lush Shenandoah foothills. In charge of bringing the new students to White Hall, Tom sat in the front of the bus. Justin saw that the intelligent-looking boy, the one who might build a time machine, sat a few rows ahead of him. As they rolled along, the boy turned around for a moment and glanced at Justin. Their eyes met and the boy turned back around. Who was he?

Halfway to White Hall, Tom walked down the aisle, stopped in front of Justin, and thanked him for supporting Mel in the airport.

"I hope that unfortunate incident didn't give you a bad impression," he said.

"To the contrary," Justin said, eager to please, "it showed me more than ever that I must support the White Hall community."

This response elicited a warm smile from Tom. Such flattering notice from the Knight president transported Justin beyond every care.

"Just between us," Tom said, "the Knights review incoming students, and we know something about your background."

Hearing this, Justin was near panic. Did Tom and the Knights know of the near-destitution of the Davis family? Tom continued, "I mean to say that we are aware that you were state champion in several martial arts. And that you have real scholastic ability, when you try. Impressive. Anyway, thanks again." Tom gave Justin a friendly slap on the shoulder and returned to his seat. Justin was struck with wonder.

A girl at his side in the window seat had been eagerly gazing at the lovely landscape and completely missed Justin's encounter with Tom. She now turned to Justin and pointed with admiration at the rich, equestrian estates lining the winding roads. Justin gave a courteous reply without knowing what he said. He could think only of the kindness he had just received from Tom Walker.

As the bus approached White Hall, Justin did feel the excitement, and he gave increasing attention to the scenery. And Joey would demand details.

Twilight cast a mystic glow on the Albemarle countryside. As they glided through the tiny village of White Hall, a few miles away from the school, the majestic Shenandoah Mountains suddenly loomed before them. Behind darkening peaks, the sun's last golden rays fanned up through the clouds. The bus rolled into Sugar Hollow, bucolic as its name. After a few more miles, Justin saw up ahead lighted domes of different colors, similar to those at Harvard. This was White Hall! The elegant campus sat beneath the southern slope of Pasture Fence Mountain.

They passed under a noble archway decked with a welcome sign and rumbled to a stop by a big green quadrangle bordered by elegant Georgian buildings, artfully lit for the occasion. Justin sighed. Bracing mountain breezes thrilled his body and mind. This was heaven.

Expensive cars streamed into the campus. Proud parents and excited students lugged suitcases, boxes, plants, computers, groceries, and sports equipment up the steps of historic residence halls with gables and turrets.

White Hall staff, smartly attired in polo shirts emblazoned with the school shield, bustled about with tablets and cellphones, answering queries and urging everyone to enjoy the fine refreshments.

Prestige and excellence gloriously suffused the air, as palpably redolent as the scent of surrounding forests. This was a higher world.

Justin's feet hardly touched the ground as he floated to the registration table and received a White Hall welcome folder with keys to his room in Oxford Hall. Eager to move in, and not seeing Scarlet, he went straight to his room.

He walked up the stairs to the third floor and found the door to his room ajar. He entered and found a boy sitting at a desk. It was the boy who had noticed him in the airport, and on the bus. Finding this remarkable, Justin assumed it was meant to be. He went forward gallantly with outstretched hand and introduced himself.

The boy scrambled up from his chair and warmly grasped Justin's hand. "Hi, I'm Luke Tester from Pasadena, California. Great to meet you."

Pleased by Luke's genuine friendliness, and experiencing a strong sense of knowing Luke, Justin spontaneously said, "Luke, have we ever met?"

"I don't think so," Luke replied. "You probably saw me in the airport. But to be honest, I do feel like I know you. That's why I looked at you. Sorry about that."

"Not at all," Justin said. Eager to be considerate, he added, "Well, I won't keep you from your work. You must be busy."

"Oh, I was just texting my parents to let them know everything's fine here. You know how parents always worry."

Justin agreed, and concealed the pain that this innocent reminder of his father caused. "In fact," Justin said, "I'd better call my family now."

His phone didn't work. He came back into the room and apologetically asked if he could use Luke's phone.

"Hey, let me see your phone," Luke said. "I can usually fix things."

"Really?"

"Yeah, my dad's a big scientist and I think I got it from him. My mom is all humanities, which are also important, of course."

Justin smiled and handed Luke the phone. In a matter of moments, Luke handed it back. "No problem," he said. "It's fixed."

"How did you do that?"

"It's a gift, I guess. I know we just met, but I feel strongly that I can trust you."

"Absolutely," Justin said, and he meant it.

"Well, I earn money as an ethical hacker. Companies hire me, even government agencies. I don't talk about it much, but I feel I'm doing good, exposing vulnerabilities so that good people can protect themselves."

"I agree," Justin said. "You really have a valuable skill. Excuse me just a moment, my mom wants to hear from me."

"Of course."

Justin stepped into the hall and spoke to his mother and brother, who hung on every word as he described the amazing events that occurred in but a single day. Joey could hardly believe that Justin met Tom Walker, his sister Scarlet, and Mel. By this time, Joey was well on his way to memorizing the Knight-site.

"Sherri and Ben, and everyone else asked about you," his mother said. "Please keep calling. I need to hear from you." Justin promised he would.

When he returned to the room, he noticed with pleasure that Luke had filled his bookshelves with volumes of philosophy, history, theology, and even a book on Plato. This was going to be a very interesting semester.

Justin took out the only book he brought, *The First Avatāra*, and held it in his hands. Luke came over and asked to see it. Justin could not refuse, and he did further calculate that Scarlet already saw the book, but if too many people saw it, and mentioned it to others, Justin risked becoming known as an eccentric with weird interests. He had not yet lost the power to stand back and watch himself calculating, but he could not stop himself. Still, it was all for the best.

For now, he must let Luke read the book. Justin would look far weirder if he did not let Luke read it.

"Of course you can look at it." Justin handed his book to Luke. "I warn you, it's a bit esoteric. My mother got it for me, and..."

"Thank you!" Luke eagerly took the book in his hands.

"And maybe I'll take a look at some of your books, if you don't mind," Justin said.

"Mind? Quite the opposite. I'm starving for serious discussion."

"Really?" Justin asked. "I thought White Hall was a smart place."

"Oh, it's very smart," Luke replied, "as you'll see. But it's mostly surface smart. You won't see hundreds of students walking around here wondering what life's all about. They already know. Life is about worldly success."

Justin felt admonished by Luke's words, though nothing in their tone suggested such an intention. Luke studied the cover of *The First Avatāra* and said, "The cover art is excellent. I feel like that blue guy is looking at me. Did you ever feel that when you looked at the cover?"

How much could Justin safely reveal? Luke might repeat Justin's words to the wrong person.

"Well," Justin said, "the cover art is quite striking. It does lend a lifelike quality to the figures on the cover. And the prince on the cover is Kṛṣṇa. Ancient texts say that his complexion was the color of a rain cloud."

Luke smiled. "I definitely want to read this."

"Great. Hey, Luke, if I could pursue your previous point, you mentioned that most students here are a bit superficial in their ultimate concerns. If that's true, I'm curious as to why you chose to study at White Hall. It's a sincere question."

"Of course, you can ask me anything. My parents both studied here and after all they've done for me, I wanted to please them. I'm also getting a fantastic education."

"That makes perfect sense," Justin reasoned.

"Thank you," Luke said. "I'm not sure what I'll do with my education. I would like to help the world in some way. Things are so crazy now on our planet."

"I admire your intention," Justin said. "I would also like to help this poor planet if I could. But is it even possible to promote wisdom at a place like White Hall?"

"Good question. I think it is possible. White Hall is open to new ideas, if they are presented intelligently. The students are not hopeless, though most are stuck on life's surface."

"Very interesting," Justin said. "Anyway, I'm curious to know what you think of that book, if you find time to read it."

"Oh, I'll make time," Luke said.

Justin smiled and nodded. *Very interesting roommate.* He finished his unpacking.

When Luke saw that Justin settled in, he said, "Hey, would you like to take a little walk on campus, since we've been traveling all day?"

"Absolutely." Justin was eager to learn more about Luke. He seemed modest and kind, yet shrewd and observant. And he might understand the book.

The two new friends strolled about the hushed campus, which now took on an elegant, nocturnal mystique. Justin was thrilled, almost incredulous to be here at White Hall. As they entered the grassy quadrangle, staff were removing the last tables and tents. A few students and parents lingered in the fresh night air.

Justin gazed at the graceful old stone chapel standing on the green's east side.

"That's the All Faiths Chapel," Luke said, "built in the English style. It's quite impressive inside. If you like, we can see it now. It's always open."

Justin nodded. As they stepped forward, a familiar figure approached—Scarlet Walker.

"Justin!" she cried.

Justin joyfully greeted her. Big smiles spread across both faces. Luke stepped back.

"So, Justin, how do you like White Hall? Don't you love it?"

"It's like a dream," he said, hoping not to wake from this one.

"Oh, I see you're with a friend," Scarlet said.

"I am. Scarlet, this is my roommate, Luke Tester. Luke, this is Scarlet Walker, whom I met in Dulles."

"Hi, Luke." She smiled. "I've seen you on campus, and we had some classes together."

Luke smiled and said, "Yes, I remember you."

Justin saw that behind these smiles, Luke and Scarlet studied each other.

"Tell me," Scarlet said, turning back to Justin, "what were you doing at the chapel? Are you religious?"

"I don't think I would call myself religious," Justin said, wary to reveal too much till he knew more about Scarlet's views. "The architecture drew me here. It's a handsome old building."

"Were you going to pray?" she asked playfully.

"I hadn't decided," he said, adopting her playful tone.

Scarlet nodded as if approving his chess move in response to hers. "Of course, I respect everyone's freedom of conscience," she said. "Do you want to know my views on religion?"

"Sure, I find everything about you interesting." Justin hoped he did not seem too forward in stating what he really felt.

"I'm happy to tell you," she said gaily. "I believe I am a mild, but not extreme, skeptic."

Justin and Luke both listened intently. The darkening sky now turned a luminous deep blue that reminded Justin of the Avatāra's complexion. He waited a moment to see if Luke would reply, but he nodded in deference to Justin. This was Justin's game to play. And so, he replied to Scarlet, "So that I can understand your skepticism, in regard to what are you mildly skeptical?"

"Excellent question," Scarlet said. With both hands, she swept her glistening auburn hair from her forehead. "You may find my answer less than excellent, but here it is. For me, you and I exist here and now, and that is all we can know with certainty. Therefore, we should make the most of the present, with a view to predictable future events, such as our future need of a satisfying career, and a satisfying long-term relationship. I am not a blind, foolish hedonist. I am more of a classic epicurean."

"That is extremely interesting," Justin said. "I assume you agree with Epicurus that pleasure is life's goal, and to maximize pleasure one must live moderately, to avoid the suffering that comes with overindulgence."

"Very well stated, my friend," Scarlet replied. As she spoke, cool mountain breezes scattered the evening clouds. Silver moonbeams now revealed the beauty of Scarlet's features. Justin inaudibly sighed.

"May we also assume," Luke ventured, replying to Scarlet, "that you agree with Epicurus in ranking the pleasures of the mind above mere physical sensations?"

"You may freely assume that." Scarlet laughed. "I see that you two gentlemen have read your Greek philosophy."

"I've read a bit," Luke said.

"But Scarlet," Justin said, "we still don't know in what sense you are a moderate, and not an extreme skeptic."

"Of course," Scarlet said. "I am not a severe skeptic because I believe that within the here and now, we can have real knowledge and happiness. I am a moderate skeptic because I doubt future lives or higher worlds. And that, my friends, is life as I see it. Now, you can both condemn me for my impious views."

Justin and Luke protested that they did not condemn her, and that they respected her freedom of conscience as much as she respected theirs.

"Thank you," Scarlet said with a happy, confident smile. "Now, Justin, it's your turn. What is your view of life?"

She had trapped him. He could not refuse to reciprocate with Scarlet, and she would instantly detect any insincerity in his reply. He glanced at Luke, who gave him a good luck smile.

Justin began, "In my view, a rational human being should believe or doubt wherever he or she has a good reason to believe or to doubt. And ultimately, a good reason must be based on self-evident experience that may be physical or metaphysical, and which one cannot fairly dismiss."

Scarlet and Luke listened intently. But seeing that Justin would say no more, Scarlet said, "Well done, Justin. I am sincerely impressed. You gave a very safe answer, without being overly evasive. And now, please go see the lovely chapel if you wish. I'll see you tomorrow."

Justin instantly recognized Scarlet's last words as yet another test. "Oh, I can see the chapel any day," he said. "I'd rather talk to you."

"But I'm going to bore your friend, Luke."

"Not at all," Luke said.

"Thank you, Luke," Scarlet said. "However, since it is getting late, perhaps you two gentlemen can escort me back to my residence hall."

The two gentlemen were delighted to escort her to the Steventon Hall door, handsomely framed in white granite with red sandstone accents.

"I would gladly invite you up for a cup of herbal tea," Scarlet said, "but boys are not allowed to come in except on special days. And this is not one of those days. So, I must bid you good evening."

With a joking curtsy, Scarlet walked into the dormitory without looking back, closing the door behind her. For a minute, Justin stood staring at the door till Luke said, "Justin, let's go back to Oxford Hall. They're starting to turn off the lights on campus."

Justin found it hard to sleep that first night. As cool mountain breezes drifted down the river into his open window, visions of Scarlet, Tom, and the Knights danced in his blissful mind. As crickets fiddled, he rejoiced with wonder at his fortune. White Hall was Bhū-loka without the Asuras, or perhaps with tiny Asuras like the bikers. Their threat did concern him for his friends' sake. But he had too many other topics to think about.

To balance his giddy joy, he admitted to himself that there were various problems. When he first met Scarlet, he gave her a false impression of his family's situation. Also, there seemed to be a mutual attraction between him and a girl admired by the Knight vice president. Seriously displeasing Mel, or her, could instantly terminate his Knight candidacy. White Hall was a high-stakes environment. This was not Tucker County High School.

Yet these problems were manageable. Indeed, before long, he thought, he would conquer White Hall the way he did Tucker County High School. He was up for the challenge. He would deal with problems, whether bikers or love triangles, if and when they arose. He looked forward excitedly to tomorrow's start of classes.

He had heard a rumor that Senator Hunter Clay might visit campus soon. Some said he might appear the next day at the school assembly. Winning the favor of Senator Clay would be life changing. Justin would make every effort to meet the senator and win his favor.

CHAPTER 20

T he next day, the White Hall semester began as it always did, with an assembly of students and faculty. Classes would start later that day. Justin and Luke arrived early and chatted in the auditorium lobby. Justin hoped to see Scarlet, who swore she would come at the last possible second to such a boring affair. True to her word, she was the last to enter, but her entrance did not please Justin. She came arm in arm with Mel. Justin forced a smiling greeting, bestowing one each on Mel and Scarlet. Serenely free of romantic interest, Luke sat with Justin.

White Hall's president and alumna, Dr. Jill Lofter, spoke all the words that one expects to hear on such occasions—the warm welcome, the high hopes for each and every student, the wish that students take full advantage of the unique opportunities of a White Hall education, and of course, the word to the wise that students must comply with all school rules.

Finally, Dr. Lofter again wished each and every student much success, and ended the assembly. Eager to avoid Scarlet and Mel, Justin hurried back to his room, put on hiking boots, and headed for the hills. He needed time alone, to think. He missed his solitary time at Blackwater Falls, but Pasture Fence Mountain would do for now.

He feared his growing attachment to Scarlet. On the one hand, it made him vulnerable to painful disappointment, as well as daily, almost hourly, anxiety. On the other hand, Justin feared that Scarlet might be another Su Varṇa. Yet, as in Bhū-loka, he was attached. His interest in Scarlet was sincere. Were she not Tom Walker's sister, he would be just as interested in her.

But to make matters worse, he could not even openly compete with Mel for her affection. That was too dangerous. He must passively wait for Scarlet to show her preference, and that went sorely against his nature. On top of that, he found it demeaning. He would moderate his attachment to Scarlet, without any perceptible change in his behavior toward her. If she liked him as much as he liked her, she would declare it.

If he showed any coolness toward Scarlet, he might offend or hurt her. He had no wish to do that. She might conclude that his interest in her had been whimsical or insincere, which was not at all the case.

As if that were not complicated enough, offending Scarlet was no more dangerous than offending Mel. This was the White Hall Academy. Justin was clearly not in control here as he was back home.

Tired of such thoughts, he used the time remaining before his first class to walk through the wonders of the White Hall campus, admiring the variegated gardens—English, French, Japanese, Mediterranean, and of course, Virginia Colonial. A creek curved through campus, creating lush, landscaped islets linked by little bridges. Pink brick paths led to waterside patios with umbrellas of bright colors.

These natural charms delighted him, and gave him a strong sense of the privilege and prestige of his new school. In this happy mood, he received Scarlet with all the easy, natural affection she expected when their paths suddenly crossed.

They were chatting with enthusiasm when the sound of a motorbike on the mountain broke the still air. Justin saw a bike lunging straight up the steep slope.

"That," Scarlet said with a touch of mocking sarcasm, "is Manly Branley!"

"What?"

"That's an inside joke. It's manly Brad Branley on his super Rokon Trail-Breaker."

"He's a Knight?" Justin asked, trying to sound casual.

"Yes, and he will be the next Knight president after Tom. Not that I'm ecstatic about it, but so it is."

"But Mel is the vice president."

"I obviously know that. But Mel will graduate with Tom. The Knights only allow seniors as president or vice president. Brad is a junior and the executive secretary. And the ES becomes the new president."

"I see," Justin said. He needed to pay more attention to Brad Branley.

"Did you ever drive his super bike?" Justin said, synching with Scarlet's irreverent tone.

"Oh no," she said. "Lord, no! I guess you don't know Brad yet. No one touches Brad's stuff, especially his Rokon Trail-Breaker. If anyone so much as looks at it too long, they will have problems with Brad."

Justin smiled. "I will definitely keep that in mind."

"And, he is the White Hall martial arts champion, so no one gets in his way."

Justin made due note of this. He would take care not to compete in the same events as Brad, since once a fight started, Justin had trouble holding back.

"Does he have a girlfriend on campus?" Justin asked.

"Wow, what questions! I will assume you are jealous for me and so I will take your question as a compliment and answer it. No, he does not have a White Hall girlfriend. Manly Branley thinks he's too good even for White Hall girls. They say he's got a lovely young heiress in Manhattan."

"I see."

"And that is more than enough of Mr. Branley," Scarlet said. "Not another word. Tell me what you chose for your last class."

CHAPTER 21

T he last class period was an elective course that each student chose according to their interest. Justin planned to take a course in Renaissance history. But Scarlet praised a course she was taking on nineteenth-century romantic novels.

"The teacher is excellent," she said. "He's going to deconstruct the naïve romantic credulity that characterized much of that century."

Intrigued, Justin read the course description:

Nineteenth-Century Romantic Novels. Instructor: Dr. Angeloff

Course description: Are we inexorably selfish? When we claim to love another, or to act selflessly, do we really pursue our own pleasure? Does selfless love exist? Is there such a thing as pure altruism? We will consider how nineteenth-century romantic novelists might answer these questions.

Scarlet insisted he take the class with her, and he could not say no, nor ask if Mel would also take the class.

"Sure," he said, "I'll meet you there."

Scarlet gave him an approving smile and ran off to her first class. Justin found himself looking forward all day to the last class. When he arrived at the classroom, he was disappointed to see that Mel was also there. Had Scarlet invited him too?

Justin met Scarlet and she arranged to sit between him and Mel, who seemed as unsatisfied by the arrangement as Justin. Excited anticipation filled the air, as students filled the seats and stood in the aisles.

Finally, young and handsome Dr. Angeloff strode in, looked around with a cocked chin, walked briskly to the podium and nodded at his own notes, like the God of Genesis who saw that his creation was good.

Professor Angeloff then looked up and broke the pregnant silence with the words, "Well, well."

As he greeted familiar students with smiles and quips that provoked laughter, Brad Branley strolled into the classroom and stared at a young student till he stood up and gave Brad his seat. Justin studied him. Brad was tall and very well built.

The campus bells pealed and Dr. Angeloff began. His manner was relaxed, confident and entertaining as he introduced himself and the course and launched into his lecture. At first, he impressed Justin, till he found that the teacher's skeptical views seriously differed from his own. Justin enjoyed great literature, but Dr. Angeloff seemed to enjoy theories about literature, especially theories that were boldly irreverent and tended to discredit metaphysical assumptions. In that mood, the professor turned to love.

"I have long been fascinated," he said, "with a topic I mentioned in the course description—the possibility, or more likely the impossibility, of pure love, sometimes described as pure altruism. We will raise these issues in our reading of romantic novels. Let me touch briefly on love itself."

Several young ladies leaned forward in their chairs. Scarlet leaned back in her chair and smiled.

"My view of love," Angeloff said, "also found in *Leviathan*, by the great philosopher Hobbes, may be called psychological egoism. As I see it, at every moment, we all seek our own interest, our own pleasure. We are never purely unselfish; hence, there is no pure love. We may believe we act selflessly for another's benefit, but consciously or unconsciously, we seek our own interest."

Scarlet raised her hand. Not waiting to be called on, she said, "Do you mean there is no pure love?"

The professor seemed to know her and smiled at her question. "Well," he said, "if we take love in the dictionary sense to be 'an intense feeling of tender affection and compassion,' we certainly do experience love. But whenever we love, we ultimately seek our own satisfaction."

"We certainly do!" shouted a muscular boy in a football shirt.

Several students laughed. Justin did not.

"So," Professor Angeloff concluded, "are there any questions on this view? Or objections?"

Justin glanced at Scarlet. The teacher said, "All of you, feel free to say what you really think."

Justin hesitated. He was new at White Hall and did not want to be seen as challenging a popular teacher. Also, he wanted to please Scarlet, but he would not totally abandon his own intellectual integrity. Sensing his doubt, Professor Angeloff looked straight at Justin and said, "Please tell me what you think," then hunched forward as if ready to do battle.

"I don't mean to argue," Justin began, "but I do have a problem with that theory."

This little preface roused and even alarmed the class. Heads turned; eyes bore down on the rebel.

"What is your name, young man?" asked Dr. Angeloff.

"Justin."

"So, Justin, go on, please."

"Well," Justin said, "the fact that love, or altruistic behavior, gives us pleasure does not prove in itself that we seek that pleasure as our primary motive when we love. The joy of love, at least in some cases, may be the natural effect, rather than the principal motive, of a loving act."

Justin plunged the room into silence. Dr. Angeloff said, "You express yourself well, young man. Then I assume you object to a Freudian analysis of romantic novels."

"It certainly may apply in some cases," Justin said, "but not in all. To insist otherwise would run the risk of circular reasoning."

Dr. Angeloff's admirers, including Scarlet, now stared at Justin. Had he offended them all by his bold assertion? Or had he impressed them?

A glance to his side showed him the feelings of at least one student. Scarlet was not pleased. But was she displeased? The answer was on its way. Scarlet raised her hand and this time waited for the teacher to call on her. When he did, she spoke in a cool tone. "Since the nature of all human beings is to be selfish to some degree, why posit a theoretical, unrecorded state of mind in which one loves with no selfish interest?"

Indignant, Justin wanted to retort, "Why? Because I met such a person with pure motives, and however rare, such people exist." But of course, he said nothing, lest he seriously damage his career.

"Wait," cried another student with mock excitement, "Justin has given us a great new theory. We'll call it the love theory of literature."

At this, several students broke into boisterous laughter. The teacher tried to regain control of the class.

No one had dared publicly mock Justin at Tucker County High. Only Billy Skinner had tried, and he paid the price. White Hall was different. No one feared him here. They openly mocked him. It was a new pain and challenge, one he had not learned to master. Justin gave way to anger and hurt, even with so much at stake.

Then Brad Branley spoke up and said, "Justin is sadly mistaken, but his theory is clever—a clever illusion."

Justin noted the combined insult and praise, but did not react. The bell rang, ending class. The students stood up to leave. "Wait one moment!" Mr. Angeloff shouted over the students' bustle. "Wait, this is important." The room hushed. He looked at Justin and said, "Justin, you made a good point. I do not share your view, but you stated it well, and that is what White Hall is about. Thank you for having the courage to say what you really think."

Justin nodded and thanked the teacher. Some students looked abashed. Scarlet looked apologetic. Justin darted away before she could speak to him. His diplomacy and tolerance had their limits. He was too disturbed to speak to anyone. He craved solitude and went to a secluded corner of the campus, down by the river. Even for Justin Davis, White Hall was to be an intellectual baptism by fire.

Under a crisp blue sky, Sugar Hollow glowed with autumn charm—the rushing river, tall, leafy trees, and ever-present Shenandoah peaks high in the west. Justin sat with his back against a giant boulder, and hurled stones into the ceaseless current of the clear, restless creek, as he had done with the bigger waters of Blackwater Falls in Davis.

Clouds formed. The mountain air cooled and so did his mind. With a shudder, he now saw the obvious—he might have ruined his hopes for Knighthood. He scorned Scarlet when she wanted to reconcile with him. Now, cold river wind brushed his skin like heralding hands of social death.

Not finding peace by the river, Justin brooded over where he might go. An unexpected and exciting thought entered his mind. Justin vividly recalled his yoga practice in Bhū-loka, under Devī's guidance. Yoga there had definitely been peaceful. In fact, it had been too peaceful. But Justin needed peace now. Why not take a yoga class? The teacher would not be Devī, but it still might calm his nerves. He walked briskly back to campus, entered the athletic center, and went straight to the yoga studio. It certainly did not compare to Devī's mountain ashram, but still, the atmosphere was peaceful. A friendly girl at the front desk, apparently seeing his distracted manner, asked if he had ever taken a yoga class.

"Not in this millennium," he said with a smile.

She laughed. "I like that. Not in this millennium."

"So, what do I do?"

"Place your shoes in the rack, and come with me," she said. "I'll show you."

They entered a room with a polished wooden floor, furnished only with a small table with a little burning candle and a small brass Buddha. The girl led Justin to an equipment area and handed him a mat, blanket, strap, and block.

"There you go!" she said, and returned to her post at the entrance. Justin spread his mat and sat anxious and quiet.

A student couple stretched and conversed, waiting for the class to begin. A large girl came in and sat down on her mat, sticking her legs out in front of her. She then looped a strap around her feet, leaned forward and touched her head to her knees. As Justin stared straight ahead at the brass Buddha, a graceful feminine figure glided up, rolled out a mat, and sat beside him. It was Scarlet. Startled and happy, he began to greet her when a voice called out from the back:

"Hello, everyone! Namaste!"

It was the yoga teacher, Serena Silver from Charlottesville, a thin woman in her thirties with large, mascaraed eyes and short, frizzy hair. Serena spoke at once to Justin.

"Well! We have one new student. Welcome! What's your name?"

"Justin."

"That's a nice name!"

"Thank you."

"Thank you for coming, Justin!"

After this effusive greeting, Justin glanced at Scarlet out of the corner of his eye, but her eyes were fixed on the teacher. Why sit next to him, if she wouldn't look at him or speak to him?

"All right, everyone!" Serena said with her default exuberance, "I want you to sit comfortably, take a deep breath, and be present here and now. Close your eyes and let all your cares and worries slip right out of your mind. Let them fly out the window!"

Justin struggled not to laugh. Serena closed her eyes. Seeing this, Scarlet whispered to him, "You actually made a good point today in class, even if I don't agree with you."

"Thank you."

"Just relax," sighed Serena, eyes still closed. "No words, no thoughts, no cares!"

"I'm glad you feel that way," Justin whispered.

"We can't talk now," Scarlet said, her own eyes closed.

"Sorry."

Serena Silver opened her eyes.

"Did you say something, Justin?" she asked sweetly.

"No," he replied. "I think I was breathing too loudly."

"Oh, that's very good. I want you all to be conscious of your breath. Breathe in. Breathe out. Watch your breath. Hear your breath. Feel your breath. All right, we're going to begin today with a delicious twist! This will feel so good. Now lie down on your back and extend your arms straight out to the side, along the lines of your shoulders."

Scarlet playfully slapped Justin's hand.

"Now extend your legs straight out," Serena said. "Keep your legs together, bring your knees up toward your chest, and then let them fall to your right side as you turn your head to the left, and twist!"

Justin did this. Then he quickly turned his head back to the right so that he was looking straight into Scarlet's eyes.

"Perhaps we could talk after this class," he said.

Scarlet held her finger to her lips.

"Justin!" cried Serena. "Your head is turned the wrong way."

"So?" Justin whispered to Scarlet, as he turned back to the left. Scarlet smiled. And so it went. Whenever Serena spent a minute on the other side of the room helping a student, Justin and Scarlet turned to each other. And so, despite all Serena's vigilance, by the end of the class, Justin and Scarlet were better friends than ever. They went to the campus café, sipped tropical smoothies, and forgot they had ever disagreed about anything.

The next day, Justin said to Scarlet, "Maybe I didn't explain myself so well in that class."

"Oh, I think you did," Scarlet said with an arch smile, "but I still insist that whatever you said then, or now, is in pursuit of your own happiness."

"Perhaps," Justin replied.

"But if it makes you feel any better," Scarlet added, "I studied this topic after class, and I was glad to discover that I am an altruistic egoist."

"Kindly explain." Justin smiled.

"Simple. I believe that the rational pursuit of self-interest is compatible with—in fact it requires—benevolent actions and motives. That is, to be truly happy, I must make other persons happy. It's just the nature of life."

"Granted," Justin agreed, "but still, if I care about you because it pleases me to do so, then my ultimate concern is not about you; I care about myself."

"Precisely. That's why it's altruistic egoism." Scarlet smiled.

"Personally, I wouldn't call that love."

Why not?" Scarlet narrowed her eyes and playfully poked him.

"Professor Angeloff explained it all perfectly." In a deep voice, she imitated the teacher. "'Love is an intense feeling of tender affection and compassion.' So, who cares why we feel it? Why ruin such a lovely feeling with–ugh–philosophy? Well, aren't you going to argue with me?" She pushed his shoulder and laughed.

Justin leaned back in his chair and smiled at Scarlet. She had not proved her point with philosophical rigor. She seemed to disdain philosophy, at least in jest. But she spoke with charm and affection. They were closer than ever, or so it seemed.

After the incident in the class, and his quick reconciliation with Scarlet, Justin's political instincts resumed control. He would not again let pride or anger interfere with his goals. He would excel in all his classes, just as he did at Tucker County High School.

Having said goodbye to Scarlet, who wanted to study, Justin made his way back to Oxford Hall. A thought struck him. In a sense, Dr. Angeloff's views were those of the Asuras, who deny an ultimate truth or meaning to our life, beyond the selfish pursuit of pleasure. But clearly, the teacher was not an Asura. Perhaps Asura qualities had really infiltrated the minds of otherwise good people.

Justin entered his room to find Luke reading *The First Avatāra*. Justin asked him in a tone of forced calm how he liked the book.

"Quite interesting," Luke offered.

"Do you think any of it might be true?"

"Why not?" Luke said with a contagious smile that Justin had to return. "You see, I believe we live in a multidimensional universe."

"Please explain," Justin asked.

"All right. Imagine you had an appointment in town at 10 Main Street. You go there and can't find the office you seek. However, you don't know that 10 Main Street is a ten-story building. You're searching the lobby, but the office you seek is on a higher floor."

"Continue," Justin urged.

"I mean that the world we normally see might be just the ground floor of a multidimensional reality."

"Yes," Justin said, "and if that were true, we must find the stairway, or perhaps the elevator, that goes to the higher floors."

"Precisely," Luke agreed.

"And what are the stairs or elevator?"

"I suppose it must be some form of higher consciousness. It would be like coming out of a cave into the sunlight."

"You refer to Plato's cave?" Justin asked.

"Yes. Have you read it?"

"Yes," Justin said, "many times. Of course, other books offer other metaphors, and various techniques to attain higher consciousness."

"You probably know more about that than me," Luke admitted. "I would like to ask you about—"

Justin's phone rang. It was Scarlet. She wanted to talk. Higher truths must wait.

CHAPTER 22

J oey eagerly texted Justin that news of his friendship with Scarlet and her brother, the Knight president, had spread all over Tucker County. Joey insisted there was no pressure, but everyone in the county expected Justin to achieve Knighthood. *No pressure.*

That weekend, Justin eagerly accepted Scarlet's invitation to walk with her, Tom, and Mel. Justin was pleased that Mel, still grateful for Justin's zeal to defend him in the airport, wanted to get to know him better. It was a very significant gesture. Justin appreciated it and not only because of its significance for his Knight candidacy. Justin suspected that Scarlet, eager that all her friends be friends with each other, had orchestrated Mel's piety. The four friends happily strolled along the sparkling river where the green-grass-carpeted bank rolls gently into the clear waters.

In the midst of lively talk and frequent laughter, Tom suddenly raised his hand and stopped the group. Forty yards ahead walked a small gaggle of girls in tattered gray uniforms—Stonies. Tom had them wait till the dangerous girls walked far ahead.

The friends continued their walk. Minutes later, they saw another girl whose beige skirt reached her ankles. Large sunglasses and a sky-blue beret pulled over her forehead effectively hid her face. Tom and Scarlet joked about her long dress. Mel looked curiously. Who was she?

The girl walked up a neat brick path to the respectable Wolfe residence, and knocked on the bright red door. The friends paused to watch. Mrs. Wolfe came out, looked at the girl, turned as red as her door and shrieked, "What are you doing here? You're a Stonewood girl. Get out of here! Get off my property! My daughter warned you never to come here again!"

Tom said to Mel and Justin, "Come with me to the house. That Stonie may attack Mrs. Wolfe, or try to rob her. Scarlet, stay here."

As the men approached, to their surprise, the Stonewood girl replied in a gentle and educated tone, "I'm very sorry, Mrs. Wolfe. I believe there has been a most regrettable misunderstanding."

These conciliatory words did nothing to placate Mrs. Wolfe, who grew increasingly furious and terrified. Justin thought her in danger of a stroke. She tried to slam the door shut, but her hand trembled and slipped off the knob. She stepped back into the house and screamed, "Ronnie! Ronnie! The witch is attacking me." Turning back to the girl, she screamed, "Never speak to my daughter again! Do not even look at her. Get off my property! I'm calling the police!" She did just that on her cell phone, as the girl turned to leave.

Scarlet approached, despite her brother's vigorous hand signs to stay back, and said to her friends, "What is going on? Why did Mrs. Wolfe call that girl a witch?"

By this time, a burly young man, presumably Ronnie, emerged from the house yelling vulgar oaths at the girl, who now retreated down the brick walkway with its neat rows of bright flowers on each side. Spotting the White Hall boys, she pulled her beret down so they could not see her face, and hurried past them.

She was moving away down the main road when Ronnie, still shouting profanities, leaped into a Chevy Camaro, and revved the motor so loud that Justin could not hear what Scarlet said to him. The White Hall friends watched in horror as Ronnie roared past them, racing straight at the girl, who deftly stepped behind a big oak tree.

Thwarted, Ronnie screeched to a stop, backed up, and shouted at the girl, "Stay up on your mountain, witch, or I'll kill you!" Having given this terse warning, he again revved his engine, backed up, and shot his car at the girl, who was walking peacefully down the road.

As he did so, he thrust his hand out the car window and tried to direct a derogatory hand sign at the girl. In doing so, he lost control of the wheel. The car turned sharply, flew into the air, flipped over, and landed upside down on the riverbank.

Smoke poured out of the car. People poured out of their houses. Mrs. Wolfe rushed to the scene, screaming that the witch caused the crash by her witchcraft.

As voices shouted not to move the victim, the victim himself climbed out of the car and wobbled on his own feet before collapsing onto the riverbank. With a gasp, Mrs. Wolfe identified the victim as her nephew, Ronnie. Her neighbors gasped in reply and rushed to Ronnie's aid. Ronnie again stood up and seemed to suffer no serious injury apart from a fracture of the expressive fingers of his left hand.

Every set of eyes turned on the hapless girl. She tried to walk away but people blocked the road and shouted at her to wait till the police arrived. An ambulance, siren blaring, rushed into the Hollow. Paramedics jumped out and attended to Ronnie, assuring the crowd that he did not appear to be seriously injured, but was likely suffering from shock.

The crowd grew in size and anger. Rough voices threatened the girl from all sides. She moved toward the forest, as if to escape. A sheriff's car with flashing lights arrived.

The sheriff spoke through an impossibly loud speaker mounted on the car's roof: "All right, everyone, stay where you are. Young lady," he said, referring to the girl, "that means you too."

The girl complied, as did the White Hallians. A tall sheriff got out of the car and conferred with Mrs. Wolfe, whom he seemed to know. He walked up to the girl and asked, "What is your name?"

"Jane Rivers," she said.

"I thought it was you. What did you do to that boy?" he demanded.

"It is rather what he did to me," she said, stating exactly what happened in fine English.

The officer said, "Do you have any proof of that?"

"Someone must have seen it," she said, glancing around. She looked straight at the White Hallians, as if waiting for them to come forward and tell the truth. Justin looked at his friends.

Mrs. Wolfe shouted, "Don't anyone be fooled by this girl. She's not just a Stonewood girl. She's the worst of them, the infamous witch in the ghost house on the mountain."

The witch on the mountain! This epithet, which everyone but Justin seemed to understand, produced an instant effect. Mel froze and his chin dropped. He gaped at the girl.

"It's her, it is the witch," cried many people who recognized her name. Even the sheriff stared at her as if ready to pull out a gun if she attacked. He took a deep breath and said, "Did anyone besides Mrs. Wolfe here see the accident? Any witnesses?"

"What should we do, Tom?" Scarlet asked her brother. "The girl is telling the truth."

"I know," Tom said. "But it's the witch. This could be dangerous. I'm worried about your safety."

The White Hallians looked at each other, clearly trapped in a moral dilemma.

Mrs. Wolfe gestured and shouted wildly, insisting that the deadly witch almost killed her nephew and the sheriff must arrest her. Some neighbors stepped up to confirm her story. Others shouted that they would get their own guns and take care of the witch if the sheriff didn't.

The girl, Jane, reasserted her innocence in a manner so utterly calm and fearless that Justin began to suspect she did indeed have some power. The sheriff took off his cap and scratched his head. The neighbors grew bolder and demanded that the sheriff arrest the girl. Tom and Mel looked at each other. Scarlet looked at Justin. He thought of his father. That settled it. Whatever the consequences, Justin would not allow this injustice.

"Excuse me," Justin said to Tom, "I'll be right back."

Justin charged forward, demanding that the crowd be quiet and let him speak. Intimidated by the force of his passion and his White Hall uniform, the crowd hushed, much to their own surprise.

Justin said to the sheriff, "Sir, I was close to the accident. I saw exactly what happened."

The neighbors' ears perked up. Despite their angry testimonies, they had no idea what actually happened.

Justin went on, "That fool…" pointing at Ronnie being loaded into the ambulance, "that fool threatened this girl," he pointed at Jane, "ran her off the road, and almost killed her. He crashed because he was trying to show off his car, make an obscene gesture, and terrorize the girl—all at the same time."

His face taut with anger, Justin put his hands on his hips and dared anyone to deny his version under oath. No one came forward. The crowd was shy of perjury, and assumed that any White Hallian could summon fearfully expert lawyers. No one, sheriff included, trifled with White Hall. Justin noticed that the girl seemed to be staring at him. It made him uneasy and he did not return her gaze.

Finally, in a calm, respectful voice, Justin said to the sheriff, "Sir, I respect you and I respect the work you do. But if you arrest this girl, it will go viral all over the world as hashtag witch hunt. This girl, whoever she is, was thirty yards from the car. You cannot arrest her on charges of witchcraft. Your career might not survive it. I don't mean to offend you."

The sheriff smiled, took Justin's name, noted his statement, and asked if he was sure of his story. Justin nodded. The sheriff then turned to Scarlet, Tom, and Mel, and said, "Do you dispute Justin's account?"

They shook their heads no.

"So, Justin spoke the truth, right?" the sheriff asked.

Tom and Scarlet nodded. Mel nodded and looked away.

"Well," the sheriff said, "that's four witnesses right there." Turning to the girl, he said, "You just wait here for a moment till I finish my report. I have some questions to ask you." He turned to ask the medics a question. When he turned back, the girl was gone.

"Where did she go?" the sheriff asked, his voice trembling.

"I told you, Sheriff," Mrs. Wolfe said, "this girl is of the Devīl."

The White Hallians stared at each other. Tom said, "Did anyone see her leave?"

No one had. Even Justin shivered. The witch of the mountain.

"Let's get out of here," Tom said. The friends gave their names and phone numbers to the sheriff and hurried back to White Hall.

Scarlet, Tom, and Mel kept silent. Justin did not dare speak. He had taken the lead to defend the most dangerous Stonie, a girl feared by all, one who might possess some dark power. Was he right to defend her? By his action, he had forced his friends to corroborate his testimony. Had he defended evil in the name of justice? Had he ruined his chance to be a Knight? He could not put his mind at ease nor come to any conclusion.

Back on campus, at the first opportunity, he spoke to Tom alone.

"I hope I didn't do anything wrong," Justin said.

Tom put an arm over his shoulder. "I respect what you did. I also fight for justice in my own way. But Stonies are just too dangerous. And what if that girl really is the mountain witch that even Stonies fear? I know it sounds crazy, but what if Mrs. Wolfe is right? It's just too risky."

"Thanks, Tom." Justin hardly believed that Tom Walker had his arm around his shoulder. "I'll be careful. I really appreciate you talking to me."

"Sure," Tom replied, "but do me a favor. Go talk to Mel. Let him know you understand and respect his feelings. And do exactly what he says."

"Yes, of course," Justin agreed.

He flew to Mel's room. Mel let him in and when he sat down, pointed to a big picture of a handsome young man in a Knight jacket and cap. He wiped a tear from his eyes and said, "That's my brother Mike. I loved him. A Stonewood girl killed him. Do you get it?"

"Yes, I do," Justin said softly, lowering his head. "I can't imagine your loss. I have a brother that I'm very close with and I don't know how I'd live without him. Forgive me if—"

"It's okay," Mel said. Justin sensed that Mel liked him less than Tom did. Mel's interest in Scarlet sufficiently explained it. But Mel was fair and had a grudging nobility about him. He looked Justin in the eye. "I will be fair and give you one and only one warning: never involve yourself again with Stonies. My brother died because he wanted to be a nice guy. He thought they weren't all bad. Do you understand me?"

Justin assured Mel that he did, and with real feeling for Mel's loss, he begged his forgiveness, promising to follow the rules.

Mel shook his hand and all was okay. For now. That meant a lot. Justin had survived the strange incident. He returned to his room with the picture of Mel's lost brother etched painfully in his mind. He thought of Joey and shuddered. He agreed with Tom and Mel. It was too dangerous to trust any Stonies. If Jane was a witch, she might easily have the power to walk and talk like an educated girl, and thus trick the innocent. Mel's brother lost his life to a ruthless Stonie, and the Stonies themselves were in terror of this girl, as everyone said.

How did Jane Rivers earn her infamy? Even more troubling, why did she stare at Justin? Would she now target him? What might she do?

The next day, when things were calmer, Justin asked Scarlet what she knew about that witch.

"I know that the other Stonies fear her," Scarlet said. "She stays in the haunted house. People regularly see lights up in the house. Some people watched it with a telescope and actually saw her there. A few times, the sheriff went with a heavily armed posse to make her leave, but they can never find her at the house. She always knows when they are coming."

"But why do other Stonies fear her?" Justin asked.

"Apparently, when she first came to the school several years ago, some girls tried to bully her. That's normal at Stonewood. But everyone who bothered her, even teachers, suffered strange accidents and almost died. Now, no one will look in her eyes and she hardly ever shows up at her school. She roams the mountains. You have to be careful if you hike up near the ridge. They say that is her domain."

"So, Scarlet, do you think she really is a dangerous witch?"

"I cannot say she is not a witch, nor that she is not dangerous. Since I don't know, I don't say. But I stay away. Abundance of caution. However, to be fair and honest, there is another side. Some people say that she is an heiress, that her parents were the richest family in the region, and that the witch house is a fabulous mansion that she will inherit. I've also heard that Jane, as she calls herself, really never goes to Stonewood, but the school is afraid to expel her. She really lives in that mansion, if the stories are true."

"What a strange story," Justin said.

"Yes, and some people, believe it or not, claim she is an alien who came from another world and that's why she has powers." She paused. "Don't look at me like that. I didn't say I believe it. I'm reporting what they say."

"Scarlet, I never thought for a moment that you believed it. It's just so very strange."

"Yes, and you would be surprised to see the respectable people who are convinced she is an alien. And one very strange point—the few persons outside of Stonewood who actually saw her all say she is beautiful. As you may have noted, she always covers herself in public. If she is so beautiful, why always hide her beauty?"

"It is truly strange," Justin said.

"It truly is. But I left out a crucial point. The ghost house where she lives is less than a mile from our campus, right on the ridge of Pasture Fence Mountain."

"Seriously?"

"Very seriously. If you ever step foot on that property, White Hall will expel you. That's how serious it is. But Justin, tell me what *you* think."

"First, in the face of all these stories and accusations, I sincerely admire your integrity in not committing yourself to any story you cannot verify. I know less than you, so I will adopt your attitude, which is the only rational one in this case."

"I hope you mean that and are not just trying to please me," Scarlet said.

"I mean exactly what I said—about your integrity, and about my own earnest decision to emulate it."

Scarlet's smile told Justin that he behaved like a gentleman and that pleased her. He liked Scarlet very much. He had never met a girl like her. But who was the so-called witch?

CHAPTER 23

A few undramatic weeks passed. Justin's initial White Hall euphoria settled into a calmer joy. Having studied them with utmost discretion, and frequently spoken to them, Justin increasingly understood his new friends.

Tom was serenely confident, but not arrogant. Though clever, he was not inclined to abstract philosophical complexity. He sought a career in government administration. For Tom, strict adherence to a rational social contract formed the basis of a good and just society. Fair rules and laws, not the whims of public or private persons, must prevail.

Tom was a natural leader. He liked to help others. He believed in his success, and success always came easily to him. He was diplomatic and loyal, a team player. And he demanded as much from those he admitted into his circle, or with whom he worked on various projects.

Tom was generally good-natured and easy-going, not as intense as his sister. Tom reacted to his parents' nasty split by becoming a peacemaker. A natural leader, he inspired cooperation. Now his world centered on White Hall. Respecting White Hall and its traditions anchored his other virtues.

Scarlet admired and followed her brother in public affairs, but she was fiercely independent in her pursuit of business administration. She saw herself as the future head of a multinational corporation that interacted importantly with governments. Eminently pragmatic, she found Justin's complex mind to be nearly inscrutable, which fascinated her. But, like Tom, she found Justin's metaphysical musings a bit ethereal, and she was not shy about telling him so.

Scarlet was smart and proud, but she could laugh at herself. She liked to spend money from her bottomless trust fund, but followed Tom's example, and conscientiously gave a regular percentage to charity.

Scarlet responded to the parental split with a fiery determination to forge her own life. She resented her mother and stepfather, and loved her independence. She would only listen to Tom, but he knew just how far he could push her.

Proud and coquettish, but kind, Scarlet truly cared about her friends, and all those who sincerely solicited her help.

Scarlet and Tom would each inherit a fortune from their father, who had divorced their mother with deep mutual acrimony, and so left nothing to his former wife in his will. Scarlet told Justin, "I'm a great catch, don't you think? Rich, beautiful, and above all, witty and charming."

When Justin shook his head with amusement, she burst into laughter and said, "I hope you know me well enough to know that I am not really the shameless narcissist I just appeared to be. I do know my limits, and I may know yours as well."

He smiled and said, "Really? What are my limits?"

"You don't really have any," she said with mock reverence. "Do you agree?"

"Of course not. I have serious limits. For one, I mistake my body for my real self."

"Now that was clever," she said. "Proselytizing in the guise of self-deprecation! Bravo, Justin. Well done."

Scarlet, like Su Varṇa, did not want controversy or danger in her life. She wanted the normal life of a powerful, rich woman. She relished her banter with Justin, but she was intensely focused on her career. Therefore, getting involved with Justin's esoteric interests was a distraction from, and possible risk to, her carefully planned career path.

Justin began to decipher Mel's attitude toward him and Scarlet. Mel was too proud to give in to jealousy. A girl that did not return his regard did not deserve its continuance. He did struggle to apply this maxim to Scarlet, for as Justin plainly saw, Mel was deeply attached to her. Still, Mel would not sacrifice his honor by jealous revenge or endlessly unrequited attentions.

Mel Trayhem sought a career in sports medicine and cosmetic surgery. He valued good dressing and grooming, health, and fine appearance. He was a competitive tennis player. In short, his life was focused on the body.

Lacking Tom's serenity, and Scarlet's confidence, Mel could be anxious and fretful. He worshiped his late older brother, but was painfully aware of his own inferiority in looks and abilities. He did not resent his brother's superiority, but constantly strived to prove himself worthy of him. He was prone to anger, but loyal and ethical. Mel, Scarlet, and Tom, like almost all White Hallians, were smart, and highly ambitious.

By now, Justin saw what he always knew in theory: White Hall was what Joey once called it: a very sophisticated cave. Luke was right. Few students or faculty at White Hall seemed to regularly, or even sporadically, worry about life's ultimate meaning.

So be it. Justin must save his family. Cave or not, he could not abandon his mother and brother to a life of misery. He himself would never return to a life of disgraceful poverty, a life that wore down body and mind. That was inhuman. He must go forward. He might be spiritually weak, even a hypocrite, but it was far better than his only present alternative. He would eventually follow his father and do good in the world. His plan was a good one. No change.

Lest other students suspect Justin of a backwoods upbringing in rural West Virginia, he studied them and precisely reproduced their manner of walking and talking. Still, Scarlet teased him by saying, "My fair Justin, I will be your Henry Higgins."

Justin wished Scarlet to be part of his grand life plan. She would make him happy and one day might accept higher knowledge. Perhaps old age was the best time for spiritual transcendence, after a long life of leading and serving the world.

In fact, Justin fantasized that Scarlet might someday be his partner and ally. So far, Scarlet only smiled and occasionally laughed at Justin's metaphysical ideals. It would take time. He would wait. He was becoming attached to her.

At times, he feared that it was all happening again, just like in Bhū-loka. He would forget any spiritual vision, and simply try to enjoy this world. "I will never find enlightenment," he sometimes muttered to himself. "I am simply trapped in this world."

If Justin preserved a tenuous link to his book and his Bhū-loka dream, he gave the credit to Luke Tester. Of all his new friends, Luke Tester deeply intrigued Justin, though ostensibly Luke could do least to advance Justin's career. By some strange twist of destiny, Justin's roommate seemed to share Justin's interest in the book. Indeed, Luke's interest might even have exceeded Justin's at that point. He and Luke got along very well, like old friends. They both noticed that.

Justin's first impression of Luke in the airport was now confirmed. Luke was intelligent and inquisitive. He was modest and ambitious in the best sense of each. Justin's respect and affection for Luke steadily increased.

One other White Hall student began to play a role in Justin's life. Brad Branley was not only a Knight, he was slated to be Knight president when Tom graduated. Brad also actively served within Hunter Clay's elite Youth Corps.

Brad was taller than Justin, very muscular, and captain of the White Hall martial arts team. His strongest event was karate. Justin did not enter that event, to avoid fighting, and perhaps embarrassing, a very influential Knight. Justin focused on judo.

Justin maintained a constant disguise in a critical area of his life, ever implying, if never explicitly stating, that his family was like all of theirs. Justin wondered how the truth of his dirt-poor condition might affect his friendship with the Knights and Scarlet. He did not worry about Luke. Justin assumed that it would not matter to Luke. Still, Justin lived in constant anxiety, fearing detection and exposure.

One day, Tom said to Justin, "Scarlet told me you live on a beautiful country estate by Davis, West Virginia. It's only two and a half hours from here. I'm surprised you flew to Charlottesville. Anyway, Scarlet thought we could go for a weekend outing at your estate, if your mother doesn't mind. We'll pay for our food and all that."

"Oh...that would be great," Justin said, trying not to sweat. "It would be an honor for me and my family. We would love to host you. Unfortunately, my mom...has not been well. Health problems."

"I'm really sorry," Tom said. "Of course, we won't trouble her. I pray she gets well soon. Please send her my best wishes."

"I will. She will appreciate it, I'm sure."

The White Hall Academy was mostly a school for rich geniuses, and even the car issue constantly worried Justin. All his friends drove luxury cars. They wondered why he didn't as well. Justin's eco-alibi was rather thin, but it seemed to work—he was reducing his carbon footprint.

Justin received a scholarship that barely allowed him to preserve a façade of normalcy. And he sent half of that to his family. He lied to his mother and told her the school gave him extra for his family because of their health issues. His mother would send it back at once if she suspected he was depriving himself.

With that modest addition, Star Davis was able to work less, and her health slowly improved. She assured Justin that someday soon she would be able to write again. Bursting with pride in his brother, Joey's high spirits seemed to improve his health as well.

Justin would not deprive his mother and brother. The money he sent made a big difference to their lives. But this essential frugality threatened to expose him. How could he keep up with the White Hall social scene and sustain his Knight candidacy on his shamefully small budget?

He snuck into the scholarship office every time he went to collect his money. And he always implored the staff to keep his financial status strictly confidential. They assured him they did. But how long could he pretend that he was like other White Hall students, like his friends?

A few days later, Justin was speaking to his family on WhatsApp when Luke entered the room. Having told his family so much about Luke, and Luke so much about his family, he was anxious for them to finally meet. Handing the phone to Luke, Justin watched happily as Luke conversed graciously with Star Davis, and made Joey laugh.

After the call, Justin thanked his friend, who made Justin promise to speak soon with his parents, a promise eagerly given. Luke then looked gravely at Justin and said, "Did you notice that your phone is bugged?"

"Bugged? What do you mean?"

Luke nodded with complete assurance. "I mean someone has tapped into your phone and monitors your calls. Did you notice your phone makes little clicking sounds?"

"Yes, but I thought that's because it's old."

"Not those clicks. Does your battery run down faster than it should?"

Yes, but I thought...so those are signs that someone is tapping my phone?"

"Exactly. Now we should test your mother's phone. Call her from my phone and let me listen on the speaker." Justin did so. He exchanged a few words with his mother and looked up at Luke, who nodded again. "Your mother's phone is also being tapped."

Alarmed, Justin said, "What can we do?" In all his success at White Hall, he had not worried about an Asura attack, but now fear for his family struck him.

Justin called his mother at once, told her what Luke had discovered, and urged her to change her SIM card immediately. Both Justin and his mother changed their cards. For now, the problem seemed solved. But

Justin was reminded in a most disturbing way that forces beyond his power were likely observing him, and with threatening intent. Justin must alone bear the weight of this danger. To whom could he explain it, without calling into question, in their mind, his own sanity?

Justin now looked for possible danger everywhere. His friends noticed his anxiety and inquired. He replied that it was just a "little family problem, nothing serious." His friends seemed satisfied with this explanation and Justin endeavored to seem like his normal self.

A day later, something happened that gave him both joy and increased anxiety. Scarlet said to Justin, "We have known each other for a while, yet you never ask me out. I must conclude that you do not really enjoy my company." Justin knew that behind her teasing formality, she was displeased. He tried to placate her by treating her complaint as nothing but banter.

"That would be a very wrong conclusion," Justin said, with a chivalrous bow. "Indeed, I treasure your company."

"Well spoken, Prince Justin. So now I authorize you to ask me out."

"I always wanted to," Justin said, more seriously, "but I feared offending Mel. You know how he feels about you."

"Oh, don't worry about that," she replied. "I already spoke to Mel. You see, White Hallians have a strict code. We respect each other's freedom. I am determined to choose who I will be, and with whom. Mel honors that. He would never act against you if I chose to go out with you. And since you are so shy, I will ask you to go out with me."

"Of course! I would be delighted. Really."

"Excellent. We can go out Friday evening. And since you don't have a car. I will drive. Tell me again why you don't have a car."

"Well," he said, forcing a smile, "it's an environmental statement."

"Justin, you're joking, right? Get a hybrid!"

"You know, I thought of that, but...well, even to manufacture a hybrid in a factory...there's a lot of negative impact on the environment."

"Well, you are a rabid ecologist. I assume you won't object to traveling in my motorized vehicle. You did fly here from West Virginia. Or was that on the back of a large bird?"

Scarlet said this with utmost gravity, and then burst out laughing at him.

He forced another smile and said, "It was a large metal bird. Where would you like to go?"

"To a great French restaurant on the downtown mall in Charlottesville, next to the theater. We'll do dinner and a play. And we'll each pay for ourself. Okay?"

"Sounds great!" His face smiled, his heart sank, his mind was in turmoil.

"Come to my dorm Friday at seven p.m. Goodbye, Justin, I have to study. Oh, and by the way, wear nice clothes. We dress semiformal for dates. Do not embarrass me."

As soon as he was alone, Justin found the restaurant and theater online and saw the prices. Then he looked up semiformal dress. He would need a dark business suit, dress shirt, tie, faux leather dress shoes, and dark dress socks. Well, he had dark socks.

This was an unmitigated disaster. For other White Hall students, the cost would be nothing. For Justin, the date would eliminate his semester savings. It was money his family desperately needed.

What would he tell Scarlet? His fragile hoax was crumbling. They would all say he lied, or at least misled them. Justin collapsed onto his bed, overcome with shame and worry.

This was a crisis. He would deeply offend Scarlet if he did not go out with her. He might lose her forever. Of course, Knighthood would also be over. He could not say no. He must eagerly accept her invitation, which he did. And he really wanted to go out with her. But how was he to pay for the date?

He was trapping himself in a web of deceit. Again and again, these words from Scott's *Marmion* haunted him: "Oh what a tangled web we weave, when first we practice to deceive!"

In the midst of this, he noticed that the first fall colors glittered on the high slopes. Desperate to escape the mounting pressures of White Hall, and desperate over his coming date with Scarlet, Justin left the campus after classes and hiked to the ridge of Pasture Fence Mountain. As he ascended, his body responded joyfully to the challenge. On the summit, he found a scenic ridge road. The dreaded witch house lay to the west. He went east, delighting in the sudden freedom, vast views, and pristine air.

Then a daring curiosity gripped him. Without breaking White Hall rules, he could behold dreaded Stonewood from a safe perch. He had binoculars!

With quickened pace, he strode the ridge till he stood high above the chaotic, crumbling campus of the Stonewood School for Girls. It lay in a cramped, dark glen, impervious to sunlight. To this benighted academy, the state of Virginia consigned those girls whose drug addiction, thievery, violence, and prostitution were judged implacable.

He studied the shabby clearing dotted with old, ramshackle structures. Once handsome, they were now plagued with broken walls and windows, and encircled by jungled lawns. He watched gray-clad girls range the glen.

Immersed in surveillance, sure of solitude, he did not notice that he was not alone, till a hostile voice chilled his nerves. "Like the view, White Hall boy?"

Ten feet away, a muscular Stonewood girl glared at him.

"Sorry," he said. "I was just out for a walk."

"Don't be stupid," she said. "Now pay for the view, rich boy."

"I'm not rich," he said, "and I don't pay for public views. Sorry again."

"You're mocking me," she said.

"No, I just told you the truth." Justin tried for a minute to reason with her, but only succeeded in making her angrier.

"I've had enough," she concluded, "so now I'll pay you."

She pulled out a knife. "Now get on your knees and beg."

This was crazy. "Look," Justin said, "I'm going now, so don't bother me. I don't want to hurt you."

She called him several remarkably vulgar names, and tried, rather amateurishly, to stab him. He easily evaded her. Again she thrust and he danced away. This went on for a while until he realized she would not stop. And she blocked his way home. So, he grabbed and twisted the wrist of her knife hand until she dropped her weapon, which he kicked a good way down the mountain. As the raging girl shrieked maledictions, he ran so fast along the ridge toward White Hall that she could not follow him. He understood even more clearly now the widespread perception of Stonewood and its scholars.

As he started down the mountain toward campus, Justin heard the unmistakable roar of Brad Branley's Rokon Trail-Breaker. Brad was zooming up and down the hills near him. A chilling thought froze Justin's heart. He had spoken with a Stonie, grounds for expulsion from White Hall. Of course, the girl had threatened him with a knife, but he had not instantly left, he had stayed for a minute to amuse himself, before disarming her. Brad was riding nearby and could have seen him.

There was more danger. Local people walked the hills with binoculars and zoom cameras. What if someone took his picture with the Stonie? It was a remote possibility, or maybe not so remote.

Then, as soon as he crossed down into cell range, he received a text from the White Hall administration. He was to come at once to the school president's office. This was crazy! How could they know? Justin hurried down to campus with catastrophic visions assaulting his mind.

CHAPTER 24

J ustin's stomach churned as he hurried to the president's office. If
White Hall expelled him, his life was over. He could never face family
or friends in Davis. He would live as a hermit in the hills. He must convince them he was innocent of whatever they were going to accuse him of.

As he neared the administration building, he saw several black
Cadillac Escalades with tinted windows parked at the entrance. Two
big, strong men in dark suits and dark glasses stood by the entrance.
They were obviously high-level bodyguards. But for whom?

Entering the building, he saw two more of these guards just outside
the president's suite. What was going on? As he approached the door,
an agent stepped in front of him, politely asked his name, and checked
his photo ID. Satisfied, the agent smiled, opened the door for Justin,
and said, "Go right in. They're waiting for you."

President Lofter's secretary also smiled at him, and ushered him
into the president's grand old office. Justin respectfully greeted her.
And she also smiled. "So, you are Justin Davis," Dr. Lofter said, both
asking and telling him.

"Yes, I am," Justin said with a slight bow of his head.

"Very good." She then led Justin's gaze to a couple sitting on the
other side of her office in a living room setting. On the couch, looking
steadily at Justin, sat Senator Hunter Clay and his wife, Dr. Barbara
Clay. What was this?

President Lofter led Justin to the celebrated couple and said, "Please
allow me to introduce our very distinguished alumnus, Senator Hunter
Clay, and his wife, Dr. Barbara Clay."

Astonished, and hardly knowing what he did, Justin gave the Clays
his little bow. The senator said, "Glad to meet you, Justin," and stretched
out his hand. Justin rushed over and shook it. He then shook his wife's
hand. The couple's relaxed, smiling demeanor almost put him at ease.

"It's an honor to meet you," Justin said with his own best campaign
smile. This was supremely high stakes for Justin's career. Every nerve
was on alert. Justin sat in the chair that Dr. Lofter indicated for him.

Senator Clay smiled. "It's a pleasure to meet you, Justin. I heard from various sources that you showed real courage at the airport, that you wanted to fight the bad guys. Thank you for standing up for our White Hall family, for the Knights, and most importantly, for justice."

Before Justin could mumble something humble, Dr. Lofter added, "Justin was a state champion in martial arts."

"So we've heard," Barbara Clay said with a glittering smile. Behind her smile, a steady, probing gaze showed Justin that she was no less alert and inquisitive than her husband.

Justin could not fail to be impressed by the handsome, famous couple, stylish and elegant, exuding the steady charm of perennial campaigners. The senator was a large, powerful man, who moved as if in excellent physical shape. He was about the age of Justin's late father, in his mid-forties. It was a supreme priority for Justin to ingratiate himself with the Clays, and they seemed eager to give him that opportunity. They wanted to know more about him. He prayed they would not ask where he was from.

I know you're from a small town in West Virginia," Barbara said.

"Yes, I was born in Davis, West Virginia."

"Of course," Senator Clay said, "Barbara and I attended your dear father's funeral. I'm so sorry about his passing." Hunter glanced at Barbara.

"Yes, what a terrible loss," Barbara said.

"It was most kind of you to attend the funeral," Justin said. "It meant a lot to all my family."

"We were glad we could be there," Barbara said. "And your family is still there in Davis?"

"Yes, my mom and brother," Justin explained.

"Yes, what a terrible loss," Barbara said. "I'm so sorry for you, Justin."

Senator Clay lowered his head sadly. "I'm so sorry. I'm sure he's looking down and very proud of you now."

Hunter, as he insisted Justin call him, quickly changed the topic, and after some small talk about White Hall, said, "Justin, Barbara and I are interested in you. We help deserving White Hall students, and we would like to help you. That's why we requested President Lofter to invite you here."

Dr. Lofter praised the Clays' generosity, mentioning their recent gift to expand the student health center.

"And now," Dr. Lofter said, "this magnanimous couple wishes to do even more. They expressed a wish to help worthy students who could use a hand, and we told them about you, Justin. And out of the goodness of their hearts, Senator and Mrs. Clay want to significantly increase your scholarship. What do you say, Justin?"

Dr. Lofter nodded reverently to the Clays and leaned forward in her leather chair.

Justin's jaw dropped. "I...I'm very grateful," he stammered. "Senator and Mrs. Clay, I'm most grateful. I don't know how to thank you. This will mean so much to my family and me."

Dr. Lofter smiled approvingly at this fitting response. Senator Clay smiled kindly, and said, "Barbara and I have done well in life and we like to help deserving young people who need a little assistance."

Senator Clay nodded to Dr. Lofter. She nodded back, and handed Justin a document showing that the senator's gift would triple his available funds for October and every succeeding month. Justin received it with a joy and gratitude that pleased the Clays. His troubles were over. He could now dress like the other students, take out Scarlet, buy a decent computer, and give up his fear and shame.

"As we say," Senator Clay said, "use it in the best of health. There will be an equal check every month, as long as you are in White Hall, and that includes your summer vacation. I want you to go out, enjoy yourself, and help your family."

Justin eloquently expressed his heartfelt gratitude. The adults seemed fully pleased with him. Justin sensed that the meeting was about to end and was looking for a signal to get up and leave, when Hunter said to him, "As you may know, I created a national youth alliance called the Youth Corps. We help exceptional young people get involved in the political process. They work in my campaigns, serve as Senate pages, and help to spread our message. Our goal is to serve our country in the best possible way. Perhaps you might be interested, Justin. Young people join the Corps by invitation only."

Many thoughts flashed through Justin's mind in an instant. The Corps was a fast track to major success in the world. It also earned fame for its absolute loyalty to its founder, Hunter Clay. To join meant certain success, but at a price.

As if reading Justin's mind, Hunter said, "I know it's a big step for you, Justin. Give it some time, discuss my offer with your family and friends, and then let me know. Here's a card with my secretary's number. I'm sure you will respect my wish that you not share this number with anyone, not even your closest friends or family."

"Of course, sir." Justin took the precious card. "I will absolutely respect your privacy and wishes. And I sincerely thank you for the honor of your offer. As you said, it is only fair that I discuss this with my family, since it is such a big step in my life."

Justin had dreamed of a bright career. But his dreams were manifesting at a speed he had not imagined. Hunter Clay was widely expected to run for president next year. Polls showed that he was the strongest candidate in the country from either party.

But there were dangers. Would Justin come under the control of a mission that was not exactly his own? Would he lose his independence? Would the senator approve of Justin's serious metaphysical commitments? All of that remained to be seen. But Justin was hopeful. The potential for rapid ascension captivated his mind, even as worries remained.

"One last thing," Hunter said. "Barbara and I would like to invite you to visit Clay Campus, my estate, just over the mountain. When you come, we can discuss my plans and yours, and hopefully they will be compatible."

Senator Clay and his wife stood up and the others instantly followed. He and his wife warmly shook President Lofter's hand and thanked her for her time. She could not thank them enough in return. He then gave Justin a firm handshake and patted him on the shoulder. After Barbara shook his hand, the couple quickly departed with their escort.

When they were gone, President Lofter said to the somewhat dazed Justin, "Congratulations, young man, on your extraordinary good fortune. Use these gifts wisely."

Justin was cordially dismissed and headed back to his room in Oxford Hall, his feet hardly touching the ground. Tom and Scarlet intercepted him in the quadrangle and eagerly questioned him regarding his meeting with the Clays, about which they had been informed. The White Hall Academy was a tight network indeed.

Justin told his curious friends what took place, though he spun the extra scholarship money into a story that concealed his poverty. Justin said that Hunter gave him a grant to be used at his discretion to further his career goals.

"Well, Justin," Scarlet said, smiling, "the rich get richer. I'm surprised the Clays didn't give that grant to a needy student. Anyway, I'm glad for you, and it is certainly an honor. And the Clays do help poor students. But you don't need the money. The real news here is Senator Clay's invitation to join the Youth Corps. That is amazing. What did you tell him?"

"I thanked him, of course," Justin said, "and I told him I would speak to my family."

"Speak to your family?" Scarlet asked, incredulous. "Justin, do you know what we're talking about here? Tom, tell him."

"If you have any plan to enter politics," Tom said, "this will put you on top of the world.

"On top of the world?" Scarlet said. "That's an understatement. Hunter Clay will be the next president of the United States. The Youth Corps will have extraordinary opportunities to serve the country."

"You're right," Tom said. "Look, Justin, I'm personally not interested in a purely political career, but it seems that you do have interest in that area. The Youth Corps is a super elite group."

Justin was speechless. "Tom," Scarlet said, "tell him to do it."

"To be fair to Justin," Tom said, "I will say this. Senator Clay can offer you unlimited political and economic opportunities. But you have to be his man. He demands absolute loyalty from those who work with him, and certainly from the Youth Corps. You have to fully trust him."

Justin knew that he could never really give up his own judgment and blindly follow anyone, no matter how powerful. But for now, how could he reject this golden opportunity?

Scarlet again urged him to accept the offer. Tom urged him to read up on the senator, and make sure he could join with a clear conscience.

Justin thanked his friends and, still somewhat dazed, made his way back to Oxford Hall, where he again explained it all to Luke. The two friends then busily researched Hunter Clay. The senator seemed to take moderate positions, though he also spoke grandly of the need to reinvent American democracy, to make America the first fully scientific Republic, with the best possible life for all.

He would think more about this later. For now, he dreamed of his date with Scarlet. When he took her out, he would do so as a respectable White Hall man. He owed it all to America's most powerful couple, Senator and Dr. Clay!

CHAPTER 25

Justin eagerly bought semiformal clothes and fake leather shoes (on ethical grounds) for his evening with Scarlet. The other couple had to cancel for unstated reasons. Scarlet drove Justin in her luxury hybrid. With wit, laughter, and over-the-table high-fives, they enjoyed their vegan dinner. Scarlet liked the play more than Justin, but in her company, he was glad to endure it. If Mel respected Scarlet's right to choose, and if Scarlet chose Justin, he would happily choose her as his partner.

When she dropped him off at Oxford Hall that evening, Scarlet was kind, merry, and formal, and they ended the evening with a most cordial handshake. It would not be easy to fully win her heart.

Justin soon had another serious concern. The White Hall Academy's annual Parents Weekend fast approached, timed to coincide with peak fall colors. Justin sat with Luke on the emerald quadrangle by the bell tower. Luke asked, "Will your family come to Parents Weekend?"

"My mother is still not well," Justin said. In fact, Star and Joey Davis yearned to come, and Justin longed to see them, but it was too dangerous to invite them. His White Hall friends would ask his family about life in Davis. Star Davis would try her best not to embarrass her son, but she lied poorly, and God only knew what Joey might say. It was not safe. Anyway, Star Davis still did not enjoy great health, so Justin's excuse was not far from the truth.

Scarlet also enquired whether Justin's family was coming, and he gave the same answer.

"I really hope your mother's health improves," Scarlet said. "My mom and stepfather are coming. It's no consolation for you, but they both want to meet you. My stepfather, Randy, can be annoying, but he insists he just wants to meet you. You will be here, won't you?"

Justin planned to spend Parents Weekend deep in the hills, where he would not suffer by seeing happy, whole, respectable families. He didn't want to even hear the festivities. But he could not refuse Scarlet. He knew that she could only invite him to meet her parents with Tom's permission, and Justin took it as a most pleasing honor.

Scarlet and Justin agreed that before heading for the hills, he would join Scarlet, Tom, and their parents at Saturday brunch, since their parents were leaving Saturday night. As Tom's friend, Mel was also invited.

The day came, and hordes of luxury cars paraded onto campus. White Hall bustled with proud parents. The administration, faculty, and staff were out in full force, with their unique White Hall blazers. With kind words and smiles, they answered questions, gave campus tours, and of course graciously accepted gifts for the school endowment.

As Justin walked to the brunch, he thought of his mom and Joey. He called them and spoke for a minute. That helped. He thought of his dad, and for an instant, the old pain washed away all the new charm of White Hall. He still needed justice for his dad. That need did not go away. Even White Hall could not cool that fire.

This family day was bad for him. Peals of laughter and live music pursued him on the path. Parents Weekend was in full swing. He would leave after brunch and return when the music was over and the family bliss had ended.

Tom and Scarlet's mother and stepfather, Linda and Randy, perfectly matched Justin's image of Palm Beach snobs. Impeccably stylish, tan and healthy, they exuded casual arrogance, as if they stepped out of the pages of an airline magazine article on Palm Beach glamour.

As the brunch conversation unfolded, Justin saw that suspicion, not kindness, sparked Randy's interest in him. If Scarlet subtly probed Justin, her stepfather dug out Justin's life like a human backhoe.

With a gauzy veneer of smiling curiosity, he asked Justin to confirm what he heard about "your fascinating life in Davis." Randy was so sorry about Justin's father, and the family's subsequent financial collapse. He actually said that. And he sincerely hoped that Justin's mother would find more satisfying work. It must be wearing on her to clean other people's houses. And was Justin quite sure that it was safe for his family to live in an old trailer? Those old trailers were firetraps.

"What are you talking about?" Scarlet shouted. "What do you know about Justin?"

"My dear, calm down," Randy said. "Justin lives in a very small town, and anyone can just call the local Dollar General store, or the Shop and Save." He pronounced these names with thinly veiled disdain. "In fact, you can call any restaurant or hotel or gas station in Davis, and everyone knows the Davis family very well. I'm a bit surprised that you would ask such a question."

"What is your purpose?" Justin said, his face white, his heart stopped. "My purpose, whether Scarlet agrees or not, is that she go out with a boy on her level."

Burning with shame and rage, for himself and his family, Justin shot to his feet, almost knocking over his plate of bagels and butter. Controlling his desire to flip the table onto Randy's head, and not even saying goodbye to his friends, he stormed away, not seeing or caring where he went. He walked till he was stopped by people shouting his name from behind. He turned and faced Tom and Scarlet, who followed him for some distance.

Tom looked embarrassed. He put his hand on Justin's shoulder and said, "I apologize for Randy's malicious behavior. It is none of my business, nor his, where you and your family live, or what your mother does, and I really don't care. I care about you."

Tom brought Justin back to life with the kindness of an older brother. Scarlet, shaking with anger, waving clenched fists, cursed her stepfather and said to Justin with real compassion, "I am sorrier than you can imagine. I'm too angry to speak. Forgive me for ever inviting you to meet that disgusting person."

As Justin was trying to articulate his gratitude, Scarlet suddenly turned her anger on Justin. "Why didn't you tell us the truth? You must think Tom and I are so shallow that we would judge you by your family's income. I thought you knew us better than that."

"Scarlet is right," Tom said. "Why didn't you just tell us the truth? I also believed that we all knew and trusted each other. You didn't directly lie, but you allowed, even encouraged, us to think a certain way. That's why I suggested going to your estate."

"And that's why I suggested you take me out to an expensive place," Scarlet said.

With emotion he could barely contain, Justin said, "I didn't tell you the truth because for me the truth was humiliating. Scarlet, I sincerely felt that you deserved much more than I could offer. Who was I? A destitute young man who could not afford to take you anywhere beyond a nature walk, or even accompany you and pay his own way. Somehow, I thought that if you felt half the shame about me that I felt about myself, you would not want to be seen with me. If I offended you in thinking that way, then I beg your forgiveness. But this is all so new for me. I'm so different, so out of place, so embarrassed about my situation. Yes, I was weak. I lacked the courage to declare openly that I grew up like all of you, but I lost everything. I lost my father, my home, my respectability. Everything was taken away. I'm sorry. Forgive me." Justin could not contain his tears, which only added to his anguish.

Scarlet and Tom stood in silence, moved by Justin's agony. Finally, Scarlet said, "Justin, you read those spiritual books, and spiritual people don't care so much what others think. Even I know that and I'm a sworn materialist."

Justin laughed at this through his tears and confessed that he was not really very spiritual. "There was a time when I thought I might pursue a spiritual path, but I guess I failed."

Tom said gently, "Justin, come what may, most important is that we be honest with each other."

Scarlet added, "Tom is right. I do admit that had I been in your situation, I would have been strongly tempted to conceal the truth. But I would not have concealed it from my real friends, and I thought we were real friends. Justin, I would not have exposed you to public embarrassment and I will not do it now. Tom and I have trusted you. We revealed to you extremely sensitive facts about our own lives, facts that we would never want to be generally known. But you did not trust us as we trusted you."

Justin had no answer. Shame colored his face.

"Yes," Tom said, "in the future, be completely honest with us. We must be able to trust you."

Scarlet agreed and insisted, "You must swear that you will never deceive us again."

Justin swore. She then playfully punched him in the shoulder and said, "Let's forget about this. Take your walk in the mountains."

"Yes," Tom said, "take your hike. When you go up the mountain, keep checking your compass. It's confusing up there. Stay away from the ghost house where that most feared Stonie lives. The house is actually less than a mile from campus, so be extremely cautious."

"Yes, I will. Scarlet told me how close the house is to White Hall."

"The owners of that estate died years ago, and the property is trapped in a Bleak House lawsuit. It's against the law to even step on the property. I know you understand."

"Completely," Justin said. "Count on me."

"I do. Now we have to get back to our mother and evil stepfather."

Justin repeatedly thanked them from his heart, and the friends parted. He was grateful. He was miserable.

His wearied mind turned to another grave concern. He must reply to the illustrious Senator Clay. If Justin joined the Youth Corps, he would forfeit some of his freedom, but he would gain the greatest opportunities. He would end the family's disgrace, and the poverty that threatened his mother's and brother's health.

He must give Hunter an answer. He called his mother and explained the situation. She asked him what he wanted. He wanted to help his family, to make them healthy and happy. And he would not stop until he achieved his goal. She thanked him with much love, but urged him to think about it, and do what he felt was best. "It was very kind of Senator Clay," she said, "to come all the way from Washington to honor your father at the funeral."

"Yes," Justin said, "and if I don't accept now, I may look indecisive or even ungrateful." The fiasco with Randy, which Justin did not share with his mother, was just a sample of what his mother must experience every day. He could not bear to think about it. He told his mother that he must do all he could to help her and Joey, and that he would be all right. He would take care of himself.

"I know you," Star said, "and I see you want to do this. Hunter Clay has so much influence. He could help your career enormously."

Justin took this as permission. He had another powerful motive that he could not share with his mother. He and his family might well be in danger, and Hunter Clay was probably one of the few persons in this world that could protect the Davis family. Back in his room, he nervously called Senator Clay's secretary and declared his wish to join the Youth Corps. She thanked him and said that a member of the Corps would contact him soon about his candidacy. He thanked her.

So, he was merely a candidate. He overstated his status to his mother. Thirty minutes later, there was a knock at his door. He opened it and was startled to see the Knight Brad Branley, who was scheduled to be Knight president after Tom graduated. Justin invited him in. Brad strode in and sat in Luke's chair. He said, "As you may know, Justin, I am a member of the Youth Corps and I work closely with Senator Clay. I've come to speak to you about your candidacy for the Corps. You are a candidate, right?"

"Yes, I am," Justin said, certain that Brad came at the senator's order.

"Good. Naturally, we want to know you better, and we want you to know more about us. Does that make sense to you?"

"Yes, it does."

"Good. We want you to visit Clay Campus and see a little of what we do there. Is that all right with you?"

"It would be an honor," Justin replied.

"Excellent. The campus will send a car for us. I will go with you as your guide."

Elated at this prospect, Justin profusely thanked Brad and asked him to convey his gratitude to the senator.

"I certainly will," Brad replied. "I'll let you know the day and time of our visit. That's it for now."

He rose, walked to the door, turned, and said, "One last thing, at White Hall, Senator Clay only accepts Knights into the Youth Corps. At other schools around the nation, he accepts students only from the most selective student groups. I think you know what that means."

"Yes, I do. My candidacy for the Corps depends on my being accepted by the Knights."

"That is precisely correct," Brad said coolly. "Good luck, Justin."

Without waiting for a reply, he left the room.

Justin had stood when Brad stood up, and he remained standing, trying to understand what just happened. He was thrilled at the invitation. He was amazed that Senator Clay would send a car for him. That a future Knight president, and current Corps member, would come along as his personal guide was also wonderful. But this last wonder Justin had to attribute to Hunter's wish to investigate him further.

Justin sent a text to his mother and brother with a moderate version of what just happened. But that moderate version was enough to enflame the hopes and imagination of Joey, who in rapid fire sent back text after text with questions, hopes, congratulations, and speculations. His mother expressed herself with more cautious joy and congratulations.

With all this, Justin forgot about evil Randy. He still wanted to escape, not to nurse his wounds, but to savor positive events. He packed a water bottle, compass, and energy bar. He picked up the book and almost put it in his backpack. But it was too heavy for a long trek. He put it back on the shelf. Next, he proudly put on his White Hall windbreaker and cap, both powder blue and gold, and even indulged in a moment of self-admiration in the mirror.

He headed for the door, but it suddenly opened, and Luke entered with his parents. Justin had promised to meet them in the evening, but now impromptu introductions took place, and all expressed their joy at the sudden meeting. Luke explained that he thought Justin would be gone by now. Justin smiled and explained that he had had an unexpected visit, but was delighted to meet Luke's parents.

Luke's father, Dr. Matthew Tester, taught physics at Cal Tech in Pasadena and also worked for NASA at the nearby Jet Propulsion Laboratory. Like his son, he was serious but friendly. Luke's mother, Claire Tester, had authored a well-known series of historical novels set in nineteenth-century New England. More outgoing and talkative than her husband, she was delighted to hear that Justin's mother was an aspiring novelist. "I must meet her someday," Claire Tester said. "Send her my sincere greetings and let me know if I can help her in any way. I mean it."

These were welcome words. Justin promised to convey her message. Luke's parents then suggested that they all go hiking together. The Testers were enthusiastic trekkers and preferred the quiet mountains to the noisy events on campus. "Unless, of course," Luke said, "you want to be alone, Justin."

Justin did prefer to walk alone, but Luke was his friend, and his parents had shown him kindness. He could not refuse them. He told them how happy he was to have their company. So, it was settled. The whole party walked to the west, up to nearby Sugar Hollow Reservoir, a mirror lake ringed by wooded hills and backed by Blue Ridge Mountains. Clear water columns rushed over the reservoir dam. Dr. Tester took pictures, but mercifully did not ask the others to pose in them.

With Justin as their guide, they turned north and began hiking toward the southern ridge of Pasture Fence Mountain. Reaching the summit, they enjoyed the exquisite view of the White Hall Academy, through a wide break in the tree line.

Justin and Luke wanted to go farther along the ridge, but Claire Tester needed to rest. It was quickly agreed that Dr. and Claire Tester would stay there on the soft grass of a clearing and wait for the boys, who would explore further.

Justin and Luke happily ranged the ridge, discovering crystalline springs to the east. They explored for some time till Luke realized they had been gone over an hour. The boys headed back at a quickened pace. As they approached the grassy clearing, they saw from a distance that Luke's parents were speaking with a girl who sat with a canvas on her lap and drawing pencils spread at her side on a cloth.

"Luke! Justin!" Claire Tester cried. "We've met a wonderful young lady. Come and meet her."

As the boys came forward, they suddenly stopped and looked at each other. Claire Tester was speaking with a girl from Stonewood. Justin's first thought was for the safety of Luke's parents. Seeing herself exposed, the girl might attack in the hope of getting money from their group. Like the other Stonie, she might pull a knife. Fortunately, Justin never left home without a weapon or two of his own, and he patted a knife hidden on his side.

CHAPTER 26

"Shouldn't we go?" Luke asked.

"Luke," Justin said, "you cannot leave your parents alone with a Stonie. I know she seems very different. And if she really is, I wish we could be her friend. But we can't take a chance. You can't leave your parents alone here. What if other Stonies come? Your parents could be in danger. Let's just stay here till your parents are ready to leave."

Seeing the boys standing back at a distance, Claire Tester said, "Don't be afraid, boys, she's not going to hurt you. Her name is Sara, and she's quite an artist. Come see the lovely drawings she's done of White Hall. And she knows all about the architectural styles of the campus. She was telling me how White Hall integrates three distinct periods of English architecture—Stuart, Georgian, and Victorian. We had quite a vigorous discussion, and she knows her architecture. Just look at this lovely sketch she did of your campus. This girl is brilliant."

Indeed, Sara, the Stonewood girl, did not look dangerous. Her frame was slight and delicate. She stole a glance at the boys. Justin looked back and was startled by the depth of mortification he saw in her face. Justin whispered to Luke, "We can't talk to her. You know the rules."

With his index finger, Luke beckoned his mother to come to him. When she hesitated, he motioned and scowled till she came. In yet another whisper, he told her the problem, and the possible consequences for him and Justin.

Seeing all this whispering, Sara turned white and looked as if she actually might die of shame on the spot. "I was just leaving," she gasped. With trembling hands, she began to hurriedly pack up her art equipment. But she was so disturbed that her hands shook. She struggled to place her many pencils in their box, but the box fell from her hands and the pencils spilled all over the ground.

"I'm sorry," she said, as if struggling to breathe. "I'm going, I'll be gone in a moment."

She again tried to gather her colored pencils, but she could not grasp them in her shaking hands. After several fruitless attempts increased her desperation, Sara's trembling legs would not support her. She sat on the ground, lest she fall, and burst into tears, covering her face with her old, gray shawl.

Everyone stood and stared, speechless. Justin did not doubt that the girl was in profound anguish. Justin glanced at Luke and saw him transfixed by the sobbing girl, as if holding back his own tears at her plight.

Claire Tester bent down and held the convulsing girl in her arms, till she stopped shaking. Her husband stooped over and picked up the pencils, placing them neatly in their box. A new thought flashed in Justin's mind: some Stonies might be victims, not perpetrators. But what could he do?

Claire Tester asked Sara, "Has anyone from outside your school ever spoken to you? Have you ever had a chance to tell your story to anyone?"

The girl shook her head.

"Well, I want to hear your story, if you will tell me."

Through her tears, Sara said, "Now? In front of everyone?"

"Yes, exactly. I trust my intuition. It's always led me straight, and I have a very positive feeling about you, young lady. And I think it's good for all of us to hear you."

Luke's father said, "I definitely want to hear her story."

Mrs. Tester turned to the boys and said, "Young men, I am not a White Hall student, and I will speak to this girl if I wish, and I do wish. I know all about Stonewood, I've heard it many times, but this girl is different. She's just as smart as you, or maybe smarter. She's a lovely, gentle young lady, and I want to know her story. Now, you boys can either go home, or you can stand behind a tree and listen to what she has to say. Does that violate your rules?"

Justin turned to Luke and said, "Is it technically against the rules for us to listen, if we stand at a distance and don't speak to her?"

Luke said, "No, there's no rule against that. We just can't speak to her or converse with her. And personally, I want to hear her story. You can go back if you prefer."

"Well," Justin said, "I want to hear too, if it doesn't violate any rule."

With Claire Tester's encouragement, indeed, her gentle insistence, Sara began her story. Her father was an artist, her mother a teacher. Sara grew up in a happy home, till the day her parents died, victims of a drunk driver. Having no family able to raise her, Sara became a ward of the state and was placed in the hands of a very kind but tragically inexperienced social worker, Ms. Beth Holiday.

"I remember so well," Sara said, "the day that Ms. Holiday brought me to Stonewood. On the way there, I wrote a poem. It began,

'It was a warm day in late spring
Crickets fiddled their chorus
the creeks ran low, the land thirsted for rain.'"

Mrs. Tester stared at Sara. "My dear, how old were you when you wrote that?"

"Ten."

Claire shook her head. "Please continue your story."

"As I mentioned," Sara said, "I came to Stonewood with Beth Holiday. It was her first solo case for Albemarle County Social Services. She was new to the area. We drove out in her old blue Ford Taurus. She drove so slowly along Garth Road that a line of cars behind us began honking. That made Beth nervous, and she went even slower. Finally, I suggested she pull over and let the people pass, which she did. As Beth resumed driving, she said to me in a cheery voice, 'Don't worry, Sara. I'm sure you'll be very happy at this school. See how lovely the countryside is here in West Albemarle!'"

Dr. and Mrs. Tester looked at each other and shook their heads. Sara continued, "I sat so straight in that seat, as if good behavior would be rewarded. I wore my favorite yellow suit, and I put a yellow flower in my hair. Beth kept telling me I would be happy at Stonewood. I didn't reply. I didn't believe that I would be happy anywhere without my parents."

"You poor girl," Claire said. "Please go on."

"When we passed the Mt. Moriah cemetery and came to the village of White Hall, Beth said she was confused and stopped to ask directions in the country store. She asked a big, burly man at the counter for directions to the Stonewood School. The man twisted his puffy red face and said, 'You sure you wanna go there?'"

Sara imitated the burly man's voice in a way that made Claire and her husband laugh. Luke laughed quietly behind the tree. Justin stared. Sara continued, "Anyway, as we left the store, the people there started buzzing, saying the word *Stonewood* with disgust. I asked Beth why they spoke that way, and she claimed she didn't hear anything, and that Stonewood must be a very nice school."

Comfortable in her narrative, Sara now imitated Beth Holiday's voice with skill that impressed and thoroughly entertained Justin, though he had never heard the original Ms. Holiday. Luke seemed mesmerized by Sara.

"We drove a few more miles," Sara said, "till we came to a road that led to the loveliest buildings and gardens I had ever seen. I was ecstatic! This was my school, my new home. This was Stonewood!

"Hand in hand, we went straight to the school office. Beth asked a well-dressed, middle-aged lady sitting behind an expensive desk if this was the Stonewood School. Outraged by the question, the lady angrily told Ms. Holiday, 'This is the White Hall Academy. Our students have absolutely nothing to do with Stonewood! They are forbidden to even speak with Stonewood girls, so you had better leave at once or I will call campus security.' Ms. Holiday and I were shocked. She squeezed my hand and asked directions to Stonewood. The lady replied, 'Go back the way you came! A mile on your left. No sign. Just a barbed wire gate.' And a few minutes later, we were there."

Sara stopped to catch her breath. Justin and Luke looked at each other. "I know," Justin whispered, "it's unbelievable how well she speaks, and what a victim she was."

Luke nodded. "When she speaks, it's like literature."

Sara continued. "Passing the gate, we jounced and jerked down the road. Ms. Holiday almost hit several big trees before we came to the school. I was so eager to see it that I had my nose against the window. I discovered that Stonewood is a small, round clearing spotted with rundown houses and one large construction. We went into the little office and we met Ms. Lancine Howell, the principal and proprietor of Stonewood. She is a lady of medium height, with a stronger than average build. Her features seemed to show the cumulative effect of a lifetime of frowning."

Luke almost burst out laughing. He contained himself by making a coughing noise. Sara looked his way and Luke hid behind a tree. She continued.

"All the girls said that when she was young, Ms. Howell suffered in an abusive relationship, and then gave up all hope of happiness. She worked hard, saved her money, and bought a crumbling girls' school, Stonewood. She seemed determined to prevent in everyone around her the happiness that was denied to her. I believe that Stonewood's seclusion in a narrow, wooded glen with almost no sunlight appealed to Ms. Howell. I always felt sorry for her, despite her cruelty. I'm sorry to speak of her that way, but it is the truth."

Dr. and Mrs. Tester looked at each other, shook their heads, and then assured Sara they believed her and urged her to go on. She did. "My first meeting with Ms. Howell was almost risible."

"Where does she get words like *risible*?" Justin whispered.

"Sshhh, listen," Luke said.

Sara said, "Poor Ms. Holiday had no clue. She took me to Ms. Howell and said, 'Sara just loves horses. I noticed lots of horses in the area, so perhaps she can go horseback riding. And she plays classical flute, so I'm sure you'll want her to perform at school events.' Ms. Howell just stared at her and said, 'Ms. Holiday, I see that no one told you about Stonewood.' The principal's only concern was to get state money for me. She took away my yellow suit and all my other good clothes and dressed me in the gray rags you see before you. She even took the yellow flower out of my hair and threw it in the trash. Oh, those were the days."

Sara stopped to wipe her eyes, and Luke's parents took advantage of the break to wipe their own tears. Sara resumed. "For the girls, Ms. Howell is just a natural complement to a dismal, humiliating environment. Many of the girls have known little else. They take it as the nature of life itself. For me, too, Ms. Howell is just one of many painful indignities, the worst being that the world scorns and despises me, not caring who I am or what I feel, what my abilities or virtues might be. I am an untouchable outcast because a young social worker took me to the wrong school and there was no one to rescue me. No one knows or cares that I was like them, that I spent most of my life in a good, loving family, till my parents were taken from me."

Overcome with emotion, Sara paused again. Luke wiped tears from his eyes. Justin stood motionless, almost forgetting to breathe.

Claire Tester said, "My dear girl, how did you survive all these years? It must be five or six years now."

Sara took a deep breath and steadied herself. "Yes, ma'am, it was six years. I'm sixteen now. When I arrived at Stonewood and realized I had no escape, that I would be there for years, my spirit sank into deep depression. I was hopeless, until I met another ten-year-old girl, a very special girl. By some mysterious light or power, she held firmly at bay the scabrous community around her, even defying Ms. Howell herself. That girl befriended me, and my life changed forever."

"Who was that girl?" Dr. Tester asked.

"Everyone called her Jane."

"It's the witch!" Justin whispered to Luke, who held a finger to his lips. Sara continued, "Jane arrived a few months before me. She stayed in a big house that everyone called the ghost house. But when I arrived, she started coming regularly to Stonewood, as if she were coming to find me. I first saw her in the lunchroom. She sat alone in a far corner. She was so pretty."

This confirmed that Jane was the so-called witch, and also confirmed what Scarlet heard—the witch was very lovely.

Sara sighed and went on, "Jane seemed to be in a world of her own. She was so different from the other girls who were loud and vulgar. I asked a girl about Jane and was told to keep away from Jane, that she was dangerous, and terrible things happened to 'anyone who messed with her.' So, I didn't speak to Jane. I was afraid."

"Do you know what terrible things happened to those who bothered Jane?" Mrs. Tester asked.

"Yes," Sara replied. "Apparently it began with a girl named Reena Rykes, the school bully. Reena was the oldest girl in the school, the biggest and toughest and she harassed everyone. Reena once declared that she would finish Jane. Reena planned to push her into a barbed wire fence and called all the other girls to watch. But when she went to push Jane, Reena slipped and fell into the fence herself. She struggled to get free and it got messy. Reena spent weeks in the hospital and never returned to Stonewood."

"So, Jane did not personally attack Reena," Mrs. Tester said, pushing back her hair and tying it with a band.

"No, she didn't."

"This Jane sounds dangerous," Justin whispered to Luke. Luke did not take his eyes or ears off Sara, and did not hear Justin's words.

"Is there more?" Dr. Tester asked anxiously.

"Yes. Once there was an English teacher at Stonewood, a Ms. Ogilvy, who hated Jane with a passion, and always called her a heathen. Jane was in her class, but Jane knew the subject better than Ms. Ogilvy, and rarely attended. She generally spends very little time on campus. Anyway, Jane's failure to attend class, and her superior knowledge of the subject when she did attend, infuriated the teacher. The girls warned her, 'Don't mess with Jane,' but Ms. Ogilvy insisted that she was not about to fear heathen witchcraft. Ms. Ogilvy really hated Jane and decided to humiliate her. The next time Jane came to class, Ms. Ogilvy seized a rod and struck Jane on both arms for failing to carry out an impossible instruction."

"And what happened?" Mrs. Tester asked anxiously.

"Well," Sara said, "the next day, Ms. Ogilvy was coming down a path. She tripped and fell and broke both her arms exactly in the place where she struck Jane. She was carried away to the hospital and was never seen again at Stonewood. After that, even Ms. Howell feared Jane and never tried to force her to do anything."

"So, again Jane did not personally attack Ms. Ogilvy," Claire said.

"No, she didn't."

"And how did Jane behave after that?" Dr. Tester asked.

"When they left her alone, Jane never bothered anyone. She never looks for trouble. But at that point, I still feared and avoided her, though I always watched her closely. Somehow, she fascinated me. Jane seemed innocent and lonely. At last one day, though still filled with fear, I said hello to her. She smiled, as if she were waiting for me to say that. She treated me very kindly. We were both only ten years old. The other girls saw what I did and decided to punish me for speaking to Jane. I had broken their rules. The next day, when Jane had gone, I was walking and skipping through the woods. I heard demonic laughter and shouting. A gang of older girls approached me. They locked hands in a circle, trapped me in the center, and wouldn't let me out. Then the circle moved toward the stream. It was late fall and the water was bitter cold. The girls planned to throw me into the stream onto the rocks. If I drowned it would be an accident. I screamed at them to let me go, but that made them wilder and angrier. Stonewood girls had years of practice in this form of harassment and they executed it efficiently. They dragged me to the stream bank and were just about to throw me in when suddenly Jane appeared and walked boldly into the circle. All the girls ran. Jane took me by the hand and led me away, up into the hills."

"So, Jane saved you." Mrs. Tester leaned forward.

"Oh yes," Sara said, "and that was just the first time."

"And she was only ten years old, like you."

"Yes." Sara smiled. "And she has a beautiful mansion up on the ridge. I began to spend most of my time there."

Justin jabbed Luke in the side and whispered, "That's the ghost house! Jane is definitely the witch. But she sounds like a good witch."

Mrs. Tester said, "Sara, I apologize for asking you so many questions. I think you're tired."

"Please don't apologize," Sara said, clearly delighted with Luke's parents. "Since I lost my parents, no one in the outside world has been as kind to me as you and your husband. You can ask me anything."

"Well," Mrs. Tester said, sitting up straight and stretching for a moment, "at your kind invitation, I will ask, because I am truly fascinated by your story. What happened after that with you and Jane? She must also be sixteen now."

"Yes, she is. To answer your question, Jane became my real teacher. I had special gifts of which I was unaware, but Jane showed them to me."

"Special gifts?"

"Yes. I'm shy to speak about them, but I assure you they are all benevolent, and not malevolent. They are the power of good. I'm afraid to say more."

At this point, Sara did seem emotionally spent. Her shoulders slumped, and she took a deep breath. Claire Tester sat down next to her, put her arm around her, and urged her to rest.

"Luke," Justin said, "this is all more than amazing, but I have to get back. What should we do?"

"You may think I'm crazy," Luke said, "but I feel like I know Sara. I've never in my life felt this way about a girl before. I'm confused."

"Luke, I understand, but you heard Sara speak about Jane. Jane is the witch, or the girl everyone calls a witch."

"But, Justin, you heard Sara explain that Jane never directly attacked anyone."

"Gray area, Luke. You know that. Jane may have remote powers."

"But you heard Sara speak. She's brilliant. I'm sure she's a genius, and she has a heart of gold. Surely you saw that."

"Everything you say is very likely true, but it's so dangerous. You don't know what you're getting into. You don't know what power these people have. You know what people say about Jane."

"Yes, I do. I've heard it all. Justin, I respect your feelings. And I'm very concerned not to do or say anything that could get you in trouble. So, with all sincerity, please go back to White Hall. I will not tell you, now or in the future, what I am contemplating in regard to Sara. I just know that there is something extraordinary between us, something that I cannot deny unless I deny myself. So, the less you know of my plans and actions in this regard, the better for you. I promise I will be careful. I will avoid any real danger."

Justin looked at his friend. What more could he say to Luke?

"Justin, please go," Luke insisted. "I can't risk any harm to you. Our situations are different. My future does not depend on White Hall. For your own sake, return to campus. I'll deal with my parents."

Justin embraced his friend and headed back to campus. He feared for Luke and admired him at the same time. Having just promised Tom and Scarlet that he would be fully transparent, he appreciated Luke's clever refusal to let Justin know what he planned to do. Justin need tell no lie, nor hide any secret. In fact, he did not know what Luke intended. White Hall did expect students to divulge any observed rule-breaking, but Justin had seen none.

CHAPTER 27

The next morning, Saturday, an unprecedented reserve reigned between Justin and Luke. Justin was afraid to ask Luke what he was thinking or planned to do, and Luke was equally afraid to speak about the one item that absorbed his every thought—Sara.

Justin was to meet Brad Branley in the main quadrangle. Senator Clay would send a car to take them to Clay Campus. Justin planned to appear at the meeting point ahead of time. He was glad to escape the sadly tense mood in his room where Luke quietly studied.

Brad hailed Justin as he approached. Brad had come even earlier. Justin made a mental note.

Punctual to the appointed time, a black Cadillac Escalade stopped in front of them. Justin recognized the driver in his black suit and dark glasses. He was one of the large bodyguards who stood outside the White Hall president's office where Justin first met Senator Clay. The driver welcomed Justin and introduced himself simply as Jack. A circle of curious students gathered round the car. As Justin got into the car, one of them shouted jokingly, "Hey, Justin, are you being arrested or what?"

Justin laughed with the students, then said, "Not yet. Senator Clay sent this car for Brad and me. See you guys later."

As the amazed students stared and whispered, Justin's driver smartly turned the car around, moved slowly through the campus and headed east on Sugar Hollow Road. As they drove, Jack was happy to converse. His speech was not cultivated like that of Senator Clay, but his eyes and manner were sharply observant, and he knew a lot about the region.

"You can ask me anything," Jack said, as if expecting Justin to inquire.

Thinking it would be impolite not to ask something, Justin ventured, "I know that Senator Clay represents a western state. I suppose he finds his Virginia estate a convenient getaway, being so close to Washington."

"Exactly right, young man. The senator flies his executive jet to the capital in thirty minutes; he goes several times a week."

"My father used to fly his plane to Morgantown, West Virginia," Justin said. "He taught there at the university."

"Oh, did he?" Jack replied. "That's interesting. Of course, Senator Clay has a beautiful place in DC as well."

"Of course," Justin said. He saw that Jack had little real interest in him and wanted to keep the conversation on the senator, as he always called him.

"The senator deserves the best, and he can afford it," Jack said. Justin gave the praise that Jack expected, and he nodded his approval at Justin's ability to engage in this shallow diplomatic small talk. Brad stayed silent, carefully watching and listening. Justin smiled to himself. He knew he was under double surveillance.

Seeing Justin quiet, Jack turned to Brad and said, "How you doin'?"

"Very well, Jack. We're on track, if you know what I mean."

"Oh, I do know. All on track."

Justin assumed that this code referred to the senator's ambitious plans. After two and a half miles (Justin measured on his phone map), Jack went north onto Sugar Ridge Road. Passing the White Hall Vineyards, he turned back to the west on a small private lane, about halfway from White Hall to Mountfair. With one hand on the wheel, Jack wove easily through forested hills till they reached the regal gates of Clay Campus. Inside the guard booth, a man in black waved to Jack and the gates opened.

Jack waved and smiled and the Escalade rolled slowly through a half mile of handsome orchards, gardens, and vineyards. Jack looked on with approval as Justin put down his window and stared and spoke with open admiration of the handsome grounds. But where was the main campus?

As they came around a curve, three large, elegant buildings, each handsomely situated within its own green park, loomed before them.

Jack parked by the building on the left, whose lawn sign read, "Guest Reception and Suites." Jack unlocked the car doors. Justin stepped out. Jack came briskly to his side and said, "Welcome to Clay Campus. Brad, I will leave you to show our guest around."

"My pleasure," Brad said with a nod to Jack, who hurried off on foot to another part of campus. "Are you ready for a tour of Clay Campus?" Brad asked.

"Yes, thank you," Justin replied, struck by his serious, precise manner.

"First of all," Brad said, "I will explain the three large buildings you see in front of you. Right in front of us is the Guest Reception. We will finish our tour there. To its right, up on that little hill, is Senator Clay's personal residence and command headquarters."

The Hunter mansion, situated majestically beneath the eastern slope of Pasture Fence Mountain, had a large central area with two symmetrical wings. To its right, the third building was the Research Center and Library. All three buildings were newer constructions in the French Provincial style. Manicured lawns and gardens separated and surrounded the buildings.

As Brad spoke, he watched Justin with a vigilant gaze. Clearly, Justin thought, Hunter asked Brad to study him, hopefully as a serious candidate for Hunter's Youth Corps.

"We will proceed to the west," Brad said, "toward the mountain. Clay Campus encompasses more land than White Hall itself, and we won't see everything, but you'll get a very good idea. You will notice that the Youth Corps consists of both prep students like ourselves and college students from the best schools and clubs. Our staff features a seamless progression from prep school to college to professional politics."

Saying this, Brad set out briskly, with Justin at his side. Clay Campus was more businesslike than White Hall. It bustled almost silently with handsome staff moving quickly about, sometimes stopping to converse in hushed tones inaudible to passersby. Everyone dressed stylishly in khaki pants, buttoned shirts, and blazers. Some, like Brad, wore a gold Youth Corps pin on their lapel. Armed guards discreetly patrolled in battery-driven jeeps bearing an elegant Clay Campus insignia on their sides.

Passing the three main buildings, Brad pointed out several cafeterias, a botanical garden, and a first-run movie theater. They walked by athletic fields, tennis and basketball courts, a bowling alley, and a shooting range. Pointing to a small gymnasium, Brad said, "That is a dedicated facility for martial arts. It should interest you. We'll stop on the way back."

At the back of the campus, on a hilltop, stood a small observatory. Justin asked about it. Brad replied that the senator was an avid amateur astronomer.

Next, they entered the extensive woods of Clay Campus and came to a secluded hunting lodge below the observatory. There Brad proudly pointed out Senator Clay's extensive rifle collection kept safe by elaborate security measures. Brad had keys and codes and showed Justin an array of rifles, many with precision scopes.

"It's a fine rifle collection," Justin said, trying to sound approving.

"Yes, Albemarle County offers excellent hunting. The senator is a serious hunter, and some of the best game is right around here."

Justin smiled. Now was not the time to argue with Brad about the need for animal rights and veganism.

Brad then took Justin up the slope to the highest point of the estate to show him the most impressive view of the campus and all the surrounding area.

"This is as high as we go," Brad said. "The ridge is half a mile straight up the slope."

Justin asked about a glare of reflected sunlight atop the mountain.

"Oh, you noticed," Brad said. "That light is from what the local people call the ghost house."

"I've heard. Did the senator say anything about it?"

"He warned all his staff, all of us, to stay away from the ghost house. He said it's dangerous to go near it. The ghost house property includes a large piece of land, and it's illegal to trespass there."

"Of course," Justin said. Intrigued, Justin looked again, careful not to seem too interested.

The walk back to the guest center offered a commanding view of the entire campus, which was impeccably landscaped.

"So the ghost house is right above the senator's campus."

"Yes," Brad said with a rueful smile. "Less than a mile. Fun neighbors!"

"Is there a road from here to there?" Justin asked.

"No," Brad said sharply. "There is no road from here to there. To be honest, I did hear there was an old road that used to go up the mountain, but it's now blocked and unpassable. Be grateful for that."

"That's fortunate," Justin said.

"Yes, it is."

As they walked back to the main campus, Justin expected Brad to lead him to the Guest Reception building. Instead, Brad turned to the left and walked toward another building. He said, "Up ahead is the martial arts gym. I know you're good, and I need a challenge. So we'll spar a bit, just for fun, a test of men."

Justin dared not object though he had no desire to fight with Brad, who was himself a martial arts champion. Justin did not fear losing to Brad. He feared defeating him and damaging his candidacy both for the Knights and the Youth Corps.

With Brad directing every step, the two young men changed into fight attire, with headgear and thin karate gloves.

"What are the rules?" Justin asked.

"Not many," Brad replied. "Freestyle. We don't break bones or kill each other. And we stop if the other submits by tapping out."

As they entered the ring with its padded floor, Justin noticed cameras on the ceiling. Perhaps the senator, or one of his lieutenants, was watching them now. This was all part of his test.

As other fighters watched, the battle began. Brad struggled to strike Justin with punches and kicks but Justin danced away. He renounced opportunities to pummel and finish his opponent.

Justin concealed his superior technique for two reasons. First, he didn't want to humiliate Brad, who had significant power over his life. Second, he didn't want Brad, or whoever was watching by surveillance camera, to know the full extent of his power and technique. Justin could not predict the future, and he must keep powerful surprises in reserve.

When Brad shouted that Justin should attack him, Justin made a fairly credible show of trying to strike Brad. After ten minutes, Brad ended the match. They went to shower and change. As they dressed, Justin tried to avoid speaking of the fight, and said, "Brad, I can see how dedicated you are to the senator."

"I would give my life for the senator. I will fight anyone who fights the senator. That's my path. And, it's time to go to the guest center. You may actually meet the senator."

As they walked back, Brad suddenly turned to Justin and fixed him with his eyes. "Are you seriously considering the Clay Youth Corps?"

Justin quickly recovered from his surprise at this question, the way he always quickly recovered from an opponent's unexpected strike. He said, "Yes, I am very seriously interested. That's why I'm here."

"Good answer," Brad said with a brief smile. "I'm sure you know that to join us, you must embrace Senator Clay's vision for America, as we all have."

Justin knew he was being tested. He would not say too much before he fully understood the game. For now, he said, "Could you tell me about the senator's vision?"

"Sure. We use the term *hedonic humanism*. The human animal, if I may use that term, is the natural center of life on earth. Therefore, we seek to maximize human pleasure in rational ways. So, for example, preserving the environment maximizes human pleasure. The ultimate goal is what we call a rational republic, a society free of superstition and myth, and rather based squarely on meritocratic principles at all levels."

"You do make a cogent case," Justin said, determined to win over this influential White Hall Knight whose vote might determine his future. "I have looked over the senator's writings, and you represent him well."

"Thank you." Brad smiled. "I'm still learning, but I hope I grasp the basics. Perhaps you will join us someday."

"I hope so," Justin said. Brad knew well that only a Knight could join the Corps. Justin must do all he could to gain this Knight vote, especially from the future club president.

In these talks, Justin deployed an innocent tone to conceal his ambitious goals. He gave his words an air of unselfish sincerity. At the same time, he added enough passion to persuade Brad that he felt more for these views than he actually did.

Awash in calculated diplomacy, Justin worried, in a flash of uncalculated sincerity, whether he was entirely losing his spiritual bearings in his march toward worldly greatness. He concluded he was not. He did admire Hunter Clay, and the senator's political philosophy did not seem to directly oppose Justin's spiritual goals, or what was left of them.

Knighthood, combined with the Youth Corps, would send Justin flying to greatness. Senator Clay was the man of the hour, and the future. Justin would be next in line, the new generation. He could build on the senator's platform and thus achieve his own goals. No, there was no contradiction, no serious problem. Justin felt fiercely determined to achieve Knighthood, and with it the Clay Youth Corps. This was an infallible path, but the consequences of failure would be dire, for himself and for his family.

Justin saw some vehicles moving on an internal road that led to the north and wound behind a hill.

"Where does that road go?" he asked.

"I see that you're curious," Brad said. "That road leads to a highly restricted building that is, let us say, the inner sanctum of the campaign."

Justin had heard this word *campaign* several times as a jargon for the senator's ultimate plans to improve the global condition of humanity.

Brad continued, "That's where the senator meets with his inner core to plan the world's future. The security around that building is impenetrable. It also serves as an elite campaign headquarters for upcoming political campaigns. Only very special people are invited. I hope to be invited there one day."

"So you've never been there."

"No, not yet. But one day..."

They reached the Guest Reception area and Brad declared the tour over. Jack would take Justin back to White Hall. Brad would stay on Clay Campus till evening.

Justin thanked him and concealed his disappointment at not seeing the senator on this visit. But Justin's conclusion proved to be unfounded. Brad received a call, nodded, said, "Right away," and hung up.

"Well," he said, "this is your lucky day, Justin. The senator just sent word that he will see you in his own house. That is a real honor."

Brad led him straight to the great mansion where Senator Clay and his wife, Barbara, resided. He escorted him past the entrance guards and ushered him into a handsome waiting room.

The floor-to-ceiling windows, facing out, afforded a lovely view of the lush gardens. The doors facing in revealed the wide, gracefully curved central staircase. Brad told Justin he would see him back at White Hall. Justin again warmly thanked him for the tour. Brad nodded and left.

Justin sat and waited, trying to organize his thoughts about all that was happening. His mind kept returning to one powerful fact. Justin was sitting in the house of the man that would likely be the next American president. Moreover, Hunter Clay led a political wave extending beyond his own candidacy and country. His friends and allies were leading candidates in regional and national offices, both in the US and in several other leading countries.

Justin could not but admire the senator's wealth. Justin grew up with affluence, but the Clay Campus spoke of wealth and importance beyond anything Justin had experienced. Indeed, he now sat waiting in the largest private residence he had ever seen.

Absorbed in such thoughts, he did not notice the passing time, and before he expected, he saw Senator Clay come down the stairway with an entourage of male and female assistants with whom he conversed. At the bottom of the stairs, the assistants hurried to their tasks and the senator strolled straight into the waiting room and greeted Justin.

As he did at their first meeting, Justin felt the power of this large man who was intimately connected to world leaders, and would soon become the greatest world leader. Yet the senator handled his wealth and power in an elegant, effortless way that inspired Justin's admiration. Justin rose to meet him. Hunter Clay was dressed casually in slacks and a polo shirt. He was just as handsome and charismatic as Justin recalled from their first meeting.

The senator shook Justin's hand with an easy smile, motioned for him to sit, and sat facing him. He began with small talk.

"So, Justin, we meet again. Thanks for coming. I believe you met Jack."

"Yes, sir. He was kind enough to drive me here."

"And Brad showed you around the campus?"

"Yes, it was very kind of him."

"Good, good. Jack has been with me from the beginning of my career. He is fully dedicated to my mission. I value loyalty above all else."

"Of course."

"Excellent. I must say that I derive a special pleasure from our Youth Corps. If I may speak a bit personally, my wife and I were always so busy with our mission that we never took the time to raise kids of our own. I guess that's why I love working with youth now."

Justin nodded. "I'm sure that many deserving youth around the country are grateful for the opportunity you've provided."

Hunter smiled, as if taking a moment to savor Justin's words. Justin felt at that moment that Hunter Clay was everything that Justin could wish for—a role model, a father figure (though never replacing Tark Davis), and a generous patron of worthy, ambitious young people. Serving his mission was obviously the best way for Justin to pursue his own dreams. At that moment, Justin again affirmed his determination to do everything possible to achieve Knighthood and then enter the Clay Youth Corps.

As if reading his thoughts, the senator said, "Justin, the sky's the limit if you dedicate yourself to me. I would even consider you as a senate page in the nation's capital, as long as I remain senator."

"That is incredibly kind of you," Justin said, "even to consider that."

"Of course there are legal requirements," the senator said. "Tell me, are you sixteen or seventeen?"

"I will be sixteen very soon."

"Good. And I believe you are finishing your junior year in high school."

"Yes, sir."

"And do you have at least a 3.0 grade average?"

"Yes, sir, I exceed that requirement."

"Excellent. You pass all the legal requirements. I should also mention that as a personal rule, I always appoint young men who are Knights to that position. I believe Brad mentioned that to you. I also appoint qualified girls from the Knights' sister organization, the Lorelles. So that would be your test. You must be accepted by the Knights."

"I'm aware of that rule, sir," Justin said. "Brad mentioned it."

"Very good," the senator said with another easy smile. "We do insist on a high level of achievement and loyalty. They are key to our mission."

"Of course, sir," Justin said. "It makes perfect sense."

"Thank you, Justin. I know you will also respect the fact that I cannot and will not interfere in the Knight selection process at White Hall or any other school. Each local chapter chooses their new members with full autonomy. And I respect their decision. The national coordinating body for the Knights, of which I am a member, merely sets general standards for new members."

"Thank you for telling me, sir. I understand and honor those standards. They are self-evidently judicious. I will do my best to earn Knighthood."

The senator was then briefly interrupted by a call from the Speaker of the House in Washington and left the room. Justin took advantage of this pause to again marvel at where he was, with whom he was speaking, and the opportunities that were opening for his future. Looking around, Justin thought, "If Scarlet's wicked stepfather could see me now!"

Several minutes passed and Justin wondered how long the senator would be. But then Jack appeared and conveyed the senator's apologies. He must attend to urgent senate business. Jack would take Justin back to White Hall, if he was ready.

Of course Justin was ready, and they were soon driving back to White Hall. Jack asked him a number of questions, all focused on ascertaining Justin's experience at Clay Campus. Justin gave most positive answers, and Jack nodded approvingly.

Then Justin asked Jack how he got involved with the senator. "Did the political philosophy attract you?"

"No, I'm not much for philosophy. I'm a simple guy. I just do whatever the senator tells me. It's always been that way between us. I believe in the senator, and I'm glad to do what he says. Good enough for me."

Back at White Hall, Justin hurried to his room to avoid any questions from students and instantly began to ponder and evaluate all that he had experienced that day. These were his thoughts:

Clay Campus breathed world power. It was so different from Davis or Morgantown. So different from the White Hall Academy, which, for all its elegance, was just a school—an excellent, prestigious, influential school, to be sure—but with no ambition beyond being a great school.

Ever since his return from Bhū-loka, Justin had dreamed of success and power. Now he stared into the eyes, perhaps into the teeth, of world power. This would be his life. Was there a more spiritual, or even a more human, way to wield such power, or was this the naked, real form of it?

And what were the consequences of rejecting power? Would it mean death for all his family? Would it mean a terrible fate for the world? The image of Devī came into his mind, so vividly that she seemed to stand in front of him. But in an age of nuclear weapons, of monster corporations, of technology that threatened to replace the human race, what could Devī do with a fire-shooting staff, or even the yoga power to slay an Asura?

The Avatāra himself had eventually slain Kaṃsa, but what would Kṛṣṇa do against the industrialized, digitized, legally globe-striding Kaṃsas of this world? Perhaps one must fight fire with fire. Perhaps Senator Clay was right. The only way to confront the super-efficient forces of predatory, heartless materialism was an equally efficient, driven, and potent army of public servants, precisely like that mustered and mobilized by Senator Hunter Clay. Perhaps a squeamish aversion to Clay Campus was just another way of failing the call, as Justin did in Bhū-loka. What if Hunter Clay was the Teacher for this age, and there was no other practical, real way to fix the world? After all, Justin had recoiled at Devī's extreme gravity, and with horrific results. If this was the new test, he must not fail merely because of the machinelike efficiency of Clay Campus.

CHAPTER 28

T hough strongly inclined to take his destiny in his own hands, for now Justin saw no other course but to defer to fate's initiative in his life. Justin had fears and dreams, but little power, for now, to change the course of events. At all costs, he must not repeat his tragic blunder in Bhū-loka. He could not bear to see more innocent people suffer, when he might have had the power to rescue them. Whatever malign forces might be stalking him, and, God forbid, his family, he must do all in his power to acquire greater power, so that he might engage it in the defense of all he knew to be good and true. Beyond this, he saw no present options, no existential electives.

It was Saturday, the night of the Fall Dance. As Justin and Luke dressed for the event, Luke quietly mentioned that he would leave the dance early. He was going to meet someone. Justin looked at Luke and Luke nodded. Both understood that Luke was going to meet Sara. Both understood that if Luke did not explicitly mention Sara, White Hall rules did not require Justin to report Luke to the authorities.

But Justin could not stay silent when he felt his friend might be in real danger. As they walked to the dance on the far side of campus, Justin said, "A few days ago, a girl who shall remain unnamed said that when she met her special friend, she felt that her friend knew everything about her. This worries me, Luke. What if that unnamed girl is under her friend's control?"

"If that's the case," Luke said, "then I want to help that girl."

"But Luke, what if her friend really is a witch?"

"Do you think it appropriate to call her a witch," Luke said, "when we don't really know anything about her?"

"It may not be appropriate, but is everyone really making this up about how dangerous she is? The unnamed girl herself admitted that she's dangerous, at least when provoked. Surely, you don't doubt her account. Maybe there are good and bad witches, but this friend really sounds like a witch. Luke, this is too dangerous at many levels."

As they approached the dance hall, Luke paused and stepped to the side to let other students pass. Justin joined him. Luke sighed. "Justin,

I understand your concern. But when I think of that girl, I just know I have to see her again. Even my parents agree, and they are not normally foolish."

"Luke," Justin insisted, "I would never think your parents or you are foolish. But you recall that day I saw the girl known as the witch. Well, she speaks in the same intelligent, plausible, refined way. What if both girls are...into the same things? I know there's a connection." Justin turned his back to the sidewalk leading to the dance hall. None of the passing students could see his tense expression or hear his impassioned appeal to Luke. "Don't take chances. Maybe it's all a bunch of superstitious nonsense, and maybe it's not. I'm worried about you."

Luke made clear that he appreciated Justin's concern, but could not turn back. Justin promised not to mention the topic again. Sadly, he saw that his dear friend Luke might now be a liability. Justin was rising at White Hall, especially because of his budding connection with Senator Clay. Justin, and his family, had far too much to lose to risk any trouble. If he were seen to be close to Luke, and Luke were caught with Sara, it could seriously damage, even destroy, Justin's career. Guilt by association.

Justin shone at the Fall Dance. Lorelles and other leading ladies took advantage every time Mel danced with Scarlet to walk his way and start a conversation. And Justin chivalrously asked them to dance. He was an excellent dancer. And his political and social skills burned brightly. Nothing could stop him—nothing but a lethal attack like the one that took his father's life. This constant worry galvanized his determination to seek powerful allies like Senator Clay.

Forty minutes after they arrived at the dance, Luke made a nod that only Justin could understand, and silently slipped away from the dance. Luke was indeed a dear friend, and Justin was not happy that he might need to distance himself. But he might have no other choice. And Justin truly feared for his friend's safety. Jane must be that most dangerous of Stonies.

In the days that followed, Luke began disappearing whenever unavoidable duties did not prevent it. Justin knew that he was meeting with Sara, but Luke never talked about it, and Justin never asked. He feared that through Sara, Luke was coming under Jane's control. At what point should Justin intervene? Should he report Luke to the school for his own good? No, he would first contact Luke's parents and alert them to the danger. Luke might be furious and break off their friendship, but Justin's first concern must be his friend's safety. *Or*, Justin asked himself, *am I succumbing to irrational paranoia?*

Yet another fear troubled Justin. Would he ever become a Knight? Tom never talked about his candidacy. And no one else did. His relationship with Hunter Clay depended on Justin's achieving Knighthood. And Justin had not heard a word. The Knights proudly kept their selection process completely secret. One could not apply; the Knights must invite one to candidacy. Justin could do nothing to further his chances. He must simply wait. For this reason as well, Justin was extremely sensitive about any negative repercussions of his close friendship with Luke. Perhaps that friendship had already alarmed the Knights, who, like Senator Clay, demanded total loyalty. Justin did spend time with the Knights, and even ran errands for them. But he also spent considerable time with Luke. That might be an issue for the Knights, and it could easily become a fatal issue for Justin should Luke's friendship with Sara be exposed.

Justin's persistent anxiety and endless conjecturing about his Knight candidacy were finally relieved in a conversation with Tom Walker, who approached him and said, "Justin, it's my duty to discuss something with you. Do you have time?"

Justin certainly did. They sat down together on the central lawn. Tom began at once.

"I'm aware that Senator Clay's generous gift enabled you to take Scarlet out on a somewhat regular basis. Correct?"

"Yes, correct."

"I'm happy for both of you. As you know, Scarlet is extremely popular with the Knights, and any guy she likes has a big advantage with us. She is also an heiress, as you know. Justin, I want to be clear that I don't suspect or accuse you of anything. I have no reason to doubt your integrity or motives. I'm just doing my duty to my sister. I won't let any guy use my sister to become a Knight, or for any other purpose. You and I need to be clear about this, man to man. Scarlet stood up for you. Now, decide if you are serious about her. I won't let any guy play with her feelings. And I will add that I had this same conversation with Mel, since he also goes out with Scarlet. I'm sure you understand. Absolutely nothing personal."

"I do understand," Justin said, "and I sincerely honor your dedication to your sister. To be personal, I deeply care about Scarlet. She's the loveliest, smartest girl I've ever met." He could hardly tell Tom about

Su Varṇa or Devī. "I'm grateful, very grateful, that she likes me at all. I will always be honest with Scarlet and tell her my real feelings."

Tom smiled and punched his shoulder. "You're okay. And now that we've cleared that up, as I knew we would, I have something else to tell you. I invite you to be an official Knight candidate. I'm not promising anything. This doesn't mean you will be a Knight. But we will be looking at you very closely, more closely than ever. And we will now regard you as a candidate. Remember, not all candidates make it."

Justin was thrilled beyond words. Tom smiled and left. Within an hour of their talk, Brad approached Justin to convey the senator's invitation to return to Clay Campus in a few weeks and learn more about the Youth Corps. Jack would pick him up as before. Hunter Clay must be keeping close tabs on Justin's Knight candidacy.

Justin's official Knight candidacy and his second invitation from the senator thrust him even more into the White Hall spotlight. He was now somebody at White Hall. It was like his rise at Tucker County High School, but with much higher stakes.

Justin kept in constant touch with his family. Star Davis refrained from spreading the news of Justin's candidacy. She must spare him all possible embarrassment if he was not successful. Joey, however, whispered the news to his best friends, and soon everyone knew.

Tucker County, West Virginia, was proud of Justin. Here and there, people made little gestures to help his mother. They recalled how generous the Davis family had been in better times.

Some old friends in Davis were trying to arrange a desk job for Star Davis with the county government. She was grateful, but her real dream was to write.

Once, when they were alone, Justin asked Tom if he had ever considered the Youth Corps.

"Yes, I did," Tom said. "I deeply admire Senator Clay, but I'm not fully convinced that all of his policies are good for the country."

"What do you mean?" Justin asked.

"I'm a little busy now, but later I'll tell you about my concerns."

Later, Justin asked Scarlet what she thought. "I see this as an invaluable opportunity for you," she said.

"Your brother has concerns."

"I know. I've heard about the senator's Rational Republic. I hope it's not a slick, new version of social Darwinism. But if you can, why not tolerate some of Hunter's idiosyncratic views? It seems that many voters are willing to do so. Once he's elected, he'll probably swing back to the center and govern as a moderate, and a chance like this may never come again."

Justin gladly agreed, eager to justify the sagacity of his decision.

Justin continued to worry about Luke and Sara. He remembered how kind the Asura, disguised as Lokeśa, had been in Bhū-loka. The Asura Vyādha had been as affectionate and kind as the real Lokeśa—until he tried to kill Prince Jaya.

Sara was indeed a brilliant, charming, and naturally modest girl. Nothing could be easier than to see how and why Luke was in love with her. But who was she really? And who was Jane?

CHAPTER 29

On a Friday afternoon, just a few days before his second visit to Clay Campus, Justin went for a long, solitary hike in the mountains. He needed a break from his constant academic and social duties. He wanted to think deeply about his life, and check his bearings.

He knew it was healthy, even important, to occasionally do some serious soul-searching. But lately he had floated so happily on the lovely lake of success that anything resembling introspection had bounced off his bliss. But today he was resolved to think deeply about life, at least during one good hike.

He relished the rising fortunes of his family. He would never let them down. But he admitted his addiction to prestige and power. He saw clearly that the pleasure of his growing status at White Hall was a gateway drug to an ambitious adult life.

As he walked across campus toward the mountain trail, he saw Scarlet.

"Where are you going?" she asked.

"I need to get away and think, so I'm going up the mountain. Of course, you are most welcome."

"I would, but I have to study. Justin, be careful! A bad storm is coming. It should hit White Hall by sundown. Come back early. That's an order."

"I promise," he said, flattered and charmed by her attention. "See you soon!"

He doffed his White Hall cap to lovely Scarlet, who laughed and hurried away. Off he went on his introspective mission, thinking only of her.

His body had never been in better shape. He walked quickly and soon stood high above the campus, beholding White Hall's signature turrets and halls through colorful trees. *How small the students are,* he thought, *yet how big we think we are.*

Eager for a challenge, he decided to trace the source of White Hall Creek on the high slopes of Pasture Fence Mountain. He left the marked trails with their predictable loops and made his own way through the wilderness. Buoyed by freedom, he still took care to note landmarks for his return—the twisted old tree, the giant cleaved boulder.

Thrilled by nature, he could not focus on the non-physical self. In high spirits, he fought his way up beneath towering trees, seeking the source of the waters.

He found the waters—not on earth but in the sky. A raindrop poked his eye; another hit his nose. It was not yet noon. Indeed, above his rapturous head, dark clouds swirled and massed. The storm would come much later. Eager to keep exploring, he trusted the weather forecast, ignoring what he saw above.

As the rain began to pelt him, he realized with a groan that the forecast was for the valley below. He had almost reached the ridge, almost three thousand feet above White Hall. Here the rain came sooner and harder. Indeed, an ugly storm, borne by livid clouds, now barreled into the ridge.

Cold winds lashed him. The temperature plummeted. In his light coat, he shivered from head to foot. Showers pounded tree crowns, as if gods dumped heaven's bucket on the slope. A deafening bolt ripped open the sky, loosing shearing sheets of deluge.

Justin turned back toward White Hall, fighting for footing as fiendish flows gushed about. Earth melted into grasping mud. Water blinded his eyes, choked his nose and mouth, tripped his legs. Bolts slashed jagged paths to earth, as if to obliterate him.

He grew up in a mountain town. He knew this was bad. The steep slope ran like a river. He could not risk a descent to White Hall. His only hope was to reach the level ridge just above him. Daylight vanished, smothered by clouds.

A cruel gust whirled him around. Racing mud and hidden vines tripped him. Fighting for balance, his feet flew up from under him. He crashed into a boulder. He heard his flashlight shatter. *Don't panic.*

He stood up, but his sense of direction dissolved. Stories of lost hikers found dead did a devil's dance in his mind. He trembled violently. He saw but inches past his face. He must find a cave, an overhang, any shelter at all from blinding rain and freezing wind.

He tried to pray, but he was unpracticed and little came out. A line from "California Dreaming" flashed in his mind: "Well, I got down on my knees, and I pretend to pray."

Should he pray to the Avatāra? Not now. He was in no mood for self-serving, near-death piety. For a moment, the rain slackened. He looked up. Someone was running on the ridge thirty yards above him. There might be shelter nearby! Justin fought his way up, shouting again and again. The young man stopped, turned, and saw him coming.

Gasping for breath, Justin screamed over rain and thunder, "I'm lost. Is there shelter?"

The boy nodded yes. He was dressed for the storm, but anxious to keep moving, presumably toward shelter.

"Please take me there," Justin said. "I'm freezing."

The young man hesitated. A brutal bolt struck near them.

"Please!" Justin said. "Take me to shelter?"

The boy nodded and motioned for Justin to follow him. The sure-footed youth knew the mountain well. With remarkable agility, he raced along the ridge with Justin in close pursuit till a faint light appeared in front of them.

The youth went straight to the light, which came from a big house atop the ridge. An ancient stone wall circled the estate. An iron gate guarded it. A huge sign glared at them: "No Trespassing!"

Justin's heart sank. It must be the dreaded ghost house. But there was no other shelter. The freezing wind was unbearable. He would die without shelter.

Pushing past the gate, the boy ran up the old steps and opened the large front door, waving him in with a quick gesture. Heart thumping, Justin entered.

The boy slammed the door behind them, flew to the hearth, and deftly roused a fire. Justin looked around. The ghost house was a magnificent mansion. But he could not think of that now. He turned to the boy, and to his utter horror saw a long skirt under the boy's coat. Long locks of hair slipped from the hood. Justin had seen those locks before. He was not a boy. He was the so-called witch, the Stonewood girl who terrified other Stonies. As if to confirm this, thunder shook earth and heaven and Justin shuddered with them.

For all his courage and martial skill, Justin was shocked. What if Mrs. Wolfe had been right? What if Luke was wrong? What if Justin was trapped in the house of a deadly lady who cloaked black arts in fine speech? What if she created the storm to ensnare him? His mind ran wild. She kept her back to him, tending the fire.

He had to escape. He told her, "I must go. The storm is abating."

"No, it's not." She kept her back to him. He moved toward the door. She spoke in that same clear voice, "Truly, you won't make it."

Was that a threat? Would she try to stop him? Could she see him with her back turned? He shivered. He must flee at once. He gently pushed the door, hoping to leave quietly. But the ancient iron hinges screeched every inch of the way. He stepped onto the covered porch.

She called out, "I assure you it's not safe."

Of course not, he thought. *You made it unsafe.* "No problem!" he shouted back.

In fact, the storm raged on. Rain fell harder than ever. Never mind. He could not return to that house. He would make it back to White Hall if he had to swim there. The storm would subside. He was young and strong. He had no choice. As he descended, the cold would decrease.

The instant he stepped off the porch, the storm drenched him. *Great beginning! Whatever. Go!*

He charged ahead, sloshing forward about ten feet. But with a shocking crash, a thunderbolt split a huge tree in front of him. The bolt's raw power spun him around, flinging him face first into a deep, muddy pool. He rose choking for air, wiping mire from eyes and mouth.

Rain pounded his naked head. He searched for his White Hall cap and found it deep in mud. A fiasco! All about, flashing bolts gored the earth. Raging water concealed every path. In his light jacket, he could not bear the wind chill. He could go no further. He ran back to the covered porch. He would stay outside the house, till the rain actually abated.

But bitter wind whipped and froze him. Fighting for breath, caked in mud, he went inside but stayed by the door. She sent the lightning to trap him, just as she sent the rain. But if she did anything strange, he would rush out and die a free man.

She kept her back to him and tended the fire. She knew he would return. *Oh God. Now what?*

The room warmed. Keeping her back to him, she slowly lowered her hood, freeing lovely locks that fell about her shoulders. For the first time, he would see her full face. At Mrs. Wolfe's house, she concealed herself behind big, dark glasses and a low blue beret. In the storm, a hood shielded her features. But now he would see her. Every nerve in his body braced itself. Every horror movie he ever saw hissed that she would shed her human disguise and reveal her true ghastly form. Was she a devīl?

She slowly turned to face him. He waited with one hand on the doorknob, the other on a knife in his back pocket. He would run straight into lightning before he fell prey to evil power.

She faced him. Her beauty startled him. Her big, piercing eyes opened wide. She seemed even more astonished than him. What did she see?

"It is you," she said. "I thought I recognized you at Laurie's house, but I could not believe it."

"I don't know what you mean," Justin said, trying to be civil, but ready to run.

"You don't recognize me, do you?"

"Recognize you? Who are you?"

"Look carefully and you will see. We met long ago. I am Devī."

CHAPTER 30

S tunned beyond speech, Justin stared at Devī. Either it was indeed a witch who had assumed the form of Devī—for it was Devī in all her features—or it was Devī herself, Devī of Bhū-loka, who miraculously stood before him.

"Please," she said, with urgency, "come and stand by the fire. You're shivering and about to collapse from hypothermia."

The kindness in her voice further astonished him. It was Devī, but softened in manner and tone. And his body was indeed shaking. She placed a chair by the fire for him. As he moved to the chair, she modestly retreated. He thanked her, though in his utter confusion, he hardly knew what he said.

Devī said, "You need to drink something warm. I will bring it."

He thanked her and she flew to the kitchen. As the warming fire began to restore him, he marveled at how Devī's manner was so changed. She had never spoken to him in such gentle tones, so free of condescension and impatience. Yet, as memories of his offenses against her flooded his mind, his discomfort increased. He felt he did not deserve such kindness from her.

Again she had saved him. But why did people call her a witch? A simple, plausible answer presented itself. In rural Virginia, it would not be surprising that her yoga powers were seen as witchcraft. And her link to the Stonewood school made such an interpretation all the more credible.

But was he still on earth, or was the door of Devī's house a portal to some supernatural land where Devī now resided? A quick glance through the window confirmed that he was definitely still in White Hall, Virginia.

But why were they again brought together, for this could be no coincidence? His vow! The Avatāra must have sent Devī back to Earth to claim his vow. But Devī seemed surprised to see him. She had not planned this meeting. The White Hall Academy seemed a million miles away. But it was really just a mile down the mountain, and at this very moment, Justin was in grave violation of school rules, and of his sacred vow to his dearest White Hall friends. Yet it was Devī!

Lightning crashed outside. He could not leave. He prayed that this was really Devī. And if it was truly Devī, he was still too weak, too shocked, and too shy to ask her the myriad questions that flooded his mind. How could she possibly be here in White Hall, Virginia? What were her intentions and wishes? What were his feelings toward her, and hers toward him? She too seemed startled at their meeting. If it was Devī, then with all her powers, she did not plan this reunion between them.

Or had he gone crazy? Was he in fact helplessly under the power of a true witch that scoured his mind, and duplicated the image of Devī that still dwelled there and exercised a powerful influence over him?

Another rather serious problem intruded into his still-astonished mind. No matter who this extraordinary young lady was, any discovery of his association with her would end at once his White Hall career. But he could not think of that now. He could think only of Devī. If anyone in the world could empower him to fight the Asuras and save his family, it was Devī. If only she would accept him again. He had renounced her, and she rejected him. But here they were together on the ridge above the White Hall Academy. Devī had come! The Avatāra could not be far behind. What would they ask of him? Could he satisfy them?

For now, he must calm his mind. Absorbing the fire's saving heat, he looked around at the palatial room. Varieties of books, some very old, lined mahogany shelves. The so-called ghost house was in fact an elegant mansion, decorated and furnished with refined good taste.

But, several months ago, he dreamed of Bhū-loka. Devī was in that dream. What if he was dreaming now? What if in fact he had fallen delirious in the snow, and now lay on a frozen mountainside in the final stages of terminal hypothermia, again dreaming of Devī?

But he had no evidence of that. And as he grew stronger by the minute, he accepted as a working hypothesis that in fact he was not lying delirious on a mountainside, experiencing psychotic visions as he froze to death. He was in a beautiful mansion with an excellent library. He was with Devī, reborn on Earth.

As if to confirm this, Devī returned with hot vegetable broth, similar to what she gave him in Bhū-loka. She set it in front of him on a small table by the fire. She helped him to grasp a large spoon and bring the broth to his lips with his still-tremulous hands.

Where did she get this food? Naturally, she answered before he asked. She had friends in the area, ladies who gave her vegetables from their gardens, and homemade bread.

He thanked her from his heart. Unlike in Bhū-loka, Devī's benevolence was now untainted by sarcasm and disdain. She was gentler than he would have thought possible, and this continued to amaze him. As Justin ate, Devī sat on the other side of the fire. As in ancient times, the flames lent a magical glow to her face and hair, though even without fire, Devī glowed. The fire's heat, and Devī's supernatural broth, began to restore his strength.

When he could eat no more, and the initial shock of their meeting had somewhat subsided, Devī looked at him caked with mud—the result of his attempted escape—and she laughed. He understood and laughed with her. They had never laughed together before. It had been unthinkable in Bhū-loka. Her cordial ease astonished him almost as much as finding her here at all.

"You must change into clean, dry clothes," Devī said. "Wait here for a moment." She soon returned and said, "Follow me." She led him through the house toward a large and well-appointed ground floor suite with a fire burning. Along the way, he saw more wonders of the so-called ghost house—fine paintings, carpets, and furniture, all in elegant good taste. It was a far cry from Devī's rustic cottage in Bhū-loka. Everything he saw increased the questions he longed to ask her. But with Devī, even the new, friendly Devī, he must proceed cautiously.

In the suite, he found a clean change of clothes neatly laid upon the bed. She then left him to bathe and dress. After showering, he cleaned the marble floor, leaving it immaculate. He dressed and sat in the room by the fire to gather his thoughts. He rummaged in his backpack and pulled out his cell phone. It still worked! His phone hurled him back to reality. He was a White Hall student. He had a family in Davis, and friends on campus who must be worried sick for him. His Earth brain began to function again.

His situation was astounding, inspiring, but dangerous. Worst-case scenario: *Tom sees I'm missing and tells the school, who call the police, who send a search party that busts me in this house, destroying my life.*

At once, he took evasive measures, texting Tom and Scarlet: *trapped in storm, found shelter, don't worry, back asap.*

Before they could reply and pry for details, or worse, insist on coming for him, he added, *battery dyin...* He thought it clever to curtail *dying*, as if his battery had died that moment.

Scarlet instantly texted back anyway: *take care please!! keep in touch!!*

Scarlet and Devī—two worlds collided. This was Bhū-loka 2.0! At last able to think with a modicum of calm, he realized that he had absolutely no idea what to do. Contact with Devī would destroy his White Hall career. But what if only Devī could save him and his family from the Asuras? Then again, what if the Avatāra whisked him away to another world? What would his family do then? And Justin had been to enough worlds this year.

He had no idea what to do. Then it got worse. His phone pinged. Tom texted: *WHERE R U???*

Justin did not reply. What could he say? *Tom, I just had a delicious vegan dinner up in the ghost house. My charming hostess is the witch that all Stonies fear. But don't worry, she's actually a yoginī from another world.*

No, Justin would not send that message. Not today. White Hall could never imagine who Devī was. For now, he would go with the dead battery scenario. So, no reply.

But Justin must leave before they sent a search party. The second the storm abated, he must leave. If the storm howled on past daylight, he would have to spend the night and leave at dawn, if weather permitted. To return in the dark was far too dangerous. He dearly hoped that he would be forced to stay here. He longed to speak to Devī, to apologize, to try to ascertain the cause of her kinder demeanor, to learn, if he could, what the Avatāra would demand of him.

In any case, he must not be found here. For now, he must not keep Devī waiting. He first stretched out his wet clothes before the fire. He needed them for his return to White Hall. New clothes would prompt questions he could not begin to answer.

Justin had yet another grave duty to perform, a duty to his close friend Luke. Clearly, Devī was the so-called Jane, the close friend of Sara. For Luke's sake, indeed, for Sara's sake, Justin must understand as well as possible Devī's true identity and intentions. For this and many other reasons, he was eager to speak again with Devī.

Justin then returned to the great room, and found Devī patiently waiting for him. He took his seat by the fire facing her. He tried not to stare but he could not take his eyes off her. Her celestial beauty had only increased since he saw her in Bhū-loka. And she really did behave far more like Devī than a dangerous witch. But how could it be Devī? His memories of their time together in Bhū-loka rushed into his mind. He could no longer wait to ask her the questions that so intrigued him.

"Devī," he began, "I am glad, very glad, to see you. But how is this all happening? Please, tell me."

She fixed him in her inscrutable gaze. "Somehow, Kṛṣṇa brought us together again."

He yearned to hear more, but thought it his duty to inform her that several months before he had relived in a dream the time they spent together in Bhū-loka. She nodded as if she already knew.

If only he could be absolutely sure that it was Devī, that he was not dreaming again. Before he could express his lack of complete certainty, Devī said, "You are not dreaming now. You relived your life as Prince Jaya in your dream. But now, all this is really happening."

He nodded. He had no power or reason to challenge her version. He recalled in painful detail the terrible words he spoke to Devī long ago, after she twice saved his life; he vividly witnessed in his mind how he failed her test and could not help a suffering planet. And he remembered his vow to the Avatāra. If this was truly Devī reborn, he would have another chance to fulfill his vow, to realize his eternal self. How could she be here for any other reason? But Devī had rejected him. Would she accept him now? And if she did, where would his life go now? What about White Hall? Only Devī could answer these questions, but he hesitated to ask them. Not quite yet.

He felt that both his body, and their relationship, had thawed enough to begin with a small question. "Devī, where did you get these clothes for me?"

"They belonged to my father."

"Your father. Of course. Thank you. I heard you are an heiress in this life. So, this was your family house?"

"One of them. My parents were quite affluent."

Justin nodded. Devī had truly gone from rags to riches. He said, "I heard this house is legally shut down. How can you live here?"

"The sheriff helps me."

"The sheriff? But..."

"Yes, he acts unfriendly to me in public so he won't lose his job or create suspicion. He knew my parents well. They were kind to him."

"I see. Of course." He gathered his courage. "So, I was Prince Jaya, and now I'm Justin Davis."

She nodded. Then a smile crossed her lips. "Sorry to preach philosophy at such a time, but in a higher sense, you are neither Jaya nor Justin."

"Really?" He braced for another dimensional shift.

"I only mean," she explained, "that you are an eternal soul, taking birth in different bodies with different names."

He leaned forward in his fireside chair. "Then who are you?"

"An eternal soul, like you."

"Of course," he said. "Of course. And do you recall all that happened when we met so long ago?"

"Yes, I do."

That was embarrassing. "And you know that I recently relived that time in a dream. Several months ago."

"Yes. It sounds as if you remember everything," she said.

"I do." His face reddened. He was ashamed of what he had done and said in Bhū-loka, but he could not dwell on the past. He must look to the future and find out Devī's purpose in returning to Earth. For he did not doubt that she had come by her own plan. He must push on with his inquiry. His and his family's fate, indeed, Earth's destiny, might well be revealed in her answers to his questions. He must begin, awkward as it was. "Devī, I have no right to ask you this, but please tell me if you can, how or why are you in this world? I remember that you were headed to a higher world, to the World Beyond. That's why I'm surprised to see you here."

"I will explain," Devī said. "I will tell you everything."

CHAPTER 31

T hey sat on facing chairs by the fire, at a respectful distance, of course. As Devī spoke, Justin saw all she described within the fire. Devī's words had that power.

"When the Avatāra left this world, he granted my wish to join him in the World Beyond. That world is beyond material time."

"So," Justin said, deep in thought, "time did not pass there. Hence you did not forget our meeting."

"Yes, exactly," Devī said. "You do understand these things."

"I'm not sure about that, but if I may ask another question…"

"Of course," Devī said, her large eyes steadily gazing at him, "please ask."

"Thank you." Justin was anxious for a status update on his vow to the Avatāra. He thought it best to first broach the subject indirectly. He breathed deeply and began. "You told me once that the Avatāra travels to many worlds, helping people. Yet you joined him in the World Beyond. Does he no longer travel around the universe?"

Devī smiled. "That is an excellent question." If this was truly Devī, it was a far more amiable version. Perhaps her time in the World Beyond had softened her. She continued, "Kṛṣṇa eternally dwells in the World Beyond, and simultaneously travels to many worlds in the material realm."

"How does he do that?"

Devī smiled again, as if bemused. "Kṛṣṇa expands into many forms, yet he is one person. The Avatāra can do such things."

So, the Avatāra was still active in this universe. Justin assumed that his vow was still outstanding, and to be claimed. Eager to learn more, especially about Devī and her possible role in Justin's future, he said, "Forgive me if this question is inappropriate, but why did you come back to this world after achieving the highest destination, an eternal home?"

Devī hesitated. With both hands, she pushed back her hair, exposing her handsome forehead. Then she looked into the crackling fire and said, "I became aware of much suffering on Bhū-loka. The people of Earth, as you call it now, forgot how much Kṛṣṇa did for their world. They hardly remember the Avatāra and the wisdom he taught. You and I both know the cruelty that now abounds on this planet toward virtually all life forms. And among the human beings, countless souls live in fear and hardship."

Justin nodded, unable to take his eyes off Devī. He saw the accuracy of this portrait. "That is all true," he agreed. "So, what did you think when you saw all this?"

Devī closed her eyes. So deep was her concentration that Justin suspected she was looking into her own soul, or perhaps looking at Kṛṣṇa within her heart. After a long moment, she opened her eyes. "Bhū-loka was once my home. I had to try to help. Kṛṣṇa granted my wish and I returned here. I felt I must develop greater compassion for this world before I renounced it forever. You thought that about me, when we met in Bhū-loka."

These words struck Justin with force. A voice inside him asked whether his rebuke of Devī in Bhū-loka, ignorant as it was in many ways, had reached her heart in some way. She had then considered it a degradation to descend the mountain to the human world below. Now she had postponed her own final liberation in order to help those she once scorned. He admired her for her decision. And he wondered if her decision was somehow related to his own fate and future. Devī continued and he listened carefully.

"I asked the Avatāra if I could return and he granted my wish, though he said it would not be easy. And now, as you see, I am back on Earth." She looked up, as if gazing upon the Avatāra in a higher dimension.

Justin looked at her intently, keenly aware of the significant difference in their levels of consciousness. He appreciated her more than ever. He was proud of her, and could not help saying, "Devī, you gave up so much and came down here purely out of compassion. I honor you for that."

Looking embarrassed by his praise, she turned her eyes back to the fire. In the time remaining to them, he longed to learn more about his possible role in her mission. The fire's steady heat, and Devī's powerful presence, had restored much of his strength. He sat up straight in his chair. Still shy to ask about her role in his life, and still afraid to directly broach the subject of his vow to Kṛṣṇa, he pursued another angle, hoping that as they talked, Devī would answer his most urgent questions.

"If I may ask," he said, "who were your parents in this world?"

At this question, Devī's eyes moistened, as if with fond recollections. She nodded. "I will explain. The Avatāra arranged for a kind and wise couple, sages living on Mahar-loka, a higher world in this universe, to come to Earth to be my parents. They agreed to take care of me until I was eleven years old and gained full use of my powers."

"And your childhood with those sages?"

"As you can imagine, with such kind and wise parents, I lived happily. Kṛṣṇa supplied my parents with all we needed, and more. The Avatāra is most generous."

"In coming back to Earth, Devī, you acted with true generosity," Justin said. "I profoundly admire what you did. You are a worthy associate of the Avatāra."

Devī shook her head. "It is kind of you to say that, but I don't deserve such praise. I've done very little here, though I tried. I now wonder if I should have come at all."

"Really? What happened? I'm sure you tried to help people find their true self and happiness."

"I tried," she said, with a stoic sigh. "But that is about all I accomplished. As a child, I sought to help other children, but their parents feared me and my strange ideas. It was hard for me to fit in with ordinary human beings."

Justin understood. A voice within told him that he, Justin, could help Devī to fit in. And she would enlighten him with her teachings. He was mastering the outer world, and Devī had mastered the inner world. A dream team! But he was too shy to bring it up, and she did not suggest it. Officially, they had renounced each other in Bhū-loka. And despite Devī's warmth and kindness, she had said nothing to indicate that she would rescind her decision and renew their formal relationship. If he brought it up, she might reject him. He preferred to wait and see, if he could, her intention. Had she intentionally returned to this world at the same time he did—for they were near the same age—or was it mere coincidence? Or had the Avatāra himself brought them together? For now, it was safer to continue inquiring from Devī, if she allowed him, and search her words for clues to his future. Beyond that, Devī fascinated him more than ever, and he wanted to learn all he could about her life here on Earth.

He said, "Devī, forgive my asking, but given your birth to such excellent and affluent parents, how did you come to Stonewood? Do you have a legal guardian?"

Devī's head pulled back at his question, but then her features softened. She sighed. "Of course, you must ask that. I will explain. When my parents departed this world and returned to Mahar-loka, my aunt and uncle gained legal control over me. I do have an ongoing problem with them. For their own reasons, they insisted I come to Stonewood. I agreed because it's near this house, and I really live here. I rarely go to Stonewood."

Justin was sorry to hear of Devī's problem with her aunt and uncle, her legal guardians. But he was glad that she trusted him with some detail of her personal life.

"Can I help?" he asked. "Is there anything I can do?"

Devī thanked him for his offer, then leaned back pensively in her chair. With inscrutable gravity, she said, "I won't bother you with my problems. I'm sure a White Hall student cannot be involved in a Stonie problem."

She spoke matter-of-factly, without resentment. Justin feared that Devī might need help, but would not seek nor even accept it. She had regularly saved him, yet he could do nothing for her. Worse, she was not trusting him with details of her predicament. He did not persist on this subject.

Rather, he simply asked, "What was it like for you when you came to Stonewood?" He wanted to see if she would mention the confrontations so vividly described by Sara.

Devī sighed. "The Stonewood girls were generally not eager to learn from me. In fact, some of them, and even a teacher, sought to harm me."

"And what happened?"

Devī smiled. "You ask what you already know. I believe you heard the answer from Sara in the forest."

Justin's face reddened. Why had he asked such a foolish question? Of course, Jane would tell Devī everything about their chance encounter. Justin apologized for his silly question. Devī nodded, in a way to put him on his guard against further breaches of trust. Justin asked her to please tell him more about her experiences since coming to Stonewood.

"As you already know," Devī said, "only Sara wanted to learn from me, and we again became very close."

Justin wondered why Devī said again, but he did not want to interrupt her.

Devī continued, "I often wear normal clothes outside the school, and I did meet some young people with whom I could speak. But something always went wrong. There was Judy, who loved the idea that she was an eternal soul in a temporary body. But then the boy of her dreams began to notice her, and she decided that for now she needed to be her body and forget the soul."

"I understand," Justin said with a smile. Devī continued.

"Melanie wanted to learn about the Avatāra, but her mother found out and medicated her till she forgot I existed. And now Laurie Wolfe wanted to meditate with me. She said her mother would be gone. But her mother came back, and you saw the rest."

"Yes, I did."

"Of course, to protect Laurie, I didn't reveal the truth, that she invited me."

"I appreciate that," he said.

"So, you see," Devī concluded, "I'm not very good at helping people." She looked at him, as if to say, "You already know that about me from our experience in Bhū-loka."

He protested that she only needed time and a fair chance, but his heart and brain told him that, for all her spiritual superiority, she needed him to help navigate the material world.

She thanked him for his generous words, but they both knew the truth of the matter. The real question was whether Devī would ever ask for his help, or whether he should offer it. For now, he had to find out more.

"Devī," he said, "you are still aloof from the world here. Does that still please you?"

Her eyes silently acknowledged the acuity of his question. "It does not please me like before," she said. "In the days of Bhū-loka, I often had the company of other sages. There are sages in the world today, but not here. I must be of age, legally independent, to associate with them. But even then, I won't go back to the life I had long ago. I don't want to shun the world."

"You don't?"

"No. I think I care more about the world now. I just can't seem to help very much."

Devī's profound concern for the suffering creatures of this fallen world formed a remarkable contrast to the aloof philosophical concern she evinced in Bhū-loka. Had his words in Bhū-loka affected Devī? It was too much to hope. But the change was clear. And hearing her speak of her frustrated mission, a part of Justin wanted to cry out, "Devī, I will help you. You're not alone. We can do this together." But he could not speak those words. He feared Devī's rejection, and he also knew that if White Hall discovered his collaboration with Devī, he would be sent back to West Virginia in disgrace, and would also be unable to see Devī. Yet, he must help her in some way. He must not fail as he did in Bhū-loka. He found that he cared deeply about Devī and her mission. Most earnestly he said, "I truly admire your concern for the world, Devī. But why don't you just use your powers to change the world?"

"If only it were that easy." She sighed. "Souls have free will and must choose their own destiny. I cannot change their hearts and bring them to the Avatāra with mere carnival tricks. Even if I did impress them in that way, they would give up their devotion as soon as a better carnival came to town. No, people must knowingly revere the Avatāra for his perfect goodness. They must understand who he truly is. Otherwise, they will try to use him, or me, to gain personal power, not out of real devotion."

"Very true." Justin winced inside. Devī had given a perfect description of Justin's own attitude toward her in his life as Prince Jaya. Both Justin and Devī knew it. She was too polite, and he too embarrassed, to utter this truth. The situation was awkward for both. On a hunch, he changed the subject, hoping to lift her spirits, and flatter his own. "Devī, did you know I would be here in this world?"

"No, I didn't."

Well, that answer humbled him. Whatever divine plan there might be, Devī did not come back for him. But could it be mere coincidence that they met again after so long? If he could somehow induce her to speak openly, he might discover a clue to the meaning, if any, of their reunion.

Justin now identified a fear in his heart. He felt a chilling premonition that Devī would soon leave this world. She already expressed doubt about the wisdom of even coming to this world. And he did not doubt her power to transcend this world at will. He must try to learn more about her plans.

"Devī," he said, "do you know how long you'll stay on Earth?"

"That's difficult to say."

This confirmed his fear. It would be terrible if she did leave, though he had no time now to examine his own feelings on this. Grasping at some way to keep her in this world, he thought of Devī's close bond with her friend. "What about Sara?" he said. He wanted to speak casually, but these words came out more blurted than smooth and they startled Devī. He had touched a nerve, but had no idea how. Devī quickly recovered, pulled the veil over her feelings and said sedately, "After I met Sara, I knew I must help her. But if I do go, I will leave Sara in good hands."

Was this a reference to Luke? Had Devī herself arranged their meeting?

"So, to answer your question," Devī continued, "I don't know how much longer I'll stay in this world, but perhaps not long."

Devī fell silent. She was trying to be gracious, but Justin knew well that distant look on her face. For now, it would be futile to inquire further on this topic, or perhaps any topic.

As Devī remained silent, Justin pondered his own feelings and thoughts. Devī was definitely far kinder now than in Bhū-loka. He wanted to believe this change was real and lasting. Yet for all her kindness, Devī did not fully trust him, not yet. Several important topics—how long she would stay, her difficult aunt and uncle, and now Sara—clearly had a deeper story that Devī would not reveal to him. He had forfeited her trust in Bhū-loka, and now he seemed to have only partially regained it. Further, his situation at White Hall, with its limits and dangers, did not allow him to do all he yearned to do to regain that trust.

He was anxious to speak more with her, but he could think of nothing further to say. Devī watched him as he tried to think of some question, some observation, that would keep their conversation going. For the first time, his ingenuity, his mastery of words failed him. And Devī remained silent. She must see how tired he really was.

Physically exhausted by his ordeal, emotionally confused by his reunion with Devī, Justin reluctantly joined her in fixed silence. In that state, they sat for some time. Fortunately, the storm raged on till darkness swallowed the mountain. He would spend the night here. It was almost like old times.

Finally, Devī spoke, but only, as he expected, to insist that he rest. "You cannot leave tonight, and you must rest. You've been through so much."

He protested that he was fine. But she smiled and shook her head. If he could only think of something to say. But he could not. Instead, he grew drowsier. He repeatedly thanked Devī for saving him again, bid her good evening, and reluctantly walked back to his designated room. As he settled in beneath a warm mass of blankets, he tried to understand what he now thought about Devī. He rejected as absurd his fear that she might be a witch impersonating Devī. No, it was Devī herself. And any resentment he had ever felt toward her was completely gone. His own behavior in Bhū-loka had been immeasurably worse than hers. And her present kindness softened, indeed erased, every unpleasant memory.

In fact, at that moment, as Justin lay silently pondering it all, he could think of no one, apart from his own parents, that he admired as much as Devī. But what path should that admiration take? It seemed impossible that Devī had come all this way, that they had met like this, through sheer, blind coincidence. No, that was surely preposterous. But why hadn't Devī mentioned his vow? Could she be as reluctant as he was to bring up old points of contention? What did she think of him? Did she still see him as an essentially mundane young man who, despite his sincerity and concern for her, could never really live a spiritual life in this world? She had welcomed him into her house, she had fed him, but she had not renewed her offer to teach him. Her rejection of him as her student seemed to endure. Justin knew of Devī's almost frightening determination. It seemed that she would never go back on a vow, once made. And she had vowed to never teach him again. He feared that she would never go back on that vow, not even to help him fulfill his own vow to the Avatāra. This thought pained him, threatened to break his heart. Never before had he so valued, as he did now, what he had thrown away in Bhū-loka.

But what if only Devī could protect Justin's family? Should he ask her, beg her, if necessary, to protect his mother and brother? If Devī made no offer, however slight or indirect, to accept him again as a student, then for his family's sake, not his own, he would plea for her help. His own pride was nothing compared to the safety of his family.

And what of his vow to the Avatāra? Devī herself taught him that the Avatāra never forgot those who once vowed to serve him. Perhaps, Justin must try again with another teacher. But his heart told him that only Devī could teach him.

Finally, he thought of Luke, who seemed most fortunate. Sara was Devī's best friend, and for Justin, Sara could receive no higher recommendation. Luke would be a most fortunate man if he won Sara's heart, and from the frequency of his absences from White Hall, he must be doing just that. Devī even hinted that Sara would now have a new protector. That must be Luke.

And in this state of confusion and despair, Justin drifted into deep sleep. His last thought was, *On what planet, in what eon, will I awake?*

CHAPTER 32

M uch to his relief, Justin awoke on earth, in the same house, on the very next day, before dawn. Everything was normal. Yet, it was all so strange. He was with Devī in the so-called ghost house, and this fact alone amazed him almost as much as if he had awoken on another planet.

He had slept for hours, yet his bedroom fire was still going strong. Devī, goddess of fire, must have interrupted her own sleep to feed it throughout the night. For his sake. He deeply regretted every unkind word he had ever spoken to her.

But where was Devī? He listened hard. Only the fire broke the silence. The storm had died. He must leave at the crack of dawn, before searchers found him there. He had so little time to spend with Devī. He went to the great room, looking for her. She always rose early in Bhū-loka.

He warmed himself by the main fire as it licked and chewed mountain timber. He heard singing and strained to listen. From another room, another realm, a melodic, angelic voice rose above the fire's snap and sputter. Devī sang! Beautifully. Who could have imagined!

But as soon as he listened, she stopped. She knew he was listening. Her shyness must have ended her devotional song. As if to confirm this, she came to the great room and greeted him with a bashful smile and upturned palms that seemed to say, "I'm sorry, but I can't sing when you listen."

They greeted each other kindly, if awkwardly. Devī's new gentleness had at least survived the night.

Unsure of where to look, or what to say, he turned his eyes to a painting of Kṛṣṇa. Just as on his book cover, Kṛṣṇa definitely looked back at him and even seemed to wink. Justin remembered his vow. He glanced at Devī, who surely saw it but said nothing. Time was passing. Dawn approached. He had so much to ask, but he felt as shy as Devī. He walked to the library shelves, pointed to rows of old Sanskrit texts, and asked, "Do you read these, Devī?"

"Yes, I do."

"In Sanskrit?"

"Of course."

"Of course." He shook his head at his naive question.

She told him that she had already prepared breakfast. He would need strength for the journey back to White Hall. They both knew that he must leave soon. He thanked her from his heart; and on a tray, she brought two bowls of hot oatmeal with fruit. They ate together in silence. He recalled their meals in Bhū-loka. He insisted on washing the plates.

He returned to the great room and they sat by the fire. Every few seconds, he glanced out at the sky fearing the dawn. He was desperate to learn more about her life on earth.

Devī glanced at him. Their eyes met for a moment. Justin was sure that she knew his feelings. If only *he* knew his feelings. And hers. He wasted a precious minute in awkward silence. When could he see her again? He must find out if they would meet again. So much depended on it, certainly his spiritual life, and perhaps even his material life and the lives of those he loved most. But apart from what he might gain from Devī, he cared about her more than he could express, perhaps more than he could admit to himself. If he was ever to render important service to this world, it must be with Devī's help. As he again felt the power of her presence, he realized how absurdly unfit he was alone to make a real difference on this planet. Yet his situation in life, as a White Hall student, made association with Devī virtually impossible for the foreseeable future.

"Devī," he said, "I must leave soon, for reasons you can well imagine, and…I feel deeply that had I been a true friend to you back then, you would now be my oldest friend."

His words affected her. She tried to conceal her emotion, but he knew Devī well enough by now to see that she was affected. Hopeful of a frank dialogue, he continued. "Devī, please tell me how we can ever meet again, at least in the next few years, given your situation and mine. Forgive me if I speak too boldly, but I really want to know what comes next."

She hesitated and looked away. "So you really want to know?"

She asked with innocent uncertainty. With all her powers of penetration, Devī could not imagine how highly he had come to regard her.

He took the plunge and told the truth. "I ask because despite my failures, my inability to embrace your teachings, I truly admire you.

And I am sure that wherever you go in the universe, or beyond it, there must be a higher purpose that guides you. And despite the present circumstances, I wish that I could help in some way. That's why I asked."

Devī looked at him with embarrassed surprise. He had never seen her so unsure of what to say. She closed her eyes, as if searching her own heart for the answer. She quickly recovered her composure and said, "If you truly wish to keep your vow, the Avatāra will show you the way."

He longed to tell her that he could not serve the Avatāra without her, but he had no right to say that, considering the past. And so, to spare her any possible embarrassment, he changed the subject and said, "Were your parents sad to leave you?"

"Perhaps, but they know me well and why I came here. They told me I would face challenges but that Kṛṣṇa would protect me. We all trusted in Kṛṣṇa's plan."

Justin nodded. An ancient clock rang the hour. Justin looked at it and sighed. He gazed at Devī. "And what is Kṛṣṇa's plan?"

"To again save this world."

Justin admired the unwavering faith and devotion of these rare souls, all the more because he did not possess their faith or devotion. Devī continued, "Out of love for me, my parents used their power to gather resources, so that I would have all I needed for my mission."

"Resources? You mean wealth, assets, properties, stuff like that?"

"Yes," Devī said, briefly showing her lovely smile. "Stuff like that."

"That is fortunate," Justin replied. "So, you are an heiress."

"Yes."

A silence followed. Devī sat in perfect serenity, her mind focused deep within herself. Justin admired, but could not imitate, her. Instead, he brought up a delicate point.

"Devī, if I may be open here..."

"Of course." She glanced at him inquisitively.

"...I have often noticed that you possess, or certainly seem to possess, the power to read my mind, or to know what's going to happen."

"I do have some advanced cognitive abilities," she said, "but I also have a strong ethical sense. I try not to invade the privacy of others, at least not in confidential or intimate matters."

Justin was intrigued. Did she know how he felt about her? Perhaps not, since he himself could not understand his feelings for her.

"And only Kṛṣṇa knows everything," she added. "Sometimes he likes to surprise me."

Justin ran his hand through his hair. "I see. Devī, you mentioned that your legal guardians, your aunt and uncle, placed you in Stonewood."

"Yes, that's right."

"They cannot really care about you. They cannot love you. In fact, it seems their feelings are the opposite."

"That's correct." She folded her hands in her lap.

Justin must learn more. Amazing as it seemed, Devī might need his help.

"Devī, forgive me if you find these words inappropriate, but I actually do care about you. I know you are far more powerful than me, but if you recall, I'm the worldly one, and I have powerful contacts." Here, Justin thought of Senator Clay. He would surely understand that Justin had to take shelter in this house. And when he learned that Devī came from a most respectable family and was a victim of greedy relatives, he would help her.

"Devī," Justin said, "please tell me about this family problem."

"I didn't want to mention it…I didn't want to bother you."

"Please give me some little chance to help you after all you've done for me."

Devī sighed. "I thank you for your kind wish to help. I will tell you more about my family. When my parents left, my relatives fought to control my estate, each seeking their own advantage."

"And you knew what they were doing," Justin said.

"Of course. But I could do nothing. They acted selfishly, but within the law. Well, all those relatives died rather quickly and mysteriously, till only one couple, an aunt and uncle, remained."

"My God!" Justin said. "Do you feel that your aunt and uncle somehow caused the death of your other relatives?"

"Oh yes, I know they did. And once the other relatives were gone, they gained full legal control over me and my estate. They were determined to destroy me, and steal my estate. They placed me in the most dangerous school they could find, Stonewood. And they even purchased a nearby estate to closely monitor me. Their plan was to win over or bribe the neighbors, teachers, and local authorities, and with their support, have me declared mentally incompetent and committed to an institution. They would then seize my inheritance. For that same purpose, my aunt and uncle spread rumors that I am a witch. You saw how people fear and loathe me. They actually believe that I'm a witch."

"But if you knew your aunt and uncle killed your relatives, and plotted against you, why didn't you go to the police or sheriff, or a lawyer?"

"What could I tell the authorities? That my aunt and uncle killed all my other relatives? That would confirm my insanity since I had no proof, and it would facilitate my aunt and uncle's plan. They hoped I would accuse them. That would make their work easier."

"But why not use your powers to prove their guilt, or just stop them?"

"This is a particularly difficult case," she said.

Surprised, he waited for her to explain how a mere aunt and uncle could be difficult for Devī. But she said no more. He said, "I will have to trust you there. Did you ever think of running away?"

Devī sat back in her chair with a stoic smile. "I have no money now. If I run, and live as a beggar, they will find me and make things worse. It was best to stay here and wait for my inheritance. I have my house; people leave me alone. I have complete freedom."

"Your life is so different now," Justin said softly. "I mean no offense."

"Of course," Devī said. "I know what you mean and you're right. My life is very different now."

"And why do you undergo this? Why risk your life for that inheritance? I thought you disdained material wealth."

"I must be practical," she explained. "In past ages I lived freely in the forest. If I do that now, I'll be arrested for trespassing or vagrancy. Nowadays, one needs one's own home."

This was a new Devī. "I admire your pragmatism," Justin said.

"Justin, nowadays we need resources to live and to help save this planet."

"I absolutely agree," he replied. "And I know you will use all you have to serve the Avatāra."

"Exactly. So why not protect an estate that my parents lovingly left for me, one which I hope to use for the best purpose?"

"You are so right," he agreed. "Absolutely right."

"I may not always have been so pragmatic," she said, "but the world was so different then, in the days of Bhū-loka."

"I am grateful that you are explaining this to me," Justin said.

Devī nodded and almost smiled, but then her face turned grave. "There is something more about this that I must tell you. It was not simply my powers, nor luck nor chance, that despite all the efforts of my relatives, my inheritance has been preserved intact and I will inherit it soon when I turn sixteen. Kṛṣṇa helped me, through the extraordinary kindness of a very special soul."

Devī paused and hastily wiped a tear from her eye. Justin was stunned. He had never seen Devī cry, weep, or shed a tear. What could move her in this way? Justin waited breathlessly. She resumed her narration.

"Kṛṣṇa sent a most noble gentleman to help me. He was an old friend of my father, and I first met him while my parents lived. He was a brilliant lawyer, and when my parents left this world, that friend took up my cause at his own expense, and even at his own risk. It is thanks to his courage, skill, and kindness that I will inherit my entire estate."

"I'm glad that Kṛṣṇa sent that kind man to help you. From what you say, I admire him greatly."

Devī nodded, but kept her eyes away from his. She fell silent. Justin said, "But with your aunt and uncle so actively resolved against you, how did you manage to create a life for yourself in this mansion? They must have legally fought to restrict and harass you. Did you simply use your powers to thwart them?"

"Yes, I did and still do. But my aunt and uncle also have powerful ways to achieve their will. Here, too, my lawyer friend, who in my heart was a dear uncle to me, defended me in court. And when my aunt and uncle tried to send me to a remote school, far from my home, that same friend fought in court to keep me here so I could live in my own house, in peace."

"Devī, how fortunate you are to have such a kind and brilliant friend."

Devī again looked down, apparently mute with emotion. Justin suspected that something tragic had happened to this wonderful man, but Devī did not speak about it, and he was afraid to ask. It seemed too sensitive a topic.

Instead, he said, "Is that a special room where you were singing?"

"Yes, it's my sanctuary."

"Oh. Am I allowed to see it?"

"Would you like to see it?"

"Very much. Thank you." This was promising.

Devī led Justin into the sanctuary. Above a black marble fireplace, on a blue onyx shelf, sculpted candles shed soft light on silver-framed pictures of Kṛṣṇa and what Justin assumed to be enlightened teachers. This was Devī's altar.

She bowed before it, touching her handsome forehead to the floor. Justin did not bow. He expected to be admonished for his pride, as he was in Bhū-loka, but Devī said nothing. Feeling safe from her censure, Justin asked, "Why do you bow?"

"I bow so that with my whole being, I offer respect and gratitude to the source of my existence, Kṛṣṇa."

"I see," he said. "That sounds quite reasonable." She smiled. He felt a pang of self-reproach for the pride that would not let him bow.

They sat below the altar, facing each other. He tried to understand his feelings toward Devī, but could not resolve the paradoxes. He felt most natural in her presence, yet he felt most awkward. He trusted her, yet he feared her.

He knew he deserved far less kindness than she now offered him. That thought humbled him. He missed his own soul, neglected in the pursuit of worldly goals. He looked closely at the altar. Neither of them spoke. After a few minutes, Devī indicated they would return to the great room.

Before leaving the room, she bowed to her altar as she had upon entering. As before, he did not bow.

With her forehead still resting on the floor, Devī suddenly turned her face toward him and insisted, "Justin, get down. Lower your head."

He could not pretend, not even for Devī. "I don't bow the way you do," he explained.

She shouted at him: "Justin, get down! Lower your head!"

Why this sudden shouting? Had Devī not really changed? After all her kindness, she was actually yelling at him.

"Don't shout, please," he said. "I'll think about it."

"Get down, Justin!" She was screaming at him.

He would comply this one time before she went completely crazy. He bowed his head, just as a bullet whizzed by, singed his Caesar-cut hair, and slammed into the temple wall. He threw himself down before the altar as a barrage of bullets blasted through the window and tore up the opposite wall. Justin's heart raced. He held his breath. The shooting stopped.

Hugging the floor, he asked Devī if she was all right.

"I'm fine," she said, sitting up on the floor. "It's safe now."

Utterly shocked, Justin sat up and faced her.

CHAPTER 33

"**D**evī!" he said. "This is serious. Someone just tried to kill you, or me, or both of us. And you knew what they were doing. What is going on? I beg you, tell me. I want to help you. And I have to protect myself. Devī, tell me what just happened."

So earnestly did Justin speak these words that he startled himself, no less than Devī, who stared at him as he spoke. She hesitated, looked away as she always did in these situations, then looked back at him, took a deep breath, and said, "I warn you that I have heavy things to tell you. I wanted to tell you and now I must."

"Of course. I must know. Our lives are in danger."

"Yes, you have a right to know. I will explain. First, as you may suspect, my aunt and uncle just tried to kill me. You were a secondary target. They fear you will help me."

"Oh great, your relatives are out to kill us. But how did they know I'm here? That's impossible."

"I told you, they are powerful people. And now I see they are growing even more aggressive. They clearly know that you are here. I didn't explain everything before because I didn't expect them to escalate so quickly."

"Powerful people? Devī, what power would tell them that I was here in your house? No human being could know that."

Devī sighed with resignation. "I cannot conceal the truth. Yes, exactly as you say, no human being could know that."

Justin's eyes opened wide and he stared at Devī. "Are you saying that your aunt and uncle, the ones who killed your other relatives, are not human? You don't mean that."

"Oh, but I do mean that."

"You don't mean they are Asuras?"

Devī stoically tilted her head. "I'm afraid I do mean that also."

Justin could not be so stoic. His stomach went queasy and his fists clenched. His mind raced into fight-or-flight mode. "Devī, after so many years, after millennia, the Asuras are hunting us. Here on Earth."

"Yes, that is correct," Devī said calmly.

"Devī, we need help," Justin insisted. "I have a powerful contact that can help us. He is one of the most powerful men in the country, Senator Hunter Clay. He'll probably be the next president. I'm sure he'll help us. We can fix this."

"I don't think he will help us," Devī said.

"He's a good man," Justin insisted. "He'll understand that I was forced to take shelter in this house. He won't blame me for that. I'll explain to him that you come from an excellent family, that you are a victim of greedy relatives. I know the senator will help us."

Devī thanked Justin and firmly declined his offer, which frustrated him greatly. This was vintage Devī, never willing to engage the world below, not even to save her own life or his. She was about to say more, but he spoke first, insisting, "Devī, if you won't accept my help, then let your wicked relatives have the money. Don't risk your life, and mine."

"Even if I gave them the money, they would still try to kill me, or us. It wouldn't help. They are determined to stop my mission."

"Your mission?"

"Yes, to help the Avatāra save Bhū-loka again."

"And your aunt and uncle understand that mission, don't they? That's why they are pursuing you."

"Yes. Exactly. Justin, you must know the full truth. My uncle is specifically the Asura that I killed in Bhū-loka, the one who disguised himself as Lokeśa, the one who..."

She paused. Justin completed her sentence. "The one who vowed that in a future life, he would kill you, and kill me if I did not surrender to him. Did you mean that Asura?"

"Yes, that Asura. And he's much stronger now."

Justin stared, unblinking, at Devī. "Oh, is that all?" he said. "I feared it might be something serious. Devī, what is going on? This is crazy."

"Of course it's crazy," she said. "But it's true."

"It's impossible." Justin shook his head.

Devī waited a moment, watching him. When he stopped protesting, she raised her hand for emphasis and said, "You must face the truth, for your own sake. Vyādha, the Asura I killed in Bhū-loka, knew that Kṛṣṇa would bring you and me back to this planet, so he took birth as my uncle, my mother's brother. His Asura wife hates us for killing Vyādha back then."

Justin felt he had plunged headlong into a deadly sci-fi movie. Yet Devī was serious. And the bullets were in the wall.

"But that was thousands of years ago," he argued, recalling fearfully how easily the Asura had defeated him.

"Sorry," Devī said. "Asuras are known to have long-term anger issues."

"Marvelous. But why hunt us now, after so long?"

Devī stretched her open hands toward him, to indicate how plausible these events were. "Justin, during the last several earthly millennia, I was in the World Beyond, which Vyādha cannot reach. And after your life as Prince Jaya, the Avatāra had you take birth on various planets, to learn life's lessons. He concealed you from the Asura. But now Kṛṣṇa brought you back to Earth to complete your task here, and, obviously, to fulfill your vow."

"The task and vow that I failed thousands of years ago."

"Well, if you must put it that way, yes. But actually, it was not so long ago. Although you did not become a Royal Sage in Bhū-loka, you and Su Varṇa did perform many good deeds. As a reward for your piety, you took birth on pious, celestial planets where time moves more slowly than on Earth."

"So," Justin said, "while thousands of years passed on earth, much less time passed on those higher planets."

"Yes. Therefore, it was not so long ago you were in Bhū-loka. And Kṛṣṇa recently reminded you, through a dream, of your vow."

"I see," Justin said. "All right, I accept. I will stop behaving like a child. But tell me, what finally happened to Su Varṇa?"

"Like you, Su Varṇa received many rewards for her good deeds. She enjoyed those gifts on other planets. And she has gone on to other heroes."

Justin felt a twinge in his heart. "I see. So, my relation with Su Varṇa is clearly not eternal."

"Clearly not." For a moment, as she said this, Devī's eyes rolled, just as they did in Bhū-loka when he did or said something that she considered silly. She raised her hand, and pointed with her index finger, as she would do in Bhū-loka when teaching him. "Justin, the love between you and Su Varṇa was based largely on your temporary bodies, rather than your eternal souls. Only a love between eternal souls can be an eternal love. That's quite elementary, wouldn't you say?"

He scolded himself for his regrets. With his heart, he wished Su Varṇa well, but theirs had not been a love between eternal souls. He had no doubt of that. Justin took a deep breath, determined to focus on his present duty. He would not be weak or doubtful, regardless of the outcome. Yet, he must act with intelligence. "Devī, Vyādha easily defeated me in Bhū-loka, and would have killed me had you not stopped him. And now you say he is more powerful. My only hope is to work with you. But that will provoke Vyādha, whoever he is now, to kill me more quickly. Besides that, if I may mention mundane details, I'm at White Hall. So, if I'm ever seen with you, I'll probably be expelled and sent back to glamorous Davis. In which case, we still can't work together for a year or two, and by that time Vyādha will probably have killed me. I really want to save my life, and help you, but how can I do that?"

Devī nodded and smiled. Asuras still did not faze her. "To answer your question, you must resume your spiritual practice and strengthen your trust in the Avatāra. You must keep your ancient vow. He surely has a plan."

"Of course. But what plan?"

"It will become clear in time. Let the Avatāra act through you and he will choose the time and place. In Bhū-loka, you tried to defeat the Asura with your own power and yes, he would have killed you. I was able to stop him because I let the Avatāra's power flow through me."

Justin shook his head. "I don't feel qualified, but I will do my best. I will not turn back from my duty."

"Thank you. Justin, you must learn to accept the power that Kṛṣṇa is offering you. Do it, Justin, for the sake of all you hold dear."

"This is all so amazing," Justin remarked. "So, none of this is a coincidence—that Kṛṣṇa had me relive my life in Bhū-loka so recently, and soon after that I met you again, and the same Asura is here on the planet with us."

"No, it's not at all a coincidence. It's a plan."

"And the plan is that I face the same Asura that once thrashed me. But I can only stop him if I take my spiritual practice seriously, learn to channel the Avatāra's power, and thus keep my ancient vow to him. And that's the story, right?"

"Yes, that's the story. For many lives, Kṛṣṇa hid you from the Asura. He gave you time to learn and grow. But now the battle will resume."

Justin nervously paced the room, fighting off the doubts and fear that attacked his mind. Devī watched him. He turned quickly to face her and said, "But why force me to do this? How is that right?" Justin asked.

"Justin, you vowed to serve the Avatāra. You gave your word. And apart from your vow, even in Bhū-loka, after we parted, you had many sincere moments in which you truly wanted to be empowered to help the innocent. You know you did."

"Devī, were you monitoring me?"

"I know whatever Kṛṣṇa reveals to me. Justin, I told you Kṛṣṇa would never forget you. And now you are needed. Asuras like my aunt and uncle are regaining control of Earth."

Justin stopped pacing. He looked at Devī. Her spiritual power was visible in every feature. He wanted to be like her. He would be like her, some day. "Devī, I want to do this, but I made my vow thousands of years ago, when I was a prince. I'm not a prince now. I'm a dirt-poor teenager from West Virginia, and I will ruin my career if I am even seen speaking to you. But it seems that I must do this."

Devī smiled and nodded. "Yes, you must. For your own safety, and that of your dear family, please resume your spiritual practice. In this difficult age, the practice is much easier. If you accept me, I will teach you. But you must embrace the practice with all your heart. Otherwise, I cannot help you."

His eyes opened wide. Devī was again offering to teach him. He had waited thousands of years to be forgiven by her. He could not turn back. He could not betray her, and himself, again.

She thanked him and reminded him of the need to protect his family. Her words struck him. Where his mother and brother were involved, he could not fail. He said, "The Avatāra must have sent you to remind me of my vow?"

"It seems like that," she replied. "I didn't volunteer, but I did witness your vow."

"But what should my practice be now?"

"In a spiritually crippled age, Kṛṣṇa kindly appears in his name. Meditate on his name. Remember his name, and his power will flow to you. He is actually present in the sound of his name, and as you advance in your practice, you will see that clearly. Surely such a practice, in private, does not violate White Hall rules."

"No, it doesn't."

"Justin, only your spiritual practice will save you from the Asura. I do not insist that you work with me. That is your choice. But for your own sake, you must be ready. You must devote yourself to this practice. You must find shelter in the Avatāra. Connect with him. That connection, in Sanskrit, is called yoga. That's actually what the word means."

Devī was even lovelier in her spiritual ardor. She fascinated him, even if her warnings and prescriptions greatly disconcerted him.

Justin thought of Scarlet and his duty to her. He must not betray Scarlet, even in his mind. He would not keep one vow by breaking another. And he had committed himself to Scarlet. Equally important, he must never betray or profane Devī by contemplating her in any way other than as a pure soul inhabiting a human body, a soul who wished to help a suffering world.

Justin could not ignore or deny that even on a human level, Devī was a very lovely young lady of extraordinary intelligence, power, and integrity. But Devī was far more than a mere human being, and that was the point. Her spiritual beauty could never be possessed, only admired. Devī could never be the object of anyone's selfish desires. Of this, he had no doubt. Devī dwelled in a very different realm, beyond the world of Justin and his friends.

Deep in thought, Justin realized that Devī was speaking to him. She said, "I really do understand that you cannot work with me now. I won't bother you about that."

"Devī," Justin said, "I deeply respect your vision. And I truly want to help you and the Avatāra and the world. I'm not quite as foolish as I was, though I fear I'm not much better. At least now, I greatly value your help and I deeply regret that my situation does not allow me to directly assist you now. But so it is. However, I promise that I will sincerely endeavor to privately resume my spiritual practice, to prepare myself, and even more important, to spare my poor family further pain. They've already suffered too much, from poor health, disgrace, and poverty. I cannot inflict more misery on them. If the Asura kills me, I don't know how my mom and brother will survive. So, I will do all I can to prepare myself, to learn how to receive the Avatāra's power."

"That is all I ask," Devī said. "I will never ask you to sacrifice your family or yourself. But trust the Avatāra, and resume your practice. He will help you. And remember that here on Earth, we are not alone. Kṛṣṇa brought all of us together on this planet to serve in his mission."

"Who are all of us? Who else is with us?"

"Didn't you recognize Sarit and Lokeśa?"

Justin realized the truth in a moment. "Oh my God!" he said. "Sara and Luke."

"Yes, of course."

"And that's why Luke will not give up Sara."

"Yes. They will never be separated again. And there are other friends of the Avatāra who have taken birth on this planet. We are not alone. Kṛṣṇa brought us all together for the mission. Kṛṣṇa will help us, but we must do our part. For the world's sake, we must not fail."

Out of astonishment, Justin sat down. Devī left him to his thoughts for a few minutes. But knowing dawn would come soon, she said, "Justin, there is more I must tell you, if you want to hear it. I warn you, it will not make you happy."

"What else could you tell me?" he asked. "Lokeśa is my roommate. I can't wait to see him, and dear Sarit."

"You must hear what I dreaded telling you."

Devī now had Justin's entire attention. He waited nervously as she began to speak. "I told you," she said, "that Kṛṣṇa sent a most excellent man, who was my father's dear friend. When my parents left this world, that friend helped me in many ways at his own expense and risk."

"You did tell me that," Justin said, fearing what he would hear next.

"I begged him not to put himself at risk, but he would not abandon me. A few years ago, my wicked aunt and uncle ordered his execution."

"That is unbearable evil," Justin said faintly.

Devī looked down and wiped tears from her eyes. He could hardly breathe. She said, "I am so sorry that I must be the one to tell you. That exceptional man, who was like a loving uncle to me, was your father, Tark Davis."

Shock, disbelief, pain, and rage seized Justin's mind. He clenched his fists, closed his eyes, wept, and gasped for breath. When he opened his eyes, he saw Devī watching him with a deep and tender compassion that he had never seen in her before.

"Where is my father, now?" Justin whispered. "Devī, you must know."

"He is receiving extraordinary rewards. I promise you that."

"You knew my father," Justin marveled.

"Yes. I loved your father. I will never forget him. Ever."

Justin breathed deeply and tried to collect his thoughts. Devī's loving link to Tark Davis filled him with pride for both of them. At once, he felt closer to Devī than ever before. She was family now! Yet, these tender, inspiring thoughts could not long detain him from filial shock and rage. Unbreakable resolve formed like steel in his mind. He would pursue cold, methodical vengeance.

But the villain was an Asura. Justin remembered the Asura's power, now increased, and he remembered his vow to the Avatāra. If Justin loved his father, and his living family, if he did not want to again be tortured by the agonized cries of the world's innocent victims whom he could not help, then he must throw all his energy, all his discipline, rage, and resolve, into his spiritual practice. He would become the Avatāra's consummate lethal instrument, democracy's version of the royal sage, free of selfish passion, replete with selfless, deadly devotion. He would die, if necessary, to bring the killers to justice. But then he thought of his suffering mother and Joey and how much they needed him, and he gave up the notion of martyrdom. Victory was the only path. They could not bear his loss. He would somehow find the Avatāra's power and let it flow through him.

Devī did not speak but watched him closely. Justin understood that she knew his mind. For now, she respected his need to grieve and plan. He made a rapid calculation. In this age, even yogīs and Asuras were subject to earthly law enforced by a strong government. Justin's friend Senator Clay had mastered those laws, and he possessed a virtual army of followers, not to speak of his soon becoming the commander-in-chief of the mightiest military force on earth. Hunter Clay could mobilize unlimited power. He was Justin's and Devī's best ally, their best hope. Justin must convince Devī to accept that help.

Dawn was coming. He had precious little time left with Devī. He had to convince her.

"Devī," he said. "I must speak to Senator Clay about the Asura. Please allow me to speak on your behalf as well as my own."

Devī suddenly looked at him with such piercing gravity that he was forced to look away. What had he said? She walked slowly about the room, lost in thought. Justin watched her. Something very heavy was coming.

"What is it?" Justin asked. "Tell me."

Devī stopped, turned to him, and spoke slowly, driving home each word. She said, "Justin, you cannot seek help from Senator Clay because Hunter Clay is my uncle. Senator Clay is the Asura that caused your father's death, and just tried to kill us. And he will soon attain terrible power in this world if we do not stop him."

Justin's jaw dropped and he stared at Devī. His worlds collided. He was stunned beyond the power of expression. Devī remained silent. He moved his head slowly from side to side, as if to physically dispel Devī's claim.

"The Clays have been so good to me," he gasped. "He's going to be the next president of the United States. I can't believe he caused my father's death. He cannot be an Asura."

"I'm sorry, Justin. You insisted on knowing the truth."

"But why? Why would Hunter do that? What could be his motive?"

Devī sighed with deep sympathy. "Hunter killed your father because he was becoming famous and powerful, and he was uncovering the Asura plot. He trusted me, and I was trying to explain to him the danger. I urged him not to pursue my case, but he was a very noble man, as you know. And he had so much faith in me. Your father would have worked with you and me. Your mother too. And Tark Davis was such a brilliant lawyer that he would have uncovered the Asura's plot, even his murder of my relatives. The Asura knew that. Justin, I'm sorrier for you than I can say."

Justin savored Devī's earnest glorification of his father, but his anger also increased. He was too stunned to speak. He waited for Devī to say something, anything.

"Shall I go on?" she asked. "Are you all right? I felt you must know these things."

"Of course, you are right," he whispered. "Please tell me all you can."

"There is not much more to tell. Hunter Clay knows that only you and I together can stop him. Otherwise, he will become the next president, and that is only the beginning. Yes, Hunter was kind to you. He is determined to either win you to his side, or kill you. He believes I will then feel discouraged to act in the world. And at that point, either he will kill me, or I will abandon this world. He also hoped that with your father gone, you might see him as a substitute father figure."

"That is evil," Justin whispered hoarsely. "It is most despicable evil."

"Justin, remember that your father is as alive as we are. He is watching you. He wants you to do the right thing. You must keep your vow, if you are to defeat the Asura."

Justin knew his duty. If the Clays were responsible for his father's death, they were Justin's mortal enemies. He would stop at nothing to avenge their crime. But could he believe Devī? Dare he *not* believe her? Long ago, Justin doubted Devī's revelation of the false Lokeśa, and that doubt almost cost him his life. He was afraid to doubt her again, but how could he defy the world he knew and accept her fantastic claim?

Through a window, Justin saw on the horizon a thin, dim line of light. Dawn. He rushed to the glass and looked down toward White Hall. A mile below, he saw bobbing lights. A search party was coming up the mountain. They must have seen the light in the ghost house. He must leave at once, knowing he might never see Devī again.

CHAPTER 34

With apologies, Justin rushed to his bedroom and changed into his own clothes. With more apologies and numerous heartfelt thanks, he expressed his intense wish to see her again. Through all this she stood and watched him, her expression inscrutable.

With a last look back at Devī, he rushed out the door and headed down the soggy-but-passable mountain trail. Its steepness prevented water from collecting during the storm. He cast frequent looks back at the house. His magical meeting with Devī astonished him so greatly that he almost doubted it had really taken place.

With more interest than the topic had ever before inspired in him, he tried to make out his feelings toward Devī. Animosity, even annoyance, were completely gone. Rather, he regretted that he ever disliked a person who, in addition to her extraordinary qualities, had regularly saved his life. In Bhū-loka, he had insulted and rejected her, and now, on meeting again, albeit under such changed circumstances, she seemed to make a real effort to be kind to him. How could he not earnestly reciprocate her own genuine interest in his wellbeing? But how could they ever meet again? Devī left it all to the Avatāra. Justin was not so pious. It was all confusion to him. Yet his life would never be the same. White Hall, Virginia and ancient Bhū-loka, he now saw, had been on a collision course, and he had now experienced the first wave of impact. The danger to himself and his family that he had feared, though only vaguely understood, now rushed into sharp relief. His enemies had names. Now, he knew them and their staggering powers.

Self-realization, spiritual understanding, was no longer a boring if pious duty. It was now the only way to save his life, and probably those most dear to him. Pure consciousness alone could invoke the power he needed to help rescue an imperiled planet. Yet he could not see Devī again, not for years. But there was a plan, Devī said.

As he quickly skated down mountain trails that hours before were deathtraps, the fact that he and Devī were in real danger pressed itself on his mind.

And as he came closer to the White Hall Academy, he dreaded his reunion with Tom and Scarlet. All of White Hall surely heard that he was lost in the mountains. He himself had texted the news to his friends, and they must have reported it to the school. Such news could not possibly remain secret. It must have spread quickly. And high up in the mountain, the ghost house was the only shelter. Everyone knew that. Thus, anyone could have easily deduced his location, and with whom he was staying. This thought chilled him as much as yesterday's storm. Tom, Scarlet, and everyone else at White Hall must strongly suspect where he spent the night.

What about the deadly attack, the rifle fire? Was it necessarily the work of Asuras? There too, a plausible alternative presented itself to his mind. Justin grew up in a county filled with hunters. And October was prime hunting season.

Moreover, deer often sleep for a short time in the middle of the night, then wake up to forage in the early morning. At that time, the deer tend to be lethargic and thus are easy targets for hunters. And that is exactly when the shots were fired. The shots came from the east slope of Pasture Fence Mountain, an area filled with forests and deer, precisely at the time eager hunters would be firing in those woods.

With every step he took away from Devī, the absolute certainty of her story faded in his mind. Her riveting tale, like a lonely ship in foggy seas, seemed to sail into mythic mists. He revered Devī, but Justin could not yet see the kind, charismatic Hunters as murderous Asuras.

If the outer storm had subsided, Justin's inner storm now turned into a tempest, tossing him between worlds. In this wholly unsettled state, he slid down the slope. And just yesterday, life at White Hall had been so easy, so simple and pleasurable. And there was still Scarlet.

Though serenely blind to ultimate things, Scarlet was affectionate and fun, brilliant in her own way. He was committed to her, and so he must remain. But what if she discovered where he spent the night, and with whom? He could not deceive her or Tom again. His heart revolted against it. How would they react? What would he do?

Lost in thought, he almost collided with Mel, who had come looking for him with Tom and Scarlet. Justin's heart raced.

"What happened, Justin?" Scarlet cried, running up to him. "Where were you?"

Justin struggled to sound calm. "I was trapped in the storm. Major flooding. Lightning almost killed me."

"Are you all right?" Scarlet gasped.

"I think so."

"You don't look so great," she said. "We'll take you to the health center."

"Thank you," he said. *Would it be this easy? No.*

Tom stared at and through him and said, "The storm wasn't as bad as you say."

"It was much worse up in the mountains," Justin said, feeling queasy as he foresaw Tom's moves.

"Oh, so you went high in the mountains," Mel said. "Near the ridge?"

"Yes."

Now Tom took over. Clearly, he and Mel had agreed on a strategy to interrogate and probably indict Justin.

Tom said, "You grew up in the mountains. You must know it's not safe to climb to the ridge when a big storm is coming."

Justin told as much truth as possible. He heard the storm would come later. He went up the slope to search for the source of the White Hall Creek. His words did not shake his interrogators' incredulity.

Scarlet shook his arm. She had been trying to get his attention. "Justin, how did your clothes dry in the freezing cold?"

Mel and Tom nodded at each other and turned to Justin, who said, "I found a shelter and lit a fire." He thought of saying he found a cave with firewood, but to directly lie would make it worse.

Tom continued the attack. "I remember telling you about a forbidden house up on the ridge. I don't know of any other house or shelter up there. Do you, Justin?"

"No, I do not," Justin said, watching the inexorable checkmate unfold.

Mel's face morphed by degrees from doubt to indignation to rage. Scarlet looked confused, anxious to support Justin, but loyal to her brother and the Knights.

Justin's only hope was to tell the truth minus Devī. He first defended his innocent desire to search for the source of the White Hall Creek. After all, he grew up in the mountains. A simple mistake trapped him in a truly life-threatening storm. He did indeed take shelter in the forbidden house, but only to save his life. He then swore that no witch was there, no crazy Stonie. Since Devī was neither a witch nor a crazy Stonie, he hoped his words would ring true.

But Tom turned on him and said, "Justin, were you alone in that house or was someone else there?"

Justin hesitated. Checkmate.

"For God's sake!" Tom shouted. "Do not lie to me. Do not try to deceive me."

Justin looked down. "Yes, there was another person in the house."

"Is that person a Stonewood student, and hence a girl?"

"Yes."

"Was it the same girl we saw that day in front of Mrs. Wolfe's house?"

"Yes, the same girl."

"Justin!" Scarlet cried. "You spent the night with that girl?"

"No, I did not. She slept upstairs and I slept downstairs. Look, that girl is not what you think. She is—"

"Shut up!" Mel screamed, trembling with rage. He clenched his fists as if he were about to attack Justin.

Tom put his arms around Mel, comforting him and physically stoppings him from attacking Justin.

"Justin," Tom said, still restraining Mel, "all White Hallians, especially Knights, act with discipline. We follow the rules. You ignored my clear instruction to stay away, far away, from the ghost house. And that led you to violate sacred rules, and to place yourself in acute danger. We stayed up all night, worried sick about you, and when we finally found you, you tried to deceive us. I can't believe you did that. You know how I feel about deceit. I am very deeply hurt, more than I can tell you. Justin, I tried so hard to help you, to be a brother to you, and this is how you repay me."

Justin saw the pain in Tom's face, heard the pain in his voice. It was horrible. Still, he owed it to himself to speak what he saw as the truth of the matter, no matter what the cost.

"I did not lie to you," Justin said. "I acted to save my life. Yes, it was foolish to go up in the mountain, but once the storm hit, it was impossible to go back down, and I would have died without shelter. I left the moment it was possible to leave."

Justin stood like a dead man, hardly breathing. Mel muttered inaudible curses. Seeing Tom's face, even Scarlet moved away from Justin and said with tears in her eyes, "I understand what you're saying, and we did not want you to kill yourself to follow a rule. But after all we've done for you, you owed it to us to be more careful. You know how Mel feels, and how Tom and I feel about these matters, and your lack of caution was at the least an indirect betrayal."

Justin hung his head. He had no clever remark to make in his defense.

Tom said, "Let's go. Justin is not dying, and he can find his own way to the health center."

The three friends left Justin in shock and misery and headed back to campus. Justin stood, slumped and silent as the sun crossed the horizon. He let his former friends get far ahead of him, and then walked back to his room, without feeling the ground beneath him, or seeing anything around him.

But Luke was there to console him. If it was really Devī he saw in that house, then Luke must be Lokeśa. Shaken by all these events, Justin desperately needed to speak openly and honestly with Luke. Justin explained all that happened from the moment he set out on his hike the day before, his astounding meeting with Devī, their conversations, and finally his meeting minutes before with Tom, Scarlet, and Mel. When Justin revealed Devī's claim that Hunter was the Asura that attacked him in Bhū-loka, Luke's eyes opened wide. He was almost as shocked by the idea as Justin.

In his recounting of these events, Justin withheld only one point, which he now disclosed. He had thought it too sensitive to mix with his general narration. Justin now revealed what Devī said about Luke and Sara, their previous lives as Lokeśa and Sarit. By now, Justin had informed Luke in detail of the dream of Bhū-loka.

Luke accepted at once the truth of Devī's words and admitted that he and Sara already suspected it was the case. In any case, Luke and Sara would always support Justin, no matter how the White Hall community in general chose to deal with him. Justin and Luke embraced, in confirmation of their unbreakable friendship.

"It will work out, I'm sure," Luke said.

"But what about Hunter Clay?" Justin posed. "It's too much for me. I don't know what to believe. What if the Asura Vyādha is impersonating Hunter Clay, or does so at times? Keep in mind that in Bhū-loka, Vyādha was a master of disguise. What if he has done it again and is masquerading as a leading political figure?"

Luke thought for a moment. "I see what you mean. He might have created a fake form of Senator Clay, as he did with me."

"Yes, exactly."

"Not likely, on several counts," Luke argued. "First, we can eliminate at once the possibility that Vyādha occasionally impersonates Senator Clay. The first time he did so, the senator would realize that people thought he was somewhere he wasn't, or said something he didn't say. No, that is not a real possibility."

"All right, granted," Justin agreed. "Option two—what if Vyādha killed the real Senator Clay and took his place?"

"Also very unlikely. I have been researching the ancient histories of the Asuras. Vyādha assumed my form as Lokeśa for a short time. Forgive me for what I am about to say, but I must say it under the circumstances. Devī claims that Senator Clay was involved in the tragic loss of your father. If that's true, Hunter has been bad for a few years. From all I've read, I don't think an Asura can hold a false form that long."

"I understand," Justin said. He knew he must suppress his anger and grief at the mention of his father. It was essential to calmly discuss these points with Luke. "So," Justin said, "Devī is either all right or all wrong about Hunter Clay."

"It seems that way."

"What do you think, Luke?"

"I don't know Devī very well. I've hardly met her in this life. I know that Sara believes in her completely. And Sara is a pure soul. But I do need evidence. My sense of justice demands it. And we just don't have that evidence. Not now."

Justin sat on his bed and put his head in his hands. "Luke, why did the Avatāra let me relive that time, and not you?"

"Perhaps because you and Devī are meant to lead us. Sarit, I mean Sara, also vaguely remembers her past life in Bhū-loka. But you and Devī know it all. You must lead us."

"I don't know what to do, Luke. I can't follow Devī now, but I also can't reject or abandon her. I'll try my best to resume a spiritual practice. Maybe that's all I can do."

"Sara wants me to do it too."

Luke said he was leaving and made it clear by unspoken communication that he was going to see Sara. Justin wanted to say, "Send her my greetings, and ask her to tell Devī that I hope she's well." But he didn't say it. He wasn't expelled yet, and he would follow the rules until he was.

Luke asked Justin if he would be all right alone. He would.

Justin heard two students speaking in the hall. The Knights had called a lunch meeting for this year's official candidates. Justin was not invited. He shut the door and locked it, but the room confined him. He must get away from everyone. He headed for the reservoir trail into the Shenandoah. But on the way, he passed Scarlet on campus. She tried to avoid him, but he begged her to stop for a moment and listen to him.

He swore to her that he never touched the girl in the ghost house, and repeated that he only took shelter there to save his life, that he was only guilty of carelessness in that he hiked too high on the slope and ran into a deadly storm.

Scarlet softened slightly. "I believe you, but you were much too careless. You did not take our rules seriously enough and now what can I do to help you? The Knights must be extremely cautious. You know Tom loved you, but you hurt him badly. I'm sorry, Justin. Tom won't listen to me on these issues. He is fully loyal to White Hall and its rules."

Justin asked Scarlet if Tom was going to report him for entering that house. To his horror, she said that he already had.

"Justin, you know that Tom's first loyalty is to White Hall and its honor code. He felt it was his duty. Through negligence, you broke a big rule."

Justin turned white. Scarlet almost took his hand. "Justin," she said, "I deeply care about you. I hope you know that. I really don't want you to suffer. And I know this is the worst time to tell you this. But it's best we not talk now. My brother is hurt, and I cannot cause him further pain."

Justin thanked Scarlet for her concern and even said that he understood why they couldn't talk for now. With a single mutual backward glance, they left in opposite directions.

As he walked along through campus, he saw that word had spread with dizzying rapidity that the Knights rejected him, and that he would likely be expelled. Students who once dreamed of being Justin's friend now walked away from him. It was worse than anything he experienced in Davis, West Virginia. In Tucker County, he had suffered deeply, but his exile was self-imposed, and after all, it was little Tucker County. This was White Hall and a pariah status was being forced upon him, crushing the very plans and dreams that lifted him out of depression and hopelessness. The very White Hall campus that once thrilled him now tormented him. He must get off campus for now. He could not bear to be here.

Walking alone by the reservoir while everyone else was busy in White Hall activities, Justin thought of Devī and her conviction that there is a plan. But a gruesome scenario was unfolding—expulsion from White Hall and a return to Davis in utter disgrace. How would he tell his family? How could he face his old friends? No, he would drop out of school and get a job, perhaps in nearby Morgantown, where his father's old friends would help him. He would send money to his family, and perhaps visit Devī. Once he was expelled, there was no further danger in seeing her. But he could not live again in Davis. Of that he was sure. He would get his high school diploma through the GED exam, and then take classes at West Virginia University. For his family's sake, he could not give up. He would fight his way to success. It would just take much longer.

But what about the Asuras, who actually seemed to exist? Would they follow him to Morgantown? Would they attack his family? Would they try to kill Devī? Did Devī have the power to stop them? She said her power came from the Avatāra, and that the Avatāra was already present in the mantra of his name. This was not a normal plan, but there was no other plan. All this uncertainty paralyzed him. It was dark now, and he returned to his room.

Justin locked himself in his room, unable to face the other students. He lay on his bed, got up, and watched his phone. It was Saturday night and the school offices were closed, but he feared at every moment a call from a school official, declaring his expulsion. So great would they consider his offense that they might even expel him on Sunday.

Justin recalled what Scarlet and Tom told him at Parents Day. Scarlet had said, "You did not trust us as we trusted you."

Tom said, "In the future, be completely honest with us. We must be able to trust you."

Scarlet then said, "You must swear to never deceive us again."

And Justin had sworn a vow, just as he once swore a vow to the Avatāra. Was Justin incapable of keeping a vow? He fell to his knees with his head on his bed, sick with confusion, trepidation, and self-reproach.

Within his exhausted mind, an answer came. For his family's sake, he must try to meditate on the Avatāra. And he would keep his word to Tom and Scarlet and reveal to them the truth about Devī. He had nothing to lose now. He would trust the Avatāra and the truth, not his own schemes.

Luke returned with a tray of vegan dinner for Justin, who, despite his misery, eagerly ate it. With a spark of energy, he sat on the floor and tried to meditate on the Avatāra's name, laboring to focus on each syllable—Kṛṣ and ṇa. Devī did not have time to write down the specific names on which he was to meditate.

But he remembered George Harrison's song, "My Sweet Lord," and played it over and over, singing along with the relevant lines that contained names of the Avatāra: hare kṛṣṇa hare kṛṣṇa, kṛṣṇa kṛṣṇa hare hare. This song lifted his spirits, but not enough to face anyone but Luke. Then he thought of his inexorable expulsion and his spirits sank again.

Luke came in, just as the music stopped. He asked if Justin wanted to hear "My Sweet Lord" again. Justin waved it away with a lifeless hand. He remained in that chair, in that specific posture, mentally numb, so long that Luke expressed serious concern.

Then Justin's phone rang. He fumbled for it with trembling hands. It was not the voice of expulsion. It was Senator Hunter Clay himself, not a secretary, and he expressed an earnest wish to help Justin overcome his crisis.

Amazed by this call, Justin still wondered if he was speaking to his father's killer, a mighty Asura who tried to destroy him and Devī several hours ago? Or was it the Senator Clay he had always believed in and admired. The sincere, confident voice on the other end of the call inclined Justin to hope it was the latter. There was still a chance. Justin could not reject anything Devī said, but his intense wish to avoid crushing social death inclined him to hope for some improbable but real misunderstanding that could be somehow cleared up. In his panic, Justin could not fail to see that with Senator Clay on his side, anything was possible. Trying to sound unsuspecting, Justin profusely thanked Senator Clay for his kindness and accepted his offer with alacrity.

Justin discussed all these issues with Luke, first making him swear that he would not share this confidentiality with a certain girl, whom they both knew to be Sara, since she would surely speak to Devī. Luke struggled but agreed.

After hearing everything, Luke swore Justin to solemn secrecy, and then revealed that he had begun a serious effort to hack into Clay Campus, despite its seemingly impenetrable firewall.

"Just to be sure," Luke said. Justin nodded, exhausted by the intrigue, the uncertainty, and the danger that swirled all around him.

CHAPTER 35

So volatile and bewildering were recent events and claims that Hunter Clay's wish to help awakened in Justin both a quasi-religious hope for salvation, and a dread of imminent doom. Was Senator Clay a godsend or a mortal enemy?

Having no clear evidence to decide, Justin opted for caution. He would insist, as diplomatically as possible, that they meet in a public place. He would not meet Hunter in a place without witnesses.

No such diplomacy was needed. Hunter stated, without asking, that he would meet Justin the next day at noon together with White Hall President Dr. Jill Lofter, and the Dean of Students, Ava Rankin. They would gather in a private, elegant room of the faculty lounge.

Villages don't keep secrets very well, and White Hall, for all its intellectual prestige and social glamor, was a village. When Justin left his room on Sunday morning, bound for his meeting with those who would decide his fate, students stopped to watch him. A personal audience with Senator Hunter Clay, at the senator's own request, might compensate for large amounts of social misfortune.

Justin did carry concealed knives to the meeting as a standard precaution. And on sudden inspiration, he had placed the book in his coat pocket. He was desperate to resolve his confusion and, if needed, he would confront Hunter with the book to see how he reacted.

As Justin approached the faculty lounge, the crowd of gawking students grew. *God only knows my fate*, Justin murmured to himself as he approached the large, black-clad guards with their dark glasses and barely concealed automatic weapons. Seeing Jack among them, Justin smiled and greeted him. Jack nodded, whispered to the other agents, and they moved apart to let him pass.

A host led him to an elegant room with a thick door. As Justin entered, the door closed tightly behind him. He was punctual. The other four persons were evidently early. He saw that Senator and Mrs. Clay were speaking seriously with President Lofter and Dean Rankin. Their demeanor and hushed voices, which fell silent when he entered, showed they had by design discussed Justin before he arrived.

Hunter and Barbara Clay looked up and greeted him with such kindness that Justin felt ashamed of his suspicions. All his doubts about Devī and her tale flooded back into his mind. Yet she was Devī, probably the most remarkable person he knew. What could he do but observe the Clays and hope for insight?

As Justin took his seat facing the Clays, the president and dean stood up. President Lofter said, "Justin, the Clays have very kindly and generously agreed to speak with you. When you are done, we will return."

Justin nodded and they left, speaking quietly to each other. When the big door closed behind them, Senator Clay said casually but firmly, "Let us begin. Justin, we all know what happened to you in the mountain. And none of us doubt your account of the events. I have confirmed that with President Lofter and Dean Rankin. So, Justin, your account will serve as the basis of our discussion here. Honor system."

Justin breathed a sigh of relief and thanked the Clays. They respected his honesty, though they must know that he had told the truth in a rather circuitous manner.

"Barbara and I want to help you," Hunter continued. "We see you as a victim of circumstances, even if your carelessness played a role in creating those circumstances. Would you agree, Justin?"

He most certainly did agree. He deeply regretted, indeed, was ashamed of, his negligence and would certainly never repeat it. Hunter smiled kindly, as if amused by Justin's adolescent foibles. Justin took that as a strong positive. Barbara Clay, with a more restrained smile, nodded her approval of Justin's words.

Hunter spoke again. "Justin, you may wonder why I take such personal interest in this case. If you assure me of your absolute confidentiality, I will explain things that are known only to Barbara and me. But what I say must never leave this room."

He paused and looked pointedly at Justin, who quickly vowed total secrecy. Hunter thanked him, leaned back comfortably in his seat, and continued.

"As you know, Justin," he said, "long before this unpleasant event, I noticed that you had unusual potential, and I decided to help you. As the president and dean know well, Barbara and I have worked for years with the White Hall scholarship committee to identify and help deserving students. Justin, you are eminently qualified. We're delighted to help you. However, in the present case, I have another important reason to involve myself. The young lady named Jane, who calls herself Devī, is in fact our niece. My late sister was Devī's mother. She and her husband, Jane's father, were very dear to us. And now we are Devī's legal guardians."

Justin nodded. The senator's account perfectly matched Devī's. So far. Justin leaned forward eager to hear every word, every intonation.

"So you can see," Barbara said, "how intimately the senator and I are involved in our niece's affairs. Jane's parents were such good people, for whom we cared deeply."

She paused, moved by remembrance of Jane's parents, and then turned to Justin. "Young man, the senator and I want to help you in your present difficulty because we suspect that you were victimized by our niece. So it is our duty to help you."

"Victimized?" Justin said. He leaned back, feeling queasy.

"Yes," Senator Clay replied. "We've seen our niece damage the lives of many innocent young men. You are hardly the first to whom she's told her fantastic story."

"Many young men? What do you mean?" Justin asked, already shocked and fully expecting to be further shocked.

Senator Clay fixed Justin in his gaze and smiled. "I mean our niece has told many young men the same story, and I imagine she told it to you. In fact, I can guess what she told you."

"You can? What did she tell me?" Justin asked, hardly breathing.

The senator and his wife exchanged knowing glances. "Oh, I guess she told you, basically, that she came to Earth from a higher world to save our planet from people like me. But she can only do that with your help. Am I correct?"

Stunned by this precise depiction, Justin had no time to feign or dissemble. There was no escape. "Yes," he said. "That is essentially what she told me."

Hunter sighed and interlaced his fingers. "Oh, and let me guess. You had a dream in which long ago you were a prince who met Devī in the mountains. She urged you to help an Avatāra save the world from invading Asuras. Then, an Asura disguised as a friend tricked you and almost killed you. But Devī saved you. Now you met Devī again and she revealed to you that I, Senator Hunter Clay, am the very same Asura reincarnated. Right?"

Justin was speechless. Senator Clay nodded and said, "Don't feel bad. As I said, you are hardly the first young man that Jane convinced of this, nor sadly are you likely to be the last. And it's always the same basic story. We've been dealing with this for years."

"Perhaps it's clear now," Barbara Hunter said, "why we feel that our niece took advantage of you, and that we have a special duty to help you. We don't blame her; that would be cruel. You see, she is not well."

Justin struggled to get past his shock and collect his thoughts. If Hunter Clay really was an Asura, he might easily know as much about Devī as she knew about him. In that case, he could easily create doubt about Devī. On this interpretation, the truth of the matter would appear to most people as fantasy. Thus, Hunter could play the part of a human skeptic, and contrast his own down-to-earth worldview, which was in fact a pretense, with Devī's version, which would appear to a typical human being as sheer fantasy. Caught in the middle, Justin could do nothing but listen and implore the Avatāra to reveal the truth. But if Devī's story was false, the Avatāra might not exist. For now, Justin had to pay attention before the Clays noticed his absence of mind.

"Justin," Hunter said calmly, putting his hands in his lap, "I've spoken to the best psychologists in the country about my niece. I spent a fortune of my own money, not hers, trying to help that girl. The conclusion of the best professionals is that she has a dangerous mix of deep psychosis and some strange but real mental power. It's a parapsychological phenomenon, similar to those studied at Princeton, and in the parapsychology program right here at the University of Virginia. Jane's psychosis makes her believe she is an ancient sage named Devī, reincarnated here to save the earth. Her mental power enables her to influence the minds of innocent victims, to convince them of her story. Unfortunately, there's a police record of Jane doing this, with many testimonies."

"A police record?"

"Yes. I'm sorry."

"And you believe such powers exist?" Justin said, keeping a calm exterior as he desperately tried to understand the truth.

"There's a lot of scientific literature confirming that some people do have such powers," Barbara said. "We just don't know enough about it yet to give a definitive explanation. But one day, we will know."

"Yes," Hunter said, "there are many documented cases. Strange but true."

With his faith in Devī under withering siege, Justin decided to test the Clays and see how they react. He said, "When I was trapped in that house with your niece, someone shot at us. I feel it's my duty to report the incident to the police."

"Please do," Hunter said. "I urge you to report it. My staff has reported many such incidents. You see, outside the White Hall campus, these mountains are home to quite a few rural, redneck Virginians. They all call that house the ghost house, as you know, and when they hunt in that area, they shoot at it about as often as they shoot at road signs, which is quite often. You're from West Virginia, so I'm sure you know that hunting season began recently."

"Yes, I do know that," Justin acknowledged.

"And you also know that deer often sleep just a few hours at night and then forage in early morning."

"Exactly," Justin replied.

"And so around the time someone shot at the ghost house..."

"Yes, I considered that myself," Justin said. "Deer are lethargic at that time, so it's prime time for hunters. So you believe it was a hunting accident."

"Exactly." Hunter smiled. "All the landowners in this area have trouble with hunters. We've filed many complaints with the sheriff, which are public record. There are many deer on our side of the mountain, and at times the hunters drink and act in an irresponsible manner. Clay Campus itself has taken a few stray bullets. The sheriff will confirm all this, just in case you think I'm an Asura." Hunter said these last words with a good-natured wink.

"Oh, I'm not saying that," Justin cried out. "Please forgive me if you think that I meant..."

Hunter laughed. "Don't worry, Justin. It's natural that you were suspicious. I've had to deal with many young men like you who were confused in various ways by my niece. Anyway, regarding the shooting, please do report it so that we can build up our case file and get those hunters banned from our area."

Justin was too confused to speak. He was not yet fully convinced that the Clays were not Asuras, nor that they were. The situation was painfully confusing. But for now, he must feign total acceptance of the senator's version, and thus buy time for further investigation. A misstep on one side, believing all that Devī said, might lead Justin into benevolent madness. On the other side, he might play into the hands of powerful Asuras.

"Don't feel bad," Barbara said. "The truth is, Jane is a very beautiful young lady, and very bright. She convinced quite a number of young men that only they could help her save the world. So, don't feel bad that you also fell into her trap."

Justin nodded, desperate to be alone to think.

"I should add," Barbara said, "that Jane always claims she will inherit a fortune. The truth is quite the opposite. Her parents were certainly comfortable, and as you saw, lived in an elegant house, though property values in the mountains are nothing like in the city. But unhappily, Jane's parents lost most of their fortune in bad investments and the rest was spent in legal bills after their lamented passing."

Here Justin thought of his own father's disastrous investments and the final blow coming from legal fees and debts. Mrs. Clay continued, "The truth is, though we don't tell anyone, that Hunter and I have been paying the taxes and upkeep on that house, for Jane's sake, though she is hardly grateful. But the truth could not be more different from what she says. We are practically monsters in her eyes. It can be quite painful, though we know the clinical causes."

Barbara Clay clenched her teeth, as if holding back tears, and the senator put his arm around her. He shook his head but did not speak.

A few very awkward moments passed in silence till Barbara said, "Justin, I want you to know that Jane is at Stonewood not because Hunter and I are cruel, but rather because we didn't have the heart to put her in a mental institution. The state tried to do it, but we fought against it. She tells everyone we want to put her in an institution, but we kept her out. You must have wondered why we allow our own niece to live at Stonewood. There's a simple answer: we begged her to live with us at Clay Campus. We offered her a beautiful suite, but she suffers from paranoid delusions. You know what she thinks of us. It is Jane herself who refuses to leave this area. Stonewood is simply the only area school that will take her. What else could we do? We love Jane, but she has special needs. We would come to see her often, if she didn't dislike our visits so much. But we love our niece and we keep trying."

Barbara's eyes moistened. "I'm sorry, but it's so upsetting."

"Yes, it is." Hunter sighed. "She's my dear sister's only child. Justin, we even arranged for the sheriff to look the other way and let her live in her old house. That was all we could do for her, apart from paying for classes she never attends, and a dorm room she never sleeps in. We even pay the neighbors to bring her fruits and vegetables for her vegetarian diet, since she won't accept food from us. She thinks we want to poison her."

Justin did not know what to think. The Clays' account of many material details perfectly matched Devī's. But the two interpretations were radically opposed.

Barbara wiped her eyes with a tissue. "We really tried. We tried so hard for her parents' sake, for her sake. We've known her and loved her since the day she was born."

Although no one outside the room could hear their words, Hunter leaned forward and said softly to Justin, "Please never repeat this, but I believe Jane's madness drove her parents to their grave. It is very hard for me to talk about it. Her parents were such good, loving people. But imagine, Justin! Their only child tried to convince them that they came from another planet to help her fight demons like us. How her poor parents suffered. That's why I call her by her legal name, Jane. The name *Devī* is a beautiful Sanskrit word, but unfortunately it reminds me of the grief she caused my poor departed sister, and my brother-in-law."

Justin knew not what to think. In his anxiety, he changed his sitting posture, then changed it again. His special book now protruded from his coat, and Hunter Clay saw it.

"What is that?" he said. "Can I see it?"

CHAPTER 36

J ustin handed him the book. Hunter nodded. "I know this book well."
"You've seen it before?" Justin couldn't conceal his surprise.

"Oh yes," the senator replied.

"Have you read it?" Justin asked.

"Oh yes. Jane manages to get a copy to all the young men she plans to meet. And they have shared it with me."

"And what do you think?" Justin was afraid to hear the answer.

"I must admit," the senator said, "that both in my view and that of some excellent scholars who know far more than I do, the book gives a rather subjective view of the actual legend."

"Perhaps you could explain more about that." Justin tried to sound calm and merely curious.

"Indeed," Hunter said, "I must be more clear."

"Now, Hunter," Barbara said, "let's not bore Justin with your academic views on ancient myths."

"No, please," Justin urged, "I would like to hear your views."

Hunter smiled. "Justin is a bright young man and naturally he's curious. So, I will explain. Most scholars agree that human heroes were the original basis for ancient myths, including Indic tales—those from ancient India. Scholars do what they can to trace these stories, to discover how they might have developed over time. In the well-known story of the Mahā-bhārata, the story of Kṛṣṇa and the Asuras, some scholars believe the Asuras were the original heroes of the story. But over the centuries, with changing historical circumstances and tribal loyalties, the story flipped, so to speak. The original heroes, the Asuras, were depicted as demons, and the villains, like Kṛṣṇa, became the heroes. I think it safe to say that modern scholars who taught these views at prestigious European universities were not themselves Asuras. I'm sure you see how mad it would be to think so."

"Yes, I do," Justin said, wondering if some European scholars could in fact be Asuras. Or had Devī actually presented a sectarian version of the history?

"I'm still a bit of an amateur," the senator said, "but I have read the essential texts. We lack hard evidence of the historicity of these ancient stories. In other words, we don't know what actually happened. The common scholarly view is that ancient storytellers wove history and mythology into a single narrative."

Justin nodded. He knew that Hunter was giving respectable academic theory. He also knew that academic theory often tilted toward reflexive skepticism.

Barbara added, "You may not know this, Justin, but in Zoroastrianism, one of the world's great, ancient religions, God is called Ahura, which is the ancient Persian pronunciation of Asura. So, in one of the world's important theistic traditions, Asura is a name of God. *Asu* means 'life,' and Asura is the god of life."

"By the way," Senator Clay said, "you'll find that meaning of *Asura* in the *Oxford Sanskrit Dictionary* on page 121. You may be surprised that we know these things, but remember who our niece is. We did due diligence to understand her imaginings. We really did all we could to help her."

Justin listened and stared. Would Devī's stature survive this barrage of arguments? He didn't know, but he must soldier on and delve further into this issue. He must find the truth. At the same time, he felt deeply honored, and even astonished, by the amount of time and attention that Senator Hunter Clay was giving him. It was an opportunity he must seize to clarify his dilemma.

"What about that evil Asura King Kaṃsa?" Justin asked. "How can we call him a hero?"

"Good question," Hunter said. "If we judge by your book, or your dream, it would be absurd to call Kaṃsa anything but an evil tyrant. However, real history, if there really was a Kaṃsa, is often very different from myth and dream."

"Yes, that's true," Justin agreed, determined to remain neutral and test the senator's theory. "So, do you ultimately consider these ancient stories to be mythology or history?"

"Another good question," Hunter said. "I admire your intellectual integrity and tenacity."

"And I admire your learning in this area," Justin said, trying hard not to provoke any suspicion. He could not be insensitive to such praise from a famous, powerful man. But Justin's reason told him that in this democratic age, the Asuras would have to master knowledge of their own past, to respectably promote their point of view. Still, at all costs, Justin must not let the Clays suspect his own suspicions. Of course, if they were actually Asuras, they might already know his thoughts. The situation was stressful, to say the least.

Hunter continued, "Regarding Kaṃsa and friends, we know that if these stories are in fact histories, they were written many centuries after the events. The tradition claims they took place five thousand years ago. In that case, three thousand years separate the writing of these stories and the events they describe—that's three thousand years of a volatile, shifting oral tradition. So, the written record is relatively recent, far distant from the alleged events. And we must consider the bias of the ancient bards who sustained the oral tradition. Clearly, they sought to exalt their civilization by creating a glorious tale of its origin. Isn't that exactly what Virgil did in writing the mythic *Aeneid* to glorify Rome through a fabled history?"

"Yes, that is what Virgil did," Justin admitted.

"Ironically, Virgil lived around the time that writing first proliferated in South Asia. So, we see a process both in Rome and Asia of popularizing epic tales that attribute a glorious origin to an important civilization."

"So, you don't believe any of it really happened?"

"There may be a kernel of truth in it, somewhere, but how can we tell since archeology helps but little here? I should add that I know about these issues because I studied Asian mythology at Cornell. As I told you in the office that day, Barbara and I met in a class on Hindu myths. We love the stories, and we agree with Joseph Campbell on the beauty and value of myth. But we must remember that we're not dealing with rigorous, literal history."

Justin nodded, surprised and impressed by the senator's knowledge. This powerful man was also a serious scholar. Justin tried to gather his thoughts. Perhaps everything Hunter said was true. Perhaps. But in fairness to Devī, Justin must give her the best possible defense.

Sitting up straight and taking a deep breath, he approached the issue of historicity from another angle. "When I read about King Kaṃsa, I felt I was there, and that he did commit those atrocities. I had a powerful dream of the events described in the book. Devī, or Jane, is on my book cover, as you can see, and I met her in my dream of Bhū-loka."

Barbara and Hunter exchanged glances. "Hunter," she said, "perhaps you can explain to Justin about that book."

The senator nodded. "Of course. As far as I know, Jane got her father to self-publish *The First Avatāra.*"

"And Devī's, or Jane's, picture on the cover?" Justin asked.

Senator Clay again looked at his wife, who nodded, as if grasping his intention. He turned back to Justin, clenched and opened his hands, and said, "I believe her dad paid a professional editor to polish the book. He also paid an artist to do the cover art. I would guess that Jane herself insisted she appear on the cover with Kṛṣṇa, her idol. Jane's dad, my brother-in-law, probably sent the book to regional bookstores, without charge, and obviously you got a copy."

"I see," Justin said, uncommitted to either version of how he got the book. Barbara smiled at Justin, encouraging him to accept the Clay version. With a friendly nod to him, she said, "Justin, a final word on your dream, if I may."

Justin nodded. "Of course. Please."

"Thank you. The truth is that Jane does seem to have mental powers, and as Hunter mentioned, all her previous friends had the same basic dream. I can't say I understand how Jane does it, but I do know that all her previous victims, at the time of their dreams, were in a deeply disturbed, vulnerable period of their lives. Justin, I swear we will never tell a soul, but tell us honestly, were you experiencing such difficulties in your life when you had that dream?"

After some hesitation, Justin said, "Yes, I was."

"I understand," the senator's wife said. Then she fixed him in a powerful gaze. "If I may be frank, young man, are you really going to tell the world that a key leader of the United States, a leading candidate for the presidency, is really an extraterrestrial demon from thousands of years ago? And you know this because a young girl told you it's true? Justin, the entire world will consider you mad, and I admit that I will too. Think carefully, young man. Don't throw your life away. Think of your family."

Justin nodded, facing the stark reality of her words. The world would indeed think him mad. Indeed, he might easily come to see himself that way. And surely his family would become, or rather remain, ruined. But Devī...

The senator interrupted this frantic introspection. "Justin," he said, "we don't have more time now, and so let me come to the point. My goal in meeting you was to give you a more objective picture of our dealings with Jane, and especially to see if there is any way that we can keep you in White Hall. I gave the reasons for our concern—our sincere belief in your potential, and our sense of responsibility for our niece's part in all this. I will be frank and admit a third motive, though the first two would certainly have justified and brought about our attempt to help you. The third motive is my strong wish to avoid any public scandal associated with my name, even indirectly through a near family member. It would not help either of us for Jane's opinions to leak into the public sphere."

"I certainly respect and share that wish," Justin said, "and I believe that you would have very kindly sought to help me in any case. I am indebted to you for your interest in my career, and I will appreciate beyond expression any help you can offer to save me from the disaster of expulsion from White Hall."

"Well spoken," Senator Clay said, nodding to his wife with smiling approval. "Well spoken indeed. I believe in you, Justin."

Buoyed by this praise, Justin dared to ask, "If I do remain at White Hall, do I still have any chance at Knighthood?"

"I'm afraid even we can't help you with that," Hunter said. "I spoke with Tom. He mentioned that you were keenly aspiring to Knighthood. Unfortunately, Tom will never ask Mel to accept as a Knight a student who spent the night with a Stonewood girl."

"But nothing happened," Justin insisted. "We stayed in different parts of the house."

"I believe you," Hunter said, "but it would hurt Mel too much, and on issues like this, Knights are fiercely loyal to other Knights. I'm truly sorry, Justin. I know how much this meant to you."

Justin nodded in mournful resignation.

"To be honest," Barbara said, "at this point, we are working hard to keep you in White Hall."

Justin could not hide his disappointment, but he expressed genuine gratitude for all they had done and were doing for him. His deepest feelings on this matter were somewhat ambivalent. If Devī was truly Devī, then his final victory would come through her, and not necessarily through the Knights. If there was any truth to Senator Clay's account, Devī could not ultimately help Justin, and the loss of Knighthood would be a loss indeed. But for now, it was natural and prudent to manifest to the Clays the disappointment he did feel.

The Clays seemed touched by his words, and Hunter said, "We gave you that scholarship because of your merit. Sadly, we have no children of our own, and so it is a great pleasure for us to, one might say, financially adopt needy and deserving students. It gives meaning to our lives."

These generous words reminded Justin of Devī's comment, that after killing Justin's father, the Asura hoped to become a type of surrogate father to him. But he lacked final proof of this, and fearing that Senator Clay might be an Asura who could read his mind, he put that thought aside. He would give the Clays and their viewpoint fair consideration. They deserved as much, after all the help they had offered him.

He tapped a button on the table before him, and in moments the president and dean entered the room. When they were seated, Barbara Clay explained why the Clays felt that White Hall should not expel Justin. "Considering the circumstances," Mrs. Clay said, "we feel strongly that the White Hall administration should perhaps put Justin on probation, and assuming he complies with all school rules, which we know he will, the probation can be lifted as soon as the rules permit."

President Lofter nodded her agreement as the senator's wife spoke, giving strong hope to Justin. "Mrs. Clay, Senator Clay, you know the depth of our gratitude to you for your exceptional service to our school. White Hall respects your views on this and all other matters of mutual concern. Thus, based on your recommendation, the White Hall administration decided not to expel Justin."

Justin breathed an embarrassingly audible sigh of relief. But his relief was cruelly short-lived.

The president said, "While the three of you were talking, Tom Walker, our student body president, came to see me. As you know, he has agonized over this case. He has great affection for Justin and therefore it took him some time to reach a decision."

"A decision?" Justin asked.

"Yes. According to White Hall rules, when the administration chooses not to enforce expulsion for certain offenses, that decision must be ratified by the student body government. It is the concept of a trial by one's peers."

"I see," Senator Clay said. "So even though the administration chose to grant clemency to Justin, the student government makes the final decision."

"Exactly. The other student officers hold Tom in the highest esteem, and given the sensitivity of this case, they declared their intention of following his decision. It was difficult for Tom, as I said, because he hates to hurt Justin. But Tom decided that White Hall rules must be applied evenly, without favoritism. He notes that in most past cases of expulsion, the student concerned did not exhibit malice or a clear intent to break the rules. But White Hall has always held that strict enforcement of such rules is necessary to maintain the proper standard. Tom felt it was unfair to break with precedent based on his personal friendship with the student concerned. Our student government agreed."

"And so..." Mrs. Clay asked.

"And so, I am truly sorry to say that apparently Justin must leave White Hall. I will mention one detail—according to our rules, the student council can only meet on weekdays. This rule is meant to assure that student leaders rest on the weekend and not overstress themselves. So, the council will make and declare their formal adjudication tomorrow, Monday. Once they do, Justin will receive the usual courtesy of three days to arrange his departure."

Justin felt dizzy and dazed. Mrs. Clay said, "Justin, we know how you must feel. We made a point of personally speaking to Tom on your behalf. He listened to us, but we have all heard his ultimate reasoning on this matter. He has such a strong sense of honor toward White Hall and its rules."

Justin nodded politely, hardly knowing that he did. He tried to force a smile but failed and fell silent. His shocked mind seemed to leave his body and spin around the room. He watched everyone, including himself, exchange kind words. He watched the Clays depart. Dean Rankin sat next to him and suggested he go back to his room and rest, for he looked quite ill. He dreaded returning in utter shame to Davis, West Virginia. And if there was any truth at all in what the Clays said, he might lose not just White Hall but also Devī. In that case, he would return to Davis with nothing but shame and impotence.

Justin felt his body rise from the chair and walk with wooden legs out the door. He arrived at his room without knowing how he got there and fell on his bed, too depressed to do anything. In this state, it was impossible to consider his views on Devī and the Clays. For now, his numb mind knew nothing but misery.

Eventually Luke walked in, saw Justin, and guessed the rest. He said, "I'm ready to do anything for you, Justin. I'll leave you in peace, but just call me and I'll be here in a minute. I won't be far. I'm sure it will turn out well." By the time Justin managed to lift his head, Luke was gone.

Earlier that day, Justin had invited Luke to join him in a meditation on the Avatāra's names. Justin had been eager to resume some form of spiritual practice. But that was impossible now. Luke knew better than to bring it up.

As Justin lay on his bed, more troubles entered his mind. For example, even the Clays acknowledged Devī's mental powers. So, she probably knew he had spoken to the Clays. How might she react? What if Devī was just a pious madwoman? Who was his friend, who his enemy?

Justin had to stop thinking about it, before he drove himself mad with conjectures. His intellectual pride collapsed. He knew only his own confusion, fear, and misery.

Justin fixed his mind on Morgantown. He could not return to Davis. The humiliation would be unbearable. He would approach his father's dear old friends at West Virginia University. They would help him find a job. He would live simply and send money to his family. He would pay their fare to visit him in Morgantown. His mother would insist he finish high school, so he would enroll in a Morgantown school after the New Year and continue working.

Justin looked up and saw Luke carefully watching him. The thought that Luke might not be Lokeśa disturbed him. *What if he is just Luke?* They would still be best friends, of course. But even that might be difficult, if Justin could not believe in Devī and Luke did. How could they differ on that point and remain best friends?

But somehow, if Luke were not Lokeśa, it would be different, as if an angel had fallen to Earth. No, that was unfair. Luke was a true and wonderful friend. But if it turned out that Luke was deluded about an ancient relationship with Sara, that must affect Justin's friendship with him. What if Devī was influencing Luke's mind to secure a mate for her dependent friend? These thoughts shocked Justin but he could not drive them from his mind.

But then Justin recalled with a start his terrible mistake in Bhū-loka of doubting Devī. But there might be no Bhū-loka. The Clays insisted that Devī created the dream to bind him through a sense of indebtedness to her.

It was too much for his mind. His faith in Devī was shaken but not destroyed. He could not resolve the matter. He could not surrender to her authority. But he could not reject her. Perhaps his expulsion was the Avatāra's doing. Once expelled, he could meet with Devī whenever he liked, and she permitted. But should he?

At the very least, Devī must have her day in court. She had a right to reply to the accusations against her. If only he could speak to her! After his expulsion, he could freely hike up to her house. But if the Clays were right, that might be dangerous.

Trapped in a state of wretched indecision and deepening depression, Justin struggled to understand, but nothing was clear. He decided to hike to the waterfall, far from Devī's house. He would get away where he could breathe and think more freely.

When he returned, he would explain everything to Luke, who had promised to double his efforts to hack the Clay intelligence network, for that was what it was. Luke had said to Justin, "A certain girl, whom I will not name, has been helping me to hack Clay Campus.

"What?" Justin said. "Does that girl (whom Justin knew to be Sara) know about advanced digital technology?"

"Remember Justin," Luke had replied, "That girl has been on a spiritual path for thousands of years. She is shy, but she has serious power. She has begun giving me suggestions that greatly accelerate our work. I'm starting to break through bits of the Clay Campus firewall."

Justin thanked his friend. Luke was a brilliant hacker, and if he did break into Clay Campus, he might quickly resolve Justin's dilemma. It was essential that Justin be fair to all parties in this matter. His father insisted that he base his views on hard evidence. Justin wanted the Clays to be innocent, and he wanted the whole problem to be a misunderstanding, so that the Clays and Devī were both good.

He sought relief in absolute neutrality, a full suspension of judgment on the Clays or Devī.

On the other hand, his dream of Bhū-loka, even if induced by Devī, inspired him to again act nobly, like a prince, and for that he must be ever grateful. Still, an incorrect choice or conclusion in this matter might easily ruin his life, and the lives of many others, including those he most loved in this world.

CHAPTER 37

J ustin armed himself well for the trek. Devī insisted that the Clays were Asura killers on his trail. The Clays insisted that Devī was deluded and dangerous. These wildly opposing claims scrambled his inner compass. As Justin walked past the reservoir in the cool autumn air, he pulled his hat down low over his face, the way Devī did the first time he saw her. Now he was the outcast, determined to avoid detection. Well, if the Clays were right about Devī, there was one advantage. Justin and his family would not be in danger from Asuras, since Asuras would not exist.

Yet, a few days before, that same Devī twice saved his life, giving him shelter from a killing storm, and making him bow beneath a lethal salvo of bullets. And that Devī insisted she was battling hostile Asuras, led by the most respectable Clays. For now, he had full faith only in his mother and brother. All other reference points were dissolving.

He wondered where Scarlet was. She slept late Sundays and then passed the day with Tom, who religiously reserved a few hours every Sunday for his sister, no matter what else was going on. Justin knew that Scarlet was giving Mel another look and invited him to join her and her brother today. Thinking about it made Justin feel sick, so he pushed it out of his mind.

The biting mountain air braced him and cooled his inner turmoil. He was a mountain boy after all, he told himself with a smile. Stripped of color, big trees swayed like blind mourners in the wind. God only knew what danger lurked on the trail. His fingertips tapped a martial cadence on his knife handles. He quickstepped down to the rocky banks of Moorman's River, and followed it into the Shenandoah Park.

He trekked the North Fork path into the foothills, zigzagging across the cold river on trekker's stones. As the path rose into the high foothills, the valley narrowed into a steep glen that propelled the river faster and louder.

Unexpectedly, the cloud cover thinned. The sun lit up fall's last sylvan colors. With quicker pace, Justin traced a track into a lovely meadowland. There he sat for some time, struggling to clear his mind, with no success. Happily, nature seemed to be doing better. The dreary clouds had whitened and shone in a rich blue firmament.

He returned to the river path and continued to ascend the glen that rose steadily toward the Shenandoah peaks. He heard waters crash and mingle. He neared the falls. He walked further and looked up to his left.

The Big Branch Creek dashed over a sheer rock face and cascaded down through a glistening chain of crystalline pools, into Moorman's River. This was a place to explore.

He climbed a path on the south side of the falls. Halfway up, he saw a young couple with University of Virginia jackets, lounging on a big rock in one of the clear pools. As Justin approached, they waved and smiled and he happily reciprocated.

"Are you going to the top?" the girl asked.

"Yes!" Justin said. "Definitely!"

"You'll enjoy it," the boy said. "It's beautiful up there. There's a big pool right at the top."

"Thanks," Justin replied with a grateful smile. He raced up the path. He would rest by the highest pool. He craved the solitude he was sure to find there.

Reaching the highest pool, which shimmered and sparkled in the sun, Justin found an array of flat stones that formed a natural bridge over the water. He stepped onto the first stone. Moving across the pool, Justin saw a girl sitting peacefully behind a large stone on which she rested her back, and which concealed her from all but those who crossed the pool. In the dazzling reflected light, he saw that she wore a smart black skirt and royal blue coat, with a sky-blue beret tilted on her lovely hair. Absorbed in her book, surrounded by crashing waters that muffled his approach, the girl did not look up.

Justin looked more closely at the girl and froze in his tracks, wide-eyed. It was Devī. Conflicting emotions whirled in his startled mind. He felt joy to see her. Yet he feared she used her power to bring him there. He could turn and run. Devī might never know he was there. But he thought of his father. Devī knew his father, or claimed to. In any case, Tark Davis would insist that Justin be impartial, fair and just, to Devī and to the Clays.

But if Justin did stay and speak to her, should he conceal it from Tom and Scarlet? *That doesn't matter now!* he thought bitterly. He would be expelled from White Hall, and his so-called friends had already rejected him. Well, Scarlet half-rejected him, but that was quite sufficient for proud Justin to consider the relationship finished. No, Justin would not deny Devī justice for a mere pharisaic compliance with the letter of White Hall law. Justin was the son of Tark Davis, not of Hugo's Javert.

But another point must be considered. The Clays attended his father's funeral. These famous, powerful people had not only been extremely kind and generous to Justin, they had honored Tark Davis. And it was they who warned him that Devī was dangerous. Would Tark Davis place his own son in harm's way, especially when real harm to Justin would devastate Tark's widow and his youngest son? If the Clays spoke the truth, Justin should leave at once. But it was Devī. How could Devī pose a threat to him? She saved his life, here and now on Earth, not just in Bhū-loka, whatever that place turned out to be.

Justin's agonizing, inner questions became moot before he could answer them. Devī looked up and saw him. Once their eyes met, he could not flee. It would be too absurd. Devī must have justice. Keeping, however, a very respectful and safe distance, he greeted her. Trying to sound casual and friendly, while studying her reaction, he asked, "Did you know I was coming?"

"No, I didn't," she said. "I would never invade your privacy, nor try to manipulate you. I thought you knew that."

Her cutting words, spoken in a cool, distant tone, belonged to the old Devī of Bhū-loka, not the gracious, friendly Devī he encountered on the mountaintop. Reasons for the sudden change were only too obvious. Surely Justin affronted her, both by his unspoken doubts about her identity, and his spoken suggestion that she hiked miles just to see him. In any case, this encounter was not starting well.

He took a deep breath, glanced at the clear water, and tried to begin again. "I'm glad to see you. I didn't mean to imply…"

"I often come here." She waved away with her hand any need for explanation. He interpreted her words to mean not that she trusted him, but that she just didn't care anymore what he did nor why he did it. This thought pained him greatly, and he began to realize how much he really cared about her.

Devī's every feature told him that she knew of his treasonous meeting with the Clays. The atmosphere was excruciatingly awkward. Devī kept her eyes trained on the flowing water, as if it symbolized the fleeting, protean nature of his relationship with her. She evinced no inclination to speak, and he had no idea of what to say. A gloom fell over them like an asphyxiating blanket. He stood in place. She sat in place. Each looked away from the other. For Justin, it was awful. His mind had no place to rest, no certainty, no clarity. He felt only a painful suspicion that he had betrayed Devī. The mute air oppressed him.

Justin grew desperate to break the impasse. He was absolutely resolved to honor Devī's right to reply to all accusations against her, whether she chose to do so or not. Still, he dreaded mentioning his meeting with the Clays, though he must eventually do it. After quick, anxious consideration, he decided to first break the silence by explaining his imminent expulsion from White Hall. Devī probably already knew, but his duty was to be open and honest with her. He would disclose everything, but gradually, gauging her response and modulating his narration accordingly.

He told the tale of his expulsion in a way that laid all the blame for it at his own door. He did mention in passing Tom's unbending adherence to the rules, but without a hint of rancor or accusation. And though his ostensible crime was entering and staying in Devī's house, Justin took eloquent pains to spare Devī any imaginable imputation of responsibility for his plight. He spoke what he truly felt.

As he concluded, his eyes returned to the moving waters. He wondered if Devī would respond with sympathy, indifference, admonition, or even a hope that they could now freely work together. Devī responded with none of these. To his astonishment, Devī shook her head firmly and said, "You will not be expelled."

Incredulous, intrigued, Justin stared at Devī. "Not expelled? But how is that possible?"

"Kṛṣṇa has a plan." Devī would say no more.

He appealed to her. "Devī, what plan?"

"You will soon see. Be patient." Her tone forbade further appeals.

Amazed by her claim, Justin forgot for a moment that he must tell Devī all he heard from the Clays. Devī quickly reminded him. "I think you have more to tell me," she said.

When Justin's heart sank and he hesitated, she said, "Justin, we must be honest with each other, and we have very little time." Devī looked down the path to the river, as if to emphasize that one of them must soon leave.

"Of course, we must," he said, disappointed that their meeting would soon end, and almost horrified that he must reveal to her face all that he heard from the Clays. The two most important girls in his life, Scarlet and Devī, both demanded honesty from him. Whatever his feelings, Devī had a right to know of his meeting with Hunter Clay, and his charges against her. Only by full disclosure would he honor her right of reply.

The wind rustled the water, and chilled him. The sun glided behind a cloud. Anxious to begin the topic in the least injurious way possible, he stated how the Clays summoned him and tried to help him remain at White Hall. Devī nodded, revealing nothing of her feelings.

Reasoning that diplomacy was not duplicity, and eager to avoid an ugly scene, Justin began with an academic point, explaining to Devī in soft tones what the Clays said about the word *Asura*, that in the Sanskrit dictionary the word indicated a good, or even divine, spirit. He fervently hoped that a linguistic point would not arouse her fury.

Devī heard him, shook her head with a sad little laugh, and in a rather academic tone of her own, said, "There is indeed an ancient Sanskrit term *asura*, derived from *asu*, life. In that sense, *asura* can be a positive term. But that word is a mere homonym of the relevant term *asura*, as it is used in the ancient history of the Avatāra. *Sura* in Sanskrit means a deity or godly person, and a-sura is the opposite—an ungodly person. The Avatāra subdues the ungodly a-suras who take life, not the Asu-ras who give life."

"I see." Justin felt both impressed and foolish. "That is significant. I guess the Clays are not Sanskrit scholars."

"That is a safe guess." Devī sat up straight. "But the best Sanskrit dictionaries are available online, and since whatever I say may be false, you may confirm what I said." She looked away from him.

Justin reddened. He could not deny the justice of Devī's sudden, cutting remark. In the immediate aftermath of his Bhū-loka dream, he doubted her very existence. After their recent reunion, he doubted everything about her but her existence. And she obviously knew it.

"I don't need to check," he said. It was painful to see that Devī knew he did not trust her, and so in turn, she did not trust him. Whatever Devī was, he had come to appreciate her very much. Even if his rational mind did not fully accept her, she was still Devī.

"What other Indological points did you hear?" Devī asked, keeping her eyes focused on the water, as if she could see Kṛṣṇa in the currents.

Abashed, and fully expecting to be refuted, Justin sat down on a smooth rock, and in acute misery, he next explained that prominent scholars argued that the Asuras were the original heroes of the history. Devī refuted this as well.

"In fact," Devī said, "that was a nineteenth-century theory, held by a few scholars and abandoned by almost all scholars in the last two centuries."

She then referred him to the works of leading modern Indologists to verify her claim.

"I believe you," Justin said quietly. "Devī, you are helping me greatly by explaining these points." In his heart, he rejoiced at Devī's victory, and he wondered about the Clays. To be fair to them, as he must be to Devī, their amateurish views on ancient South Asia did not make them Asuras, though they had been rather eager to defend Asuras.

Hawks circled overhead, casting darting shadows. Justin watched them for a moment, grateful for a brief interlude. Devī remained silent, as if waiting for him to speak. So he shyly raised a final point, anxious to hear her answer. "Scholars believe," he said, "that the stories of Kṛṣṇa and Bhū-loka are mythological, even if they grew out of real but untraceable historical events."

"Justin," she said, pronouncing his name in a cool, distant tone, "it is true that normal scholarly methods cannot trace these events. Thus, on academic grounds, one cannot affirm or deny them. I never claimed that these spiritual truths could be proved or disproved by material means. I invited you to personally experience your non-material self. As far as the historicity of the Avatāra, I urged you to experience it for yourself, not to accept it blindly. That is precisely why I always encouraged your spiritual practice."

"Very true," was all Justin could say.

Devī looked weary, as if tiring of his questions. She seemed impatient to be alone, as if hopeless that this or any other meeting with Justin Davis could remove his constant doubts about her, doubts that she could no longer bear.

With one perfectly formed hand, she lifted the hat off her head. As the sun's rays shone on her silken locks, she stretched her arms toward the sky, tired of sitting in one posture. She then replaced the hat on her head, turned to Justin and said, "Let us conclude. Tell me, please, who you think I am."

He had not foreseen this sudden confrontation. He could not lie to Devī. He must not pain her, but a clumsy attempt at evasion would be worse than anything. Any hedging, dodging, or dissembling would deeply offend her. He stood disarmed before Devī. Tact, subtlety, delicacy and cleverness all abandoned him. Wretchedly trapped, he said, "You know very well what the Clays say about you. I want to believe in you. I deeply respect you. But I am confused."

"Confused about me," Devī repeated softly. Her lips tightened. He saw pain in her eyes. To his astonishment, his words seemed to wound her. But how could that be? Since Bhū-loka, Justin had been firmly convinced that nothing he said or did could seriously disturb Devī. Her indifference to his feelings about her had been an absolute reference point. Even lately when she was kind and gracious to him in her house, he assumed that her entire concern arose from a sense of duty to the Avatāra.

How could his words surprise her? She knew his thoughts. But now he recalled that at other times, his actions and words had seemed to surprise her. She did have cognitive powers. She was often aware of remote events, but those were external. She had told the truth in claiming to never deliberately invade his private feelings. Rather, it was her deep insight, coming from a heightened, expanded state of consciousness, that often made his own, less evolved, thoughts and feelings obvious to her.

Now, Devī was deeply hurt. He saw it in every pale feature of her face, in her downcast expression. Whoever Devī was, he never wanted to hurt her. He did not know what to do or say. It was terrible.

Despite her pain, Devī was still Devī and she quickly roused herself. She breathed deeply. Strength and reserve returned to her features. She stood up straight and said in a polite but distant voice, "Kṛṣṇa has blessed me today. I told you in my house that before meeting you again, I yearned to leave this world, that I didn't belong here. But I hesitated when we met again. I thought there might be a plan that reunited us all. I admit that I hoped it was true. If that was selfish of me, may Kṛṣṇa forgive me. I am truly sorry if I pressured you to help me. I had been staying in this world for Sara. But she and Luke have reunited, though you may doubt their past identities, and I know Luke will fully support her, and she will bless his life. So, you see, I have no further reason to stay here. I am ready to rejoin Kṛṣṇa. Don't fear that I will trouble you further, nor that when I am gone, the Asuras will target you, though you doubt that such beings exist."

Appalled, Justin said, "Please don't leave this world now. Aren't you always with Kṛṣṇa, wherever you are?"

"Yes, but to personally serve Kṛṣṇa is special and..." Devī stopped, as if embarrassed by her own words. She hesitated, then said quietly, "Why do I say this to you? In your mind, all I say about the Avatāra could be merely my imagination, even madness."

What could he do or say with integrity that would matter to Devī? And with Devī, anything less than absolute integrity was absurd. Lately, his feelings for Devī had softened considerably, to the point of caring deeply about her. Still, it would be absurd to tell her anything but the truth. And the truth was too awkward to repeat. He could not hurt her again. But he could not let her leave this world, though he dared not ask himself why.

"All I can say," Justin said, "is that in my heart I know this is not right. You may consider my unenlightened intuition to be useless. And I cannot in any way justify myself. But I know it is not right that you leave."

Justin's desperate sincerity struck Devī for a moment. Then she said, "You and I are different. We belong to different worlds. I should not have interfered in your life. Forgive me. I will not do it again."

"Please," Justin said, "don't apologize to me. Who am I compared to you? How can I live with myself if even indirectly, I drive you from this world?"

"Justin, do not blame yourself. It is my wish to leave."

"Surely you won't leave at this moment. You can't."

"Not at this moment," Devī said, "but soon."

"I may be a fool, but the world needs you."

"You are not a fool." Devī shook her head. "But I don't belong in this world. I don't express myself well to people here. There are other souls on Earth who are better able to teach here, and more will come. Many persons in this world think I have no heart, at least not like other people. You also thought that. I understand why you saw me that way. I don't blame you. But I do have a heart. I returned to this planet with good intentions, but for years I have been feared, shunned, even hated. Now, I've even lost your trust. Justin, I have a heart, and this world has broken it. I can bear it no longer. I must go back to where souls are like me, where they understand and accept me."

Ashamed beyond anything he had ever felt, Justin could not speak. He knew since they met on the mountain that Devī might leave this world. But her confirmation of an imminent departure struck him harder than he expected.

Devī now said softly, "Since we will not meet again, I will explain two things that should resolve your doubts and reveal your path." She sounded ominous.

"What two things?" Justin asked, fearing the answer.

"The first is the lesser point, though it is revealing. You may recall that in Bhū-loka, the Asura's name was Vyādha."

"Yes, I recall that clearly."

"Look up the Sanskrit word *vyādha*. See what it means."

"Please tell me." Justin asked. "I will accept what you say. Please."

Devī relented. "The Sanskrit word *vyādha* means hunter."

"Hunter," Justin said with a shudder, "as in Hunter Clay."

"Yes, Hunter as in Hunter Clay. But that could be a mere coincidence, entirely circumstantial. Or it might not be. My second point suggests that the first is not mere coincidence."

"What is the second point?" Justin asked with deep foreboding. Devī's face turned grave and sad, but not distant. She said, "I deeply regret that I am the one who must tell you this."

"Please, tell me," Justin said softly, sighing deeply.

Devī nodded and fixed him in her gaze. "You doubted me when I accused my uncle and aunt of being murderous Asuras who took your father's life. You still doubt my words. So, I will give you evidence."

Justin froze, hardly breathing. *What evidence could there be?*

"You know," Devī said, "that Hunter Clay has a loyal assistant named Jack, who has been with the senator since before your birth."

"Yes, I know that."

"You also know that Jack does nothing without Hunter's approval."

"Yes, I also know that," Justin said.

"The night your excellent father's life was taken, you chased the killer and struck him repeatedly with an iron rod. Is that true?"

"Yes, it is true." Justin gasped, struck by his memory of that night, and by Devī's knowledge of the events.

"When possible," she said slowly, "look closely at Jack, and you will see on his back and neck the scars you gave him that terrible night."

Justin went numb. His body trembled. The scars were on Jack's body. Devī would never make such a claim were it not true. Justin glanced at Devī and saw in her face the same compassion he observed the night he was trapped in her house. For now, for a few moments, they were friends again.

"I am profoundly sorry," she said, "but I had to tell you this. It's the only way to convince you, and thus the only way to truly put you on your guard, and ultimately save your life. I assure you I have no other motive. I did not tell you sooner, because... I thought we would have more time. And I had to see if you could trust me. It would be dangerous for you and me if we worked together without that trust."

"Devī," he stammered, "I'm sorry. But please tell me, what can I do now? What should I do?"

"If you simply pursue your career and do conventional good in the world, the Asuras will not target you. But if you wish to avenge your father, and help save your planet from the Asuras, then you must fight Hunter. You will defeat him, or you will die. But you can only defeat him if you embrace and channel the Avatāra's power. You must do that yourself. I cannot do it for you. I have done what I could for you. I beg you, do not fight the Asura with your own power. You will die and cause unbearable grief to your family. I pray you accept Kṛṣṇa's help and keep your vow to him. Then you will avenge your father and render the highest service to your planet."

"Devī," Justin said, "I need the Avatāra, but I also need you. I beg you to stay."

"It is in your hands now. Goodbye, Justin. You must leave me now. Your friends need you."

This was far too abrupt. He hesitated. She ordered him to leave. "I told you," she said, "your White Hall friends need you. Leave at once."

"But I—"

"Go now! Go to your friends."

She seemed to say that he should not count her among his friends. This hurt him deeply. Still shocked by her claim about Jack, he was now being expelled from her presence. Again and again, she ordered him to leave. "I told you," she said impatiently, "go to your friends."

How could she end their last meeting like this? Yet so adamant was she that he left at once, deeply upset at this cold, unceremonious final parting.

He descended the path in utter turmoil. If Devī was right about Hunter and Jack, and if he had lost Devī's friendship forever, he would be helpless to avenge his father or truly help the world. In that case, there was little left in his life that could truly inspire him. The Asuras would monitor him and probably strike if Justin tried to connect to the Avatāra.

Devī said he would not be expelled. Even if that were true, though it seemed impossible, what good was White Hall after all that he learned from her about his father and the world?

As soon as possible, Justin must verify Jack's scars. If he found them, as he now fully expected, he must either fight to the death with a person far more powerful, or live a life of disgrace, no matter how great his material achievements. As he moved down the path to the river valley, he escaped mental chaos by focusing on the trail, and the surrounding forest.

CHAPTER 38

Devī said that his White Hall friends needed him. What could that mean? His only White Hall friend was Luke. Luke had Sara and hardly needed Justin. He had no other real friend in the state of Virginia.

Was Luke in danger? This fear drove his steps ever faster lest he fail to reach him in time.

Moving quickly along the valley floor, Justin soon came to a secondary path that led to the mountain meadows. Voices intruded, carried on the mountain air. He stopped and listened. The voices called to each other, pealing through the meadows. The voices were familiar. He took a few steps toward them and realized that they belonged to his former White Hall friends.

Tom, Scarlet, and Mel, intrigued by Justin's mountain treks, had often declared that one day they would also explore the mountains. Apparently, the stress of recent events finally drove Tom to get away, and naturally he took his sister and Mel with him. That much Justin could surmise.

Perhaps Devī meant these three as friends needing help, even if they no longer considered Justin their friend. Just in case, he went quietly toward them, keeping out of sight, till he saw the three through leafless trees. He stayed behind a tree where he could see them without being seen.

Should he call to them? Absolutely not. They made it clear, each in their own way, that he was no longer a friend. Still, he watched them, till a shocking sound drowned their voices.

Six big mountain motorcycles roared up the main path and exploded into the meadow, heading straight for the White Hallians, whose faces registered their shock. The bikes screeched to a stop inches from them. The bikers turned off their bikes. A hush covered the meadow, shattered the next moment by the bikers' ugly curses and taunts. This was what Devī meant. These were the friends that needed him.

Justin crept closer, tapping his knives to make sure they were all there. Six bikers with black leather jackets and knives of their own, along with a rather unkempt Stonewood girl, dismounted and surrounded Tom, Mel, and Scarlet. It was the very girl Mel challenged in the airport the day Justin arrived, the girl who swore Mel would die for his act. Now she had come with six big, angry thugs, including the two gentlemen from the airport. Flashing knives, they encircled and trapped the White Hallians, who froze in fear of death or mutilation. The meadow was deserted. Cries for help would melt unheard into the wind.

A biker grabbed Scarlet and pulled her aside. Mel bravely rushed him, but two bikers slammed him to the ground, where he lay gasping. Mel gamely got up on one knee, but the Stonie biker kicked him back down. Mel got up again, wheezing and wiping his bleeding face. The girl, whom her friends called Sam, then punched Mel off his feet. This time, he stayed down in a puffing lump. Sam came to fight.

The biker who held Scarlet pulled her close to him, held a knife to her throat, and said, "Before we end you and your friends, young lady, we all plan to have lots of fun with you."

Too scared to speak, Scarlet shook in his hands. Tom shouted and took a step toward his sister. Two bikers stepped in front of him, swung their knives an inch from his face, pushed him back, and spat out a warning that his next move would be his last.

The biggest of the bikers, the leader, said to Tom, "We didn't kill you yet for two reasons. First, we want you to see what we do to the girl. And second, you guys are going to dig your own graves, and hers."

He whistled and a biker pulled a shovel off a motorcycle and threw it hard against Tom's legs. Tom let it fall to the ground and didn't flinch. The leader demanded he pick it up, and his friend brought his knife under Scarlet's chin to emphasize the point. White with fear for his sister, Tom picked up the shovel and began digging. Mel moaned on the ground, too shocked to stand up.

From the start, Justin wanted to rush into the clearing and save his former friends, but that was too dangerous. He might precipitate their death or serious injury. The bikers might intend to only beat and scare their victims. In that case, his attack, if even slightly flawed, could provoke the bikers to kill those they would have spared. Justin might cause the deaths of those he meant to save. And since his foes were seven, it would take time to subdue them all. Yet if he did nothing, the innocents might perish.

Sam vulgarly renewed her vow to kill Mel. On cue, the bikers chimed in with equally indelicate oaths to rape Scarlet and then kill all the White Hallians. Conclusion—killing the White Hallians might very well be Plan A, and Justin must intervene fast. He quickly took inventory.

Scarlet would not fight. Mel was out of action. Tom lacked martial training, but he was strong and would help. So, Justin and Tom would have to take down six big fighters and Sam, who were all tough but amateurish. This was definitely doable, but required precision. As Tom dug, Mel moaned, and Scarlet trembled, Justin quickly made his final calculations. Mel looked up and said to Scarlet, "Since we may die here, I want you to know that I've always loved you and if I could give my life to save yours, I would happily do it."

Even in her agony, Scarlet rewarded Mel for his chivalry with a grateful, affectionate glance. Apparently not the romantic type, Sam rewarded Mel with another kick.

The leader said to Mel, "What do you mean you *may* die? You guys are already dead." To punctuate this prophesy, he kicked Tom and ordered him to dig faster. He then declared that Mel's final pleasure would be seeing all the bikers enjoy his beloved.

Ordering the other bikers to guard Tom, the big leader moved toward Scarlet, declaring in vulgar language what he intended to do to her. Tom stopped digging. His tears fell into the emerging grave. Justin's rage burned cool and violent. Justin knew that Tom would give his life in defense of his sister. He would die fighting before he allowed these men to molest her. Justin admired Tom deeply for this, but Tom would suffer a hero's death, which Justin could not allow. Now was the time to act.

Under cover of the bikers' loud threats, Justin silently approached the clearing, till he crouched behind a wide old tree that shielded him from Scarlet's guard. The huge leader came up to her and raised a hand to molest her. The biker guard exchanged a lurid word and glance with his leader. Neither saw Justin flash forward. He grabbed the guard's knife hand and plunged his knife deep into the leader's shoulder. The leader screamed and sank to the ground. The wound was not lethal, but it was seriously disabling. Justin wanted him out of the game.

His attack shocked the other bikers and gave Justin precious time. Before the guard could react from his own shock, Justin smashed his head against the tree, knocking him out, but avoiding brain damage. Justin was thrilled to be back in action. Enough talk about fighting evil.

The other four bikers and Sam overcame their shock and came at Justin, who shouted at Scarlet to run away into the forest. She obeyed. The enemies might try to take Tom hostage. To preempt this, Justin rushed straight at a confused biker, disarmed him, and threw his knife to Tom, who picked it up and leaned into a fighting pose worthy of *West Side Story*. Okay, two against five.

But fearing for her brother, Scarlet returned and called to him. Sam screamed and went after her. Tom went after Sam, wild to save his sister. As Sam lunged to stab Scarlet, Tom tackled her. She scrambled up and jumped on Tom like a wildcat. Tom was strong, and in defense of his sister, he showed frightening power. He held the girl's knife hand in his own powerful right hand, and with his left hand choked her into semi-conscious compliance.

Mel's gaze was locked on Scarlet. He struggled to his feet and ran to her. Justin tossed him one of his many knives and told him to take Scarlet away and protect her. It was an easy assignment that would rebuild Mel's self-esteem. Mel gratefully ran to Scarlet, who actually led Mel into the woods as Sam lay gasping on the ground.

Seeing his sister safe, Tom raced back to Justin. One biker ran away in fear. Three bad guys to go. Justin's rage boiled over. He charged the three bikers so fast they had no time to throw their knives. Bashing their shins, guts, and chins with fists, feet, and knife handles, Justin had just enough self-control not to end them.

As the bikers lay crying on the ground, and their leader sat in shock on the ground groaning, Tom pulled Justin away, saying, "Don't kill them. Please, Justin, let's go!"

Justin wanted to throw their bikes off a ledge into the river, but Tom dragged him away. Tom shouted to Scarlet and Mel, who came running. Tom called 911 to get a medical team and law enforcement to deal with the bikers and Sam.

The four White Hallians then hurried toward White Hall as fast as they could. With surprising strength, Scarlet supported the limping Mel who, despite the traumatic events, looked as if he were in heaven with Scarlet helping him along. Tom repeatedly offered to call for medical assistance, but Mel refused. He would rather die in Scarlet's arms than survive in the arms of a medical team. When Scarlet asked about Mel's condition, Tom insisted he had no serious injury. Justin smiled and shook his head when Tom asked if he needed medical help.

Watching Scarlet assist Mel, Justin felt only slight jealousy. Another more powerful thought forced itself on his mind. Devī had saved his friends by insisting that he go to them. That was why she abruptly ejected him from her company. Had she let him stay even a few minutes longer, his friends might have suffered terribly injury, abuse, or even death. With this proof of Devī's goodness, Justin lamented even more her imminent departure. If only his friends knew their debt to her. He would tell them, but not at this moment.

As they walked along, Tom said to Justin, "We owe our lives to you. I will report you to the school—but as a true hero. You know how stuck I am on rules, but my first rule is gratitude. I could not live with myself if I did not do all I could to repay you, though I know I never can."

Hearing these words, and remembering the events that inspired them, Justin was humbled. Devī spoke the truth when she declared he would not be expelled from White Hall, that Kṛṣṇa had a plan. The Clays had failed to save him from expulsion. But now, Kṛṣṇa, through Devī, had engineered his worldly salvation, and that of his friends. All Justin's White Hall problems were over. Tom dropped many hints that should Justin wish it, the Knights would be honored to have him. And with the same subtlety of language, Justin made clear that he still strongly desired Knighthood.

Mel then said, "Justin, I haven't always been kind to you. I apologize for that. I hope you understand my struggles. That's no excuse, but this apology is from my heart."

Moved by these words, Justin thanked Mel and expressed his sincere hope that they would always be friends.

Yet Devī was leaving, and this fact haunted Justin, even as he thrilled in the gratitude and acceptance of his friends. In his heart, Justin thanked Devī. When would he learn to believe her? In the last few weeks, she had saved him from a killing storm, bullets to the head, and social disgrace.

The sheriff was waiting to speak with the four friends. When they all gave the same story, he asked them repeatedly if they were absolutely sure that Justin alone disabled all the bikers. He did, they all stated. The bikers and Sam were in police custody. With tears and embraces, the friends parted.

As Justin walked to his room, he asked himself how he really felt about his renewed friendship with Tom, Scarlet, and Mel. The answer came to him at once. Their gratitude was so heartfelt, and their prior rejection so understandable to his rational mind, that he did not hesitate to welcome them back as dear friends.

And despite all he had recently suffered, and all the reevaluation that his suffering caused, the prospect of finally becoming a Knight still had the power to delight and enthuse him. But this joy lasted but a moment. He had to focus on looking for telltale scars on Hunter's loyal Jack. If he found the scars, which he fully expected, Devī would have proved her point about the Clays.

How would he then deal with them? If they had powers like Devī, they would know that he knew their true identity. They might try to kill him to protect their plan for global power. Devī said they would not kill him if he did not challenge them. But even looking for the scars might trigger a lethal response. Yet, how could he do nothing as he watched his father's killers seize world power?

Justin could only share his fears with Luke. How would Justin respond to an Asura attack; indeed, how could he survive it, if Devī were not there to guide him and defend him? Justin gravely doubted his ability to submit on his own to the Avatāra.

He needed Devī more than ever, but how could he contact her? How could he persuade her to stay in this world? Could she ever accept him again, if he had the courage to accept her? Luke and Sara were his best chance to send a message to Devī.

Justin rushed to his room to tell Luke everything. He found Luke eager to hear. After going over the astonishing events, they huddled over the computer screen, staring at the definition of *vyādha* in the standard Monier-Williams Oxford Sanskrit-English Dictionary— "vyādha: one who pierces or wounds; a hunter; one who lives by killing…"

CHAPTER 39

As news of Justin's heroic act raced around campus, he went instantly from pariah to demigod. Throngs of students hovered about him. Even Knights sought his company. Scarlet was proud to spend time with him.

The White Hall Academy kept the news out of the media, to avoid alarming current and prospective students, and their parents. But everyone that knew told someone, and in a remarkably short span of time, everyone knew everything.

Justin told Joey, and soon all of Tucker County could speak of nothing else. The local newspaper, *The Parsons Advocate*, honored White Hall's plea for media silence, but did use indirect language to confirm what the entire county already knew.

Since his arrival at White Hall, Justin had starred on various martial arts teams, whose tournaments were sparsely attended. Now, tickets for future tournaments were claimed in record numbers. Students, teachers, and administrators stopped to watch Justin's daily run up and down Sugar Hollow, all the way to the country store and back up to the reservoir. He was becoming a legendary figure on campus.

There were brief moments when Justin exulted in his success. But his dread of Devī's departure, and of an inexorable fight to the death with an Asura, sustained a deep, concealed sadness in the midst of social conquest. Luke did, however, ask Sara to convey Justin's fervent appeal that Devī stay at least a little longer, but Devī would not hear of it, even from Sara.

Luke did reveal what he learned from Sara, that Devī had fixed the day of her departure. Her sixteenth birthday fell in two weeks. On that day, she would legally inherit her family estate. She would leave the estate to Sara and other friends of the Avatāra, and she would leave.

This very concrete, specific information destroyed Justin's last hope that Devī might stay. Wretchedly resigned to her leaving, Justin vowed that he would never forget her and all she had done for him. She would always be his spiritual inspiration.

Despite these major troubles, one of which was life-threatening, Justin did occasionally bask in his new celebrity. The Knights extended to him an open invitation to all Knight events, a reliable precursor to Knighthood. Their grateful looks and words, the manly backslaps liberally bestowed, showed that Tom gave them a fine and true account of the great battle in the mountain meadow.

Immersed in an ocean of praise and adoration, Justin always found time to worry very much about how and when he might meet Jack. Days passed and no opportunity presented itself. Justin wondered if Senator Clay read his mind and prevented a meeting with Jack.

In the midst of all this, Justin noticed that the spark between Scarlet and Mel, kindled or rekindled in combat, had survived for at least a few days. This led him to examine his own feelings for Scarlet.

He first reasoned that for now, he was too troubled to focus on a deep commitment to Scarlet or any other girl. And he would honor his promise to Tom not to mislead Scarlet about the degree of his attachment to her. Only if he could fully commit to Scarlet would he urge her to accept him in the same way.

Despite his analysis, Justin still found Scarlet enchanting. He saw her limits, especially in the spiritual arena. But she was brilliant in other ways. If she could only appreciate a little of the spiritual wisdom he learned, he felt he could love her for her many excellent qualities— her wit and intelligence, her integrity and charm, and the drive for excellent that they both shared. Of course, he could not be sure that Scarlet would accept him, but all such considerations must wait for now.

He could not keep this resolution. He needed to further examine his feelings, and Scarlet's. So, he invited her for a walk along the reservoir, hoping that its natural beauty might foster a deeper conversation between them. Standing close together at twilight, they watched the flowing waters darken and the dancing stars ignite. Scarlet's shoulder-length auburn hair shone magically in the moonlight. Justin forbade himself to compare Scarlet's beauty with Devī's. The two girls lived in different worlds that must be kept apart.

Recalling the higher purpose of this evening stroll, Justin tore his mind from that auburn hair, those flawless features and faultless figure, and tried to interest Scarlet in his old friend Plato, a Western sage whom she might find more acceptable. Resorting to his old favorite, the cave analogy, he spoke to Scarlet in poetic terms of the soul's ascent to a higher realm of light, and very gingerly alluded to the mundane world as something less, a charming but ephemeral reflection. But to no avail.

"Justin," Scarlet said, squeezing his hand, "I really have no idea what's beyond the body. For me, it is, and will remain, a mystery. I only know that I exist here and now. I will make the most of this world with a man I truly admire and love. There, now you know me!"

He instantly assured her that he respected her views, etc., etc., but it might be interesting to just consider—

She cut him off with an affectionate smile and an apology. "I'm sorry, Justin, I prefer not to philosophize about the world. I live in the moment. That's where I find beauty."

He smiled and spared her the annoyance of further philosophy. They moved along the reservoir, hand in hand, but not exactly mind in mind. Even if they could not savor the same wisdom, they could still delight each other with kind words and tender glances that expressed mutual affection.

Justin silently mused that the other girl in his life, Devī, would likely strike him down with a thunderbolt if he even hinted that he and she might someday be more to each other than co-workers in a divine cause. This thought saved him from deeper regret than he already felt at the prospect of losing her friendship forever.

Then something unexpected happened. After their walk by the reservoir, as Justin and Scarlet bid each other farewell in the entrance hall of her dormitory, Justin had an actual epiphany—he somehow experienced Scarlet as a soul speaking and moving from within a bodily costume. He did not directly see her soul, or rather he did not see Scarlet the soul. It was like seeing and hearing a person who moves and speaks from behind a mask and costume. One does not directly see the actual person, but one does perceive that the person is costumed and masked.

On later reflection, this was the way Justin made sense of his experience. In any case, this vision startled him. He knew quite well that he could not share his vision with Scarlet, who would take it as bizarre, if not implicitly offensive, as if he were accusing her of superficiality or falsity, which he was definitely not doing. Scarlet asked what was wrong. He apologized and said he hadn't slept enough the night before and was just spacing out.

Scarlet said that she understood, but her expression and manner revealed that she did not in fact attribute his altered behavior to mere fatigue. But both were anxious to avoid anything unpleasant, and they parted as sincere friends, but perhaps not more than that.

White Hall had a long tradition of a Fall Costume Ball, held every year just before the fast-approaching Thanksgiving vacation. Justin and Scarlet had long before committed to going as a prince and princess, and they happily kept their date. However much they disagreed on spiritual topics, they both genuinely enjoyed each other's company. Mel suffered but put on a cheerful face. Justin thought that Mel bore his disappointment well.

The school administration, still shocked by the attack on the White Hallians, thought of canceling the dance, but Scarlet insisted she needed a festive occasion to help her forget the traumatic events. Tom and Mel supported Scarlet, and a few words to the administration removed all doubts. Extra security was deployed and the whole school attended. Justin played the hero's role. He felt that it was the high point of his life.

As he and Scarlet danced happily in their royal costumes, he recalled Devī's instruction, that our bodies are but costumes covering the soul, the real person. So, Justin now had a costume over his costume. Bliss, and an inescapable sense of silliness, filled him in equal measures.

Scarlet and Justin looked so good together and danced so well that the room stopped to watch. The guys envied Justin; the girls envied Scarlet. Tom smiled his full approval. Recovering from his injuries, Mel could not dance, but he staunchly remained for the whole ball, receiving endless attention from the students, especially compassionate young ladies.

Justin made sure that Scarlet spent quality time with Mel, which added to Mel's gratitude. Justin saw that Scarlet consciously preserved her stake in Mel's heart, just in case. Justin did not resent this and wondered why he didn't.

Justin danced, joked, smiled, shook hands, and accepted praise and congratulations till the ball drew to a close. But even as he gloried in his triumph, he remembered Devī's vital role in his success. He grieved within as he calculated how few were the days she would remain in this world.

Luke came to the dance at Justin's plea, and even danced a few times, though he clearly had Sara on his mind and in his heart. Justin knew him. Luke was fixed on Sara, and if necessary, would give up White Hall for her, though he would try to avoid that. His liberal parents gladly supported him with Sara, and would do so whether he studied at White Hall or another excellent school.

In the intimacy of their friendship, Justin learned from Luke that his parents were not wealthy. Dr. Tester earned a handsome salary as a senior scholar. But life in Southern California was expensive, and the Testers had been generous with less fortunate relatives. Moreover, Dr. Tester's intense focus on his career, with little time for rest, brought him both notoriety and health problems. His doctor now insisted that he adopt a lighter workload if he wished to live a long life. This further strained the family budget.

Yet, Dr. and Mrs. Tester were so fond of Sara that they now spoke of engaging a qualified lawyer to legally extract her from Stonewood. Luke's parents insisted that it was within their means to financially support an exceptional girl whom their son clearly loved, and whom his parents were coming to love as the daughter they had always wanted and never been blessed with. Sara, Luke, and Justin all received this news with a mixture of delight and trepidation. The more Sara was cared for, the easier it would be for Devī to leave this world.

Be that as it may, Justin deeply admired the entire Tester family. The parents' kindness enabled the son to follow his conscience and his heart in cultivating a clandestine relationship with Sara. It was also true that Luke had far less to lose at White Hall, as Luke himself often said.

At White Hall, everyone but Justin believed that the greatest reward for his heroism was the heightened interest and support of Senator and Mrs. Clay. The famous couple sent a personal note to Justin expressing their deep joy at the news of his valiant deed and his consequent reinstatement at White Hall, and as the leading candidate for Knighthood. The senator graciously invited Justin to visit him at Clay Campus. Justin instantly and enthusiastically agreed, though with clandestine motives.

The day came for the visit to Clay Campus, and as Justin hoped, Jack was scheduled to pick him up. Too nervous to speak to anyone, even Luke, Justin waited for the car. It arrived, but without Jack behind the wheel. The driver explained that Jack wanted to come but found he was too busy that day.

Was this Senator Clay's doing? Would Justin see Jack during this visit? Would he ever see Jack again?

At Clay Campus, Justin did see and greet Jack in the parking lot, but the day was cold. Jack wore gloves, and a turtleneck sweater under his coat. Justin could not test Devī's claim. He was deeply disappointed.

Justin met with the Clays. He studied them closely, though with utmost discretion. He found nothing suspicious in husband or wife. In fact, both were so kind and encouraging, so earnest and rational that only Justin's growing faith in Devī saved him from again doubting her. He recalled that the false Lokeśa had also been kind, encouraging, and rational—until he attacked. Devī insisted that world-famous Hunter Clay was an Asura who plotted again, with greater strength, to establish Asura rule over the world.

His meeting with the celebrated Clays was short and pleasant. And just as Justin must be fair to Devī, so his own father would demand that Justin be fair to the Clays. He still had no evidence against them. Jack did not drive him back to White Hall. *The Clays must know.* Yet he had no proof. He would not condemn anyone without clear evidence.

In the midst of this maddening web of loss, conquest, danger, and glory, one recollection haunted him in his rare quiet moments. He recalled, with a sense of tragic wonder, Devī's revelation of her own broken heart. Justin felt he had no power to mend that heart, and thus no power to keep Devī in this world. And without her, his own future looked bleak. Yes, Devī had assured him that he could simply withdraw from all heroic ambitions to serve the Avatāra and save the Earth. Justin and his family could thus live a prosperous life in safety.

This meant deferring his vow to the Avatāra to some future life. For the first time, Justin began to grasp the many ancient Sanskrit warnings about saṃsāra, the seemingly endless cycles of death and rebirth in a very imperfect world. To his own surprise, Justin realized that he was losing his taste for material glory. Each worldly life, though bringing rewards, was in its own way predictable and limited. Endlessly taking on new identities, new problems, new struggles, and new trophies—only to die at the end, and begin the process anew—this cycle of saṃsāra was definitely losing its charm in Justin's mind. Yet without Devī, such dizzying existential rotation was his fate.

But without Devī, Justin did not trust himself to face the Avatāra, and then to battle great Asuras with enhanced powers. All that was a steep mountain that Justin could not climb. Yet Devī was about to leave, and would not even hear his pleas. She had tired of his excuses, tired of his betrayal, every time his faith in her was seriously tested. He could not blame her, but he lamented his own weakness. His worldly prowess seemed trivial in the light of his spiritual weakness. He began to fear a world, a life, without Devī.

CHAPTER 40

Three days after the dance, school ended for Thanksgiving vacation. Justin and Scarlet flew together to Washington Dulles, where they first met. Scarlet would then fly to West Palm Beach, and Justin to far humbler Clarksburg, West Virginia.

Scarlet passed up a more direct connection through Charlotte, and Justin chose not to rent a car and drive home, which would have taken one-third the time. Scarlet wanted to celebrate in situ their first meeting, to spend quality time together away from the intense social pressure of White Hall. Justin could not say no, and he was happy to spend time with Scarlet, though it took all his self-command to act as if all was well in his life.

Carrying Scarlet's bags had been Justin's first service to the young lady when they met in September. With much mutual nostalgia, they reenacted that scene. Scarlet laughed at herself as she recounted how she had tried to board with all her heavy bags.

"I think I've matured a little since then," she said. "You really helped me. And you saved my life. I'll never forget that."

Justin blushed. "I'm honored that I could help you. Really. And you've helped me so much. I think both our lives have changed for the better."

At last, he and Scarlet embraced, wished each other a joyous holiday, and happily looked forward to meeting again very soon.

As his plane descended into the Clarksburg area, Justin tried to steady his racing, anguished mind. He must face his family and many friends who drove sixty-six miles of winding mountain road to escort their hero back to the tiny town that bore his family name.

Star and Joey could hardly express their joy at Justin's return. Hugs, kisses, and tears from his mother poured forth. Joey clung to Justin as if determined to never let him go. Seeing and embracing his family after months of separation, Justin knew that he could never act in a way that put them in danger of any kind. His family must come first. How then could he ever avenge his father or defend his planet?

But Justin could not dwell on such topics now, for he was surrounded by adoring old friends. Justin was a perfect gentleman as he greeted them all with personal attention. Everyone noticed and appreciated that White Hall had not made him proud. It was Justin Davis at his best.

His mother drove him back to Davis in a borrowed car, and on the way she and Joey begged to hear everything about White Hall, though Justin had already told them through various media all he was free to tell.

As Justin visited friends and acquaintances in Tucker County (no one could visit his house) the mantra on everyone's lips was: "We're so proud of you." Most solicited was a blow-by-blow description of Justin's rescue of his Knight friends and Scarlet from the bikers' attack.

Just as he had done as student president of Tucker County High School, Justin scrupulously attended to his social duties. He graciously consented when his mother told him they were to enjoy their Thanksgiving dinner as special guests of a leading Davis family. Star added, "They are making a vegan dinner in your honor. All the best families will be there, especially those who stayed by us."

The group included Principal and Mrs. Olsen. Dr. Olsen said repeatedly to anyone who would listen that Justin had fulfilled his dream for the boy. Even the Buntons, with their daughter, Sherri, and her steady, Ben, somehow wrangled an invitation and attended. As naive Ben looked on, Sherri made a few rather clumsy attempts to reignite Justin's old feelings for her, but he pretended not to notice. He did treat her nicely in every other way.

Justin regaled the group with all the tales he was free to tell. In the midst of these grand narrations, Scarlet called from Palm Beach with unplanned but nonetheless perfect timing. Hearing the dinner noise in the background, she thoughtfully refused to take him from family and friends. She just wanted to know how little Joey was doing. Justin explained that Joey's joy and pride in his brother's success had done much to lift him above past traumas, and lingering anxiety, and he looked better. Scarlet was relieved to hear this and Justin eagerly assured her that he would call back very soon.

Before hanging up, Justin passed the phone to Joey at Scarlet's request. Joey was thrilled. Justin happily discerned from Joey's words that Scarlet asked for his number and promised to call him.

As soon as the call ended, Joey announced to all that Scarlet, who just called Justin, was the Knight president's sister and was very, very close to Justin. This revelation produced knowing nods and dogged inquiries from neighbors, till Justin admitted he was seeing Scarlet and that she seemed to like him.

When further probing revealed that Scarlet lived in Palm Beach, it was time to praise the wealth and prestige of that fabulous island community and panegyrics rolled off many tongues.

As Justin endured these effusions, he remembered that Devī would soon leave this world. He thought of Jack and his scars, and a future fight to the death with a powerful Asura. As these thoughts assailed him, it took all of Justin's considerable diplomatic skill to play the part he must play with all his old friends and acquaintances.

He somehow put aside such thoughts. His family and friends expected and needed that he savor the moment with them. However, thoughts of his troubles sobered and even humbled him. He did his best to moderate the stories of his feats eagerly recounted around him. But many others were determined to exaggerate his deeds, both to please him, and to bask in his reflected light.

After the dinner, the Davis family returned alone to their trailer. Star Davis wanted only to be reassured that Justin was still Justin, that he had not in any way been harmed emotionally or morally in his time at White Hall. Justin could not reveal anything to his mother, or Joey, that would increase their anxiety and thus threaten her health.

If somehow this time, destiny allowed him to act boldly, as a hero, then to save his very life, he must keep his ancient vow to the Avatāra, the very existence of whom few in his life accepted, either in Tucker County or White Hall. Yet it was likely that he must somehow surrender to the Avatāra to save his own life.

CHAPTER 41

That night, Justin brooded alone in his still-shameful little room. Wind rustled about, shaking the creaking trailer. He called Luke to verify that Devī was still in this world. She was. Justin begged his friend for more information. Luke revealed all he knew from Sara. Devī would soon turn sixteen and receive her full inheritance. On that very day, she would meet with an old family friend, a judge who had looked after her affairs since the loss of Justin's father.

Justin asked about the meeting's purpose. Luke confirmed Justin's fear. "Devī will finalize her will," Luke said sadly. "Then, she will depart."

It was late and the conversation ended. Justin tried to sleep but sleep eluded him. He lay on his bed brooding over the future. In Bhū-loka, he had played it safe, or rather played it selfish. He had retreated from keeping his vow and defending the planet. He now saw clearly that a failed test must be taken again. It must be passed. The thought of fighting the Asura without Devī alarmed him. And yet, if Devī did leave this world, Justin would then be forced to submit fully to the Avatāra. Perhaps that was Devī's plan. Perhaps it was the Avatāra's plan. Now, he had no choice but to submit to the Avatāra. Devī had instructed him well. He knew what he must do. And how could he face his father in the hereafter if he did not bring justice to those who cruelly ended his life on Earth?

Still, Devī's imminent departure haunted him. If Devī spoke the truth and the Clays deceived him, then perhaps he, Justin, had driven away from himself and the world a pure soul who offered the greatest gifts.

Justin's mind raced from Devī to Jack, then to Hunter and Barbara Clay. He could not sleep. He quietly jumped out of bed, kneeled, and prayed for understanding. A modicum of peace came upon him and he slept.

When he awoke, his determination to avenge his father had grown stronger. He must not rest until he discovered the truth about his father's death. Hunter might try to prevent him from ever seeing Jack's scars, but Justin would find a way. But how? The answer came to him at once.

After losing his father, Justin had badgered his mother to tell him all she knew about the possible circumstances that led to the tragedy. Star Davis adamantly refused to speak about it because she feared for his safety. "I know your violent rage," she always said. "You must believe me. I do not know who the killer was, only that your father accepted a dangerous case to help an innocent person."

Justin now recalled that once, under his withering pressure, Star Davis let slip, only to instantly regret it, that his father might have left documents related to the murder. She gave those papers to the police, who examined and returned them, saying they led to no tangible leads, only untraceable suspicions.

Star Davis had revealed this hoping it would dissuade her son from further probing. But now Justin was desperate to find those papers. Based on what Devī told him, she and Justin might be the only people in the world who could decipher the papers. Only his mother might know where these papers were hidden, if they still existed. And she steadfastly refused to confirm that the papers did still exist. Justin knew his mother. She had no talent for insincerity. The papers existed. He must find them.

Fortunately, the very next day Star Davis took little Joey to the West Virginia University Children's Hospital in Morgantown for a checkup. They would be gone all day. They dearly wanted Justin to come but he insisted he needed to rest. Any hint of danger to the health of either of her sons caused instant alarm in their mother. Star Davis now insisted that Justin not come to Morgantown.

The second she left with Joey, Justin scoured the trailer for the papers. A locked box, hidden behind a broken radiator in a storage closet, raised high suspicion. He opened it with a hairpin and knife and found the precious papers within. He removed them, put blank paper in their place to maintain the box's weight, carefully reset the lock, and replaced the box in its exact hiding place.

Justin sat on the floor, spread the papers before him, and pored over them. He soon discovered a startling fact. Justin's father met Devī's father, James Brooks, at Virginia law school. They became close friends. This family-like connection with Devī struck Justin deeply. He sat back against the wall to absorb it, but soon rushed back to the papers.

He found more. When Devī's parents, James and Faith Brooks, left this world, Tark Davis helped to settle their affairs. Justin's father wrote, "The Brooks left almost all their estate to Devī. They adored her! Who could blame them? Devī is an angel. I confess here my hope that my son Justin may one day meet her. James and Faith met Justin when he was very little, so he doesn't remember."

This was extraordinary! As a young child, Justin met Devī's parents. And his father called Devī an angel, which might be close to the literal truth. Justin read on.

"The Brooks told me quite seriously that their little Devī has a mission in this world. Indeed, sometimes James and Faith spoke as if their only purpose in this world was to help their daughter and her mission. I asked about it and they promised to tell me, but suddenly they left this world."

Were Devī's parents themselves victims of the Asuras? Justin continued to read. "The court-appointed trustee for the Brooks estate died suddenly. Another close relative was appointed and also died. At this point, the police of course suspected foul play, but they had no evidence and could prove nothing. The court appointed a third trustee, who did not die, raising suspicions that this person murdered their way to their position. I tried hard to discover the new trustee's identity, to no avail. The new trustee is concealed behind an impenetrable firewall of proxies, aliases and non-disclosure agreements. However, I have one last stratagem, which just might reveal the truth of this matter. However, I have a growing sense that I am being followed and watched. It is almost as if I am challenging a powerful evil that knows what I am doing and even what I am thinking. I know this sounds crazy and it even seems so to me. I spoke to Devī about my fear and she insisted that I take no risk. In fact, truth be told, she has insisted for quite some time that I am putting myself in danger and should give up my investigation. She begged me not to risk my own safety. Now I see that she was right. I hope it is not too late. I end with this note: whoever now controls Devī's estate added a clause stating that if Devī dies, which I cannot bear to imagine, the Trustee has power to give the estate to a charity of the trustee's choice. This leaves far too much room for mischief. I fear the conspirators will kill Devī. The very thought is unbearable. Yet this amazing young girl regularly assures me she can take care of herself, and she says it in so convincing a tone that I find myself almost believing her."

Justin paused and sighed. If only his dear father had known how true Devī's statement was, he might not have put himself in mortal danger. This was an exceedingly painful thought, and it took Justin some time to recover from the anguish it provoked.

He returned to his father's text, only to be devastated again, for he read, "I sense I am dealing with a dangerous evil beyond what I can understand. Naturally, my life may be in danger."

Hardly breathing, Justin checked the date of this last entry. His father wrote it just days before his death. The killer surely feared that Tark Davis was about to learn the truth about Devī's enemies.

Anguish, rage, and a lust for vengeance overwhelmed Justin. Recalling that all his rage would be useless against an Asura foe, Justin fell to his knees and offered himself to the Avatāra as a most willing servant. He begged Kṛṣṇa to empower him to bring justice to the Asuras. He pleaded for the chance to avenge his dear father.

Then, as if in response, a figure appeared before him—it was not Kṛṣṇa, but Justin's father, Tark Davis, appearing in a vision, rather than in a tangible physical form. But the soul of his father had come to him, or was sent by the Avatāra, in a recognizable form. Justin knew that his father had appeared now to instruct him, and every nerve strained to hear his words. Just as he had always done, his father told him to battle evil wisely and fairly, lest evil absorb him into itself. His father paused, fixed Justin in his gaze, and said, "Let the higher power lead you to victory."

His father's image then vanished as quickly as it had come. Yet his words echoed in Justin's mind—"Battle evil wisely and fairly, lest evil absorb you into itself. Let the higher power lead you to victory."

These words confirmed that a battle was indeed coming, and that Justin's only hope of survival and victory lay in his full surrender to the Avatāra.

Justin also fixed in his mind his father's call for wisdom and fairness. In fact, at this moment, Justin's rage had no fair object. He had not proved to himself that Senator Clay was involved. In fact, even if Jack had the telltale scars, they might not be admissible as evidence in court. How could Justin take justice into his own hands? How could he act as a mere vigilante? He would predictably be caught, ruin his life, ruin his family's life, fail the Avatāra, and no doubt displease his father, the very person for whom he was acting.

Desperate to calm his mind, Justin thought of Devī. Through his father's eyes, Justin saw Devī as if for the first time. His father's vision of Devī as a pure soul, an angel, transformed, or perhaps restored, Justin's own vision of her.

Tark Davis gave his life for Devī. If only Devī would stay in this world, he would help her and together they could honor his father's great sacrifice. But with or without Devī, Justin could not know how to proceed until he confirmed Jack's role in the murder. He could not be absolutely sure that ostensibly good people had committed horrible crimes, people who had repeatedly helped him, without final evidence. Justin would follow objective legal standards, as his father did, before even mentally condemning other people. It was a very difficult vow, hard to keep, but he must try to be like his father.

Unfortunately, in the indeterminate time that Justin took to find evidence, *if* he found it, the villains had all the time in the world to plot against him. Once Justin had his proof, they could strike anywhere, at any time.

Justin returned to the papers and found his father's contact list. Next to the name Blake Eliot, Tark Davis wrote *Boston lawyer, trustworthy, excellent man.* This was of utmost importance. Justin immediately called Mr. Elliot, who was deeply moved to speak with the son of Tark Davis. Trusting his father's strong recommendation, Justin told Mr. Eliot, now Judge Eliot, all he had read in his father's papers.

Judge Eliot was not surprised. "Your father and I discussed these issues many times. Thank you for trusting me as he did. I never contacted you because your father made me swear on my life, repeatedly, not to reveal any of this to his family. He feared it would endanger you all, and he was probably right. That's why I never contacted any of you. But now that you know, I will not break my promise if I confirm what you learned from him. I do confirm every word. I assume you will not share this information with your family."

"No, sir, not even a word. They will never know."

"Good," the judge said. "If they knew, it would only put them in more danger than they are already in."

These words horrified Justin. "But why do they care about me or my family? We are all powerless." Justin thought it wise not to mention the Avatāra at this time to the judge.

"You may not be as powerless as you think," Judge Eliot said. "Neither of us fully understands what is going on. What I do know is that you, Justin, must be extremely careful. Do not investigate this matter any further. The consequences could be most tragic, as they already have been."

Justin assured the judge he would follow his instructions. Then he broached another vital issue. "I've heard," Justin said, "that you and Devī will meet on her birthday, December 6."

"You know that?" the judge said, astonished. "No one but Devī and me, and one other person, knows Devī's legal affairs. Well, I see you gained her trust, or that of someone very close to her."

Justin took this as praise, and confirmation that the judge would meet with Devī.

"Do you have any idea," Justin asked, "what Devī plans to do after she settles her legal affairs with you?"

"No, I don't," the judge replied. "She will not disclose that even to me. She only insisted on finalizing her will. We will do it when I come on her birthday, which, as you know, is Friday, December 6th. We will begin our work that day and conclude by early afternoon on Saturday. I told her we could do it later, but she said no delay. And when that girl makes up her mind, no one can stop her."

"I know that to be true." Justin understood exactly why Devī insisted on settling her will at once. She wanted no delay in her departure from this world. Justin shivered, but concealed his emotions.

"Anyway," Judge Elliot continued, "I would be happy to see you after I see Devī, if you have time. It would mean a lot to me to meet the son of Tark Davis. It would have to be the evening of December 7th, Saturday. Does that work for you?"

"Yes, of course," Justin said. "Thank you so much. It will be my honor to meet you. Just tell me when and where and I'll be there."

They agreed to meet at six p.m. in the White Hall faculty lounge, to which the judge had access through old friends. With a few more kind words on each side, the call ended. Justin then pondered what he had learned from this call. He recalled with conflicted emotions the judge's surprise that Devī trusted him so much. Devī knew that Sara would tell Luke, who would tell Justin. Devī's intimate trust of him inspired gratitude, but also much pain in his heart. Clearly Devī had trusted him more than he had trusted her.

This fact deepened his sorrow at Devī's departure, which even the judge seemed not to understand. Justin pondered anxiously if he should reveal this danger to the judge. He decided to wait a few more days. He would return to White Hall soon, and if Devī had not changed her mind, Justin would mobilize everyone that had any influence with Devī to urge her to stay.

Finding no other vital information in his father's papers, Justin carefully replaced them in the box after removing the blank sheets. He reset the lock, and put the box exactly where it had been.

After all that had passed between them in two different ages, Justin tried to understand his feelings for Devī. This was not a question to be easily answered. Certainly, his ancient annoyance with her, his eagerness to be free of her, had long found no place in his heart. After the Clays made their accusations against her, he had been thrown into doubt and confusion. That too was rapidly dissipating. He held her in great esteem, he admired her, he now remembered fondly their brief happy times together and lamented that such moments might never return. He knew that Devī was his spiritual superior. His deep respect for her, which bordered on awe and reverence, overcame the more tender feelings that he feared to release from the chambers of his heart. And yet, he could not deny that in some inexplicable way, he did love Devī.

He looked out at the dark, dreary sky and thought of Devī on the other side of the mountains, enduring the same dismal night. But it was foolish to pity her. She was with Kṛṣṇa. Indeed, in this mortal world, everyone but Devī was to be pitied.

CHAPTER 42

Justin returned to White Hall on Sunday, December 1st. Flight schedules did not allow Justin and Scarlet to meet again in Dulles airport, but they did arrange to arrive in Charlottesville about the same time. The weather was unseasonably warm when they happily met at the small Albemarle County Airport. Scarlet had chosen to ride back to campus with Justin on the White Hall bus. Eagerly conversing, they strolled out toward the school bus just as a familiar black Escalade slowly passed them and pulled up to the curb about ten yards in front of them. It was Jack Cutter, bringing someone to the airport. Justin tried not to shake. This was the moment. Devī told him to check Jack's scars. Scars would mean this man murdered Justin's father. Justin fought for self-control, but his chest heaved.

"What is wrong with you? What is it?" Scarlet asked.

"Oh nothing." Justin feigned nonchalance. "Must be the jet lag."

"What jet lag? You didn't even change time zone."

Justin flipped his hands in the air to make light of his remark, but Scarlet watched him closely. Justin didn't notice. He focused with every nerve on Jack. An elegant young man got out of the car and walked back to the trunk to get his luggage. Justin recognized him as Brad Branley, who was becoming an ever-more-trusted member of the senator's team.

Brad looked toward Justin, who darted behind a pillar. Scarlet followed him, a quizzical look on her face. If only Brad would enter the terminal, Justin could surreptitiously try to get a good look at Jack.

Jack, who had been on his phone, now got out of the car and helped remove Brad's luggage from the trunk. In the mild weather, Jack wore a polo shirt with the top two buttons open. No gloves. This was Justin's chance—perhaps his only chance.

Brad Branley entered the terminal while Jack rummaged through the car trunk, still with his back to Justin. "Just one second," he whispered to Scarlet. "Wait here."

Before she could answer, he moved swiftly and silently toward Jack's car till he stood close behind him. Jack leaned forward into the trunk. As he did, the back of his shirt slid down his thick neck. Taking advantage of the angle, Justin came right behind Jack and stared at his exposed upper back. Justin saw two ugly scars precisely where he struck his father's killer. Justin's heart raced wildly. He still had to see Jack's hands.

Suddenly Brad came out of the terminal and walked back to Jack's car. He instantly recognized Justin and called out to him. Jack whirled around, saw Justin right behind him, and furiously shouted, "What are you doing here? Why the hell did you sneak up on me?"

Brad stared at Jack, clearly taken aback by his language.

Justin recovered at once. "Sorry, Jack, I was just coming to say hello. I didn't mean to startle you. How are you?"

Justin held out his hand. Jack did not shake it. "Hey, Jack," Brad said, "calm down and shake the guy's hand. Here, I'll show you how to do it."

Laughing, Brad came over and shook hands with Justin. Then Justin held out his hand again to Jack, who could not refuse. Jack had a strong grip, but so did Justin. He held Jack's hand tightly, and moved it up and down till he clearly saw the scars he caused years ago with an iron poker.

Jack pulled his hand back, and giving Justin a cold, wicked smile, said, "Sorry I spoke that way. You really startled me."

Justin met Jack's gaze with a fierce stare. "Not at all, Jack, I'm really glad we met like this."

"Are you really?" Jack reverted to a menacing tone. "Remember the old saying, curiosity killed the cat. Did you hear that? Curiosity killed the cat. So here's a friendly warning, don't prowl around like a cat. Let's shake hands on that."

Jack extended his hand. At that moment, Scarlet, tired of waiting, walked up to Justin standing defiantly, staring at Jack's hand. Scarlet nudged him. "Justin, he wants to shake hands with you."

Immersed in heavy thoughts and feelings, Justin did not notice her. But another, harder, nudge from Scarlet brought him back. He saw the need to avoid public attention and so he shook Jack's hand. Jack tried to crush Justin's hand, but Justin was too strong and Jack pulled his hand back.

Scarlet saw only that Justin was not being his usual polite, gregarious self, and so to compensate, she took over the social duties. She thanked Jack with enthusiasm, laughed and said, "Justin is so excited about seeing his family! I can't get him to think or talk about anything else."

"Of course he's thinking about his family," Jack said, with a knowing look at Justin. "That's very nice. Let's hope his family is well and stays that way."

Jack spoke in his usual gruff, unschooled voice, and Scarlet took his clear threat to Justin as a sincere if crude wish for the best. Scarlet then dragged Justin away and Jack drove off. This was a rare moment, Justin thought, when Scarlet did not understand what was happening around her.

Scarlet tightly grabbed Justin's arm and whispered in his ear, "What is wrong, Justin Davis? You look crazy. Let's get on the bus before people wonder about us." Still holding his arm, Scarlet dragged him to the back of the bus, sat him in the corner, and sat next to him, shielding him from everyone's view.

"Tell me right now what's wrong," she said with genuine concern. "I'm worried about you. You were fine a few minutes ago."

Justin mumbled his apologizes, insisting that so much was going on in his life that he spaced out and forgot where he was.

"You can hardly expect me to believe that," she said. "What happened? What triggered your... state?"

Scarlet knew him well. Yet, for her own safety, he must deceive her. He revealed real problems, to lend authenticity to his deceit.

"I never told you this," Justin said, with a sad, downward gaze, "but my kid brother has serious medical problems, and we can't afford the medical care he really needs. Our insurance won't cover it. They say cheaper treatments will help as much. But they don't. I love my brother so much. I'm upset and worried. It's hard for me to talk about it."

Scarlet pressed his two hands in hers. "Justin, you should have told me. I will personally get the money for your brother. I won't let him suffer. You have my word."

At that moment, Justin felt more true affection for Scarlet than ever before. "I don't know what to say," he said, "just that you are a most cherished friend, and always will be."

She looked at him as if to say, "Only a friend?" He smiled back as if to say, you know you're more than that. They both shrewdly refrained from saying more. But he was most grateful, and Scarlet again assured him that she would help his brother. Scarlet never spoke whimsically about serious matters.

As the bus moved south on Earlysville Road and crossed the Rivanna Reservoir, Justin could think of nothing but his father's killer. Surely

Jack acted under the order of Senator Clay. Jack did nothing without Hunter's approval, and certainly not a high-profile murder.

Justin reminded himself that his father demanded justice of him. He had no evidence the Clays were involved. All along the familiar route, from Woodland Road to Free Union Road to Garth Road, Scarlet stared with real concern at Justin, who felt and looked as if he were in a state of shock.

As they neared White Hall, the piercing sound of sirens jolted them. The bus pulled to the side. Police cars, fire trucks, and ambulances all raced by with sirens blaring. There was a serious problem ahead. The bus cautiously resumed its journey. The sirens stopped. The emergency was close. Everyone in the bus put their heads out the windows to see what it was, but the curving road concealed the problem. Cars ahead of them slowed and stopped. As the bus inched its way around a bend in the winding road, they saw a tall, gray smoke plume whirling into the sky. A highway patrol officer stood in the road, signaling with open palms that all vehicles should move even slower. Justin strained to see the fire, but the road's many curves still concealed it.

Around another curve, Justin saw flames shooting up in the distance. Was a fire loose in the forest? Traffic stopped for several minutes, then moved at a crawl, only to stop again. As the bus inched its way around another curve, Justin saw that the fire flared not from the forest, but from the road itself. The emergency vehicles surrounded a crumpled, smoking heap of metal. Shocked, Justin feared the victim or victims were from White Hall, perhaps someone he knew. Many students had gone ahead in their own cars. Thank God Scarlet was in the bus.

As the bus crawled forward, Justin saw that fire crews surrounded the mangled remains of a car. Afraid to look, but unable to avert his eyes, Justin made out the remains of a black car. After a few more feet, he saw that it was a black Escalade. As the bus detoured onto the shoulder and passed the wreck, Justin rushed to the other side of the bus, stared out, and saw the remains of Jack Cutter, still sitting behind the wheel, dead and burning.

Scarlet, and many others on the bus, cried out in horror and looked away. Though equally horrified by the sight, Justin could not suppress thoughts of divine justice. Even as he quickly began to comfort Scarlet, and dealt with his own shock, Justin realized that Jack's revealing scars would never be seen in a court of law.

Justice was done. But was this divine justice, a mere accident, or a timely assassination? Could it be mere coincidence that Jack Cutter died less than an hour after Justin discovered his guilt? Had someone with extraordinary powers of perception silenced Jack forever? Had someone at the airport watched Justin watch Jack? It could have been Brad Branley or other agents of the senator. Justin had no way to assess the extent of the senator's intelligence network, but he judged from the senator's casual remarks that the network was quite extensive.

Weighing the probabilities, Justin settled on murder as his working hypothesis. Did whoever killed Jack Cutter fear that once on the trail, Justin's investigations would connect Jack to the real author behind the murder of Tark Davis? What if Senator Clay was an Asura with the same power as Devī to view remote events? Devī insisted that Asuras and yogīs have similar material powers.

Justin realized with a shock how powerful his possible enemies might be, and how vulnerable he and his family were. Jack openly threatened Justin's family. He recalled how easily the Bhū-loka Asura humiliated him, and would have killed him. Danger could be lurking anywhere. The bus might be the next target of a crazed Asura.

"Justin!" Scarlet whispered. "You look white. Your hand is shaking."

"Oh, is it?" Justin tightened his hands into fists and shook his head like a punch-drunk boxer trying to revive. "It was just the sight of that car, of Jack."

"Of course." Scarlet again squeezed his hands. "It shocked me too. And you knew Jack better than me."

"Yes, I did," Justin said, "that is true. I'll be okay."

His joyful airport reunion with Scarlet, less than an hour ago, was all the joy he would have for now. With the shock of his father's papers, his dread of Devī's departure, his discovery that Jack was the killer, and with Jack's violent end just now—it was a grim Justin Davis who rolled into White Hall on the same bus that first took him there months before.

As he walked Scarlet to her residence hall, he apologized for his state of mind. But the revelation of his brother's medical condition, and the death in the road, fully disposed Scarlet to be kind and understanding. They parted as true well-wishers, each of the other.

As Justin walked back to his room, he did not know which trauma to focus on. But he was spared this onerous decision by his phone's special ring that indicated a call from Joey.

Joey had bid his brother farewell that very morning, but now missed him more than ever. Right now, keeping Joey happy was job number one. And Joey had ecstatic news—just minutes earlier, he received a call from Scarlet, who asked about his health and even promised to help him. Seeing Joey so happy, and receiving proof of Scarlet's real goodness, Justin wept.

Luke entered their room, and Justin told him about the scars. Luke had always believed that Devī spoke the truth, but he was still shocked to hear the confirmation.

"It is absolutely vital," Luke said, "that we penetrate the Clay Campus firewall and find out what they are really doing. Your life may depend on it."

"How is it going?" Justin asked. "You've been trying to hack them for a while."

"I didn't have much trouble with their software firewalls," Luke said, "but I'm stuck on the hardware barriers that are of course more difficult. I got in the front door of their system, so to speak. but the main rooms are still locked. I'm sorry. I won't give up."

Justin thanked Luke and encouraged him to keep trying. Justin's first duty was clear. In the midst of discoveries and traumas, he must put his family and true friends first. Jack had confirmed what Devī often told him—the Asuras would target him if he interfered in any way with their project. Shaken to the core by the day's events, Justin saw that he needed the Knights more than ever. If he pulled back from his investigation of his father's death, the Asuras would likely spare him, or perhaps only harass him in ways that he could deflect with the help of powerful friends. The Knights could help protect him and his family not only personally but through their vast network of powerful contacts. The Knight Network, as it was called, could mobilize high government officials in defense of the Davis family. The Knight Network could deploy extraordinary measures. In short, Justin must become a Knight.

Monday, December 2nd, passed uneventfully, at least externally. Internally, Justin mentally rolled through his short list of crises—Devī was leaving; he knew his father's killer and could do nothing about it; and he would likely be killed just for knowing the killer.

But the heaviest blow fell the next day, on December 3rd. Star Davis called Justin from the Davis Medical Center in Elkins, West Virginia, about an hour southwest of Davis. Through her tears, she related that

Joey's health had taken a sudden and dangerous turn for the worse. His stress-related symptoms, that began with the trauma of losing his father, were the usual ones—decreased appetite, crying for no apparent reason, headaches and stomach pain, and recurrent nightmares. Justin knew that these symptoms, if left unaddressed, could lead to permanent emotional and physical consequences for a younger brother who adored him.

Justin insisted on returning home at once, but his mother explained that Joey was out of danger for now, but his future depended more than ever on medical treatment they could not afford. Joey was under sedation, but as soon as possible, Justin would speak with him.

This was too much. Justin sat on the floor of his room, weeping. Scarlet had promised help, but Justin knew from conversations with her that she needed time to take a significant amount of money from her trust fund. Luke found Justin in a broken state, learned the cause and tried to comfort him, but to no avail. Luke stayed for some time, but Justin could not speak.

"I'm here anytime you need me," Luke said softly and left the room.

After some time, Justin could no longer bear the depressing confines of his room. He walked toward the woods and met Scarlet on the way. Her expression told him that Luke told her about Joey.

"We'll do something," Scarlet insisted. "I promise you, we'll do something to help Joey. I'm working on it." He thanked her from his heart. She gave him hope.

The next day, Wednesday, December 4th, Justin woke early thinking of Joey. Desperate to help his brother, he even considered approaching the Clays, but rejected the idea. He must at all costs keep the Clays away from his family. Luke had offered to approach his parents, but Justin knew that Luke's father had his own health problems related to a stressful workload, and that his doctor demanded that he reduce it. The Testers were generous people, and had not accumulated significant savings. Justin knew they would take a loan to save Joey, but the pressure of repayment could threaten Dr. Tester's health.

Justin even considered that in a few days Devī would receive her inheritance, which might be large, and that she would give some of it to Sara and Luke. But Judge Eliot had indicated in a different context that he was unsure how quickly funds would actually be available to Devī. Still, it was a possibility. But Luke, knowing Justin's urgency, had said nothing about it, which convinced Justin that the possibility was not a serious one.

Unsure of where to turn, Justin spent the day lost in anxiety. But in the evening, Justin's mother called him with news so wonderful, she could hardly pronounce the words to tell him. A gentleman had called her that morning from a bank and enquired about Joey and the cost of his treatment. He then assured her that the money would be wired to her bank that very day. Excited and bewildered, she asked the man's name. He replied that he was acting on behalf of the actual donor, and that for now both of them must remain anonymous. He would say no more.

"Within hours," Star Davis exclaimed, "twice the amount needed came to our account! Twice the amount needed for Joey!" Mrs. Davis broke into tears of joy. "It was a most generous gift. I've already scheduled Joey's treatment. I'm sure Joey's going to get better!"

Neither Justin nor his mother could express all the gratitude they felt. Scarlet must have done this through her lawyer. He could never thank her enough. And some day he would happily repay her with interest. But for now, he would strictly honor her noble wish for anonymity. Thus, in reply to his mother's anxious inquiry as to whom they were so indebted, Justin replied that he had no idea.

Justin soon met Luke, who was startled by Justin's ecstatic mood. But Justin quickly explained everything, emphasizing the need to respect the selfless anonymity of his benefactor. Luke knew that Scarlet had offered to help Joey, and Justin smiled knowingly when Luke asked if Scarlet was indeed the donor. Luke agreed that it was a most selfless, admirable act on the donor's part.

On December 5th, Thursday, the Knights would reveal next semester's new members. Justin had received encouraging hints from his Knight friends. Thursday came. The Knights accepted Justin as a new member, to be formally inducted with other new members on Sunday, December 8th, at Knight Rite. After months of anxiety, fear, depression, scheming, and dreaming, Justin was to be a Knight. On receiving this news, which would take some time to assimilate, he called his mother and brother. More than anyone, they deserved to share his joy, and they did with ecstatic hearts and loving words. Scarlet was next, though she already knew, long before he did.

What would Devī think? This was a question he thought it best not to ponder. Devī refused to see him, and it was impossible for Justin to see her in the days leading up to Knight Rite. By tradition, from Thursday to Sunday, all successful Knight candidates, when not in class or sleeping, remained in constant Knight company as a final, grueling examination. Further contact with Devī, even if she agreed, was now impossible. That fact prevented Justin from shedding his gravity in the joy of Knighthood. In an ironic, even cruel twist, Knight Rite might well take place the day that Devī left this world, perhaps at the same time.

Another thought intruded on Justin's joy. Senator and Mrs. Clay would very likely attend Knight Rite, perhaps as guests of honor. Justin struggled to understand how he should or could deal with that. No answer came.

Luke was gone when Justin reached his room, but he soon returned and the two dear friends embraced. Justin was now convinced that Luke really had been Lokeśa, and that Sara was Sarit. With Devī's determined plan to leave, Luke and Sara were all he had left of Bhū-loka.

The two friends discussed Justin's Knighthood, Devī's departure, and the danger posed by Senator Clay. Luke was as concerned about all this as Justin himself. The two friends went over it all again and again, seeking the best course of action.

Speaking from desperation, Justin again asked Luke if there was any possible way to keep Devī in this world. Luke's reply crushed any last hope. "Devī is leaving," he said. "Sara and I are both devastated. Devī won't even speak to us about it. We would do anything to keep her with us, but there is nothing we can do. And we know it would be wrong to hold Devī back."

CHAPTER 43

On Friday, December 6th, Scarlet informed Justin that Tom and Mel had invited her to join them on a walk in the woods, during which they would go over the final arrangements for Knight Rite, to be held in two days. In fact, behind the scenes, Scarlet was managing the event for her brother, to whom she insisted that Justin come along, since on their last trek in the woods, Justin saved all their lives. Tom liked the idea, and Mel liked it because Scarlet proposed it.

Of course, Justin would not participate in the discussions of Knight Rite, but the invitation was still a great compliment and a most promising omen of Knighthood. Justin eagerly accepted.

However, another important event that day dampened the jubilation he might have felt. Today was Devī's birthday. In the afternoon, she would meet with Judge Eliot, to settle her estate. This was to be her last action before leaving the world. Her meeting with the judge would conclude the next day, Saturday. Later Saturday, Justin would meet with the judge. And Sunday would be Knight Rite. It was a chilling irony that on the very day that Justin had so long dreamed of, Devī might not be in this world.

Still, Justin owed much to Scarlet. Above all, her generous gift to Joey could never be forgotten nor appreciated enough. Justin also believed that Scarlet had vigorously advocated for his Knighthood in private talks with her brother. Since both gifts were offered anonymously, Justin was forced to repress his urge to openly thank her.

"What are you thinking?" Scarlet asked Justin, as they all set out on their walk.

"Nothing," he said, cheerfully.

"Are you happy, Justin?" she asked, as Mel and Tom discussed another matter.

"Of course," he said. "I'm with you."

"Are you really with me?" she asked with an arch smile. Scarlet was very smart. Justin could not forget Devī's birthday and all it meant.

Tom called the walking meeting to order, and sent Justin twenty yards to the rear, for which Justin was quietly grateful, glad for the chance to think over his life. The committee walked into a little clearing and sat on smooth rocks, while Justin explored the riverbank. The wind, birds, and river wove a beguiling contrapuntal harmony.

After a while, Scarlet tired of the meeting and went to find Justin. She playfully led him here and there to gaze at a variety of natural objects. She called to Mel and Tom to join them, but they shouted back that they were just about to conclude some important issues.

As Scarlet turned back to Justin, the wind calmed, the birds rested, and even the river seemed to hush. Scarlet put her finger to her lips, and they happily relished the silence around them, till a new sound drifted toward them. It was a light, sure step descending the hill in front of them. Scarlet again put her finger to her lips and whispered playfully, "Let's go see who's coming. We'll greet them!"

She grabbed Justin's arm and led him up the path. Their fellow trekker, about thirty yards ahead, came into partial view through the trees. It was a young lady.

Scarlet was in high spirits. Still holding Justin's arm, she pulled him close and whispered, "There she is. Let's go say hello!" Another few steps and they stood face to face with a lovely girl in handsome outdoor clothes. Scarlet smiled, said hello, and waved with one hand, still clinging to Justin with the other. The girl returned her greeting in a clear voice. Justin froze in disbelief. It was Devī. Scarlet nudged him, reminding him to say hello, which he did, like a startled spirit looking down at his own body.

Devī nodded in reply. Justin would have released Scarlet's arm, but that would raise suspicion in both girls. And so, he stood somewhat miserably in front of Devī with Scarlet still clinging to him.

This was probably the last time he would see Devī, the only chance to beg her to stay, yet with Scarlet fully present and holding onto him, very little could be said.

He looked at Devī. Their eyes locked for a moment. Both looked away. Justin saw that Devī's beauty and poise impressed Scarlet, who did not recognize Devī from Laurie's house.

Scarlet turned to Justin. With surprise, she saw the sudden and acute discomfort he could not conceal. He had never been so embarrassed and confused in Scarlet's presence as he was now. Behind a smiling veneer, Scarlet's eyes now radiated suspicion, tinged with jealousy.

Her eyes darted from Justin to the girl, who looked away from Justin more than would be normal for two strangers.

Throughout her acquaintance with Justin, Scarlet confidently assumed that there was no other girl in Justin's life. Justin had told her that he was still considering whether he was ready for a serious relationship. But there was never a doubt that, should he be ready, Scarlet was the only possible candidate. Both Justin and Scarlet focused on their careers, and approached a relationship with caution. But that relationship, should it come to be, could only be with each other. Scarlet did keep a small hope alive in Mel, but both Justin and Scarlet knew that to be plan B.

At the moment, to her great surprise, Scarlet saw Justin bewildered by the sudden appearance of a very lovely young lady whom he obviously knew. Scarlet's concern was palpable, though her manners toward Devī were impeccable.

Scarlet felt too awkward to chat with Devī. Justin was too stunned to speak, and Devī seemed eager to escape. Relief came to this impossible situation when Tom and Mel joined them. Seeing a very pretty young lady in their midst, and Scarlet disinclined to speak, and Justin strangely silent, Tom happily assumed the required social duties, introducing himself to Devī, and asking her name.

She said, "Devī."

They must think it's Davie, Justin thought.

"It's a pleasure to meet you," Tom said.

Indeed, Devī had never looked lovelier. A vigorous hike filled her cheeks with color. Her large eyes glowed with mystery. Something was changed that only Justin could see. Devī's shining hair, normally neat and kempt, fell untamed about her face and shoulders. And in the late fall chill, she had no hat or proper coat. But it was Justin who shivered, for he knew how to read these signs. Devī had begun to withdraw from this world. Yet Tom and Mel gazed at Devī in wonder, for in her gradual disengagement from Earth, she glowed more than ever, as if she saw no further need to publicly conceal her true spiritual status. But even in her detachment, Devī deeply scanned all that was going on, in her usual way that Justin knew so well.

Fascinated by this new acquaintance, Tom eagerly chatted with Devī about her hiking route, how long she had been out today, etc. When a chilly wind blew, Tom kindly asked Devī if she felt cold without a coat.

"Thank you for your concern," Devī said. "I've spent much time in the mountains, and I'm quite acclimated to this sort of weather."

"Are you sure? I have several layers on and I would be happy to share one with you."

Devī smiled and graciously declined. By now, Scarlet's keen analytic gears had fully powered on, and she paid close attention to every word Devī spoke. Fortunately, this gave Justin time to recover from his shock and perform a reasonable imitation of his normal self.

In Scarlet's presence, Mel had to moderate his fascination with Devī, but he did ask her, "Do you live in the area?"

"No, I don't," she said amiably. "I came to visit a friend. But it didn't work out, and I'm leaving soon."

Devī's words disconcerted Justin, but what could he do? How could he plead with Devī to stay in front of his White Hall friends? Scarlet, sharp as a razor in such matters, already saw too much. If he spoke to Devī in code, urging her to stay, Scarlet would decrypt it.

"I'm sorry you're leaving, Devī," Scarlet said, with a delighted glance at Justin. "Where will you be going?"

"I'm going to stay with my father. He's traveling, and I'll join him."

Justin knew she spoke of Kṛṣṇa.

"That's so nice," Tom said. "I'm sorry if we're bothering you with all these questions."

"Not at all," Devī said graciously. Tom smiled and nodded.

Mel was going to ask something, but a look from Scarlet aborted his attempt. Tom asked, "Where do you live when you're not traveling?"

"I'm in transition," Devī said. "My father has homes in many places, so I'll choose one."

Though Justin knew this to be an oblique reference to the Avatāra, to the other White Hallians, Devī's words sounded very much like major wealth, and this instantly captured their attention, even Scarlet's.

Devī added, "My father and I will travel together trying to do good to people who need our help."

"That is truly admirable," Tom said.

Even Scarlet nodded her agreement, which gave permission to Mel to also appreciate what Devī said.

Throughout this exchange, Justin had repeatedly tried to communicate with Devī through his eyes and expressions, for she always understood him. He begged her to stay. But this time, whatever she might have felt, Devī acted like a normal girl who could not read people's minds. She did occasionally glance at him in a way that he longed to interpret as favorable and concerned. But he doubted himself.

At the first lull in the conversation, Devī thanked the White Hallians and said, "Please forgive me, but I really must go. I wish you all the best."

Tom bid Devī goodbye most graciously. Mel emulated Tom as far as he could in Scarlet's presence. Scarlet was polite and proper. Justin wanted to say so much, but could say none of it. And so, he looked most sincerely at Devī and said, "It was a pleasure." For a moment their eyes met and Justin imagined that he saw something like regret in her expression. But then she turned away and started her journey back up the mountain.

Justin missed Devī the moment she left. On the way back to White Hall, Tom praised Devī, and asked the others their opinion. Mel agreed with Tom. Pensive and silent, Scarlet smiled and nodded. Justin yearned to tell his friends who Devī really was and what they all owed to her. But he dared not do that now. Yet, if he spoke as if he did not know Devī, Scarlet would see his duplicity. So, he simply said, "It was an interesting encounter." He then joined Scarlet in silence and let Tom and Mel carry the conversation till they reached White Hall.

When they arrived, Tom rushed off to his office to organize his notes from their meeting on Knight Rite. He insisted that Mel come with him. With great reluctance, Mel left Scarlet in the sole company of Justin.

When the two men left, Scarlet said, "Justin, I know who Devī is."

"You do?"

"Of course. She's the girl we saw at the Wolfe house. I'm quite sure you remember."

"Yes, I do."

"And she is the girl who sheltered you from the storm. Am I correct?"

"Yes, of course. Why didn't you mention it to the others?"

"Because I wanted to observe Devī. If I revealed that she was from Stonewood, Tom and Mel would have insisted we leave, and that would have hurt Devī, whom I believe is not a bad person. And it would have deprived me of a chance to learn more about a person who, I must admit, fascinates me. So, you and I are partners in crime, since we both knew who Devī was, and we both remained there. I'm not as inflexible about some rules as Tom. And I know you share my feelings."

"Yes, I do. Thank you very much. I mean that sincerely."

Scarlet smiled. "So, I had no idea who Devī was, nor did you. Deal?"

"Yes, deal!" They smiled with mutual affection, and heartily shook hands.

"Thank you. There is another point we should discuss."

"All right," he said. He knew from her tone that something serious was coming.

"Justin, it is quite clear that you have strong feelings for that girl."

Justin saw that evasion here was both futile and unfair to Scarlet. He must speak a good portion of truth.

He began, "I discovered when I was in Davis just now that my dear, departed father actually knew Devī's family. He even helped to protect her estate."

The role of that service in his father's death was too painful to speak, and so Justin moved on. "Regarding my feelings for Devī, yes, I do feel very bad that a bright, sincere girl from a good family has been a victim of cruel persecution and slander. She has been called a witch, ostracized and despised when in fact she is a most virtuous young lady."

"Virtuous young lady? Impressive. Do you love her, Justin?"

"Yes, but, not in the way that boys love girls. Devī has no interest in worldly relationships. If anyone approached her in that way, she would be offended, not flattered."

"Justin," Scarlet insisted, "I am speaking of *your* feelings, not hers."

"But my feelings cannot be indifferent to hers, or unaffected by them. I honestly can't imagine Devī in any other way but as a sort of spiritual teacher. That's how she sees herself, and no one who sees her differently can have any kind of relationship with her. Anyway, I am quite sure that I will never see her again."

"Never? How can you say that?"

"Very soon, I mean *very soon*, Devī will leave this area, and I have no idea where she's going and absolutely no means to contact her."

"Is she going to another planet?" Scarlet asked with a sarcastic smile.

"She might as well be going to another planet. Seriously."

This answer did not entirely satisfy Scarlet, but she declared it to be "good enough for now," and, thanking Justin for his honesty, hurried off to other duties.

Justin walked the riverbank alone, lamenting Devī's departure, and his own inability to offer her the simple courtesy of a birthday greeting. But two thoughts gave him some relief.

First, Justin's relationship with Devī, despite its vicissitudes, had been most valuable. She had not only saved his life, twice, she had enriched it greatly by convincing him of the importance of spiritual awareness, even if he had little of that commodity. If the Asura did attack, and if Justin was able to follow Devī's teachings and fulfill his vow to the Avatāra, she would save his life again.

Second, why lament that he could not wish her a happy birthday? Devī herself lamented the very fact of her birth on this planet. Thus, to wish her a happy birthday was most incongruous, almost in bad taste. Devī's focus now was to rectify the mistake of her birth here by leaving.

Yet, despite all that, he would have gladly wished her a happy day, had he been able to do so without involving his White Hall friends in his intimate life in a most ill-suited way.

Devī would always live on in his life as a most precious memory. Like a rare jewel, he would guard his memories of Devī in a secret place in his heart and mind.

He now recalled that brief moment when Devī appeared to look at him with regret. What did she regret? He would never know.

CHAPTER 44

O n Saturday, December 7th, Justin was to meet with Judge Eliot. This might be the last news Justin ever received about Devī. Justin would do all he could to convince the judge to join him in a final attempt to keep Devī in this world. But the judge might not even believe that Devī was leaving. Then what?

The White Hall administration, honored by the visit of a federal judge, reserved a special room in the faculty center for his meeting with Justin. Justin walked quickly to the appointment, nervous to be meeting one of his father's oldest friends and Devī's main helper since Tark Davis left this world.

They met punctually at six p.m. in the elegant White Hall faculty center. As Justin entered the building, Judge Eliot, who sat in the lobby waiting for him, stood up and, with earnest smiles, shook Justin's hand, and told him what a real joy it was to meet the son of Tark Davis. The judge was a distinguished-looking man of middle age, well dressed and well spoken. Indeed, everything about him suggested a true gentleman.

They took their seats in the private room. Judge Eliot, wasting no time, gave an alarming report.

"I met Devī for two days, and left her just a few hours ago. She was in every way kind and cooperative, and in that sense her normal self. But I believe she was more withdrawn than ever. She was so anxious to finish her legal affairs and draw up her will, as if she were leaving it all behind. I am deeply concerned."

Though miserable to hear this, Justin sighed in relief, for at least now the judge would believe him. "Thank God you observed all that," Justin said. "I came here determined to convince you of what you already said."

"Do you know Devī well?" the judge asked.

"I'm not sure that any mere mortal knows Devī really well."

Judge Eliot raised his eyebrows.

"I meant," Justin hurried to say, "and I say this with all sincerity, that I believe Devī is inscrutable because she has great spiritual depth."

The judge smiled. "I could not agree more. Devī is my favorite yogī, or yoginī, I believe is the feminine form of the word."

Justin smiled. "Yes, precisely. But in strict confidence, I must tell you that I fear your observations are entirely accurate. Devī does not want to stay in this world. I also believe she has the spiritual means to leave this world without harming her own body as in suicide, but rather…"

"Please go on. You seem to know far more than me about these things."

"I believe," Justin continued, "that Devī has the power to, well, to simply leave her body. I think she can project her soul to a higher plane. And she can do so without harming her body. It's not suicide; she'll just…leave."

Judge Eliot sighed and his eyes moistened. "I'm glad you brought this up. Now I fear I understand more clearly what Devī was trying to tell me, without openly telling me—if you understand."

"Yes, I do. Devī can be very blunt or very enigmatic."

"Exactly. So please, if you can, interpret this for me. Devī let slip that she was very tired, that she had hoped to do much good in this world, but her plans did not succeed. She now believed her mission here was over, and that she must serve elsewhere. I asked her if 'here' meant Albemarle County, or Virginia, or the United States. And she repeatedly apologized and insisted that it was difficult to explain. There was a sadness about her I had never seen before, and it really pained me. But I didn't push her. As you know, one can never push Devī."

"I do know that," Justin replied, grieved by this confirmation of Devī's state of mind. There was a pause in the conversation, a time for both men to lament. Then Justin sat up straight. "Judge Eliot, I want you to know that I came here to seek your help. I thought you might know some way we could influence Devī, make her see that her mission is not over here. There must be some way to convince her to stay in this world. The world needs her."

"If only I knew a way," the judge said. "I would most gladly work with you to help Devī. But I just spent two days with her and I could not say anything to change what appears to be her fixed resolve. I'm truly sorry, but I don't want to give you false hopes."

Judge Eliot rested his elbows on the armrests, looked at his crossed fingers, and sighed. "Justin, there is one more thing I must tell you, even though Devī repeatedly ordered me not to tell you. I can only pray that

Devī, if she learns of my deceit, will forgive me for breaking her confidence. It's just that I am sure it is for the best, that you have a right and a need to know. However, if you prefer not to hear it, I will stop here."

"Please tell me," Justin said. "At this point, we're both desperate to find some way to keep Devī with us."

So anxious was Justin to know what Devī said that he forgot to breathe as he waited for the judge to speak.

Judge Eliot began, "Devī has now legally inherited a very substantial estate. I cannot say how much. Before her sixteenth birthday, her access to this estate was limited to a small monthly stipend. However, the terms of the will provided for a much larger amount to be immediately available to Devī in case of a medical emergency. The will's terms imply that these emergency funds are meant to help Devī personally. But the wording of this clause, by your father's expert design, was just flexible enough to allow us to access funds for urgent medical care for a person close to Devī. Now, four days ago, Devī heard from Sara, who heard from Luke, who heard from you—which apparently is the normal chain of communication—that your younger brother, Joey, urgently needed medical attention that insurance would not cover. Devī called me instantly when she heard this news and insisted that I access her emergency funds so that your brother could quickly receive all the medical care he needed. She was adamant I must send the money at once. I spoke to your mother, whom I always admired, and she told me the cost. Devī demanded that I send twice that amount, 'just in case.' And so I did.

"Devī also insisted with an intensity all her own that you must never know what she had done. She greatly feared you might think she sought to influence you by this gift. For some reason unknown to me, she was much concerned about that. Perhaps you know more about her reason, but I won't pry.

"Finally, I would never violate Devī's trust, but after seeing her state of mind, and seeing how much she cared about you and your family, I felt that the more you know about Devī and her true feelings, the better chance you might have to help her. I will only add that for a son of Tark Davis, I would have gladly paid for Joey's treatment myself. But sadly, my financial situation at the moment did not allow me to provide for your brother. Only Devī had the will and the means to do it."

From his heart, Justin repeatedly thanked the judge, assuring him that the information he disclosed was extremely important to Justin personally, and would help him to better understand, and hopefully better help, dear Devī. Justin actually spoke those words, *dear Devī*. He surprised himself by openly saying what he had now come to feel strongly.

There could be no rational doubt that Devī saved Joey. It was unthinkable that the judge would fabricate such a story. Scarlet truly planned to help. But from what Justin knew of her finances, she could not give such a large amount, nor could she secure the funds so quickly. Devī alone saved his family. It was Devī who sought anonymity and thus acted from pure motives.

Judge Eliot expressed his joy at meeting Justin, praised Justin's father, and offered his unstinting support, if there was any possible way he might further help Devī. As everyone knew, a bad storm was coming the next day, and sometime tomorrow, the airport would be closed. The judge must hurry to the airport to catch today's last flight out.

CHAPTER 45

I t was Sunday, December 8th, the day of Knight Rite. A violent storm from Canada thrashed the West Virginia side of the mountains. Everyone in Tucker County was under siege.

The storm plowed east toward Virginia. It would cross the Blue Ridge and hit Albemarle County Sunday afternoon. Lying on the eastern edge of the county, White Hall would be one of the first areas hit.

On Sunday morning, heaven showed a glum, moody, deceptively calm quiet. Knight Rite was scheduled for the morning. The Knights all took it as divine favor when the weather service announced that the monster storm would hit in late afternoon. With typical bravado, the Knights insisted on holding the morning event as scheduled. Their illustrious guests would have time to fly out before the airport closed.

The morning sun made a few halfhearted attempts to shine but soon gave up. The cloud-darkened sky decanted bone-chilling drizzle, heralding deeper meteorological misery to come. Weather reports claimed the blizzard of the decade was rushing upon Albemarle County. Weather forecasts for the afternoon, already grim, grew dire. The storm would hit earlier and harder in the high mountains, as it did the day Justin was rescued by Devī.

Pacing his room, Justin's double countdown to Knighthood and Devī's departure allowed his mind no rest. Justin wanted his mother and Joey to attend his Knight coronation. But Joey's condition made that impossible. His mother must take care of him. They could not attend Knight Rite.

Justin was disappointed, Joey more so. He only stopped lamenting when Justin explained that Knight Rite would be streamed live, exclusively for families of the Knights and their new inductees. With his mother, Joey would watch live on the new computer Justin bought for him.

Scarlet's stepfather, Randy, had inadvertently, and certainly unwillingly, done Justin a favor. Having exposed Justin's poverty to all, Justin had nothing more to fear if his family came to White Hall. Thus, he lamented their absence, whereas before he would have welcomed it.

That morning, Tom put his arm around Justin and asked if he was ready. He was. Tom gave him a manly slap on the back and returned to his duties. Midmorning would bring Knighthood. Justin envisioned again and again what this would mean to Joey, to his mom, to his career, to Scarlet. But all this joy could not assuage his dread of Devī's departure and other future problems.

Justin dressed in the traditional blue blazer and beige-gold slacks of Knight initiation. Nervously awaiting his summons, he tried to read a few pages of *The First Avatāra*. After all, it was this book that began all the dramatic changes in his life. He would always be grateful to this book. But would he ever be compliant with it? Would he ever truly see himself as a soul within a body?

There was a sharp knock at the door. Justin sprang to his feet, shouted he was coming, put down his book, and quickly embraced Luke, who could not attend the exclusive event. Justin apologized for the twentieth time for even going to an event where Luke was not welcome. Luke just laughed, embraced his friend, and assured him this was all part of a great plan that would bring them even closer together.

Justin hurried off with his elite cadre of future Knights to the time-honored ritual of Final Inspection. On Hugo Hall's top floor, at the carved double doors of the Knight Library, the novitiates gave a well-rehearsed ritual knock. The big doors opened, a Knight doorkeeper confirmed their names and ushered them into a magnificent library with carved hardwood paneling, a marble fireplace, and plush, oversized chairs.

All the Knights gravely watched the new men enter, bow, and take seats on low benches. The novices received final instructions on the duties of Knights, recited the Knight Code of Honor and Nobility, gave memorized ritual answers to ritual questions, and vowed strict obedience to the sacred codes of Knighthood. Justin thought with chagrin and remorse that having failed to keep his vow to the Avatāra, a personality of cosmic significance, he now pledged a vow to a prep school boys club.

The candidates were dismissed and ordered to proceed to the White Hall Theater for Knight Rite. On the way, as agreed with Luke, Justin stopped quickly in his room for final preparation. Since the Clays were scheduled to attend Knight Rite, probably with members of their team, Justin must exercise an abundance of caution. Thus, he hid a number of deadly daggers in various parts of his coat and pants.

Luke nodded, confirming that the daggers were imperceptible. He then told Justin to stand still, and placed two tiny blue pins, the exact color of Justin's blazer, on each of his lapels.

"What are those tiny things?" Justin asked.

"Those are bodycams."

"They're so tiny."

"Precisely—undetectable. Latest tech. Here, put this little control in your pocket. Just push the raised button and you go live, back to me. I'm set up to automatically record all you transmit. I gave you two bodycams so that you have a spare. If one shuts down for any reason, the other cam goes on instantly."

"Luke, what are you doing? Why do I need all this?"

"Sara insisted."

"Oh, she did?"

"Yes. And you know that she has extraordinary power. She's leading me through the last firewall at Clay Campus."

"Well, now that I know it's Sara. Yes, let's do it. A mystic hacker! This is new for me," Justin said.

"Justin, I've learned to never underestimate Devī and Sara. Anyway, we're starting to hear strange chatter from Clay Campus. They speak in a meta-language, but Sara is deciphering it. She feels strongly that an attack is coming very soon, either on you or Devī."

"Why didn't you tell me about this before?"

"Because we are just learning about it ourselves. Justin, listen to me, if the Clays don't show up at Knight Rite, signal me at once by activating your bodycam and tapping on it three times. Hopefully, I will soon know if you or Devī are in danger, and what the nature of the threat is."

"All right, I promise. What is that in your hand?"

"Just hold still," Luke said. "Let me put this small piece of tape on your ear. If anyone asks, it's a small cut from martial arts practice. In fact, there is an invisible, high-resolution speaker woven into the tape fabric. Press the sunken button on your pocket control to turn it on, and I can speak to you. Remember, if the Clays don't show up, activate your bodycam, tap three times on it, and wait to hear from me."

"Oh great," Justin said. "It's comforting to know that I may be killed at Knight Rite, but you will have the evidence."

"Justin, you won't be killed if you remember what Devī taught you."

"And if I don't remember it?"

"My dear brother, then you may be killed."

"You don't urge me not to get involved?"

"It's too late for that. Anyway, the Avatāra will guide you."

"Oh really?" Justin smiled. "I see Sara has fully converted you."

"Justin, just do it. Please."

"Whatever." Justin adjusted the tiny device on his shirt. He glanced out the window. People were walking to the White Hall Theater for Knight Rite. It was time. He nodded to Luke. Neither had to speak.

Justin hurried down the stairs and out to the theater. Snow was falling. As he approached the grand entrance, Scarlet and Mel joined him. They were both in lively spirits. Mel was unusually kind to him, as if to make up for past unkindness.

"You look great, Justin." He slapped him on the back. Scarlet smiled, happy to see Justin and happy to see Mel being kind to Justin. A nod and wink from Scarlet, that only Justin saw, told him that she coached Mel for this moment.

"Gentlemen," Scarlet said, "you both look great, but I cannot say the weather looks great. Those are dangerous clouds covering the high slope. The storm is already hitting up there. But we'll be safe and warm at White Hall. We even have covered walkways!"

Justin smiled at Scarlet. But inside, he feared that if Devī was still in this world, she was caught in the storm. With bitter self-reproach, Justin saw that apart from other danger to both of them, he never thought about Devī's safety in the storm. But for now, he must play his White Hall part. He exchanged friendly words with Scarlet and Mel, who continued being kind to him.

Then Scarlet made a laughing curtsey to Mel and Justin, urged them to take their seats, and walked into the theater ahead of them.

Justin and Mel crossed the lobby of the White Hall Theater, entered the main hall, and walked up on the stage. Justin took his designated seat with the Knights-to-be. Mel and the other Knights sat above him, and above them sat Knight alumni, many of them famous and easily recognizable. They had all braved the weather to attend, and those who were prevented from leaving by the storm would receive luxurious accommodations in the White Hall Lodge. Several prominent alumni came over to shake Justin's hand, offer congratulations, and thank him for his heroic rescue, about which everyone seemed to have heard in detail. Justin was entering the ethereal realm of the super successful. All doors were opening.

Still, he kept looking for Senator and Mrs. Clay. The program said that Senator Clay would speak.

As the White Hall Baroque Ensemble played regal music by Handel, Justin studied the quickly filling theater. He took pictures for his family, and waved to Scarlet, who sat in the front row. But he did not see the Clays, who would naturally sit on the stage with other most distinguished alumni.

Hunter had international duties, and it would be natural for him to arrive at the last moment, or even a little late. President Lofter took the stage and shook everyone's hand. She stepped to the podium and categorically welcomed everyone in descending order of prestige. President Lofter offered her first welcome to Senator and Mrs. Hunter Clay, who would be arriving very soon. Hearing this, Justin relaxed and settled in to enjoy the gala event.

After the president's welcoming words, Knight Rite began with fine speeches that were mercifully short. Justin kept scanning the auditorium for a sign of the senator, but the bright lights of the film crews made it difficult.

Time passed. President Lofter returned to the podium and said, "Friends and colleagues, I regret to inform you that Senator Clay has been called away on urgent business. He just sent us a personal message. He requests that we read it to you. I shall do so now."

Startled, Justin instantly reached into his pocket, pressed the raised button, and went live to Luke. He then rubbed his chin, simultaneously tapping the sensor on his lapel three times, signaling Luke that Senator Clay was not coming. Justin pressed the sunken button on his monitor, enabling Luke to speak to him. By this time, President Lofter began to read Hunter Clay's message. It was as follows:

White Hallians, fellow Knights, distinguished ladies and gentlemen. It is with profound regret that I inform you that urgent international affairs have called me away from Knight Rite. I assure you I would much rather be there with you, and I offer you my sincere apologies for my absence. To all Knights, past and present, and your families, I send special greetings. To the new initiates, I send enthusiastic congratulations. May you live up to the great tradition that you now inherit. I hope to see you very soon.

With my very best wishes,

Hunter Clay

Justin had not turned on his body camera because it violated a rule, and he had seen no need to break a rule at a Knight initiation in which he was to solemnly vow to not break rules. But Hunter Clay was not coming! This changed everything. As the program continued, Luke spoke to Justin, who acted as if he were not listening to Luke's desperately urgent voice.

"Justin!" he said. "Tap your cam if you hear me." Justin tapped. "Listen very carefully," Luke said. "Devī's life depends on it, and perhaps yours too."

No pressure, Justin thought.

Luke continued, "First, Devī is in serious danger. She revealed to Sara yesterday that she was having doubts about leaving this world. She feared she was committing a mistake by giving up on you too soon. Somehow, Hunter knows this. He is definitely an Asura. He has powers similar to Devī's, but he uses them for the wrong purpose. That's why he canceled his visit to Knight Rite. He is determined to get Devī out of this world before she changes her mind, even if he has to kill her himself. And he's the only one that has a chance to kill her, especially if she no longer cares about survival here. So, in any case, he has to deal with Devī himself. He can't delegate it. Another key fact: Sara and I put undetectable surveillance cameras on the road from Clay Campus to Devī's house, and one minute ago, Hunter and his wife headed up that road toward Devī's house. Devī has lost her will to fight. She told Sara that if the Avatāra wants her to stay, he will give her a sign. She will not resist the Asura. Last point—when Sara saw that Devī was in danger, she went crazy and mentally bulldozed her way into the Clay computer. I can't explain it. It's not normal computer science. We're in now, and I can confirm that everything Devī said about Hunter and his plans is true. Do not risk your life, Justin. I don't know what you could do now. It seems too late. I spoke to Judge Eliot and he personally begged the law for help, but they insist it's unsafe to go up the mountain. Hunter has a super vehicle to get there. What can we possibly do? I must get back to Sara. I'm struggling to keep her from rushing to Devī's house and getting herself killed. Protect yourself!"

A sharp jab from Tom behind him reminded Justin he must pretend to pay attention to the program. Luke had spoken quickly and not much time was lost in his communication. Hunter was on the way up the mountain to kill an unresisting Devī.

A Knight alumnus, president of a prominent university, spoke from the podium. Justin heard not a word. He could think only of Devī in danger. An awful foreboding filled his mind. He closed his eyes in agony. He saw Devī in his mind, her unspoken sorrow when he declared he could not help her. He saw her on the mountain trail speaking to his White Hall friends, avoiding his eyes, withdrawing from the world. He saw her in Bhū-loka, scolding him when he proudly, stupidly declared he would fight with his own power, insisting he did not need the Avatāra's power. He saw Vyādha the Asura humiliating him, the same Asura that now went to kill Devī in her passive state. What could Justin do? His crushing defeat haunted and crippled him. But he must act.

He had but one chance. Finally, once and for all, he must keep his vow and submit fully to Kṛṣṇa. Justin could not stop the Asura. But Kṛṣṇa could. And so, he silently cried out to the Avatāra for strength and guidance. He recalled the lady who sat next to him on his first flight from Clarksburg. She told him that George Harrison once chanted a powerful mantra when he feared his flight would crash. Justin silently chanted that mantra:

Hare Kṛṣṇa Hare Kṛṣṇa, Kṛṣṇa Kṛṣṇa Hare Hare
Hare Rāma Hare Rāma, Rāma Rāma Hare Hare

Over and over he chanted these words. He felt a power come into his body. The room brightened. The Avatāra had descended and was filling his mind with clarity, his body with strength. Wherever he looked, he saw the image of Kṛṣṇa, just like on the cover of his book. Kṛṣṇa pervaded the room; he filled Justin's heart. Justin's fear of the Asura began to dissolve.

The Avatāra spoke with feeling, telling Justin that he must act now, that the Avatāra would be with him.

Bowing to this order, Justin focused fiercely on tactics. The slow, winding road from Clay Campus to Devī's house was a few miles long. Brad Branley's monster motorcycle stood right outside the White Hall Theater. Straight up the mountain, Devī's house was not more than a mile. Hunter would arrive there first, but not long before Justin.

He sat up straight before Tom jabbed him again. Was Justin planning a suicide mission? No. The Avatāra was present to him, within him, in a powerful way he had never experienced. It was time to fulfill the vow. Devī always spoke of Kṛṣṇa's plan. This was the plan. If not, Justin would surely die today. But he cast off his doubts, until he thought of his family. This might be a victorious suicide mission. The Earth would be saved, but his mother and Joey would be lost. His death would shatter them. But Justin fought to drive those doubts and fears out of his mind. He looked out at the auditorium, and he saw Kṛṣṇa everywhere he looked, waiting for him to act. He surrendered his body and mind to a higher power. He must go after Devī. And he must go now.

To Justin's amazement, Kṛṣṇa smiled and nodded. Justin nodded back, and some people in the front rows looked at him quizzically. Justin made his final strategic calculations. Then, as if watching his own actions, Justin saw himself turn around and whisper to Tom, "Excuse me. I'm not well. I'll be right back."

Startled by this request, Tom whispered, "What's wrong?"

Justin tried to look deathly ill. "I'll explain later."

Seated in the middle of his row, Justin hurried to the aisle, apologizing all the way as he stepped on toes and bumped knees. The famous speaker stopped speaking. The whole room stared, Tom most of all.

When he reached the aisle, Justin turned to the silent speaker and said, "I'm so sorry. I'm not well. Please excuse me." He then hurried off the stage.

"I'm really sorry," Tom said to the speaker, "but it seems that one of our new men has taken very ill. Please accept our most sincere apologies and continue. I'll take care of it."

"By all means," the speaker said, "the health of our men comes first. Please, go attend to him." He then said into the microphone, "Is there a doctor here?"

In fact, there were many doctors present. Three of them hurried after Justin; that is, they got in line behind Scarlet, who ran after Justin, calling to him in a loud whisper, "Where are you going? Justin, stop!"

Justin ran up the side of the astonished theater toward the back lobby, with Scarlet and the doctors close behind, followed by Tom. By now, waves of whispers rolled about the room, rapidly increasing in volume till it sounded very much like pandemonium.

As Justin tried to escape the lobby, Scarlet, the doctors, and Tom, rushed to him with real concern. "For God's sake," Tom cried, "what is wrong, Justin?"

To his own astonishment, Justin realized that he was on an official Avatāra mission. After thousands of years, he was keeping his vow! He knew he was supposed to do what he was doing, and he was fully aware that every other witness of his actions believed he had gone mad. Devī always promised that the Avatāra would reciprocate if he surrendered. His life now depended on the truth of Devī's words.

Justin turned to his pursuers and said, "Thank you all so much. Tom, I have to go. Forgive me."

"What's wrong?" a doctor said. "Should we call an ambulance?"

"Should I restrain him?" an NFL linebacker, and Knight alumnus, asked.

"No, please, I'm well. Really. I have to...I must try to save someone's life. In the mountains." That was a mistake, mentioning the mountains.

"Justin, what are you talking about? Whose life? What is going on?" Tom demanded. Justin saw that Tom and the doctors now feared a mental collapse.

"I can't explain now," Justin said, with anguish. Every second was precious. "I want to tell you, Tom. There's no time now. I have to go."

As Justin spoke, he fought his way through the swelling crowd to the exit. He saw the Rokon super cycle. This was the plan.

"You've gone mad." Tom pressed his palm against Justin's forehead.

"Stop him!" cried Brad Branley, moving to block the exit. Justin spent precious time trying to explain. He feared the crowd would jump on him and stop him.

By now, everyone in the theater knew there was a crisis in the lobby, and half the crowd tried to push their way into the lobby to savor the crisis more closely. The campus police stayed in the background, at the ready, but respectfully allowing the venerable Knights to sort out their own affair.

But Tom shouted at Justin, "You are not going to the mountains. I won't let you kill yourself." The words provoked an uproar.

Police stormed through the crowd toward Justin. Dean Rankin, a lean former NCAA women's judo champion, stormed right behind them, followed by school officials and virtually all of the Knights.

Back in the theater, the White Hall president took the microphone and pleaded for calm. Never in White Hall history had Knight Rite, or indeed any other White Hall event, suffered such a major disruption.

By this time, Tom, the police, school officials, and Knights completely surrounded Justin so that he could not leave the lobby. Brad continued to block the exit. With real concern, Scarlet elbowed and pushed her way through the crowd and police, till she stood before Justin and demanded to know what was happening.

Tom said, "Someone is trapped in the mountains and Justin wants to go on a suicide mission to rescue that person. He's mad."

Brad Branley stood in Justin's path. "How do you know that person is in danger?" Brad demanded.

"I know. There's no time. Get out of my way."

"Call 911," Scarlet said. "Let the police go."

"Emergency crews won't go there," Justin argued, preparing to fight his way past Brad, who seemed determined to stop him.

"Oh, but you can go there?" Scarlet said. "I agree, Tom, he's crazy. You must stop him."

"Who is trapped?" the dean demanded. "I hope it's not a White Hall student?"

"No," Justin said. "Tom, it's that girl we met in the forest. I just got a text. She'll die."

At Brad Branley's urging, a big crowd surrounded Justin, apparently determined to stop him from leaving the building.

As Justin desperately looked for a way out, Tom grasped his hands, embraced him, and said he was sorry but nothing could be done.

"The highway patrol closed all access to the mountains through Sugar Hollow and Browns Gap Turnpike," a policeman said. "There's no way to get there. I'm very sorry for your friend."

Dean Rankin, who admired Inspector Javert in *Les Misérables*, and deeply feared parental lawsuits, threatened Justin with immediate arrest if he persisted in his suicidal attempt. "I'm sure that girl has taken shelter somewhere by now," the dean added.

"Yes, arrest him before he kills himself," Brad shouted.

Tom said, "Justin, you once fought to save our lives. Now we will fight to save your life, even if we must fight you personally. Justin, it's to save you. It's because we care about you."

Scarlet knew Justin, and seeing that he was about to fight his way out of the building, she stepped forward and shouted to Tom and the others, "Before you all kill each other in order to save each other, let me talk to Justin! I can reason with him. Let me take care of this."

CHAPTER 46

S carlet spoke with such fiery authority that no one dared oppose her. She grabbed Justin's arm and dragged him away from the others so they could talk privately. This could be Justin's best hope to escape, rather than fighting his way through hundreds of people, including angry Brad Branley, and campus police.

Scarlet planted herself in front of him, her face inches from his, and said, "You said it's that girl we saw in the forest the other day, right?"

"Yes."

"You mean Devī, of course."

"Yes."

"Devī saved you from the storm and now you must save her. Is that it?"

"Correct."

"Justin, that girl is not a witch. She is divine and you know it. You've always known it. Look, I'm a proud materialist, and I know she's divine."

Astonished at these words, Justin did not speak.

With both hands, Scarlet grabbed his lapels and shook him with surprising strength. "Justin, look at me. Look in my eyes. Do you love that girl?"

He didn't answer.

She shook him harder. "Justin, answer me. Do...you...love...her? Answer!"

"In a way, I do."

Seeing Scarlet in command, and Justin nodding and agreeing to all she said, the crowd believed she was resolving the problem.

Scarlet then told Justin, "If you love her, then go and get her. I believe you are meant to do this. If you die in the attempt, I will suffer the rest of my life, but I will also suffer if that beautiful girl dies."

Justin listened to every word as if it were a revelation. "But you and I..." he stammered.

"Justin, you don't need me. You and I love each other, but we live in different worlds. I cannot live in your world, and you can't live in mine.

I've known that, since we first met and you tried to hide your spiritual book. It bothered me for a while, but now I'm okay with it. Justin, you adore her. I saw it in the forest. I see it now. You are meant to be with Devī. I will help you if you promise me two things."

"Anything," he said, "just say it."

"First, you will tell no one that I helped you to save Devī. Promise me."

"I promise."

"Second, you will turn back the instant it becomes a suicide mission. Look in my eyes and promise me."

He looked in her eyes and said, "Yes, I promise."

"Good. Whatever god you believe in will punish you if you lie to me. And I will not be responsible if you stupidly get yourself killed. I do care about you, Justin. Don't forget how other people like me will suffer if you don't keep your word. We also matter. Now listen. Brad left the key in his beast of a bike. Obviously, you will take it. I will tell everyone you're okay and keep them distracted, even the police. When I go back to them, count to fifteen and run for the bike. You know the best way to Devī. You know these mountains. But turn back if your life is in danger. Swear on your Avatāra that you will do it."

"Yes, I swear to the Avatāra I will keep every promise I made to you."

"Deal. Now, wait fifteen seconds and go!"

Scarlet embraced him, then went back to Tom and the others and shouted with passion and charm that Justin was all right. As he counted to fifteen, Justin carefully checked his knives. At fifteen he grabbed his coat from a rack and burst through the crowd. In paralyzing disbelief, everyone watched Justin fly toward the exit. But they recovered in a moment and rushed after him. He was too fast.

Brad Branley had planted himself firmly in the doorway, arms crossed over his chest, hands tightened into fists. Justin saw the false confidence he had created in Brad in their Clay Campus sparring match.

As Justin rushed to the door, Brad shouted, "You're not leaving." This time, Justin pulled no punches. He rushed right at and into his opponent. Brad raised his arms to stop him. Justin lowered his shoulder, and drove Brad's body through the swinging door, and left him on his back, gasping for air, on the raised entrance patio.

Justin raced to Brad's burly all-terrain cycle, jumped on, and revved the motor. Brad scrambled to his feet, screaming oaths, and sprinted toward Justin, who put the roaring bike in gear, and exploded out of the parking lot. In the rearview mirror, Justin saw Knights and campus security running for their cars and motorcycles.

Determined to get away, Justin skidded through the quadrangle as sirens blared, red lights flashed, and police ordered through blaring speakers that Justin stop. He accelerated.

He careened around buildings and flew over athletic fields. White Hall students poured out of their dormitories to watch the high-speed chase. The police tried to encircle Justin, forming a perimeter around the campus.

At full speed, Justin dashed past the police and forced the bike to leap off the manicured campus onto a steep trail that shot straight up the mountain. No vehicle could follow him, and he left his pursuers behind.

Heading straight north toward the ridge, Justin's roaring bike chewed up rugged terrain like a voracious beast, ever ascending the slope. It bounced along rocky creek beds, blasted through brush, and flew over logs, clawing its way up the mountain. *If I crash*, Justin thought, *Devī will die, if she's still alive.*

Desperate, Justin remembered the Avatāra and began chanting the Hare Kṛṣṇa mantra silently in his mind. His lips were too frozen to chant. He tried to surrender to Kṛṣṇa's higher power, he envisioned the Avatāra lifting the bike over the obstacles, he pleaded for supernatural endurance.

Devī would approve, he thought, as he struggled up the very path that in October led him to his startling reunion with Devī. But as he ascended, the cold grew bitter, just as it did back then. His face now felt numb and a sudden blast of arctic air took his breath away. He shivered violently.

Snow began to pelt him. His tires locked on an ice patch. He spun around twice, nearly plummeting down the slope, before banging to a stop against a tree.

"No problem," Justin said, unfazed. He dismounted and turned his bike around. He kept fighting his way up the slope. Low branches jabbed his face; snow-veiled holes clutched at his tires. Ignoring gashes and bruises, he pushed on. Wind lashed his eyes and singed his cheeks. Another blast of arctic air shocked him. Justin shivered violently. The higher he went, the darker the sky grew under blinding thick clouds and snow.

Every day, he thought, *people are trapped and die in the mountains.* He promised Scarlet to turn back if his life was in danger. He knew all about hypothermia. His time was limited. With animal fury he pushed forward till he saw Devī's house up on the darkened ridge. A few dim lights and a fire flickered on the first floor. The upstairs was dark.

Justin had lost precious time escaping Knight Rite. Hunter must be at Devī's house by now. Had Devī already left this world? Did the Asura kill her? If the latter, did the Asura lay a deadly trap for a would-be rescuer?

Justin knew that in the still mountain air, Hunter heard the roaring bike come up the mountain. He had several minutes warning. Justin had lost all the tactical advantage of surprise. This troubling fact drove him back to his mantra with increased intensity. It seemed the easiest, most natural way to keep his vow and surrender his being to a greater, wiser power.

Justin stopped about twenty feet below Devī's house. He laid down his cycle and crawled quietly toward the house till his eyes were even with Devī's yard. Hunter's armored jeep stood sentry in the snow-covered front yard. The Asura was here!

A flickering light danced in the main room downstairs where he had conversed with Devī. So, a fire burned in the old fireplace. Devī could be alive! If so, she was in critical danger. To save Devī, and to save himself from fatal hypothermia, he must get into the house. Justin did not have warm clothing, and there was killing cold on the mountaintop.

Justin silently switched on his bodycam and whispered into the mic, "I'm on Devī's estate. Hunter Clay is here; there's his jeep. I'm going in, perhaps to die."

It was clear why Hunter came himself. No one else had the power to oppose Devī. And Hunter wanted revenge, and a clear path to supreme earthly power, unopposed by Devī, or her student.

Suddenly the jeep's blinding roof lights flashed on. Gunshots blasted the frozen air. Justin darted behind a tree. More shots slashed the bark. He was being targeted. A familiar voice called out, "Who are you? You are trespassing. Leave immediately or under the laws of the state of Virginia, I will shoot you."

CHAPTER 47

I t was Hunter Clay. Devī was probably not alive. But Justin must act, whatever the consequences. Before fighting his way into the house, he would try once to be civil. He would beg Senator Clay to let him enter the house to save his own life from hypothermia. Once in, he could search for Devī.

However, to do that, he must first eliminate the twin blinding lights that gave Hunter a lethal advantage, should Justin's appeal be denied.

Justin whispered into his mic, "If I don't make it, all my love to Mom and Joey, to Luke and Sara, Tom, Scarlet, and all my friends."

Justin grasped two knives. Countless hours, lifetimes, of patient practice empowered him. In a single flowing motion, he flew out from behind the tree, hurled two knives with two hands, and rolled to safety closer to the house, behind a giant old tree. Both knives found their target, shattering the jeep's twin lights, plunging the land into stormy twilight.

Crouching and waiting, Justin readied two more knives. He saw a few flickering candles inside the house. He listened for the faintest sound of a gun. There was dead silence, then a click, and the car's headlights went on. That familiar voice called out, the voice of Senator Hunter Clay.

"I see that it's you, Justin. No one else throws knives like that. I thought you were at Knight Rite, and so I had no idea who had come up here in this storm. I'm sorry I fired that shot, but I had to be careful. I wish you hadn't damaged my jeep, but you were responding to my shot. Anyway, you must wonder what I'm doing here. So, come on out and we'll talk."

Holding his last two daggers in his hands, staying behind the tree, Justin called out, "I came because I received a message that Devī was in danger. I'm sorry about your jeep and yes, it does surprise me to find you here."

"Justin, you don't have to hide. Come out now and I will explain why we're here. You have nothing to fear from me."

Justin sheathed his knives and came out, trembling with cold. If Hunter reached for his gun, Justin would respond. Justin stepped forward with his hands hovering near his belt knives, prepared to seize them in an instant.

The great Senator Clay nodded to Justin. "You and I both came up here, risking our lives, for the same reason. Devī was indeed in danger. She was dangerously depressed, indeed, suicidal. A mutual friend of ours, Judge Eliot, called the highway patrol to report Devī's condition and an alert went out on police radio."

That was all true. Judge Eliot had called the police. Hunter continued, "I have friends in local government and they called me. I told them about the private road up here. I said I would try to save my niece. They urged me not to risk it, or to send someone else, but I could not risk anyone else's life to save my own family, my dear niece. So, Barbara and I risked our lives to save her. Tragically, we came too late. I'm afraid Devī is gone. I'm sorry, Justin. It looks like suicide. Devī opened her windows, sat in her yoga āsana and froze to death. Barbara is with her now. This terrible event sadly confirms my assessment of Devī's mental state."

Was Devī gone? The very idea shocked Justin. He shuddered from cold and despair. But what if Devī was alive?

Had Justin not seen Jack's scars, had he not learned what the Sanskrit word *vyādha* meant, he might have believed the senator. Now he was safe from that illusion. Devī might be alive! Justin must get into the house.

"Senator," Justin said, "I'm freezing. Can we talk inside the house by a fire?"

"It's best you not go in. Get in my car before you freeze to death. You can sleep tonight at our campus."

Smart move by Hunter. Justin knew he was stalling for time. Time was on Hunter's side. Justin grew weaker by the minute. And the Asura might not have the power to kill Devī, and so was simply letting her freeze to death by her own choice.

If all that were true, Hunter would never let Justin into the house. If Devī was alive and saw Justin, she would know he risked his life to help her and might decide to stay in this world. Hunter could not risk that.

Justin felt the approach of extreme hypothermia. He must try to save Devī and he must do it now. To do that, he must fight his way past Hunter, surely a fight to the death. Justin would not sit in Hunter's car and save himself while Devī might be dying, convinced he had abandoned her.

But what if he died trying to enter the house, and Devī was already dead? He would ruin his family for nothing. He begged the Avatāra for guidance. The answer came in his heart. He could not leave Devī in the hands of the very Asura from whom she had once saved him. He must try to help her. His last hope to avoid a fight to the death was to appeal to Hunter's apparent fondness for him.

"Please, Senator Clay, I beg you, let me come in the house, just for a minute. Let me see Devī one last time."

"You are too late to save my niece. I'm sorry; she's gone. Justin, we have been so kind to you. Why are you doing this?"

"I deeply appreciate all that you and your wife did for me," Justin called back. "But I have good reason to believe that Jack Cutter, your employee, killed my father. And I fear you want Devī gone from this world. I hope with all my heart I am wrong, and if I am, I will make it up to you for the rest of my life. But I will not gamble with Devī's life. I'm going in to see her."

Hunter shouted, "Your father fought for justice. After all I did for you, you owe me justice and a lot more. You have no evidence."

Yes, Justin thought, *because you destroyed the evidence by destroying Jack's body.* Hunter was again stalling for time. Devī, if still alive, would leave this world very soon. Justin grew weaker, basically freezing to death.

Near panic, Justin struggled to fix his mind on Kṛṣṇa, clinging to the mantra. In a moment, Kṛṣṇa's power began to course through his mind, and flow into his body. Fear vanished. Then something most astonishing took place. Justin could read Hunter's mind! The senator planned that Devī die in the house, and that Justin submit or die outside in the cold. He knew too much. He was too clever.

If Justin rushed the house, Hunter planned to shoot him and then claim self-defense. Everyone knew about Justin's martial power. The senator had a right to defend himself.

But as Justin's power increased, Hunter sensed it and grew visibly concerned. He had always feared that Justin connect to the Avatāra. Justin smiled with frozen lips. He read Hunter's thoughts clearly. The senator decided to kill Justin now, before his power grew too strong.

Barbara Clay rushed out to the porch and shouted, "You are too late to save your so-called Devī. She is no longer in this world. Hunter, I've been listening to this absurd conversation. Finish him now!"

Justin readied for battle. Even if he died, all that Hunter said had been transmitted to Luke.

Senator Clay said, "Justin, this is your last chance. And I imagine you came with a transmitting device, say a body camera with audio. Sorry, but the electronic gear in my jeep has disabled it. So, actually, you neither recorded nor transmitted anything. The world will believe my version. You attacked us. Your knife is in my headlights with your prints. I just defended myself. Tragically, in the blizzard, I couldn't recognize you. You trespassed. We have a legal right to be there. Devī is under our custody. And the law will compel your friend Luke to testify under oath that you believed us to be evil, mythic Asuras. The world will of course conclude that Justin Davis went crazy. And died."

Hunter pulled out a gun. "I'm truly disappointed, Justin. You are just like your father—you can't take no for an answer."

"You killed him!" Justin shouted. He hurled a knife at Hunter's gun arm. The knife bounced off his arm with a clang and fell to the ground.

Hunter smiled. "I heard in detail about your fight with the bikers. Most impressive. I knew you might find your way up here, and so I thought it prudent to put on body armor. Very last chance—surrender to me or die."

Barbara then said, "Justin, we don't want to hurt you, really. We want to work with you. We could not let you join Devī and oppose us. There is too much at stake."

Hunter nodded. "Rule the world with us. I offer you that. Only Devī stood in the way. And so, we did what we had to do."

"What have you done to her?"

"Nothing, really," Barbara said. "We simply allowed her to carry out her own plan to leave this world. I wish I could feel more sympathy for Devī, but she did kill my husband in a past life. And Devī will be happier on another planet. This planet is ours. She never liked it anyway."

Justin had to act. Hunter Clay was not Billy Skinner, nor the bad bikers. A voice inside him whispered, *Don't fight with your own power. Let my strength flow through you. Just be my instrument!*

Justin smiled. Now he would finally do what Devī urged him to do thousands of years ago. Whatever the outcome, he was keeping his vow!

Fixing his mind on the Avatāra, opening his heart fully to the source of his existence, devoting his soul, Justin felt immense power flow into his mind, his arms, his entire body. Obeying that inner voice, he walked straight toward the house, hands at his sides, tapping the last knife, hidden in his belt.

Startled and enraged by Justin's audacity, Hunter Clay pulled out his gun, pointed it at Justin, and ordered him to get back. But with his new, enhanced awareness, Justin studied Hunter's eye movements, his finger on the trigger, and his breath rate. Justin knew precisely when his enemy would pull the trigger.

A moment before Hunter fired, Justin, still walking, dove to the ground, and did a front roll, grasping his knife on the way down as the bullet flew over his head. On the way up, Justin hurled his last knife. The blade plunged deep into Hunter's exposed gun hand. He screamed and dropped his gun. Justin had not stopped his forward movement. As the gun dropped, Justin was there to grab it. Barbara cursed him, trying with a shaking hand to point her gun at him.

"Don't shoot," Hunter shouted. "You'll kill me."

Justin was frantic to enter the house. Devī might still be alive. Part of him wanted to kill both Clays, an easy task since Hunter had a knife stuck deep in his hand, and a gun pointed at his head. Barbara, for all her gun-waving, was in panic.

Should he kill them? What did Kṛṣṇa want?

Seeing Justin hesitate, Hunter Clay rushed to his feet and grabbed his wife with his good hand. They ran past Justin, across the front yard to their jeep. Justin let them go. He must find Devī. If he indulged his hate and killed the Clays, Devī might die, and he would ruin his own life. This was another test from Kṛṣṇa. Justin must act as a servant of good, not as a master moved by hate.

Justin watched them for a moment, to make sure they actually left and didn't fire at him again with the weapons in the jeep. Barbara jumped into the driver's seat and made the engine roar. As she turned the jeep around, Hunter screamed at Justin, "You'll pay for this. I will destroy you. I will destroy your family. You're all dead, like your father."

Justin wavered. If he did not kill Hunter Clay, Justin's family might die. With his left hand, Hunter tried to grab a shotgun standing up on the back seat. Barbara cried out to him, "You're bleeding. You must get back down for medical treatment. We will kill them later."

Barbara gunned the motor and rushed to the snow-covered dirt road that led back to Clay Campus. If Justin shot out their tires, they might fight him to the death. He and Devī might die. What did Kṛṣṇa want? While he pondered, the Clays made their escape.

The jeep roared down the steep, twisting road. Seconds later, at the first frozen hairpin turn, the armored jeep flew off the unfenced road and with a few awful bounces on the mountainside, hurtled three thousand feet down to the valley floor, exploding into a fireball. Hunter and Barbara Clay were dead.

Justin had no time to be shocked. He flew into the house, frantic to find Devī. She was not downstairs. Taking three stairs at a time, he rushed up to her room. The door was locked. With wild energy, he kicked it open. There sat Devī, lifeless in a yoga posture, hands resting in her lap, eyes closed, hair spread over her shoulders. She looked as she did in life but unmoving, tears frozen on her cheeks.

Staggered and heartbroken at the sight, Justin grasped the evil plan at once. Finding Devī sad and unresisting, the Clays locked her in her room and stood vile vigil as she froze to death. Had he not come, they would have then broken in and claimed they discovered her dead, an obvious victim of suicide.

With a last hope, he gingerly took her icy hand in his. He had never touched her before. Pressing her wrist, he found a very faint pulse. Devī was alive!

CHAPTER 48

Justin flew to the bed, tore off the quilt, and wrapped it around Devī. He gently picked her up, carried her downstairs, and laid her carefully on a couch, which he then pulled next to the fire. Devī was still unconscious, her pulse still barely detectable. He rested her head on soft pillows, and furiously fed and roused the fire till it blazed with life-giving heat. He rushed to the downstairs bedroom and brought more blankets to cover Devī. With alarm, he saw that her body was too weak to shiver, a sign of severe hypothermia. With despair, he saw that she had been eating little and would have little strength to recover.

Covering himself with blankets, lest he succumb to the cold, he lit candles, placed a chair by her couch, and kept scrupulous vigil as his own body warmed. He begged her silently to stay in this world. He swore he would be more serious about serious things, if only she would stay.

As the storm grew savage, pounding the house, Devī's breathing grew steady and stronger. But she did not wake. *Dear God!* Had her brain suffered irreparable damage, making it a curse, not a blessing, to keep her in this world?

Whenever the wild wind paused to mount another fury, he heard the fire licking and chewing with relish the dry forest wood. Justin kept his fearful vigil, gazing at Devī's angelic face, remembering with deep feeling what his father said about her, remembering that even Scarlet saw her as divine. How their roles had reversed! Once Devī saved him as he lay drowning in a river. Now his duty was to do all he could to revive her.

As he gazed at her celestial features in the dancing light of the fire, a truth burst upon him, a truth to which he had long been blind— almost from the moment they met in Bhū-loka, Devī had deeply cared about him. He had mistaken her reserve for indifference, or even antipathy. Justin had failed to go beneath the surface of a profound and complex soul. Devī had always declared her indifference to the world, yet she always cared deeply about its welfare. He now began to see that a soul could be detached from all the selfish gratification the world offered, yet still be devoted to the world's highest good.

From the beginning, Devī had seen Justin as he really was—an eternal soul attached to a mortal body, and eager to enjoy a fleeting outer identity. It was to this false self that Devī had shown indifference, even scorn. Yet her actions proved she always cared deeply about his true self, the person he really was, and would always be.

With painful remorse, he now acknowledged that Devī had consistently reached out to him. But he could not value it, because unlike his other acquaintances, she would not gratify his vanity. She could never accept a relationship based on selfish indulgence, and ignorance of the true self. Justin had taken this as rejection. But it was he who proudly, arrogantly rejected what Devī had always offered him—a relationship between two real persons, between two souls.

Her earnest interest in his spiritual well-being had been a true sign of friendship. She must have hoped he would earn her love by working to discover his true self and hers. She even offered to stay in a world she regarded as barbaric and mad, if he would only stay with her, in mind and spirit. Was that not love?

Justin could not recall a single time that Devī did anything unjust or unreasonable. For all her outward reserve, at times bordering on incivility, she always sought his real interest. Whatever affection she might feel for him, he knew her to be far too shy to ever express it.

With a heart full of regret and self-reproach, Justin felt her pulse. It was still weak. The wind whipped the windowpanes, and shook the old walls. The fire sputtered, calling for attention. Justin stoked and fed the flames, and returned to Devī. In soft candlelight, and flashes of fire, he watched her and prayed that wisdom had not come to him too late.

Justin kept close watch till fatigue overcame him. He then spread a blanket on the floor by the fire and tried to sleep. A burning log crashed onto another and woke him. But the riotous storm swallowed the noise in its whistling commotion, and he was able to rest, waking often to check the fire and verify that Devī was alive and as warm and comfortable as possible. As she slept, her blankets faintly rose and fell with her breath.

After several hours of alternating sleep, nursing, and fire-tending, Justin awoke to painful hunger. He had hardly eaten that day and was now too hungry to sleep. Stocking the fire with fuel, he ran to the kitchen and prepared a simple vegetable soup for himself and Devī. Justin feared she might never wake to taste it. He could not chase these morbid fears from his mind. The unflagging storm howled about, slamming the shutters.

After eating a little and leaving most for Devī, he went to check on her. A wonderful, happy sight greeted him. Devī sat on the couch, blankets pulled up to her chin, fully conscious, carefully watching him. Her eyes shone in the dim light.

Seeing him, she tried to smile, and her lips silently said, "Thank you."

"Thank God!" Justin cried. "Thank God!" Beside himself with joy, he found no words, and so he simply stood near her, tears streaming down his cheeks. She spoke softly, thanking him again, and said, "I'm sorry to trouble you, but could I eat something?"

Justin blissfully ran to the kitchen and brought a tray with a big bowl of soup. Devī bowed her head and offered her soup to Kṛṣṇa, transforming it into spiritual food. Justin did not mention that he had already eaten some of the unoffered soup in the kitchen.

With every spoonful, she grew stronger. Devī was a consummate yogī. With rest and nourishment, she seemed to be repairing her own body from within. But something had changed in Devī. The way she smiled at him, not concealing her joy to see him—all that was a Devī he had never seen before.

Of course, in these circumstances they both must feel a camaraderie, an intimacy forged in shared dangers and trials. But Justin saw something more. He feared he was seeing too much. Several times in the past, he felt that Devī was being more open with him, only to be disappointed.

Whatever the cause of Devī's relaxed, open kindness toward him, it survived a full half hour as they sat together. That had never happened before. She was still shy, to be sure, but there was something different.

Despite his boldness in other company, he was always too shy in her presence to speak of anything but practical concerns. At her request, he explained all that took place from the moment he received Luke's warning and charged out of Knight Rite in search of her. Devī listened with rapt attention, amazed by his narrative. She expressed profound appreciation for all he did, and genuine concern for all he suffered. When he told her in detail how the Avatāra saved him when there was no other hope, Devī's eyes opened wide and glistened with emotion. In her every feature, he saw how much his story moved her. When he finished, she said, "It was your turn to save me. You showed real courage, like a true prince. And you kept your vow. I'm very proud of you. It's what I always wanted."

The joy that Justin felt at these words would be difficult to describe. But when Devī tried to say more, Justin saw that she was tiring and urged her to rest.

"Oh, we can talk," she said. But the next moment she fell back on her pillow and looked up at him, as if to say, "You were right. Now, I will be a good patient."

Devī fell back to sleep under her blankets. She awoke an hour later, even stronger, and said, "Justin, what about your career?"

"You mean my former career." He smiled.

"Aren't you upset, or at least sorry?" she asked with evident concern.

"No, I did the right thing. I am forever grateful to Kṛṣṇa that he brought me here. Obviously, Kṛṣṇa wanted me to save you, and as you might put it, I acted simply as his instrument. And I have a Plan B. I will return to West Virginia, hopefully excel in school, go to a good college, and work my way up."

He hoped she would say, "If you truly leave White Hall, you will be able to work with me." But she didn't say it. Devī was treating him so kindly, but she did not bring up their possible collaboration, the mission together. This disappointed him, but he could not mention it to her.

The storm had so darkened the sky that it was only by the clock that Justin saw how late it was. Both he and Devī needed much more rest to recover from their ordeal. Devī was recovering quickly, but she agreed that both should now rest. She insisted on returning to her own room, and Justin was not so enthralled by his new friendship with Devī as to think that he could dissuade her on this point. The medical emergency was over, and her natural modesty now dictated that she sleep in a private place.

Justin did insist that Devī wait until he had a strong fire going in her room. She gladly agreed. He did it at once. Justin worried about her ascent up the stairs, but he knew better than to oppose her on this point. When she started up the stairs, he went behind her in case she fell. After a few steps, she did pause and lean on the rail as if she might come tumbling down. She turned and glanced at him with an embarrassed smile. But she resumed her ascent and soon reached her room. When she reached her door, her smile, nod, and thanks all clearly told him that his path ended there.

As she entered her room, she turned and said with feeling, "Thank you so much, Justin." Justin offered to come during the night to keep the fire going, but Devī insisted she could do it. The next moment she was in her room and Justin was on his way down the stairs, utterly amazed at all that had happened in a single day.

He lay down under many blankets next to the fire. He tried to rest. He needed to rest. But he could not quickly fall asleep. He had far too much to think about. His family, Luke, Scarlet, and all his White Hall friends, might easily believe he died in the storm. Scarlet might think that she had sent Justin to his death.

Luke must have taken the loss of Justin's transmission as a sign of disaster. He must have told Sara. Who else might he have told? Surely, he would not mention it to Justin's family. Sara must be grieving for Devī. Tom and Scarlet, everyone might easily consider him lost, a victim of the storm. If only he could tell everyone that he was all right, that he was better than ever!

Scarlet returned to his mind. He certainly admired her beauty and intelligence, though he did wish that the latter might focus more on metaphysical topics. He did enjoy her company and always looked forward to it. He felt sincere gratitude for her support and friendship. In fact, without Scarlet he might not have escaped Knight Rite, and he shuddered to think what that would have meant.

But Scarlet herself recognized that they lived in different worlds. That now seemed more true than ever.

Of course, he dared not think of Devī in any way but as a spiritual guide and partner. It was difficult to even ask himself how he felt about Devī. It was best not to think about that now, best not to cultivate any particular feeling. It was best to simply do his duty, sincerely and kindly, and forget the rest. Devī was quickly recovering and for now, that was all he needed to know about Devī.

What would Devī be when she fully recovered? It seemed impossible that she could ever think of him in any way but as a spiritual assistant, a student, maybe someday a partner. Beyond this, he must not venture, not even in his mind. She knew his mind, and if he had any wrong thoughts, there would be painful, disturbing consequences.

His mind went to another concern. Did the world know yet that one of its most celebrated couples, the Clays, were dead? More important, what did Justin's mother and brother know or think? If news of his actions got out, they must be terrified, praying and waiting to hear of his fate. This troubled him greatly. He tried his cell phone and his body-cam transmitter, but the storm had deadened both. He had no contact with the world below.

Finally, his mind turned to a most grave topic, an issue that involved not only the present moment, nor the present life, but his future in many lives to come. What was his relationship with Kṛṣṇa? Justin knew that his life could never be the same after what just happened in his fight with Hunter Clay. Having kept his ancient vow, which Justin assumed was not a one-time commitment, how could he now break it? But what did that entail? What battles, what duties lay ahead? What adventures? What would the Avatāra ask of him? Would Justin serve with Devī? Or having honored his vow, had he fulfilled and thus completed the purpose of his meeting her? Would they move on to different worlds? This last idea did not please him at all.

Devī had expressed much gratitude, and shown much kindness to him. But she had not said a word about their working together. Perhaps that was out of concern for his exhausted state. Or, perhaps she knew that their time together was ending. It was a delicate point and he feared raising it, feared what the answer might be.

CHAPTER 49

A t last, exhaustion overcame all his thoughts, and Justin slept. He slept fitfully, waking often to worry about Devī and feed the fire. The tireless storm blew unabated. He rose at dawn with the storm in full fury. No one could possibly come to their rescue now.

He quickly fed the fire and went to the stairs to look up at Devī's room. Seeing a light beneath her door, he ran up the stairs to see if she needed help. He softly knocked but there was no answer. He waited a minute and knocked again. No answer. He called through the door, "Devī, are you up?" Silence.

Alarmed, he pushed the door slightly ajar and called again. He opened the door slowly, so as not to surprise her. Devī was not there. Had she left this world after all, simply vanishing like a great yogī? That had always been her style.

Justin heard noise downstairs and ran back down. The sound came from the kitchen. Devī was preparing their breakfast.

"Good morning," she said. "I didn't want to disturb you."

"This is wonderful! You look...normal again. I mean you never look normal, but you look like normal Devī. You've recovered."

"Yes, I'm fine. But Justin, are you all right?"

"Of course. Why do you ask?"

"You look exhausted. But of course, you have every reason to be."

They had breakfast together before the fire. After eating, and carefully watching him, Devī put down her utensils and said, "Justin, you really do not look well. Please, just touch your forehead."

He did. His body was burning with fever.

"Justin, you must rest now."

"Oh, I'm okay," he said, feeling dizzy. "I'll just sit down for a minute on the couch by the fire." He found himself too tired to sit, and stretched out. In a moment, he lost consciousness.

When he awoke, he was lying on the couch, covered with blankets. Devī, sitting near him, said, "Thank God you're finally awake."

"How long was I sleeping?" he asked.

"You slept an entire day. It's Tuesday morning. How do you feel?"

"Much better, but not great."

"Touch your head. How does it feel?"

"Better, thank you, but I still have a fever. I see the blizzard didn't stop."

"No, not for a moment," she said.

"So helicopters can't fly here."

"No. And after what happened to the Clays, which must be known, no one will dare to drive up here."

"But we have enough food and water," Justin said hopefully.

"Yes, for a day or two."

"Really?"

"Yes. You must be hungry. I'll bring you something."

"I'd rather leave it for you, just in case," Justin said.

Devī frowned. "That is out of the question. You must eat now."

"Hey, this is like old times," Justin said. "I'm your patient again."

Whereas in Bhū-loka, this remark would have earned Justin a dark look, Devī now smiled and nodded her agreement. Kind, friendly Devī was here to stay, and Justin was thrilled.

Devī soon returned with a nutritious breakfast, which Justin gratefully demolished under her watchful gaze. They spent the rest of the morning reminiscing about Bhū-loka, and revisiting Justin's battle with Hunter. Devī wanted to hear it again, and Justin was eager to recount it. By late morning, Justin felt exhausted again and Devī insisted he rest.

Justin asked whether Hunter's followers would seek revenge.

"Yes," Devī said, "especially Hunter's son."

Before he could ask, Devī told Justin: "Hunter had an illegitimate son with Asura power. But the son's power is still growing. He will try to kill us to avenge his father."

"But Hunter told me he was childless."

"Hunter Clay had an illegitimate son, a fact that he carefully concealed for two reasons. First, to save his marriage. Second, his son's mother is married to a well-known world leader who is not friendly to the United States. If Hunter's affair had been discovered, it would have seriously damaged his reputation, and probably ruined his chance to be president. That son will surely try to avenge his father by attacking us."

"Who is that son?"

"Hunter used his Asura power to prevent me from knowing. Now that Hunter is dead, his son is using his own power to conceal his identity. But his power is not yet fully developed. So, I can detect him, though I don't know his name. I do know that he will attack us soon."

Justin shivered. He wanted to discuss this topic further, but exhaustion forced him to sleep. He awoke before dawn on Wednesday. He heard a strange sound, or rather a lack of sound. The storm had weakened, though it was still strong enough to prevent any attempt to rescue the young survivors.

Justin somewhat impetuously wanted to go outside to check the storm, but Devī insisted it was not yet safe.

"I'm feeling better, but I know you're right." He suddenly felt weak and sat down on the couch.

"There is another reason," Devī said. "Hunter's followers will seek revenge. Their trademark is immediate retaliation. I'm sure they have a helicopter ready, and the very instant the weather allows, they will be up here in shooting range within thirty seconds. The rescue copters will come from Charlottesville or even farther and will take longer to get here."

"I see that you're serious. The storm is abating, so very soon there will be a helicopter gunship attacking us. And it's just for revenge against us?"

"They definitely crave revenge. They also know that if you and I work together, we will threaten their global conspiracy."

Devī finally spoke of working with him, but she did not say they would, only that if they did, they would threaten the Asuras. Why didn't Devī say they would work together? Justin did not ask. It was better to wait for Devī to explain these things. He did say, "Exactly how would we threaten the Asuras? Wait! I know. Kṛṣṇa has a plan?"

Devī smiled her assent.

Did that smile mean that they would definitely work together? Justin didn't know, but he asked about another important point. "Devī, from what you say, the Asura conspiracy didn't all depend on Hunter Clay?"

"No. He was their most prominent figure to be sure, but they are still powerful. It's an international project to rule the world. And having lost Hunter, they won't hesitate to sacrifice a few martyrs to kill us and save the greater mission."

"What can we do to save ourselves?" Justin asked.

"We must stay inside. Unfortunately, this house has no basement."

"Do we have any weapons?"

"Yes," Devī said, "but not in the house. Our weapons will come."

Justin was about to enquire about this esoteric assurance, but Devī suddenly cried out, "Justin, the storm is stopping. They will be here in minutes. Please, turn that table over and pile the couches in front of it facing the big window. We must lie on the floor behind the barrier."

Justin stared at her.

Devī shouted, "We have about one minute. Please do it now."

Justin quickly did as he was instructed. The roar of engines down in the valley shattered the still air. Justin and Devī threw themselves onto the ground behind the thick barricade. The roar became deafening. Justin snuck a glance at the window and saw an armed helicopter approaching the house. The helicopter hovered about fifty yards from the house and began to rake it with bullets, shattering the large window and spraying the walls. Bullets poured into the thick barricade, shredding the outer couch. Devī whispered to Justin, "Stay down. Don't worry, Kṛṣṇa will save us."

"Really? That's great. I'm ready to be saved."

"Yes, and it will happen right about now." She pointed to a south-facing window. Justin saw a second, black helicopter swoop in from the southeast and fire a missile into the Clay helicopter, which burst into flames, spun wildly, and crashed into the mountain.

As Justin and Devī sighed in relief, the black helicopter gently landed near the house. On the black helicopter, painted in white, were the letters FBI. A moment later, heavily armed and armored agents broke open the front door and burst into the house. Justin and Devī called out to them, identified themselves, and slowly stood up.

As they did so, more helicopters appeared over the house and began landing on the mountaintop plateau. Medical teams rushed into the house. Justin tried to explain that he was fine and didn't need any help. The next moment, he collapsed. He was placed on a stretcher and carried quickly to a Medevac helicopter. He tried to ask about Devī, but no one answered. A needle was placed in his arm. He felt groggy. The helicopter took off.

CHAPTER 50

J ustin woke up lying on a large bed in a white room. Two heavily armed guards stood at the door.

"Where am I?" he gasped.

A red-haired young nurse smiled. "Well, young man, you have been sleeping for two days in the University of Virginia hospital. Welcome back. How do you feel?"

"Two days? University of Virginia?"

"Yes, right here in Charlottesville." She pointed an infrared digital thermometer at him. "Finally, your fever broke. Excellent!" Then she ran out, saying, "Wait here just a moment."

"I'll try," Justin said.

With a shout, Joey ran in, followed by his mother. The moment she saw Justin, Star Davis burst into tears and embraced him.

Joey said, "You're famous, Justin! The whole world is saying you're a hero!" Joey jumped on the bed, embraced his brother, and had to be pulled off Justin, for he would not let go.

Justin was most anxious to know what had happened, and especially where Devī was. But his mother was too overcome with emotion to speak, and Joey couldn't speak slowly enough to be understood. Fortunately, Luke and Sara walked in, as ecstatic to see Justin as he was to see them. It was most promising that Luke and Sara could be seen together in public. Some rules must have changed.

All the friends exchanged heartfelt greetings and repeatedly thanked God for saving Justin and Devī. Sara spoke to Justin with all the affection of a loving sister. She glowed with spiritual beauty. Justin thanked her for breaking into the Clay supercomputer, and she just laughed nervously. Luke, as always, treated Justin as his own brother.

Justin asked Luke about the security guards outside the door and Luke explained that the government still feared that diehard followers of the Clays might attempt a revenge attack.

"Really?" Justin sat up straight.

Luke held out his hands, urging Justin to take it easy. "Yes, but it seems increasingly unlikely." Luke sat down next to the bed. "Let me tell you the news and you'll understand." With animated gestures and tones, Luke explained exactly what happened from the moment Justin was sedated on the mountaintop and flown to the hospital. The first startling revelation was that contrary to what Hunter Clay and Justin thought, Luke had indeed recorded, and streamed to law enforcement, all of Hunter's confessions.

"But the blocking device?" Justin said with wonder.

"Oh, I expected Hunter to try that." Luke smiled. "So, I engaged a tech genius at White Hall and we bypassed Hunter's jamming device. It looked to you as if the transmission was blocked, but we were receiving it all. We arranged for your device to look like it was blocked so that Hunter would speak freely."

"Amazing." Justin high-fived his best friend. "But why didn't you tell me before?"

"Why? Because we didn't expect you to run up the mountain on Sunday morning. I was preparing this with my tech friend, and it was ready Sunday morning. As soon as I heard you were on your way to confront Hunter, we switched it on. I sent all of Hunter's confessions in real time to Judge Eliot, and he immediately relayed them to state police and the FBI. Both agencies know and trust Judge Eliot, and immediately believed what they heard. So even in the storm, hundreds of officers surrounded Clay Campus. No one could go in or out. And the instant the weather permitted, law enforcement moved in and put the whole campus on lockdown. One Clay helicopter got away and attacked you. The FBI was ready and shot it down, as you must have witnessed. There have been dozens of arrests here and around the country, and many more to come, both in the US and around the world."

"So there really was a global conspiracy to seize power," Justin marveled. "And Hunter was very close to becoming president of the most powerful country in the world."

"Exactly." Luke shook his head and exhaled with a whistle. "That is the scary part."

"Very scary," Justin agreed. "And Devī? Where is Devī?"

Before anyone could answer, the young, red-haired nurse gave Justin a phone and said that a Judge Eliot was calling. Justin eagerly greeted a true friend, repeatedly thanking the judge for his invaluable help. But the judge only wanted to hear that Justin was doing well. After his repeated inquiries about Justin's health, and Justin's repeated assurances that he was rapidly improving, the judge was finally satisfied.

He then explained that the FBI had long suspected Senator Clay, but the senator's popularity and powerful Washington influence made it difficult to investigate him. There were no cracks in Hunter's legal armor, especially with the political and legal protection of his friends, vassals, and acolytes at all levels of government. Nonetheless, the FBI had slowly, clandestinely, built their case.

Then, when news of Hunter's conspiracy and dark deeds reached the public, which it quickly did, political support for, and protection of, the now-deceased senator vanished instantly and totally. The FBI moved in at once.

"But the law has real evidence?" Justin asked, putting the phone on speaker for his friends.

"Yes, they seized highly incriminating hard drives before they could be removed, hidden, erased, or destroyed."

"This is so amazing." Justin punched the air with his free hand.

"Indeed it is. The rapid decryption of sensitive seized material yielded shocking evidence about the Clays and their international network."

"So," Justin said, "the Asura network is completely unraveling."

"Yes, Hunter's network is unraveling, though not completely. But I did not understand that word—*asura?*"

"Oh nothing," Justin said, "it's just a Sanskrit word Devī uses. It means a bad person."

"Well, in that case, the Clays and their friends were certainly asuras. I should mention that the FBI feared that Clay's followers would attack you on the mountain, so they sent an elite team to rescue you and Devī. And by the way," the judge added, "Scarlet's stepfather was involved with Clay, peripherally but knowingly."

"And Scarlet knows it?"

"Yes, she's glad he was exposed. Her mother kicked him out of the house. He may stay out of jail, but his reputation is finished."

Justin repeatedly thanked the judge for all he had done, and then asked about Devī. He feared he would hear that Devī had finished her time with Justin and was moving on alone.

"Oh yes," the judge said, "our dear Devī. She is working closely with the FBI. That's why she is gone and out of contact. The FBI is amazed by Devī's insights. She suggests exactly where they should look for evidence, and they keep finding it. And her friend Sara, who is more like Devī's sister, has amazing insights too. These two girls are quite a team. The government's investigation would have been difficult, if not impossible, without them."

"I'm not surprised," Justin said.

"Nor I," replied the judge. "I would never set limits on Devī. I know your dear late father thought the world of her."

"Yes, he did." This mention of his father triggered a very emotional reaction in Justin, and he lost his breath for a moment. Realizing that everyone was watching, and the judge was waiting, he said, "Sorry, I just lost my breath for a moment. Yes, I saw in my father's writings how much he loved Devī, as if she were his own daughter. And I agree with him, and you, about Devī. I hope I will see her soon."

"Yes, I hope you will. I don't know her plans yet."

That was disappointing. Devī had not told the judge that she planned to see Justin very soon.

The call ended with sincere assurances on both sides to keep closely in touch. Justin then asked the red-haired nurse if there was any news about Devī.

"Oh, that beautiful young girl that was trapped with you? I only know that she left two days ago. It's like magic how quickly she recovered."

"Yes, her." Justin smiled. "I'm not surprised that she recovered so quickly."

"Nor I," said the nurse, shaking her head. "Such a lovely young lady. I've never seen anyone like her. I believe she left with some FBI agents that wanted to interview her."

"Yes," Justin said, "I heard that." He glanced at Luke and Sara. "Did she leave a note or a message for anyone?"

"I don't know," the nurse said. "Not with me." Sara opened her eyes wide and spread her hands to indicate that even she had no message.

Was this Devī's last teaching to Justin—complete detachment, even from her?

It wasn't.

"Of course Devī left a message for you," his mother said. "Before she left, she told me to tell you that she would speak to you as soon as she could. She's the most wonderful girl in the world. She loves you so much."

These words left Justin quite light-headed and blushing. Devī was far too shy and reserved to ever say she loved him. He hoped it might be true. But to hear his astute mother say it based on personal observation gave him a joy he had never felt before.

"Where is she, Mom?" he asked.

His mother smiled knowingly. "As the nurse said, she is sequestered with the FBI. No communication goes in or out till they finish their business. My God, what an ordeal you and she have been through."

The nurse then said that some of Justin's close friends had come several times and were very anxious to see him.

"Please, let them in," Justin said.

Tom, Scarlet, and Mel came in with worried faces that quickly turned to smiles when they saw how well Justin looked. With evident feeling, Tom and Mel embraced him, and Scarlet planted a sisterly kiss on his cheek. It seemed that Justin was not expelled from White Hall.

"Expelled?" Tom laughed. "Quite the contrary. White Hall could not be prouder of you. But you do look different."

"What do you mean?"

"You're glowing! What happened to you up on the mountain?"

Justin smiled. What could he say that they would understand? He chose to say, "I'm just so glad to be alive and to see all of you, my dear friends."

That was true, and it satisfied his friends. Mel tossed a newspaper on his lap. "Look! You're a national hero."

The headline shouted: *White Hall Student Risks Life to Save Young Heiress from Murder Plot.*

Heiress? Justin devoured the story. He knew much of it, having been there. But he learned some amazing facts, such as that Devī's parents were both White Hall graduates. Her father was a Knight president, her mother student body president. And having just turned sixteen, Devī legally took possession of a very large fortune.

"You're a real hero," Tom said. "Despite all our opposition, you risked your life and saved an innocent girl, who is also a most worthy member of our White Hall family. And you helped uncover an evil global network. You are front-page news all over the world. Maybe one day we can talk about your spiritual philosophy. Oh, and we saw Devī again."

"We just love her," Scarlet said. "Even Mel loves her." She jabbed Mel in the side.

"Oh, yes," Mel said. "I have to admit that a revered Knight alumnus, Hunter Clay, turned out to be the worst villain, and a Stonewood girl is a true heroine. Live and learn."

"Hey, wait!" Tom read his smartphone screen. "More breaking news. Listen to this: *Heroic Student Saves Beautiful Young Billionaire.*"

"Billionaire?" Justin leaned back on his pillow. "This is getting way too serious."

"It's all over the internet." Mel frantically swiped his phone.

Deeply astonished, Justin wondered where Devī was right now. If only he could see her.

"There's more," Luke said. He explained that a news crew at Knight Rite filmed Justin's escape from White Hall, and even caught Justin's Hollywood screech-away on Brad's bike. The film went viral. That same evening, after frantic investigation, the media revealed Devī's identity as an heiress, the tragic loss of her parents, and the travesty of her virtual incarceration at Stonewood. As more details emerged, such as Justin's possibly suicidal attempt to save her, and the uncertainty of their fate, the story mesmerized the country. When to this was added the news of Senator Clay—that a man slated to be the next leader of the free world was in fact a dangerous traitor, and that he and his wife died in a fiery auto crash after trying to kill Devī—with such heroism and evil combined in the same story, the world could think or talk of little else.

When the blizzard relented and the world saw the live video of the FBI rescue of the young people, and their shooting down of the Clay copter, the story broke records for internet hits. A few days ago, Hunter had a huge national following. Now that he was exposed, millions of people insisted that they had always suspected him of something.

"And that's basically what happened while you were blissfully asleep." Luke smiled. "My God, I'm happy to see you."

The nurses now insisted that Justin's friends and family give him time to rest, which he urgently needed. Everyone quickly complied. With more hugs and kisses, the friends departed, promising to return as soon as possible. Justin's family would wait in their hotel room next to the hospital.

When the nurses were satisfied that Justin was recovering, that he had all he needed for now, and when he repeatedly promised to call them at any time if needed, they too left. As they opened the door, the security guards gave Justin a playful salute and shut the door. Suddenly he was alone in his room. It was time to think. In fact, there was too much to think about. Justin hardly knew where to begin.

If only Devī were here. All he had ever dreamed of was now his. He was a national hero. No, he was an international hero. But what would he do with it? He was suddenly so famous, so admired. He feared he stood on a peak from which every step in any direction must lead down. He feared he would disappoint the public. What would he do with all this notoriety? If only Devī were here.

Would Devī return? What would his life be now? What battles remained to be fought? And how could he ever convince anyone about the Avatāra? Justin was a national hero, but his fame would be lost in a moment, if he began to speak like a crazed preacher with magical visions. He now saw more than ever how much he needed Devī to sustain an authentic spiritual life. She really was his teacher, and of course, his dearest friend.

For now, he must behave like a gentleman and not disappoint all those who admired him. Beyond that, he had no idea where to go from here. He was certainly not a preacher. That would ruin everything.

But Justin could not deny that his surrender to the Avatāra, finally keeping his vow, had changed him. He saw the world differently. Even if his consciousness was still not pure, even if his spiritual insight was not perfect, still he was irrevocably changed, and for the better. He now lived in the Avatāra's universe, however little he understood it.

CHAPTER 51

Justin's highly trained body recovered quickly, though not magically like Devī's. After a few more days of rest, and occasional visits with his friends, and much time with his family, he was declared medically ready for an international press conference.

Finally free of his hospital clothes, he sat in his room waiting for the completion of the paperwork discharging him from the hospital. He heard a tentative knock at the door and assumed it was a nurse bringing him papers to sign. "Come in," he said.

The door slowly opened and Devī walked in, looking shyer than he had ever seen her. Startled, Justin jumped up and greeted her with joy. Devī greeted him with an awkward smile. Justin repressed an innocent impulse to embrace her. It was still Devī.

It would be difficult to say which of the two was more uncomfortable at first, but as they exchanged smiles and recalled all they had been through together, they quickly relaxed. They felt a camaraderie, a bond between them that no embarrassment could suppress. At Justin's urging, Devī sat down and respectfully asked how he felt. He felt better than ever on seeing her, and he said so. Devī looked away, but with no trace of irritation. "It was so brave of you," she said, "to risk everything, your very life, to help me. I will always be grateful."

"I owe you so much more," Justin said, "and after all the stupid things I did…"

With a little shake of her head and a movement of her hand, Devī made it clear that there was no need for him to recount the "stupid things." Justin understood and complied. They sat together, each waiting for the other to speak. Finally, Devī said, "Is your family nearby?"

"They're at the hotel packing. We're going to leave soon. But I hope we can talk, if that's all right with you," Justin said.

"Yes, of course," Devī replied. "I would have called sooner," she still had her power to read his mind, "but I was afraid to disturb your rest. And I wasn't sure that you wanted me to call."

"Really? On the mountain, I tried to show you that I do care about you very much."

"You were very kind, Justin. You were far more than kind. But you are truly a good person, and I know you felt somehow implicated in my imminent departure. I blamed myself for giving you that impression. No one could have been kinder to me than you when you came to save me. You were ready to sacrifice everything to help me. And you took care of me the first day. Yet I thought it possible that you acted so heroically out of your own kindness and compassion. And you might have fulfilled your ancient vow from your own profound sense of integrity. So, the more I understood your exceptional qualities, the more possible, even likely, it seemed that you acted selflessly, impelled by your own goodness, not by any extraordinary concern with me."

"And that is why," he said, "on the mountain, you never asked me to join your mission, as you did once before?"

"Yes. After our experience in Bhū-loka, I was resolved not to pressure you in any way. I had to respect your right to choose your own life. And you never brought it up."

"That's true," Justin acknowledged. "I was also afraid to mention it."

"What did you fear?"

"That you would reject me, or that I might fail you, and thus fail myself. I also feared that after Bhū-loka, you no longer trusted me, or that you still remembered my offenses against you. I didn't know what to think. It was very awkward for me, and now I see it was equally awkward for you."

"Yes, it was."

Now confident of Devī's desire to work with him, how could Justin overcome Devī's diffidence and show her how much he really cared about her?

Choosing his words with utmost care, he spoke from his heart. "Devī, given the entire history between us, and in light of your generous appraisal of my character, which I cannot feel I deserve, it is entirely reasonable that you felt the way you did. But I assure you with all the sincerity I possess that my feelings for you come from my soul and not from any less worthy part of me."

Devī did not reply, but Justin saw in her face that his words struck her deeply. In the prayerful clasping of her hands, in the upward gaze of her large eyes, she seemed to seek the counsel of her highest authority, the Avatāra. Justin was sure of it. And the joy that then brightened her eyes and softened her lips into a subtle smile that a stranger would not detect, told Justin that Devī accepted his words and would not reject him.

She looked at him, and of course she knew all that he knew of her, and this made her turn her eyes away in shy reserve. But that was fine. That was just Devī. He understood her now. Still, he too was embarrassed, and so he finally blurted out, "Would you like to take a walk?"

She would, but she was concerned about his health. But she knew the day was unusually warm, the sun shining, the hospital had authorized him to leave, he had warm clothes, and in short, yes, she would like to go for a walk.

Delighted at this response, Justin called his mother and asked if it would not inconvenience her if he walked with Devī a while before going to their hotel. His mother approved with joyful enthusiasm, insisting that he and Devī take as much time as they wanted. It was a revelatory reply. Justin knew his mother.

The weather was mild, but it was still December. He and Devī put on coats and pulled their hoods over their heads so no one could recognize them. Justin made a quick call on the hospital phone and told the staff he would be back soon to check out, so, "Don't worry." He hung up before they could reply.

As Justin and Devī walked down the hospital corridor to the elevator, the guards followed them at a respectful but safe distance. As they all crowded into the elevator, one of the heavily armed guards said to Justin, "I've heard about your martial arts. You've got some great techniques."

"Thanks!" Justin smiled and shook the guard's hand. Justin had spontaneously bounced right back into his I-want-your-vote mode. Devī watched, smiled, and shook her head.

The clandestine couple crossed Jefferson Park Avenue and made their way to the university's famous lawn, admiring the colonial architecture designed by Thomas Jefferson. They sat on the grass under a blue sky and watched the students and teachers go by. Then Justin and Devī leaned back against a gentle slope dividing two of the lawn's terraces. Looking up at the sky, Justin said, "Well, here we are."

"Yes," Devī said, "here we are."

They had been through so much together in two different ages. And now, here they were. Once they got past the strangeness, the newness of their situation, they really had much to talk about.

Each wanted to thank the other, but neither would allow it. So they began with a topic of easy, sincere agreement. Justin and Devī both felt and expressed deep gratitude to Judge Eliot for his invaluable help. The judge had revealed to her, when the danger was over, that by the Clays' machinations, Devī had been in more danger of losing her freedom, her inheritance, and even her life, than the judge had previously admitted, for fear of alarming her. Devī, of course, knew this anyway, but she deeply appreciated the judge's concern for her tranquility. His vigilance helped prevent those evils.

As students walked by, and a friendly sun painted the lawn a shining green, Devī and Justin spoke of many things. Devī wanted to praise Justin's father, but she first asked if it were too sensitive a topic for Justin. He replied that nothing would please him more than to hear Devī praise his father, and she did so with an eloquence, a gratitude, and deep, daughterly affection that brought tears to Justin's eyes. Tark's brave defense of little Devī stopped the relatives, including the Clays, from draining Devī's estate for legal battles, and stealing the rest through legal maneuvers. The estate remained intact and even grew with interest till Devī claimed it. More importantly, Tark's constant vigilance prevented Hunter from directly attacking Devī. And it was Tark who brought Blake Eliot into the case. Devī truly loved Justin's late father, almost as much as Justin did.

The campus bells pealed, their sound wafted about by the cool breezes of late fall. Devī and Justin paused to listen. When silence returned, they eagerly resumed their talks. Both expressed gratitude to Devī's parents for all their present blessings. And finally, Devī spoke openly about how much she loved Sara, and now Luke. Justin fully shared those feelings.

Their discussion then turned to less obvious issues. Would Justin remain at White Hall? In his mind, that depended on what Devī would do. Justin was firmly resolved to work with Devī. He would not be separated from her.

Suddenly free and rich, Devī could go anywhere. But having so long assumed she would leave this world, she had not really thought of where in the world she might like to live. With Justin's unwavering commitment to her mission, and to her, Devī acknowledged that they must find a place where both would be happy. And both had to be with Luke and Sara. And they could not be far from Justin's mother and brother, in a place with excellent medical resources for Joey.

Justin confessed that his White Hall friends were begging him to stay at White Hall.

"What about Luke and Sara?" Devī asked.

"They will be happy to stay if you and I stay. White Hall has already invited Sara to study there. But if your bad memories of this area strongly disincline you to remain, Luke, Sara, and I will all go wherever you like."

Devī smiled, touched by the love and loyalty of her friends. She then explained that despite all the trouble she suffered in Sugar Hollow, she had enough happy family memories associated with the area to incline her to stay if her friends wished it. She could easily buy a smaller house close to the school and thus be constantly with her friends.

Beaming at the thought, Justin heartily encouraged this idea. Devī did not allude to personally studying at White Hall and Justin did not bring it up. She already knew the White Hall curriculum and more.

With so much settled between them, Justin brought up a vital topic that he knew Devī was shy to mention.

"What is the mission, exactly?" he asked. "It seems difficult. I can't just go and preach to people. I'm not a preacher."

"Granted. I'm not a preacher either. But we can talk to people. And we can publish articles and books. We will share what we know with all those who wish to learn it. Justin, we know this knowledge will make people think, if they give it a chance, and that regardless of the result, we must try our best to help this planet, as long as we are here. We also know it will be hard to convince people these are not just stories. Many will think we're crazy, or proud, or both."

"True. But we must have the courage to try. And the Asuras and their allies, Hunter's associates— Will they seek revenge against us?"

"Probably."

"And we'll fight them."

"Yes, if they attack us," Devī said. "We will remain vigilant. We will monitor this country, just as other souls are doing in other countries."

Justin glanced at Devī and saw in her features the fierce determination he had first witnessed when she drove a proud Prince Jaya away from her ashram in Bhū-loka. Her courage made him confidant.

"Our task is not easy," she continued. "Long ago, in Bhū-loka, the world was divided between Asuras and Suras, godly people. But now, Asuras have legitimized, normalized their values such as vanity, envy, lust, and hatred—idolatry of the body and disbelief in the soul. These

Asura qualities are now common among the people of this world. Asuras now lead some countries and dominate some industries. Most people are still innocent, but the Asura virus is spreading."

"What can we do?"

"We can only try our best to give people this knowledge."

"Yes. But as you said, we will respond in kind to Asura aggression."

"Yes, we will. And you and I must continue to learn from each other."

"I have much to learn from you," Justin said. "But I have very little of value to teach you."

"You have taught me," Devī insisted. "I learned from you that we must go dynamically into the external world to help people. I always had courage in the spiritual realm. I have no fear there. That is the world I always lived in. But the human world, the world of illusion, always seemed strange to me. I always lost my confidence there and so avoided it. To put it simply, I once sought to renounce the world and you sought to enjoy it. Now, we have both learned that we must neither reject nor exploit the world, but rather help the world to pursue wisdom, and liberation."

"Well spoken!" Justin smiled and applauded. "But what about my career?"

"Oh, please pursue it. That is certainly part of our plan, that you become a prominent leader of this country."

"How prominent?" he asked.

"Wait and see," Devī replied. "Just do your best. In that sphere too, you must channel higher power."

"But if the Avatāra plans to save this world again, what difference does it make what we do?" Justin asked.

"The people of Earth must choose to defend and save their own planet. Kṛṣṇa will help and empower them if they want and earn that power."

"So," Justin said pensively, "Since I am also part of this world—as long as my body lives—this world depends on me as much as on anyone else."

"Yes."

Justin yearned to thank Devī for her gift toward Joey's medical care, but he deemed it best to bring that up at a later time. But there was another point he could speak about.

"Ironically," Justin said, "or perhaps naturally, now that I've achieved the fame that I always craved, now that the world is mine, so to speak,

I'm beginning to see that this world is not our real home, certainly not our permanent home. We are only here to serve. Ultimately, I want something much more, a lasting home where I can be with the people I love forever."

Devī laughed. "How nice that we meet in the middle! I accept this world more, and you are more detached from it. We both want to help the world, but not exploit it in any way."

They leaned back on the grass, savoring this meeting of minds.

CHAPTER 52

Justin and his family stayed another day in Charlottesville in the same hotel where Devī was staying. The semester had ended at White Hall, but under withering pressure, Justin agreed to stay another day in the area for an international press conference to be held in the hotel's grand ballroom. The White Hall Academy insisted on hosting the event and paying for the Davis family's hotel suite. And all of Justin's White Hall friends, along with the White Hall administration, also stayed to attend the event.

Devī was reluctant to participate. Justin tried to overcome her shyness without success, until he received a powerful assist from an unexpected quarter. To his surprise and delight, Justin saw that in a very short span of time, Joey had attached himself to Devī as his older sister, and Devī was no less fond of Joey. They were inseparable. Joey simply adored Devī, and Devī clearly loved Joey.

He was about to walk out of his room when he overheard Joey in the hotel corridor talking to Devī. He quietly cracked the door and listened.

"Devī," Joey said, "you must come to the press conference. People have never seen a goddess before. If they see you, they will know the Avatāra is real."

Devī laughed. "Your brother is very intelligent. He can explain everything."

"But there's one thing he can't explain," Joey said.

"Really? What's that?"

"He can never explain why you aren't there. Devī, he needs you there. I know he does. You and Justin have to help each other."

"You are a wise young man," Devī said. "So, if it will make you happy, I will go. But your brother must help me prepare for the conference."

"Of course he will. I promise he will. I'll bring him now."

Joey promptly went to his brother's room and pulled him by the hand to Devī's room, declaring proudly that he was Devī's official assistant. Justin smiled and happily went along.

They found Devī not at all relaxed or confident. "What if people think I'm a freak?" she said, half joking. "What if they think I'm a witch?"

"Devī!" Justin said. "Everyone knows by now that it was Hunter Clay and his wife, through surrogates and proxies, who spread all the rumors about you. It was all to isolate you so that no one would speak to you and learn the truth. Hey, I learned from Tom that it was even Hunter who told Scarlet's stepfather, Randy, about my poverty. Hunter was playing a double game, trying to win me over, and simultaneously cutting me off from other possible allies, especially from you. His goal was to control me and turn me into an Asura. But don't worry, the press has obliterated any negative idea about you. The world now understands perfectly who was the villain, and who was the heroine. And my White Hall friends all loved you before they learned the truth."

Devī gave a doubting look, but acquiesced.

A thought struck Justin. He hesitated, but he had to say it. "Devī, please don't take this the wrong way, but do you even know that Kṛṣṇa has made you very beautiful, and not just inside? Honestly, do you know that?"

"Of course, she knows," Joey said. "Everyone knows."

Devī smiled and shook her head at Joey.

"I don't mean to contradict you, Joey," Devī said, "but the truth is that no, I never thought that. I never thought about it."

"Well, you are," Joey insisted, "you're the most beautiful girl in the world, and Justin said it himself."

Star Davis then saved Justin and Devī from what was shaping up as a terribly embarrassing situation, by coming to the door and demanding that Joey come and take his medicine.

When he left, Devī and Justin were eager to drop the topic of Devī's beauty and focus instead on preparing for the press conference.

"So, the press conference," Justin began.

"Yes, what should I do?"

"Just be yourself. And please know that everyone there will be highly predisposed in your favor."

"That's the problem. I'm afraid I will disappoint them."

"You couldn't if you tried."

They rehearsed. The time came for the conference. Star Davis and Joey went ahead to take their seats. The armed guards accompanied Justin and Devī to the grand ballroom. As they entered, endless lights flashed, TV cameras rolled, and the room buzzed with expectation and the hushed reporting of reporters.

As Justin and Devī walked onto the stage, they received a long, loud standing ovation from the press and the many members of the White Hall family who attended. Justin and Devī stood at the podium waving to those they knew, and those they didn't. A waving hand caught his eye, and Justin saw in the front row Judge Blake Eliot, who was not expected to be there because of a recent medical procedure. Justin jumped off the stage, shook the judge's hand, embraced him, and jumped back onto the podium.

A famous television host began the event with this statement: "Welcome, everyone! Let me first say how joyful, and moved, and thankful we all are to see you both here, Devī and Justin. We know that you have both been through a very traumatic ordeal, and we are so grateful that you agreed to speak with us. We respect your need to rest and recover. So our program will be brief. I will first direct a few questions to Devī, and then to Justin. Devī, for many years you lived as a virtual outcast, because of the cruel machinations of your uncle. You were practically imprisoned in a school that is under state investigation at this time and will likely be closed. What do you feel now that you are finally free, now that you have gone, in a real sense, from rags to riches in such a dramatic fashion?"

Justin worried how Devī would handle this situation. She took a big breath, actually smiled at the reporter, and said, "Of course, I am very happy to be free, and to be here with all of you."

She's a natural, Justin thought.

Devī went on. "I owe an extraordinary debt to Justin, and to his dear late father, Tark Davis, the bravest, kindest man I have ever known." Devī stopped here to wipe a tear from her eye. Justin did the same. Devī breathed deeply, composed herself, and continued. "And I offer heartfelt thanks to Judge Blake Eliot, sitting here in front. His help was essential." She pointed to the judge and gave him a nodding smile. Everyone broke into applause and the judge turned around and graciously acknowledged the audience.

Devī continued, "And I must thank my dear sist...my dear friend, Sara, for her steady, loving friendship in every situation, and her old and special friend Luke, who is not really so old. Luke brilliantly gathered evidence that freed the whole world from a deadly conspiracy. Sara and Luke are also sitting here in front."

Again the audience applauded until Sara and Luke, following the judge's example, stood and thanked everyone.

"Thank you," the host said. "Now if I may ask, what lessons about life did you learn in the course of surviving such a horrific situation?"

Devī smiled again. Her radiant beauty came straight from a pure soul. She replied, "I realized more than ever that my body may be imprisoned, but my soul is always free. I also learned what it's like to be despised and rejected by people who do not know or understand me. I hope I never do that to anyone."

Heads nodded around the room. People whispered their praise of Devī. All eyes focused on her. With a meaningful glance at Justin, Devī said, "Once, I was proud of my position, proud of my gifts. Perhaps I looked down on others. I knew that we are all equal as souls, and that there is beauty in every soul, but now I feel it far more deeply. I've learned a most important lesson."

After a heartfelt ovation, another reporter asked, "What are your plans now? We hear that White Hall is eager to have you. Is that possible?"

"I'm honored by their invitation. I do have to think more about it, but I hope to speak to them soon."

That was diplomatic, Justin thought.

Another reporter asked, "Devī, apart from your studies, what other plans do you have? You are one of the richest women in America. What do you plan to do with the immense fortune you inherited?"

"I will propose to Justin," she began, "that is, I meant to say—"

The room burst into laughter. To her credit, Devī took it all with a good-natured smile.

"Let me try that again," she said. "I will suggest to Justin…" More laughter. "…that we work together to establish a foundation that will strive to make our world a more just, equal, and spiritual place for all."

Devī nodded and sat down behind the podium. The audience sprang to its feet and gave her long, earnest applause. *Well done,* Justin thought, laughing at the very idea that Devī required his help in public speaking.

The host then invited Justin to the podium, saying, "I know, Justin, that the love and support of your family, who are here today, is most important to you. Would you like to say a few words about what your family means to you?"

Justin spoke of his mother and brother with much feeling. Excited by the applause, Joey stood up and vigorously waved to the audience, which provoked more applause, and laughter. When the crowd quieted, Justin spoke of his father in words that brought tears to many eyes. He bowed his head to a portrait of Tark Davis that stood behind him.

He then said, "My debt to Devī is so great and of such a kind that I doubt my ability to express it."

In fact, Justin feared that he could not disclose his true feelings for Devī without alarming her and confusing the audience. He would not for the world embarrass Devī by publicly speaking of his growing affection for her. And he would definitely confound and even alarm the audience if he even hinted at the actual antiquity of his friendship with Devī, or that she introduced him to the Avatāra. He was afraid to even declare that Devī was his spiritual teacher, his guru.

And so, even as Justin charmed the crowd and said all the right things, in his heart he witnessed his own persisting cowardice in spiritual affairs. It had taken him thousands of years to submit to Kṛṣṇa, and it might take another few thousand before he dared to risk his public respectability by speaking like a preacher, or a true believer. He had committed to Devī's mission, but he hoped his role would be limited to battling Asuras with the Avatāra's help, and not trying to convince people of a soul or an Avatāra.

These thoughts passed through his mind in but a moment. Outwardly, he was as smooth as silk. He then named and earnestly thanked his special White Hall friends. He next praised and thanked the entire White Hall community for their support and understanding. He spoke with palpable affection of his many friends and well-wishers in Tucker County, West Virginia. He knew the whole town was watching the broadcast live.

Finally, he delighted the audience and worried his family and friends by inviting more questions, insisting that he was up to it. He answered many predictable questions in a predictable but charming way. But he staunchly declined to comment further on his relationship with Devī. He did manage to smile at each refusal. The event ended.

Escorted by the guards, Devī, Justin, and his family returned to their rooms. Justin wanted Sara and Luke to come with them, but the couple had already agreed, and firmly stated, that Justin and Devī needed to rest. Justin and Devī submitted to their unbending decision.

Joey grabbed Devī's hand in the elevator and swung it playfully. Devī laughed. Later, Joey told Justin, "Devī told me she would take me to see Kṛṣṇa!"

"Really? You're a lucky boy."

"Yes, but she said that first I have to practice self-realization."

"That sounds reasonable. We all have to realize our true self, don't we?"

"Of course," Joey said, "that's obvious."

Star Davis was in raptures over Devī, and told her elder son, "The way she speaks about your father, it made me cry. She loves him so much. And she loves you, though she will never say it. She's so shy."

When Justin lay down to rest, he remembered with trepidation that he had committed to a mission. How could he ever explain his spiritual life to others?

CHAPTER 53

At the indefatigable urging of all their old acquaintances, the Davis family agreed to spend the Christmas holidays back in Tucker County, West Virginia. Enlightened or not, Justin would rather die than return to their old trailer. So Star Davis reserved the comfortable Cottage at Blackwater Falls State Park, just outside Davis. Justin looked forward to his stay in the cottage, which was a short walk to the falls where he so often found refuge in troubled times.

Star and Justin then implored Devī so earnestly to come that despite her natural shyness, she could not refuse. She would come with Justin and a guard and would stay in the main lodge, next to the Davis family.

Justin naturally invited Luke and Sara and they fervently wished to come but they had already promised Luke's parents they would attend the festivities in Pasadena. The Testers had invited dozens of friends to meet Sara, the "newest member of the family." Luke and Sara had no choice but to go to Pasadena. Justin was delighted to hear of the festivities in Sara's honor.

By agreement, Star took Joey and went a day earlier to Davis in a fine rented car to prepare the family stay there. After the new year, the entire Davis family would return to Albemarle County.

Star and Joey left on time. That evening, Devī spoke to Justin in a quiet corner of the large hotel lobby. "On our drive tomorrow, please dress for action, in case something comes up."

Justin's eyes opened wide. "We're driving through the mountains, but I don't think you're referring to a hike."

Devī smiled. "No, I'm not."

"Do you suspect we'll be attacked on the way?" Justin asked.

"It's not impossible," Devī replied. She paused and briefly closed her eyes in deep thought. "I suspect Hunter's son will try to avenge his father."

"His illegitimate son."

"Yes. To save his marriage, Hunter kept the boy's paternity concealed. This served another purpose. If Hunter were to die, his son would continue the mission. It was Hunter's contingency plan, to train his son, but keep him concealed, so that the father's enemies would not also target his heir."

Justin stood up and paced in front of his chair. "So, the son knows who his father is."

"Yes, he does, and he is fanatically loyal. He inherited a lot, though not all, of his father's power. He will stop at nothing to avenge his father's death, which undoubtedly he blames on you and me."

Justin returned to his chair and nodded stoically. He could not miss the irony. For years, Justin sought his father's killer. Now, although he did not kill Hunter, his son saw him as his father's killer, and sought revenge. Where would the cycle end?

"You know," Justin told Devī, "the police and White Hall arranged for an off-duty officer to drive us to Davis. If you foresee danger, we'll ask for more security, not just one guard who also will drive."

Devī nodded, gazing earnestly at Justin. "I understand your concern, but in this case, it's better to go with one guard. If we take more security, the villains won't attack. They'll wait till they think we're vulnerable. Justin, we can't live like that, always worried about them. It will put your family in danger as well. It's better we encourage them to make their move now."

"And you're sure that's not too dangerous?"

Devī smiled with gravity, as only she could. "I'm quite sure."

This was the old Devī, the Devī who slew Vyādha in Bhū-loka. "We just have to remember Kṛṣṇa," she said. "If they attack, there are three of us."

"Actually four," Justin said. "We have the Avatāra."

Devī's eyes sparkled and she nodded. "I will add that you will receive a more advanced test this time."

"Really? I thought I passed the test in my fight with Hunter."

"You did pass a test. But as you pass greater tests, you receive greater power."

"All right, that's reasonable. But what's the test? Or is that a secret?"

"No secret. You must be able to use violence with compassion."

"In what sense?"

Devī gazed into his eyes. Justin felt as if Kṛṣṇa gazed at him through her eyes. "Justin, you must see that within the heart of your worst enemy there is a pure soul who has forgotten his or her true self. You must truly care about even those with whom you battle."

"In Bhū-loka, you taught me, though I was not a great learner, that all souls are unique individuals and yet we are all one. One and different. You said it was the mystery of life."

"You remember!"

"Yes, from my dream. I didn't appear to be listening, but you once said that all souls are one with the Avatāra, with Kṛṣṇa, that the quality of all souls is equal—eternal, conscious beings. And yet, Kṛṣṇa, as the source of all beings, has infinite consciousness, whereas our consciousness is pure, powerful, but finite. Nonetheless, we are all one as pure conscious beings."

"You remember everything," Devī said. "I'm proud of you."

These words meant the world to Justin. He was ready to fight for Devī and with Devī.

"So," he said, "the higher test is to fight these bad guys, but never forget their ultimate spiritual identity."

"Yes. In ancient terms, you must act like a Royal Sage."

"…with compassion for people I may have to slay."

"Exactly. And hopefully we won't have to slay them. Remember that the Clays caused their own death. Our present foes are not as powerful as Hunter. His son is dangerous, but not on his father's level."

Justin slept that night as best he could, with Devī's warning and counsel fixed in his mind. He meditated on Kṛṣṇa, who would soon test him again.

Morning came. Justin arrived early at the meeting point in the hotel lobby. Their driver, Bob, also came early. Bob was a young, muscular off-duty Charlottesville policeman who seemed ready for action. Justin chatted with him about their route, which took them west past Crozet and Interstate 81, onto US Highway 250 that led straight to West Virginia.

The two men also discussed martial arts. Bob knew about Justin's feats, and he himself practiced, though not on Justin's level. Bob was an excellent marksman and brought several very efficient guns for the trip.

Devī appeared exactly on time, lovely as ever but dressed in loose-fitting hiking pants, an outdoor jacket tight at the waist and reaching halfway to her knees, and new hiking shoes. Justin's eyes opened wide. He had never seen Devī in Western fighting clothes. She was serious about possible action in the winter mountains.

Bob invited Justin to sit in the backseat with Devī, where they would be able to speak privately, and he eagerly agreed. It was amazing just to see Devī riding in a car. This was not Bhū-loka. But he must talk to Devī, and there was but one topic to discuss—the possible attack.

"So?" Justin said in a low voice. "What is the threat level?"

"High," Devī said. "Hunter's son is on his way."

"How close?"

"Close."

"You don't mean our driver?" Justin whispered.

"No, our driver is a good soul. He wants to protect us. But Hunter's son will attack, soon. You must be ready, spiritually and materially. If we let Kṛṣṇa act through us, we will survive. You know the rules."

"Yes, I do."

"There's a powerful weapon hidden under your floor mat. Lift it quietly. I will talk to Bob to distract him."

Devī proceeded to chat with Bob. She asked him about his family, his future plans. Honored to receive such attention from Devī, he eagerly chatted with her, answering all her questions. As he did, Justin lifted the floor mat, saw a secret compartment, and carefully opened it. Inside he found a small but potent assault rifle, loaded with ample ammunition for any situation. Justin quietly placed it between himself and Devī, covering it with a coat he didn't need in the mild weather.

Devī nodded and asked Bob, "Do you know this area well?"

"Fairly well," Bob said. "I grew up in Staunton, the town up ahead. Did you know that Woodrow Wilson was born there?"

"Yes, I did," Devī said.

"I'm not surprised. You know, I used to hike this area."

"Nice," Devī replied. "Now, if someone were trying to ambush us, where would they do it?"

Bob whirled around and stared at Devī. "You're serious?"

"Very," she said, "but please watch the road."

"Of course," Bob replied. As he pondered the question, Justin said, "Last night I happened to study a topographical map of our route. I believe the best area for an ambush is the four-mile stretch between Road Hollow and Salthouse Hollow."

"Precisely," Devī said. "Though I would give preference to the last two miles between Ford Edward Johnson and Salthouse Hollow."

"Exactly," Justin agreed. "The road twists more, and the up-and-down slope surrounding the road appears to be steeper…"

"Thus facilitating any attempt to trap us," Devī said.

"My thought exactly," Justin replied.

Bob's head whirled back to them and he stared at his passengers. "Who are you two?" he asked. "All right, I know, eyes on the road." He turned back to face the road. "You people are really serious about this danger," he said. "I suppose there is some danger, or why am I driving with you?"

"That's correct," Justin said. "There is real danger."

"Okay, young man, I'm not supposed to tell you this, but I know you're a great shot. There's an assault rifle hidden under your floor mat."

"Do you mean this one?" Justin held it up.

"I should have known." Bob shook his head. "Yes, that's it. I pray to God we don't have to use it. Anyway, I'm going to stay on my radio and talk to local law enforcement in all the towns we go through. If anyone's looking for a fight with us, they'll get a fight, that's for sure."

"Yes, they will," Justin agreed, endeavoring to fix his mind in Kṛṣṇa and surrender his ego to a higher power.

As they drove past Staunton, Bob talked to local law enforcement on his radio, and they promised to discretely stay alert to possible trouble. A few miles later, they entered a mountain valley, passing through Churchville, population 194, the last village before the mountains. Ten miles later, they drove through West Augusta, a tiny mountain hamlet and the last valley village. Now they rose into the mountains. The road grew lonelier by the minute. They saw a small sign for Road Hollow. Justin and Devī looked at each other. They had entered the prime danger zone. The road continue to narrow and rise. Thick forests blocked their line of sight.

Devī whispered, "The enemy is close. Hunter's son is leading them. We must stop them. If not, they will harm us and those we love. And for the world's sake, we cannot turn the other cheek. Yet these villains are souls like us. But they cannot remember now. We must not forget. All souls are capable of good, despite their present condition. And ultimately, we are all equal. So, if we hate any soul, we are hating ourselves. Justin, this is your test. Fight with fierce courage and determination. Hate injustice. But do not hate any soul."

"I understand," Justin said. "Easier said than done."

"Justin, you must pass this test. If you hate another soul, your power will turn dark, and it will destroy you. The Asuras failed to persuade you, so now they will try to induce you to hate. If they succeed, you will come under their power and become one of them."

"Well, no pressure," Justin said with a deep breath. "But to not hate them, I must truly believe that even Asuras will wake up some day and embrace their true, virtuous selves."

"Exactly."

They reached the site of old Fort Edward Johnson. There was a small highway plaza where travelers could enjoy the lovely hilltop view. But today the area was strangely quiet, deserted.

They now entered the most vulnerable stretch of mountain road, two miles on a narrow ridge, down to Salthouse Hollow, where there was room to maneuver. As Justin and Devī focused on their surroundings, Bob picked up his radio mic and said, "I'll call ahead to the Highland County sheriff down in Monterey, Virginia."

"Yes, please call," Justin urged.

Bob did so, but received no answer. He called again. No reply. He tried a third time, and gave up.

"We have a problem," Bob said.

"What kind of problem?" Justin asked.

"I can't get through. The Monterey station doesn't hear us. Someone is jamming our radio. It's called subtle jamming—everything seems normal to me, but we don't get through. It's a crime to block us. That means either my radio failed, which is most unlikely, or we've got some bad guys after us. By the way, my cell phone doesn't work here. What about you?"

"We're all out of range," Justin said. "They picked their spot well. How far away is the sheriff's office?"

"About sixteen miles, that's twenty-five minutes on this road. I can make it a lot faster if necessary."

"An attack is imminent," Devī warned.

"In that case," Bob said, "it's time to get ready." He pulled the car over to the side. "I've got an assault rifle."

"There was a big automatic pistol down there too," Devī said, holding it up. "Perhaps I'll just keep that with me."

Bob shook his head. "All right, young lady, whatever you say. I've heard about your powers."

"So what is our plan?" Justin asked.

"We'll try to get to the sheriff's office, in Monterey. If the bad guys attack before we get there, we'll leave the car at once and run into the mountain, where we have good cover. This is not a bulletproof car. If they come with lots of guns, and we're inside the car, we lose. We die.

Anyone have a better plan?"

No one did. The plan was settled.

"Devī," Justin said, "do you have a sense of where the attack will come?"

"Not a precise sense," Devī replied. "Hunter's son will lead the attack, and his Asura blood makes him hard to read."

"Asura blood?" Bob stared at Devī.

"Devī and I have our own jargon," Justin explained. "That was just shop talk, to say that these guys are mean."

"Okay," Bob replied, "I hope your seat belts are fastened." He accelerated to the top survivable speed on the twisting mountain road. Devī and Justin hurriedly tightened their belts.

Devī whispered to Justin, "Now is the time to invoke the Avatāra's power. We will need it."

Devī and Justin bowed their heads. Each in their own way connected to the source of their being. Justin felt Kṛṣṇa's power flowing into his body and mind, just as in the battle with Hunter Clay. Devī glowed with power. This was going to be interesting.

Justin saw Bob watching them in the rearview mirror.

"Oh!" Justin said. "Devī and I do this little mindfulness exercise. It makes us more spiritual…and more lethal."

"Well," Bob said, as he screeched around curves, "whatever it takes, I guess. To be just a bit more mundane, stock up on water and energy bars. We may be in the mountains for a while. And take your warm clothes."

"We're ready," Justin replied. "We have water, protein bars, and guns. That should do it."

Bob nodded. As he entered a blind hairpin turn, the roar of a big motor startled them. A big black van came at them. As they all grabbed their weapons, the van rushed past them, slammed on its brakes, swerved to its left and stopped, blocking both lanes. There was no escape to the rear.

"They're not alone," Justin said. "Get ready to run for the hills."

"Hold tight," Bob said, "I'll try to get away." He stepped on the gas and their car leaped forward. But as it flew out of the hairpin turn, another big black van, three hundred yards ahead, made the same maneuver, swerving to its left to block both lanes in front of them.

"We're trapped!" Justin said. "We need to move now."

"The bad guys are coming!" shouted Bob as the three allies scrambled out of the car and raced into the hillside, trailed by enemy gunfire.

Armed men with black ski masks, eerily reminiscent of Bhū-loka Asuras, poured out of both vans and ran into the woods in pursuit. The two enemy groups closed in on the fugitives, tightening the noose around their quarry.

"Let's head for high ground," Bob said, "we have to stay above them."

Justin shook his head. His mind was working faster than ever. "No, we can't do that. They must have men waiting up there above us. They know they can't outrun us in the mountain, so they will try to force us into an ambush."

"Justin is right," Devī said calmly. "They have limited time. They know that when no one hears from us, the law will come looking. The only way the Asuras can defeat us quickly is through an ambush from above."

As if to confirm these words, shots rang out from above, ricocheting off trees and rocks.

Bob anxiously asked, "What do you suggest?"

"We form a triangle," Justin replied. Then, pointing with his fingers, he said, "We face the bad guys coming from the left, right, and above. As Devī said, time is on our side. So, if we stay here, they must come to us, and when they do, they will expose themselves."

"Do we shoot to kill?" Bob asked.

"We must at least disable them," Devī said, "or they will kill us. We can shoot below the waist and stop them, without killing them."

"I agree," Justin said. "Bob, are you a good shot?"

"They call me the sharpshooter. If you want these guys, let us say, temporarily disabled, I'll be happy to do my part. I don't like bad guys. Never did."

"All right," Justin said. "Let's take secure positions and form a triangle, not too close to each other, so we're not a big target, but not too far away, so we can come to each other's aid. Bob, what side do you want?"

"I'll take the land above us, unless someone else wants it."

"That's fine. Devī?"

"I'll take our right side."

"Then I'll take our left," Justin said. "Devī, you look sad."

"I'm afraid," she said, "there may be a slaughter."

"You fear they're going to kill us?" Bob said.

"No, I fear what we may have to do to them."

"Let's move, now!" Justin said. They each found a well-shielded spot behind a wide tree. They agreed they would not pursue the enemy, to force the bad guys to approach them. They didn't have to wait long.

Shots came from all three sides, but the bullets smacked into outer rings of trees in the dense forest. Devī laughed and told the others not to worry.

"That young lady is as cool as they come," Bob called to Justin.

"Bob, you have no idea," Justin called back.

Another coordinated volley of shots slammed into the trees, but the thick forest protected the defendants. The assailants now spoke through a loudspeaker mounted on a van roof: "You are trapped and have no escape. No cars will come this way. We blocked the road on both sides. It's just you and us. You cannot call for help. Surrender and save us the trouble of hunting you down. We promise you a painless death."

In reply, Justin took careful aim and with a burst of bullets, demolished the van's roof speaker. No more announcements.

"That was impressive," Bob called out.

Justin almost said, "Kṛṣṇa helped me," but Bob wouldn't understand, and this was not the time or place for a metaphysical discussion. Time was elapsing. The Asuras would have to attack more boldly.

CHAPTER 54

Racing against time, the foes did cast away caution, and moved more aggressively against the besieged friends. Devī had been telling the two men to hold their fire. Now she said, "I prayed they would desist, though I knew they wouldn't. We must begin now to disable them. I regret it, but we have no choice."

At her word, Bob and Justin began picking off the attackers who made their way forward. Bob and Justin were both accomplished marksmen, and now Justin fought with enhanced consciousness. Devī could not miss.

As the foes rushed the defense, they became easy targets, and the three friends quickly disabled them. As if in a dance and obeying a master choreographer, the Asuras fell to the ground, one after the other. Devī and Justin exchanged glances as they fired. Bob did his part, immobilizing the foe with shots to the legs and arms. All around lay wounded young men, some crying, others shrieking curses, still others weeping in agony.

Justin glanced at Devī and saw that she wept for those who could not understand themselves, nor the value of goodness. Devī then shouted, "We must get help for these men or they will die." Justin urged Bob to go down to the road, destroy the jamming device in the vans and use his radio, or use the van's radio, to call in medical help for the wounded.

Bob was about to run down when a terrible voice shouted from below, "I will kill all of you. You will pay for this."

"It's Hunter's son," Devī said. "He's the deadliest of all, and I don't think he's wounded. This will be a test."

Bob wanted to stay with them till this last foe went down.

"Let me take care of Hunter's son," Justin said to Bob. "These people will all die if you don't go now. They have families. They don't know what they're doing. We can't let them die. Please, go now."

Bob went. Devī rewarded Justin with a heartfelt smile of approval. He was passing the test, and he was doing it sincerely.

Hunter's son moved cautiously forward, firing and ducking for cover. Justin returned fire but could not stop his steady advance. Devī watched, ready to help, but Hunter's son demanded a fair fight, one against one.

After several minutes, Bob came running back, darting from tree to tree, to avoid enemy fire. He arrived panting and said, "I destroyed their jammer and used my radio to call for help. Medevacs are on the way. I said we've got at least a dozen men down here and they need help now or they'll die."

Devī and Justin thanked him earnestly. Suddenly heavy fire broke out from above them. Bob and Devī turned in that direction, leaving Justin to deal with Hunter's son, who now shouted at Justin, "I'll never surrender. I will take you down, Justin. I will have revenge for my father's death."

"I didn't kill your father," Justin shouted back. "I saw proof that your father arranged to murder my father. My father was the victim."

Hunter's son did not reply. Then he shouted, "Whatever my father did, I will fight for his honor. You held back in our fight, but so did I. We both concealed our real power. So, no more faking. Do your best. I'm coming to kill you."

"The police are on their way!" Justin shouted. "You can't win."

"Perhaps, but I can kill you before they get here." He then unleashed a deafening volley of bullets that came perilously close. Who was the son of Hunter Clay? Justin heard him creeping closer but his movements were too fast and quiet to stop.

Having subdued the last remnant of the group above them, Bob and Devī headed toward Justin, but with bursts of gunfire, Hunter's son forced them to stop at least forty yards from Justin.

"Stay back!" Justin shouted. "I'll take care of this. Please check on the wounded. Try to save their lives."

"Your life comes first!" Bob shouted.

"I'm not in danger," Justin replied. "Please help the wounded."

"This is more than danger!" Hunter's son shouted defiantly. "You and your friends will die, be assured." And he kept coming closer.

"Be careful," Devī said. "Let us help you."

"I won't put you in danger," Justin vowed. "And you must try to save the others. Let me take care of this. The Avatāra will be with me."

"All right," Devī said. "None of the others will die. I'll see to that."

"How?" Justin asked.

"Is that a serious question?" she said.

"No, sorry."

"Be careful!" Devī said, and she ran with Bob to nurse the wounded.

Justin had spoken brave words to Devī, assuring her that the Avatāra was with him. Now, fearing for his life, he meditated deeply on the Avatāra, surrendering his body, mind, and soul to a higher power. At once, Hunter's son seemed to move in slow motion. Justin saw him leave the cover of one tree and head to another. In that second, and not more than a second, Justin fired.

Hunter's son fell, shrieking in pain, crying out, "Damn you! Damn you!" The sound of his voice carried far in the still forest.

"Don't approach him," Bob shouted. "He's still too dangerous."

"I'll be careful," Justin shouted back. He heard Hunter's son dragging himself forward, firing at Justin. The foe was indeed wounded, but Justin dove for cover as bullets whizzed by him.

"This has to stop!" Justin shouted. "We can't keep killing each other."

"You killed my father!" his son shouted.

"That's not true!" Justin shouted back. "Your father tried to kill me. I could have killed him when he was fleeing, but I didn't. I did not cause his death. Your dad's man Jack murdered my father. You know that. I have every reason to kill you. The law won't think it was a crime, when I tell them that I killed you in self-defense."

Silence followed. Justin quietly circled around Hunter's son, who lay immobilized, till he stood behind him. Justin stared at the son of Hunter Clay, dressed in dark fatigues and a black ski mask, facing the wrong way. Justin fired warning shots just above his head and called out, "Drop your weapon. Now! Or I will kill you."

Clearly suffering from his wound, Hunter's son tried to turn around to face Justin, but he collapsed in pain.

"Drop your weapon or I will shoot you," Justin ordered. "Don't tempt me. You are a threat to me, to my family, and many other innocent people. We will not kill your friends if we can avoid it, but I am so ready to make you an exception."

"So, the great hero is going to kill me."

"That is a real option. Now take off your mask. I want to see who you are."

Hunter's son hesitated, but a burst of bullets close to his head motivated him. He slowly peeled off his mask and painfully turned to face Justin, who stared in shock. Hunter's son was Brad Branley of White Hall, who was to be the next Knight president.

"So, now you know. It makes no difference. My father is dead, and my life is over," he said. "You might as well kill me. Or I'll do it myself."

Justin remembered what Devī had told him, that his test would be to use force with compassion. Searching for that compassion in his heart, he said, "I want to help you, Brad. Killing you is Plan B."

"Why would you help me? You know who I am. You know what my father did to your family."

"I won't give you a sermon," Justin said, "because that would probably be worse than death for you. But we're all souls. We're all family. If I hate you, I'm hating myself."

"That sounds sentimental," Brad said, but his quivering lips showed that he heard the message.

"Whatever you may think," Justin said, "that's the kind of soul I want to be."

"What do you want from me?"

"I want you to stop doing bad things. It's bad to harm innocent people; it's bad to sabotage free societies."

"I understand. But I'll go to jail now. I'd rather die. I can't bear it."

"Make a deal. Tell your comrades to turn themselves in, every one, all over the country. Make a plea deal. I know a great lawyer, in fact, a judge. I'm sure he will help. And those of your friends who want to keep fighting us—turn in their names. Help us find them. We give everyone a chance, and then the incorrigible have to pay. It's fair. I beg you, don't make me kill you."

Brad threw his last weapons away. "All right. I'm not my father. I have a human heart along with my Asura blood. Whatever evil thing I am, I do keep my word. I accept. But if you want to help me, act now or after all this talk, I'll die here anyway. I lost a lot of blood."

Justin shouted to Bob and Devī, who came running with water and basic medical supplies. As they treated Brad, he stared at Devī and gasped, "You look like an angel. A real angel. Forgive me for what I've done."

Devī nodded, and he fell unconscious. Minutes later, police and medical helicopters landed on the road.

Justin, Devī, and Bob helped place the wounded on stretchers and carry them down the hill. Some were unconscious, some sobbed uncontrollably. Brad was semi-conscious and silent. The medical staff believed that all the wounded would be saved, though they could not have survived another few minutes without care.

After speaking extensively to the police, Justin, Devī, and Bob resumed their trip in silence. There was too much to say. There was nothing to say. On the road, Justin called Judge Eliot and explained everything. The judge would not discuss any future plan until he was assured that Justin, Devī, and Bob were well. Once that was settled, he quickly agreed to help Brad and his accomplices. The plea deal that Justin suggested struck the judge as a good plan. He finally spoke to Devī and was clearly moved to hear her voice.

Justin then called his mother and explained that he would be late, due to car trouble that was now fully resolved. Everyone was safe.

CHAPTER 55

All Tucker County received Justin with the greatest esteem. Even Billy Skinner asked for their autographs and was almost proud of having been thrashed by Justin. Sherri Bunton relished the renown of being Justin's ex-girlfriend.

All of Tucker County was in awe of Devī. She was praised knowingly as a very spiritual young lady, and a soul that was not of this world, in a good sense, of course.

Sara and Luke spent the holidays at the Tester residence in Pasadena, where they did not have a white Christmas, much to Sara's joy.

In the midst of such joy, one last source of dissatisfaction troubled Justin. Despite Devī's generous gift to help Joey, the Davis family had no steady source of income. Justin knew that Devī would never let the family suffer, and the family felt and showed no lack of gratitude. And yet, dependency itself, even on the kindest and most generous of donors, could not satisfy them.

An unexpected call from Judge Blake Eliot remedied this final problem. As the FBI and other agencies drilled ever deeper into the labyrinth of the Clay conspiracy, they found that Hunter Clay himself had engineered the financial ruin of Tark Davis. It was to be but partial revenge against him for his efforts to protect Devī.

Judge Eliot believed that he could recover in full the original Davis fortune, which was very substantial. He assured Star Davis that the law was all in her favor. He had consulted judges and legal experts in and out of the government, and their consensus proved to be correct. With public and government opinion so ardently in favor of the Davis family, the wheels of justice turned with striking rapidity. Soon the original Davis fortune was restored to Star Davis, with interest, from the immense Clay estate.

Apart from his ill-gotten gains, Hunter Clay had acquired a large, legitimate fortune. It was from those legal assets that the Davis family was fully compensated and made financially whole, that is, rich. Under gentle prodding, Devī finally admitted that she had urged the most willing judge to pursue this legal remedy for the Davis family as a first priority. Once more, Judge Eliot revealed what he was bound to conceal, that Devī paid all the legal expenses in the case.

"I wanted so much," Devī later told him, "perhaps as much as you and your mother, that your family be financially independent. You never spoke about it, but I knew how you felt. After all, you and I were both reduced to poverty after a very comfortable childhood. And there's another point. I knew you would never work with me for money. Please don't think I ever imagined you capable of that. But I want you to have absolute freedom to do whatever you like. Work with me only if you really wish it."

Justin did really wish it, and he communicated this to Devī with so much genuine feeling and conviction that he overcame even her strong natural diffidence in such matters.

Star Davis now bought a lovely house in Charlottesville close to the university medical center, whose world-class facilities offered Joey all he needed for a full and rapid recovery, which soon took place. And the new Davis home was an easy drive to White Hall. After all the family had been through, they were determined to stay near each other and near Devī.

As she once promised, Luke's mother, Claire Tester, met Star Davis, read some of her writing, and truly loved it. The two ladies formed an instant bond that would grow over time. As a respected, published author, Claire committed to helping Star publish her work. This and all the other good fortune that suddenly fell upon her dramatically improved Star's state of mind. Her physical health quickly followed. Crushing anxiety, fear, and desperation for her children, and herself, had robbed her of health and happiness. But these now quickly returned, to the joy of all who knew and loved her.

The White Hall Academy urged Devī to enroll there. As part of that conversation, Devī took various tests. Her scores revealed that in fact she already knew basically all that White Hall taught. So as a goodwill gesture on both sides, Devī became an honorary White Hall student, free to attend any class, use any school facility, or participate in any White Hall event.

Devī bought a lovely cottage on several acres adjacent to White Hall, with two hundred yards of secluded river frontage. Devī and Justin were now a two-minute walk from each other. Whenever Devī went to campus, students whispered and pointed at her. Apologies flowed in from all who had ever unfairly or unknowingly offended her.

The White Hall community generally admired her beauty, stood in awe of her intelligence, and felt her power. Students and teachers asked Justin about her, and he found that the easiest way to teach them wisdom was to simply explain Devī and her life to the many eager to know about her.

Sara happily accepted White Hall's offer of a full scholarship. Sara was brilliant, but unlike Devī, she did not yet know everything that White Hall taught. Within the principles of their serious spiritual practice, she and Luke continued to be inseparable. After a separation of several thousand years, they had much to talk about.

The dramatic events involving Senator Clay and Devī inevitably led to a full exposure of the sordid state of the Stonewood School. This situation could not be allowed to continue. The Commonwealth of Virginia closed the school and sent its students to better schools, where they would receive the attention they needed.

Devī bestowed on Sara an endowment so generous that she would be positively wealthy for the rest of her life. Both Sara and Luke eagerly declared their intention to dedicate their lives to the mission they shared with Devī and Justin.

Brad Branley kept his word and fully cooperated with the FBI and other law enforcement branches. He supplied investigators with a treasure trove of information that enabled them to dismantle the most sophisticated and dangerous clandestine society in America, if not the world. In return, Brad received a new identity in an undisclosed part of the country, where for years to come, his actions at home, in the world, and online, would be closely monitored by advanced electronic devices attached to his person. Brad's accomplices received various degrees of leniency and witness protection according to their history, needs, and level of cooperation.

The Asura network in the United States was broken. Justin and Devī could now focus on normal, earthly evil, which was more than enough to keep them very busy.

The Knights were stunned and humbled to learn that the next Knight president was to be the son and follower of Hunter Clay, who was now seen as the worst traitor in American history. The Knights also noted with due remorse that Devī, whom they now held in the highest esteem, they had once slandered and vilified. But the Knights were still young and able to learn these valuable lessons.

Scarlet adored Justin, but when it came to the point, she preferred a boyfriend who accepted her completely, rather than one who admired her beauty, wit, and charm but merely tolerated her spiritual skepticism. In Mel, Scarlet found complete compatibility. Inspired by Scarlet, Mel prospered beyond what he had dreamed possible. Scarlet was his perfect muse.

Scarlet began to appreciate Justin's attempts to discuss philosophy with her only when his attempts subsided. She then told Mel that she wanted a boy who was intellectually interesting. Miraculously, Mel's grades began to improve, and he always carried an intellectual book under his arm.

Tom continued to advance on his career path. Compared to his sister and friends, he was a bit of a late bloomer in matters of romance, but he did finally and joyfully notice that a particularly gifted and lovely young lady at White Hall had been desperately trying to get his attention for the last two years. And much to everyone's surprise, Tom manifested a keen interest in Justin and Devī's spiritual teachings. At their invitation, he began, with his new lady friend, to attend the little spiritual gatherings of Devī, Justin, Sara, and Luke. Joey also came whenever his mother could bring him.

Devī predicted in all seriousness that one day Joey would be a great Teacher in the world. And Joey's enthusiasm for all things Avatāra, and his unconditional devotion to Devī as a beloved older sister, boded well for him. Sara and Luke also doted on Joey, who was thrilled with all his new friends. Yet with all these dear new friends, Joey continued unwaveringly to model his life on that of his older brother.

During spring semester at White Hall, one often saw television vans parked on campus, and reporters interviewing students and faculty who knew Justin and Devī. The school did all it could to protect them from the media so they could have a normal student life.

Despite these earnest efforts, Justin and Devī had to accept a good deal of media attention, and the constant presence of guards, who tried to stay at a distance. Justin took naturally to the life of a modern prince. And with his steady support and encouragement, Devī was able to tolerate fame and fortune with reasonably good humor.

Justin found that as long as his old friends were allowed to joke about his spiritual practice, and as long as he laughed along with them at his own expense, they were all comfortable and happy with his spiritual practice and could even listen for very brief periods to philosophy.

After one such very brief discussion with Scarlet and Mel, Justin said to Luke, "Many people only talk about the soul at funerals, and perhaps at an occasional wedding."

"Welcome to Earth," Luke replied.

Devī, Justin, Sara, and Luke formed an Avatāra club on campus and some other students, including Tom, joined them. At their meetings, they often discussed ways they might spread the knowledge, though no one wanted to be an open preacher.

Once, on a sunny day in early spring, Devī, Justin, Sara, and Luke hiked to a secluded meadow above the waterfall where Justin and Devī once unexpectedly met. The friends lounged happily on the emerald grass and breathed pure mountain air. They spoke of intimate recollections and future hopes.

Cool river breezes ruffled their hair. Under a rich blue sky, Justin followed Devī's gaze and looked into heaven. He knew that Devī lived in a multidimensional universe. She saw what mere humans could not see, and she transmitted her vision to those who believed in her. Devī dwelled in a bigger, more enchanting cosmos, at times dangerous but always full of wonders. Justin longed to see what she saw, and to dwell in the higher dimension that she so gracefully inhabited.

Hunter Clay had fought to keep Devī and Justin apart, knowing that Devī would give him extraordinary power and vision. By surrendering to her wisdom, Justin overcame Hunter Clay, and his son. Now he longed to advance further. He yearned to see, as Devī saw, the soul that lives in the body of every living being, and animates it as an actor moves a costume.

Justin knew that with progress, he would perceive greater dimensions of this world, and greater worlds beyond it. He experienced that the more he practiced Devī's ancient teaching, the more Kṛṣṇa drew back the curtain of illusion, Māyā. Justin marveled at what he saw. But he knew that he still had much to learn.

Now, up on the meadow above the waterfall, as the four friends lay on the soft grass, Justin thought of Plato's words about the soul:

And when any prisoner is freed, he leaves the cave, and outside his eye turns to a greater reality. But he must grow accustomed to the sun's light, to the sight of the upper world.

Justin was gradually growing accustomed to the light that Devī shone on him. As he increasingly devoted himself to his practice, his relationship with Devī continued to blossom in a way that only those who understand true spiritual love can fully appreciate.

Lying on the grass, he turned his head and said to Devī, who was now a mere five feet away, "I have two questions for you."

"Yes?"

"First, what about the book?"

"The book?"

"Yes, *The First Avatāra*. How did that book end up in a bookstore in Parsons, West Virginia?"

"Kṛṣṇa put it there."

"Kṛṣṇa. And you had nothing to do with it?"

"Not so much. I imagine the late Senator Clay told you that I produced the book and sent it out to other victims."

"Yes, he did." Justin laughed.

"So," Devī said, "place a notice online that I will give one million dollars to anyone who can show us a second copy of that book. See if anyone comes forward. I'm serious."

"I think there is no second copy."

"No, not of that book. There are other books, about Kṛṣṇa, but I'm not on their cover."

"So this book was just for me."

"Yes. What is your second question?"

"The second question is this—how did it all begin?"

Devī turned to face him. "How did all what begin?"

"How did the Asuras first come to this world so long ago? Why did they come to this planet? Why did the Avatāra choose to help us? And exactly how did he defeat the Asuras? Is he still in our universe and will he ever return to Earth? And all the souls who helped him—where are they now? I would really like to know all this, if you don't mind explaining it."

Devī smiled. "Thousands of years ago, when Kṛṣṇa came to this world, another great soul came with him, a fully enlightened sage. His name was Vyāsa, and he journeyed to this world precisely to document the extraordinary history as it truly happened. He explained all the Avatāra did in our world, and the destiny of those who helped him. Vyāsa taught this history to his students, and they taught it to other sincere souls. That chain of teachers and students continues to this day. It is called param-parā."

"Devī, you must be part of that chain."

"Yes, I am. And so are others. And now you are a student in that same disciplic succession. In your turn, you will become a Teacher."

"Only with your help," Justin said. "But now, I want to hear the entire history."

"And so you shall," Devī said. "Let us begin."

ACKNOWLEDGMENTS

No author is a literary island, and I welcome the opportunity to acknowledge here my profound debt and gratitude to those who have directly or indirectly enabled me to write this book. My first and deepest gratitude must go to my spiritual teacher, Bhaktivedanta Swami Prabhupada, without whom I could not have written anything of real spiritual substance or merit.

I tried my best to learn how to write by studying great writers, especially those of the early and mid-nineteenth century. Among them, I owe a special debt to Jane Austen.

With much gratitude, I acknowledge the invaluable assistance of my late parents, H.E. and Ann Resnick, and of my brothers Allen and Robert Resnick, whose loving help enabled me to devote my time to this project.

The seed of this book was planted in my mind decades ago, and in that initial, exploratory phase, Kṛṣṇa-priya (Hollie Kennedy), Devāmṛta (Devi Thompson), and Brahma-tīrtha (Bob Cohen) rendered valuable help, for which I am grateful. Brahma-tīrtha continues to help in many important ways.

More recently, I am grateful to Pāñcālī (Sol María Videla), working from Santiago Chile. She has devotedly managed the publication of this and my other books, in several languages. I also wish to thank Taruṇi (Tal Patalon), Naṭeśa (Natacha Bourgel), Śyāmala Kiśorī Engelhart, Māyāpriya (Mayapriya Long), Devala Ṛṣi (Donald Neumiller), Dāneśa (Daniel Laflor), Ānanda-līlā (Amanda Possato), Preṣṭha (Fred Grave), Nīlācala Zabala, Adwaita Candra (Euclides Vergilato), all the members of our Global Publications team, and my gifted editor, Elizabeth Ridley.

My thanks and apologies to all those who helped and do not find your names here.